Praise for L. R. Braden

Eric Hoffer Book Award—SciFi/Fantasy category
First Horizon Award—Debut Authors
Next Generation Indie Book Award—Paranormal category
Imadjinn Award—Best Urban Fantasy (for multiple books)
Colorado Authors League Award for Writing Excellence
—Fantasy and Paranormal categories
Finalist: *Colorado Book Award*—SciFi/Fantasy category
Finalist: *Chanticleer International Book Award*
—Paranormal and Fantasy categories
Finalist and Top Pick: *Killer Nashville Silver Falchion Award*
—Supernatural category

* * *

"This book starts with a bang and really never lets the reader go . . . Another well-written, engaging, non-stop action thrill-ride."
— Penny N., NetGalley review on *Lies and Illusion*

"Great plot. Loveable characters. Heart-pounding action. Just great."
— Lauren Davis, Saints and Sinners Book Blog on *A Drop of Magic*

"What an amazing and often brutal world this author has created . . . Well written, intense and twisted, this is a book you will remember."
— Karen F., NetGalley review on *Courting Darkness*

"I'm dying for more of this world. It is incredibly compelling with vivid world-building and fascinating, well developed characters!"
— Witch-at-Heart, Amazon review on *Demon Riding Shotgun*

Other Books by L. R. Braden

The Magicsmith Series

A Drop of Magic, Book 1

Courting Darkness, Book 2

Faerie Forged, Book 3

Casting Shadows, Book 4

Of Mettle and Magic, Book 5

Chaos Song, Book 6

Lies and Illusion, Book 7

Shadow's Bastion, Book 8

The Rifter Series

Demon Riding Shotgun, Book 1

Personal Demons, Book 2

A Demon Faerie Tale, Book 3

Dancing with a Demon, Book 4

Shadow's Bastion

by

L. R. Braden

Magical Realms Press

Copyright

Magical Realms Press
PO Box 24
Broomfield, CO 80038

Copyright © 2026 L. R. Braden
Print ISBN: 9781968414238
Ebook ISBN: 9781968414221
Published in the United States of America.

We love to hear from readers!
Contact us at:
MagicalRealmsPress.com
LRBraden.com

Cover design by 100 Covers
Interior design by David Braden

Dedication

In loving memory of
David Ritchey Braden IV
June 16, 1952 – January 23, 2025

"The world we experience, the pattern of interactions in which we find ourselves, is the result of all the choices of all the organisms that have ever lived. The pattern will be different tomorrow because of the choices we living organisms make today."

—David Braden

Thank you for the choices you made and the life you lived,
I was fortunate to be a part of it.

Chapter 1

MY MIND GLAZED over as my eyes skimmed down the list again, not really registering the contents. Not that I needed to; I already had them memorized. The Aery delegate required the summit to take place in a building at least five stories high with access to a landing pad on the roof. The Church council insisted iron screens should separate each attendee as a precaution against the use of magic, while the Lord of Enchantment wanted to create a ritual circle around the room that would prevent the attending humans from lying. The UN chairman needed to live stream the negotiations to the leaders of every represented nation, while the Lord of Illusion believed the entire summit should take place behind closed doors. One group demanded meat be served with every meal, while another called for an entirely vegan menu. And on and on. . . . I felt like a crisis negotiator in a room where every person was both hostage and gunman, trying to decipher which concessions I could get away with and which might make someone snap and start shooting.

I set the paper back on its stack and rubbed my eyes. Between days spent at the Paranatural Task Force headquarters helping David sort out the details of the largest interspecies conference ever attempted and nights spent trying to imbue amulets that would protect vampires from sunlight, I couldn't remember the last time I'd slept for more than two consecutive hours.

"Yes!" David, seated on the other side of his desk, thrust his fist into the air, exposing the Mediterranean tan of his forearm. Dark curls bounced around his ears and forehead, emphasizing his enthusiasm. He grinned, showing off straight teeth that couldn't have gotten that white without help and brown eyes that crinkled at the corners along well-established laugh lines.

"Good news?" I sat up a little straighter, shaking off my stupor.

He set down his phone and brushed imaginary dust off his security chief uniform, looking remarkably pleased with himself. "I just secured a viable location for the summit."

"Seriously?" I asked. "You found something that meets *all* the parameters? Where?"

"A new resort that's being renovated just outside of Colorado Springs. It's owned by Cole Barlowe."

"Why does that name sound familiar?"

"He's an entrepreneur who does a lot of philanthropic work for One Earth. He's sort of become their unofficial spokesperson."

"Right." I could picture him now—a stocky, compact man with dark hair, a square jaw, rectangular glasses, and custom-tailored business suits. I'd last seen him shaking hands with Ann Hayworth, one of the founders of the One Earth movement, on the evening news. He'd donated a sizable amount to the organization's global outreach project to promote interspecies tolerance. He was exactly the kind of public figure we needed to back this conference. "Good work."

"Actually, he contacted me," David said.

I frowned. "Let me guess. He wants One Earth to have a seat at the table?" I looked at the pile of request forms in front of me and sighed. One Earth members tended to have open minds, which could improve our chances of securing the peace I was hoping for, but my head was already threatening to explode from trying to manage all the attendees' conflicting requirements.

"That puts us at six confirmed fae in attendance, representing Illusion, Shadows, Enchantment, the Undine, the Aery, and the Shifters." I raised one finger for each. "Four seats for the humans—the Paranatural Task Force, the United Nations, the Unified Church, and now One Earth." I stared at the last finger I'd raised. "Shit. If we let One Earth attend, Purity is sure to demand a seat as well."

"Relax," David said. "One Earth doesn't want a seat. Barlowe gets a PR boost for his new resort, and we get a location at which to conduct our business. Win-win."

I narrowed my eyes at him. "That's it?"

"That's the deal." David returned my glare. "Speaking of seats . . ."

Uh oh.

"All the major fae realms are confirmed," he continued, "as are the significant human players. We have the practitioners and werewolves covered." His eyes softened with sympathy. "We can't wait forever, Alex. If the vampires want to be included, they'll need to make themselves known."

I looked away.

Last month, my boyfriend, James, and I were whisked away by representatives of the vampire council to stand trial for crimes against their species. I'd bought forgiveness with the promise of induction into the Paranatural Alliance and a seat at the summit where the fate of all paranaturals in the Mortal Realm would be decided. The fact that most humans didn't realize vampires were real presented a problem. The fact that the fae were all too aware of vampires and objected to their very existence presented another. But neither issue was why I was dragging my feet on making the necessary introductions.

I bit the inside of my lower lip and twisted the woven fabric ring on my left hand. Images of James danced through my head—memories of our time together bound to the ring by magic to make the distance between us more bearable. I strummed the silver thread anchored to my soul and felt a whisper of response from half a world away—too far for words, or even feelings, but enough to know he was still alive—a cold comfort that highlighted the terrible ache in my heart caused by his absence.

I released the ring, and the memories faded. In their place I pictured the towering pile of scrap metal stacked at the end of my workbench at home—my failed attempts to free James from his current imprisonment. So long as James was the only vampire capable of walking in daylight, he would be the council's figurehead, their puppet, and their prisoner. He'd also have a target the size of Texas painted on his back for every Purist vigilante with a grudge against magical beings and every fae who wanted to prevent vampires from being seen as more than monsters. Our dream of a quiet life together would go up in smoke.

There were three and a half months until the agreed-upon date for the summit. I had to provide the council with an alternative before then, but all the sleepless nights in my studio had proven fruitless so far. By the terms of our deal, I needed seven functional daywalking amulets to buy James's freedom. I had yet to make a single one.

"I just need a little more time," I said. "Once I get James out of the hot seat, we can bring the vampires' petition to the Paranatural Alliance and let them take it from there."

David frowned. "You can't keep burning the candle at both ends like this, Alex."

"I know."

"I don't think you do. You're running yourself ragged."

My cell phone rang and I swiped to answer, grateful for the interruption. I knew I couldn't defer the moment of revealing the vampires' desire to join the summit forever, but once I kicked that first stone it would become an avalanche that I couldn't stop. I had to get James clear first. I lifted the phone to my ear.

"Hey, Alex."

"Maggie!" My spirits lifted, as they always did when I heard Maggie's London accent. "How are you?"

"I'm home."

"Wait, what?" My mind stuttered. Maggie, her husband, and my fae court tutor had taken on the task of weening a group of goblin fruit-addicted children off the deadly faerie drug and returning them to their families. I knew they were wrapping up, but . . . "I thought you weren't getting back until *next* week." I frantically tried to map the past month in my head. Had I lost a whole week somewhere amid all those long hours and sleepless nights?

"We moved up our timetable."

"Why?" I asked, suddenly panicked. "What happened?"

"I'll tell you at dinner. My place. One hour. Bring David."

I glanced at David. "How did you—"

"I need to get back to cooking," Maggie said. "One hour. We'll talk then."

* * *

DESPITE DRIVING SEPARATELY, David and I walked side-by-side up the concrete path to Maggie's narrow, three-story townhouse. The orange glow of half a dozen streetlamps spaced evenly along the road pushed back the vast purple twilight of the star-studded sky. The moon had yet to make an appearance. A cool breeze brushed my face and ruffled my hair. I tucked the wayward strands behind my ear and stepped onto the stamp-sized porch, raising my hand to knock.

The Tardis-blue door swung open before my knuckles made contact.

Maggie stood two inches shorter than me, though the bouncy halo of her black curls more than made up the difference. The warm tones of her dark skin conspired with the rosy light of her hall lamp to give her a reddish glow. She wore white slippers, gray sweatpants with an elastic panel at the top, and a pink shirt stretched tight across a belly that looked ready to burst. She glanced at her watch. "Only three minutes late. I'm impressed."

"A whole week early," I reminded her.

She grinned and pulled me into a tight embrace, made all the tighter by the bulge of her pregnant belly.

I accepted the crushing hug, receiving with it a faceful of hair that carried a strong floral scent. "It's good to see you, Mags."

She stepped back and said to David, "Charlie could use a hand in the kitchen."

"Yes, ma'am." David gestured as though tipping an invisible hat, a habit he'd picked up from his latest boyfriend, and slipped past us.

Maggie pulled me inside and closed the door. "You look knackered," she said.

I arched an eyebrow. "And you look ready to pop. How are you feeling?"

She chuckled. "My ankles are swollen, my hips hurt, and I have to pee every five minutes, but I wouldn't trade it for the world." Maggie jerked. "Oh!" She grabbed my hand and pressed it flat to her swollen stomach. "You have to feel this."

I tensed, uncomfortable with the strangely intimate contact, but before I could pull my hand away, a wave of motion rippled under my palm. I froze, staring at my splayed fingers. The rippling motion happened again. My gaze snapped to Maggie's.

She beamed at me. "We've decided to name him Alexander, after his Auntie Alex, who's doing her best to make the world a better place for the next generation."

My throat constricted. Tears pricked my eyes. I shook my head. "I don't deserve that."

"Bollocks," she said. "You're the kindest, bravest person I know."

I snorted. "Funny. I could say the same thing about you. I got dragged into this mess, but you. . . . You voluntarily put your life on hold to take care of other people's sick kids." I shook my head. "You're amazing."

"Well, it wasn't entirely altruistic. As you may recall, my life here had already hit a bit of a dead end, what with Purists vandalizing my bookstore every other day and Charlie losing his job for being a One Earth supporter."

"A weaker person would have taken that as a sign to cut ties with paranaturals, not jump in deeper."

Maggie shrugged. "No one gets to decide who I care about but me."

An overwhelming sense of gratitude swept over me. I hugged her again, hunching to avoid pressing too hard against the precious cargo sandwiched between us. "Thanks for being my friend, Maggie."

She returned the hug, then stepped to arm's length. "You're not a friend, Alex."

I stiffened.

"*Auntie*, remember?" She squeezed my shoulders. "You're family." She folded her arms and leveled her "no-arguments" stare at me. "I fully expect you to spoil this baby."

I laughed. "I'll remind you of that when he becomes an unholy terror."

Shaking my head, I gazed at Maggie's abdomen and imagined the baby inside. I'd known Maggie was pregnant for months now, but seeing her ready to burst like this, feeling the baby move, knowing his name, it finally felt *real*. Knowing Alexander would be opening his eyes soon filled me with a rush of joy, protectiveness, and . . . envy.

James and I had never discussed having children. From my forays into his memories, I knew he'd had children as a human—children who'd died before his transformation. Maybe he didn't want any more. I wasn't sure if vampires could even have children in the traditional sense. If he could, would I want that?

I imagined trying to protect a child throughout everything that had happened in the past year: being hunted then hired by the PTF; deadly parties and secret prisons; large-scale battles and quiet betrayals. Even a purely human child would face dangers. For someone like me to have a child, well . . . What would that child even be?

I shook my head, trying to shake off my spiraling thoughts. *The point is moot unless I can get James away from the council.*

The clink of porcelain drew my attention through a doorway that led to the dining room at the back of the house, where I spotted my one remaining roommate, Emma. She wore a tie-dyed hoodie with the sleeves pushed up. Her short black hair had grown out enough to drape her forehead in a mohawk-like swoosh that stopped just short of her clouded eyes. A quiet smile curved her lips as she circled the oak table, laying out plates as confidently as any sighted person.

"So . . . *all* the kids have been returned to their families?" I asked.

Maggie followed my gaze. "We dropped the last one off this afternoon," she said quietly.

"Emma was there?"

Maggie nodded.

The last child . . . Emma's sister, May. I recalled the anguish in Loni's expression when she told us her daughter was missing. Yeah, having kids was terrifying.

"How did it go?"

Maggie gave me a small shove in Emma's direction. "Ask her."

She waddled into the kitchen, where I could hear David and Charlie talking. I headed for the dining room.

"Hey, Alex," Emma said without looking up. She set a fork on a napkin. "How goes the summit prep?"

"David may have secured a location," I said.

"That's great!"

I nodded, knowing her otherworldly awareness would convey the gesture despite her lack of conventional sight. She and her practitioner-mentor Luke were still trying to figure out how Emma's new abilities actually worked, but she seemed to be able to sense patterns in the Rift—the chaotic realm of energy from which magic was channeled.

I grabbed a pile of knives from the center of the table and started laying one beside each fork. "How's May?"

Emma hesitated, fork halfway to a napkin, then she completed the motion. "She's good. Healthy. Maggie and Hortense did a great job purging the goblin fruit."

"And Loni?" I asked more quietly.

Emma set the last fork down and straightened, looking straight at me with her distant, unfocused gaze. "Mom was . . . okay. She's relieved to have May home."

"You didn't stay," I noted carefully. When May went missing, Emma's mother had blamed Emma, claiming that by taking and passing the practitioner test, Emma had painted a target on their whole family. Loni wasn't wrong about magic-users being persecuted, but in that case it had been Emma's connection to *me* that put May in the crosshairs, not magic in general. And since magic also *saved* her daughter, Loni had seemed a little less hateful the last time we spoke. I hoped, now that May was home, Emma and her mom could mend that bridge.

"Mom and May have a lot to catch up on, and some important decisions to make. They need time." She crossed her arms, hugging herself. "But Mom suggested I should come back in a day or two. Once May is settled."

I smiled. "That's progress."

I finished the final setting, then I frowned and counted the plates. Six. "Who's the extra seat for?"

"That would be mine." Hortense swept into the room behind me and settled herself at the head of the table.

Even fully glamoured to look like a harmless old lady, the river hag Hortense made an imposing sight. She sat ramrod straight with her bony fingers folded neatly on her lap. Her pointed chin and high cheekbones hinted at the true shape of her face, but her pale, age-spotted complexion was nothing like the leathery green skin I knew hid under the shimmer of her magic. Long steel-gray hair was twisted into a complex collection of pinned braids atop her head, showing off the magically rounded tips of her ears. Dark eyes, devoid of their natural red hue, found mine, and when she spoke, the tips of her teeth were blunted. If not for the brocade Victorian dress she wore, the fae tutor would have fit right in at any human town.

I smoothed my hands self-consciously over my wrinkled T-shirt, glad I was at least wearing jeans without holes in them. "I thought you went back to Enchantment through the Appalachian Reservation as soon as the kids were clear of their goblin fruit addictions."

She looked down her nose at me. A neat trick since I was standing and she wasn't. "I've agreed to stay in the Mortal Realm a while longer to help Margaret write her book."

I blinked. "Her what now?"

"Surprise," Maggie chimed as she led Charlie and David into the dining room, each carrying a tray of food. The smells—sweet, savory, and a little tart—made my mouth water.

Maggie's husband, who was my height but quite a bit softer around the middle, set an earthenware bowl of garlicky sautéed Brussels sprouts and onions on the table. He patted me on the back. "It's good to see you, Alex."

"You too, Charlie," I mumbled, but my attention stayed fixed on Maggie.

"Remember how I told you I was starting a new project?" she said.

I nodded.

"I'm compiling a survival guide for humans interacting with fae flora and fauna."

I stared at her for a moment, then swung my gaze back to Hortense. "And you're *helping* her?" From what I'd experienced, fae were extremely protective of their secrets. I couldn't imagine a project like this would go over well with the courts and their lords.

The fae tutor smiled. "I won't be giving away any military secrets," she said. "And it's refreshing to share my knowledge with a student who actually *wants* to learn."

Ouch.

"Okay, but is that really a good idea right now? I know you never had a proper visa to begin with, but since the PTF revoked all fae rights in the Mortal Realm, Purity has gotten a lot more ballsy. If they find you, it could not only cost you your life but lead to trouble for Maggie and her family as well."

"I have permission *and* protection from the PTF," Hortense said. "Mr. Nolan here was kind enough to procure paperwork for a special dispensation."

My jaw dropped. I snapped my teeth closed and turned to "Mr. Nolan." "I thought special dispensations were only for diplomatic liaisons integral to planning the summit."

David set a platter of cherry-glazed pork chops beside Charlie's sprouts and took a seat, motioning for me to do likewise. "Technically, a special dispensation can be granted to anyone who is doing work that the PTF deems 'invaluable.'"

I settled into a chair, giving him a shrewd look. "Maggie's book—"

"Is something the PTF is very interested in seeing published," he confirmed. "Director Harris approved the paperwork last week."

Having first-hand accounts of some of the dangers of the faerie realms *would* be invaluable. I certainly could have benefited from a guidebook on the occasions I'd found myself bumbling through other realms. I still couldn't believe Hortense had agreed to share information like that with a human.

I turned to Charlie as he slid a juicy pork chop onto his plate. He'd lost some weight and gotten some sun since the last time I'd seen him. His pale skin had burned rather than tanned, making his freckled cheeks redder than his orange hair. "Where do you fit into all this?"

He smiled, crinkling the corners of his sky-blue eyes. "My corporate job paid well, but I'm looking forward to being a stay-at-home dad for a while. I have enough squirreled away to last a few years."

I clamped my mouth shut, trapping my opinion about his "corporate job" behind clenched teeth.

A few months ago, Charlie's architectural firm had been trying to secure a lucrative government contract. Since the governor of Colorado was a Purist, having a lead engineer whose wife employed paranaturals was a deal-breaker. The firm chose to cut Charlie loose rather than lose the contract. I hoped the greedy bastards went bankrupt.

"Emma mentioned Chase isn't living with you anymore." Maggie dropped a steaming biscuit onto her plate and passed me the basket. "Something about keeping an eye on his sister?"

I inhaled the buttery aroma, took two rolls, and sent the rest down the line. "Chase is helping Targe rebuild Crossroads."

Hortense's eyebrows pinched together. "And you were worried about *me* drawing Purist attention?"

"I didn't say I approved," I grumbled. Hiding at my cabin in the woods was one thing, but opening a fae bar in the middle of Boulder? That was just asking for trouble. "I tried to talk them out of it, but Targe is . . . determined. Ava's sticking with her uncle, and Jynx is sticking with her wife, so Chase moved in to make sure his little sister doesn't end up in some Purist's trophy case." I slid a juicy pork chop onto my plate. It smelled heavenly, but a cold, hard knot at my center stole my appetite. So many of the people I cared about were beyond my reach right now.

"What about Malakai?" Hortense asked. "Has he returned from Enchantment?"

Another knife through my heart. Thanks Hortense.

"Not yet," I said, keeping my voice carefully neutral.

In all honesty, I'd expected Kai to come back by now, permission or no. Or at least send word. His complete silence since leaving the Mortal Realm had me worried.

"He's probably waiting until the visa program is reinstated," Maggie said.

"He *was* one of the few fae who followed the rules." David gave me a pointed look. One of the major concerns the human delegations had voiced about the upcoming summit was how to enforce a new treaty. Fae couldn't lie, but they were very good at finding loopholes. Luckily the legal phrasing of the deal was someone else's problem. David and I only had to make sure everyone showed up and no one died.

"Maybe you could get him one of those special thingies," Emma said, "like you did for Hortense."

We all stared at David.

He froze with a heaping mound of Brussels sprouts on his fork, looked back at us, and set his fork on the plate. "We'd need to make an argument that his presence is both necessary and beneficial to the PTF. I don't think 'because we miss him' is going to fly with the director."

"As a court knight, he's interacted with tons of high-level fae," I said. "He knows a lot about their complicated etiquette. Way more than me. His advice would be invaluable."

David pointed to Hortense. "She originally came here to teach you court etiquette, right? So wouldn't she know more than Kai?"

"Considerably," Hortense said.

Emma glared at David. "Whose side are you on?"

He raised his hands in defense. "I'm just saying, it's not a bulletproof argument."

"Hortense will be too busy working with me to advise you on fae etiquette," Maggie said.

"Kai can also help with security," I pointed out. "He has experience working big events attended by lots of important fae who want to kill each other."

"Fine," David said. "I'll see what I can do."

I leaned over and kissed him on the cheek. "Thank you."

"I was planning to make a trip to Enchantment to retrieve some of my reference books," Hortense said. "I'd be willing to impart your offer to Malakai while I'm there."

Emma set her fork down and turned her unseeing gaze on me. "Alex, you should go with her."

"I'm sure Hortense can deliver the message on her own." I touched the ring on my finger, thinking of James. "I have too much going on right now."

Emma shifted, seeming to consider her words. She pinched her lower lip between her teeth, then she exhaled and said in a rush, "I think it's time to ask your grandfather for help."

Hortense locked her shrewd gaze on me. "What do you need help with?"

I glared at Emma. I'd learned the hard way that keeping my friends in the dark never ended well, so when I returned from my stay with the vampire council, I told Emma and David what I could about the deal I'd made, leaving out only the most dangerous details that could get us all killed if I blabbed. Hortense was another matter.

Hortense knew my boyfriend was a vampire. That didn't mean she approved. Given the longstanding animosity between fae and vampires—namely that the fae wanted to eradicate every vampire from the face of the Earth—even a friendly fae would likely find the idea of outfitting the vampire council with daywalking amulets reprehensible, no matter my reasons. I stared at the old tutor for a long moment before opening my mouth.

"Never mind." She raised her hand to forestall me. "If it takes you this long to answer, it's probably something I don't want to know about."

I exhaled, grateful, but my relief was short-lived. Unlike my hesitance with Hortense, it wasn't fear of disapproval that stopped me from talking to Bael. Having produced the original daywalking amulet that James wore for decades, my fae grandfather clearly could, and would, disregard public opinion when it suited him. He was the Lord of Enchantment, after all. Still, I'd avoided seeking his aid because, while he *could* help me, I feared what that help might cost.

"I'm managing on my own," I mumbled.

"No," Emma said, "you're not." She crossed her arms. "Every second you're not planning the summit with David, you're working in your studio."

"That's—"

"You don't sleep," Emma barreled on like a playground tattletale reporting to a teacher. "You forget to eat. It's ridiculous. Yesterday, when I brought you that snack, I found you passed out at your workbench, drooling all over your sketchbooks."

My face warmed.

"You've clearly hit a dead end," Emma said, "but you're too stubborn to acknowledge it."

"We're worried about you," David added.

"What is this, an intervention?" I looked at Maggie. "Is this why you came home early?"

She patted my arm. "We know what you're doing is important, Alex, but you need help. Help that, as much as we love you, no one here can provide."

I looked around the table, taking in my friends' concerned expressions. "I'm sorry I worried you all, but asking Bael for advice isn't something to be taken lightly. Nothing's ever free with the fae."

Hortense gave a curt nod. "I'm glad to see *some* lessons stuck."

"You don't think he'll help you?" Maggie asked with a frown. "Even though you're family?"

"If she weren't family, he wouldn't even speak to her," Hortense said.

I drummed my fingers on the table. Bael *would* speak to me if I went to him. How helpful he'd be would depend on what I was willing to trade. But I'd been hitting my head against a wall trying to understand these amulets for months, even before my deal with the vampire council. I was clearly worrying my friends, and I was running out of time to extricate James from the vampire council before they forced him to become their poster boy for the children of the night. Perhaps it was time to negotiate.

I sighed and looked at Hortense. "When do we leave?"

Chapter 2

COLORADO'S SOUTHWEST FAE Reservation was nestled in the Sangre de Cristo Mountains near the Great Sand Dunes National Park. Dust devils flared and faded along the high desert road as I sucked the last dregs of coffee from my travel mug and squinted into the low morning sun. Early as it was, heat shimmers already danced along the crests of the towering dunes where the sand glowed golden. Warm air whistled through the Jeep, causing my hair to lash my face and pulling shorter strands loose from my ponytail as I sped along the empty road. Now that I'd settled on paying Bael a visit, I was eager to get this trip over with.

I turned east, angling toward the shadowed mountains north of the dunes. Hortense shifted in the passenger seat, holding stiffer than usual as we made the turn. My vehicle was not designed with fae comfort in mind. Despite much of the interior being molded plastic, there were enough steel components to make the tutor wary of bumping exposed metal, lest she get a nasty burn.

The tail end of the song "Chlorine" became a garbled mess as we headed deeper into the mountains, skirting the tiny town of Crestone—the nearest human outpost. Failing to find anything recognizable as music when I cycled through the stations, I turned the radio off.

The terrain grew steeper. Densely packed pines, drought-dry sagebrush, and groves of aspens thick with the yellow-green of new growth on their branches masked the presence of the reservation fence until we reached the gate station. Two buildings, one set to either side of the actual gate, bordered a large dirt area. The gate itself was constructed from two ten-foot, iron-mesh panels rigged with a motorized device for opening and closing. Three PTF guards stood on the human-controlled side of the gate, iron swords strapped to their hips and iron-round rifles cradled in their arms. A fourth guard sat behind a window in the smaller of the two buildings. A collection of vehicles was parked along the south side of the larger building, and I pulled my Jeep in alongside a beige Humvee.

The guards watched Hortense and me approach. None raised their weapons, but their eyes tracked us, and the tension in their stances sang of alertness.

"Good morning." I waved to the three gun-toting guards then directed my focus to the person behind the window. "I'm Alex Blackwood. I need to enter the reservation." Unfolding my PTF documentation, I passed the papers through a trough under the plexiglass window. Hortense waited quietly beside me.

The agent behind the window looked over my papers. Her hazel eyes darted to me once or twice as she read. Finally, she lowered the documents and tucked a lock of straw-blond hair behind her ear. "What's the reason for your visit today?"

"A confidential matter regarding the upcoming negotiations." I gestured to the signature visible at the bottom of my PTF document. "Feel free to call Director Harris if you need to confirm my authorization."

I held my breath. Harris would most likely authorize me to enter the reservation even though I hadn't mentioned my travel plans to her, but the director was a busy woman, and a call would cause a delay.

The agent jotted something in the visitor notebook then looked up to meet my gaze. "Intended duration?"

I exhaled. "Probably two or three days." Ideally, I'd only be in Enchantment for a matter of hours—just long enough to get my answer from Bael, grab Kai, and skedaddle—but the time difference between the two realms meant I'd lose significantly more time on this side.

She nodded and added another note to the journal. "You understand that entering the reservation may put your life at risk? PTF jurisdiction ends at the gate. We will not be able to assist you once you're on the other side."

I glanced at Hortense. Once we set foot on the reservation, her presence would grant me more protection than all the guns in the world. "I understand."

The guard made a final mark on the page, turned the book, and said, "Print your name, sign, and date." She tapped the page, indicating the locations for all three pieces of information, then she slid the notebook and my PTF documentation under the window.

I signed with a flourish, pocketed my paperwork, and stepped aside for Hortense to take her turn.

The agent behind the glass took one look at the special dispensation that identified Hortense as a fae, blanched, scribbled something in her notebook, and passed the form back without a word. She nodded to the guards at the gate and pressed a button on the wall beside her desk. The PTF was there to keep fae *in* the reservation. I imagined Hortense's paperwork would garner more scrutiny when she tried to come back out.

Metal rattled as the motorized panels slid apart, echoing across the quiet mountainside. By the time we reached the armed guards, there was a six-foot gap in the fence. Only one guard watched our approach. The others had turned and lifted their guns, ready to fire on anything that dared take advantage of the breach. I almost wanted to laugh, knowing as I did that the fae had secret avenues of getting on and off the reservation, but the fearful focus in the guards' eyes and the way their fingers hovered over the triggers of fae-tuned guns was enough to wipe the smile from my face.

"You sure you want to go in there?" asked the agent who'd kept his attention on me.

"We'll be fine," I said. "Diplomatic immunity."

He snorted and adjusted his grip on the gun in his arms. "I wouldn't trust a piece of paper to save my life if I were you." He jerked his head toward the gate. "Not from what lives in there."

Hortense snorted and marched past the guard.

"We'll be fine," I repeated and followed her through the gap in the fence. The hum of the gate's motor changed in pitch as it slid closed behind me. Ten steps later, silence fell over the mountain.

We followed a rocky dirt trail, a holdover from when these mountains catered to mortal hikers. The air became thicker, richer, with every step. Where the pine trees on the mortal side of the fence had displayed signs of drought and beetle infestation, the trees in the reservation were vibrant green. Scraggly brush gave way to lush bushes. Quaking aspens were joined by a wide variety of other deciduous trees, including some I was pretty sure weren't supposed to grow in Colorado. Birds, bugs, and squirrels created a backdrop of ambient noise that kept the quiet from becoming oppressive. I could almost imagine I was out for a stroll on my own patch of mountain back home . . . except for the tingling itch on the back of my neck.

I glanced over my shoulder. The gate and its human guards were well out of sight. I squinted into the dappled shadows under the trees then lifted my gaze to the branches overhead. Nothing stirred. I rubbed my arms, trying to smooth the bumps that textured my flesh.

Hortense stopped beside me. "What's the matter?"

"We're being watched," I whispered.

She arched an eyebrow. "Of course we're being watched. The reservation guardians wouldn't serve much purpose if they didn't keep an eye on visitors."

I scanned the forest around us. "I don't like that I can't see them."

"Be glad you can't. When you see them, that's when it's time to worry."

I shuddered. I'd come face to face with two elemental guardians—one of water and one of air—in my travels to other reservations. I'd also seen the aftermath of an earth elemental's counterstrike, after an attack against a reservation in Europe. I wasn't sure what type of elemental protected the Colorado reservation, but Hortense was right—I didn't want to meet it.

Clearing my throat, I said, "Let's get to the portal."

Hortense led the way, veering off the path after about five minutes of brisk hiking. With the sun climbing higher, I was starting to sweat. Hortense didn't seem to have that problem. Neither did her copious amounts of fabric seem to catch on any of the thorns on the bushes we pushed through. I, on the other hand, suffered multiple scratches and had to constantly pause to disentangle my clothes from the grasping plants.

"I don't think the flora here likes me," I grumbled.

Hortense glanced back. One corner of her lips twitched. "Perhaps they can tell that you don't want to be here."

"Will that be in Maggie's book?" I asked as I carefully lifted a bramble branch out of my path. "Placating plants through attitude."

"Perhaps." Hortense stepped through what seemed like a solid wall of heavily thorned gooseberry bushes with no trouble at all.

I glowered at the plants. Pointing my finger and feeling like a fool, I said, "I belong here. I have every right to pass through."

The bushes weren't impressed, and they let me know it by closing in around me as soon as I tried to force my way through them. I tripped as a branch caught my laces, dropping me to my hands and knees. Lines of heat flared across my skin as I received a dozen new scratches. I dug my fingers into a blanket of decomposing leaves and took a deep breath to keep my frustration in check. The crisp air became saturated with the musty smell of organic matter. I exhaled and pressed forward. Each step was a struggle, but eventually I tore loose from the last of the grasping branches and stumbled into a familiar clearing.

Hortense posed like a statue, but I could see the laughter in her eyes as she watched me straighten my clothes.

"I think I liked this trip better in the winter," I grumbled, pulling twigs from my hair. "Then all I had to contend with was the cold."

That lip twitch returned, and Hortense quickly turned to gesture at two trees that occupied one end of the clearing—a towering oak, its branches bursting with new leaves, and a sprawling ash whose limbs twined with those of the larger tree to create something like an archway between them. "After you."

Scowling, I tromped across the wildflower-speckled grass and passed under the arch.

The air was snatched from my lungs. I lost all sense of direction and my physical body as I was flipped around and turned inside out. Panic surged as I recalled the last time I'd felt this way, when I'd been catapulted through the Rift without a stable portal. It had been blind luck that I'd landed in a physical realm rather than being lost to the chaos of the Rift itself. Not that I'd felt particularly lucky at the time. I screwed my nonexistent eyes shut, clenched my nonexistent fists, and tried to remain calm.

The symptoms of crossing the Rift passed as quickly as they started, and I dropped to my knees in a field of bluish, knee-high grass interspersed with silver flowers that rang like tiny bells when they shook. My breath caught and stuttered as I inhaled the soothing floral scent and blew out the lingering tension shaking my limbs. I sat back on my heels.

Hortense appeared beside me, stepping out of thin air. Back in her home realm, she'd dropped the glamour that made her look human. Her silvery hair turned charcoal black. Leathery skin the color of pond scum clung like cellophane to her wiry frame. Thick claws tipped each of her long fingers. She peered down, pinpoints of darkness finding me in the red orbs of her eyes. "You're still affected by portal travel?"

I stood and silently brushed off my knees. There was no use pointing out that I *had* been getting better at traveling through portals before my wayward Rift incident, that my current reaction was more akin to a panic attack than a simple upset stomach.

"I vote we visit Kai first," I said to change the topic. "That way he can pack and say his goodbyes while I have my chat with Bael."

"*Lord* Bael," Hortense corrected. "Remember where we are."

As if to reinforce her point, a sidhe soldier in green-and-brown livery stepped out of the woods with a broad tip arrow knocked and pointed squarely at my chest. His purple skin was an almost perfect match to the shadows from which he'd emerged.

"Lord Bael," I conceded, raising my hands.

"State your identities and business," demanded the guard. His question echoed the PTF agent I'd spoken to half an hour earlier, but his expression was closer to the soldiers holding the guns than the clerk in the window.

Hortense didn't raise her hands in surrender. She simply shifted her disdainful gaze to the new arrival and said, "Hortense, Court Tutor, and Lady Alyssandra Blackwood, kin to Lord Bael. We seek an audience and various supplies."

The soldier let out a shrill whistle—a signal to other guards I couldn't see but knew must be hiding in the surrounding forest—then relaxed his bow. "Well met."

I lowered my arms.

"We require two mounts," Hortense said without preamble.

The guard returned his arrow to its quiver and made another whistling sound, this one more like a bird call.

Another guard, this one an eloko who resembled a three-foot walking bush in leather pants, emerged from the trees with reins in either hand. He led two large, six-legged beasts into the clearing. Each gaala stood over five feet tall at the shoulders, with another two or so feet of antlers spreading above their long faces. The reins the eloko held out to me belonged to the paler, slightly smaller, of the two beasts. It had a beige pelt nearly the same color as its blond mane and tail. The gaala Hortense mounted had black fur and a glossy purple mane.

The eloko offered their cupped hands to help me mount, for which I was grateful. I'd never been much of an equestrian. The gaala skittered sideways when my weight settled, pawing the ground with one of its six hooves and tossing its head, which brought its antlers disturbingly close to my face.

I choked up on the reins and called to Hortense. "Okay, let's get to the keep."

Hortense frowned at me. "I thought you wished to visit Malakai first?"

"Yeah," I said. A sinking feeling sapped the heat from my limbs. "Doesn't he live at the keep?"

She gave me a condescending look. "He resigned his service as a Knight of the Realm. Why would he still live under Lord Bael's roof?"

"Then where does he live?" I asked, flustered.

"Why would I know where Malakai lives?"

"Because . . ." I floundered for an answer. "You were both members of the court."

She exhaled, long and slow. "Do you have any idea how large the Court of Enchantment is?"

Since there was no way to answer that question without looking like even more of a fool, I kept my mouth shut.

"A scholar and a guard," Hortense continued. "Do you imagine our paths crossed often? Did you picture us sitting down to drink tea together and discussing our respective days?" Hortense waved a hand. "I'd barely been aware of Malakai's existence before our concurrent stay in the Mortal Realm. I have no idea where his family home might be."

"Then how are we supposed to find him?"

"Perhaps, in the year you spent together, you should have asked him about his life before he met you," Hortense said. "There was, after all, quite a lot of it, from your perspective. Nearly a century."

"Okay, yes, I'm a terrible, self-centered friend. I get it." I ran a hand over my hair. "I'll work on that. For now, how do we find Kai?"

"I suppose we must go to the keep first after all. Though he's no longer under her command, Captain Rhoana should have some idea where to find Malakai."

The shadowy archer coughed into his hand, drawing our attention. "If you seek the ex-knight Malakai, his family estate is in Falaiche, on the southern border of the forest.

Hortense glanced at the sky. The sun was just approaching its zenith. "That's quite a detour. We'd best get moving if we don't intend to stay the night."

She tugged lightly at her reins and made a clicking sound. Her gaala started to trot, then gallop across the meadow. I nodded to the guard who'd given us a destination and urged my mount to follow. Shortly before reaching the trees on the far side, the gaala rose off the ground. Hooves tearing at empty air, we soared over the treetops and into the clear sky.

Even knowing what was coming, I felt as if I'd left my stomach in that clearing. At least I managed to keep my hands on the reins. I took a deep breath, free of the odors of industry that so permeated my world, and rocked to the motion of the gaala. The better I matched that rhythm, the easier it was to keep my seat.

Trees spread beneath me in a riot of blues, greens, reds, and purples. Distant peaks to the west ringed the dense forest, tapering to foothills as the range curved south. Hortense turned her gaala toward those lower hills, and I nudged mine to follow. Wisps of smoke rose from tiny clusters of buildings far below. Thin streams and raging rivers split the landscape. I shivered as we flew. The tips of my ears ached. The only sound this high was the howling of the wind as it whistled past. Dark specks that must have been other gaala dotted the sky. A few other shapes—fae with wings or other flying creatures—skimmed just above the leafy canopy. After half an hour, a flash brought my attention to a break between the hills, where afternoon sunlight danced on pearlescent waves as they crashed against a red sand beach.

Hortense's gaala began a lazy spiral, dropping closer to the ground with each pass. My mount took the same winding trajectory. As we descended, I could pick out a city nestled among the trees. Fae walked along paths through the forest—some races I recognized, some I did not. A hawk called from my left and took wing as Hortense set down in a clearing similar to the one we'd left behind. My massive mount's hooves touched down, light as a feather. My wind-tousled hair settled against my back, tangled into a lumpy snarl. I turned my face to the sun, giving my chilled skin a chance to warm up. The breeze was damp and carried a heavy scent of salt.

The hawk who'd taken wing dove toward the ground, seeming to melt just before impact. A woman with light-brown skin and eyes so dark they were nearly black unfurled from the dissipating feathers. She wore a tan dress with a dark leather apron and leather boots. Shorter than I, and with a more slender frame, she had full, rosy cheeks and wild black hair.

"I wouldn't have expected to meet a shifter in Enchantment," I said as I dismounted.

"They're not unheard of." Hortense was already on the ground. She leaned close to her mount and whispered something into its ear before turning and walking toward the woman. "But that woman is no shifter. She's human."

"What?" I scrambled to catch up. Studying the woman who'd been a bird a moment before, I dropped my voice. "Then how did she—"

"An enchantment," Hortense explained curtly. "Likely she's indentured, paying off some foolish bargain."

I bit my tongue as we approached the woman.

"Well met," she said.

"And you," replied Hortense. "We seek an ex-knight named Malakai whose family lives in this area. Do you know him?"

"Young Sir Kairn," the woman said. "His family resides in a manor near the shore. You'll know it by the horses over the front lintel and the orange trumpet vines that climb its side."

Hortense inclined her chin in acknowledgment of the information.

"Shall I see to your mounts?" The woman gestured toward the gaala.

"We will not be staying long," Hortense said. "They can remain where they are until we return."

The woman lowered her gaze and bobbed a curtsy. "If that's all." She erupted in a cloud of feathers, and where there had been a woman, a hawk winged into the air.

I flinched away from the bird as it soared over my head, then I turned to watch it—her—land on an upper branch in a nearby tree.

"I didn't think humans were allowed to live in the fae realms."

"Not on their own," Hortense confirmed. "That woman is the property of some fae who lives here. That is altogether different."

Feeling queasy, I tucked that piece of information away for later and turned from the enchanted woman. There were so many details to sort out between the humans and the fae, not to mention those of us who fell between, that the idea of negotiating peace between the races felt overwhelming even at the best of times. Realizing humans were being kept as slaves even in realms that were relatively modern-minded made the whole concept seem downright impossible.

But we have to try.

"Let's just hurry up and find Kai so we can all go home."

Hortense huffed softly. "Assuming Malakai *chooses* to return to the Mortal Realm."

I frowned, the anxious knot in my gut twisting tighter. "Why wouldn't he?"

She leveled her condescending stare at me, and it took every ounce of stubbornness I had not to look away. "You forget, Alex, that Malakai and I will not be going *home* with you." She spread her arms, gesturing to the multi-hued trees, the pale sky, the blue-green grass speckled with silver bell blooms. "*This* is our home. This place you dread coming to and can't get away from fast enough."

I did look away then, but everywhere I turned I was confronted by her truth. I tended to view the Realm of Enchantment, all the fae realms, really, as somewhere I was occasionally forced to visit. I spent my time there counting the seconds until I could return to my own world.

"Learn from your friend Margaret," Hortense said. "Perhaps if you took the time to get to *know* our home, you would not fear it, or us, so much."

I had no response to that, so I studied the gently swaying grass around my feet and listened to the soft tinkle of silver bells.

It is *beautiful here*, I thought, but I couldn't shake the feeling of being out of place or the prickle between my shoulder blades that warned of danger lurking beneath the beauty. I glanced once more at the hawk-girl, then I turned toward the distant crash of ocean waves.

Hortense and I picked our way down a steep stone staircase built into the side of the hill that led from the field where we'd landed to the heart of the seaside city. Towering trees lined cobblestone paths that bent to suit the environment instead of cutting through it. Smaller walkways led to stone houses tucked between the trees. A variety of flowering bushes filled the middle space, and the ground around the weathered rocks on which we walked sported a thick carpet of springy moss. A group of children—one panotti, two sidhe, and a pooka—ran across the street in front of us and darted into the dappled forest on my right, trailing laughter behind them.

Do fae children go to school? It had never occurred to me to ask. *I really do need to learn more about the Realms if I hope to facilitate peace between the fae and humanity.*

The trees became fewer and farther between as we walked. More buildings appeared, larger and closer together. A carved and painted wooden sign depicting a sparkling horseshoe dangled above one doorway. The mouthwatering scent of freshly baked bread wafted out of the next, and a display of colorful confections tempted me through a large window.

An eloko wearing an oversized brass bell on a necklace cradled a covered basket as she made her way to the shore. A nymph in nothing but her own skin strolled under the trees, trailing her fingers along their bark and speaking softly.

A pale-skinned sidhe in an outfit that could have come right out of a human's closet whistled a tune as he walked, hands stuffed in the pockets of cutoff jeans and foam flip-flops slapping his heels with every step. Something that I mistook for a large, mossy boulder rumbled into motion, taking one ponderous step before settling down again as if to catch its breath. No one gave Hortense or me more than a passing glance.

The path we were following split on a low rise that dropped to the beach. Grass and moss petered away as soil was replaced by burgundy sand streaked with pinks and browns that created a tiger-like pattern along the red dunes. The rhythmic crashing of waves against the shore filled the air with a fine mist that clung to my skin and left the taste of salt on my lips. I glanced to either side and spotted a large building on my right with a pair of carved horses rearing over the arched entrance. Bright orange flowers with long, trumpet-shaped petals clung to the stone walls. I inhaled and found a sweet floral scent mixed with the salty air.

"Alex?"

I spun to find Kai staring at me, mouth hanging open. A simple tunic-style shirt and leather trousers covered his slender frame, cinched at his waist by the sword belt that held his sheathed katana. The handle of a wicker basket piled high with produce dangled from the crook of one arm. His unkempt, chestnut hair had grown enough to cover the pointed tips of his tapered ears, and the swirling galaxies of his eyes stared from amid the sharp angles of his unglamoured face.

"Wha . . . what are you doing here?" he spluttered.

The grin that sprang to my lips wilted. "That's not exactly the greeting I was hoping for."

"Sorry." He shook his head. "It's wonderful to see you, of course. I'm just . . . surprised." He glanced over his shoulder, as if worried what his neighbors might make of this visit from a mortal.

I shuffled my feet. *Is he annoyed that I'm here?* I glanced at Hortense, recalling her earlier reprimand that Enchantment was her and Kai's true home. *Maybe the reason he didn't come back to the Mortal Realm . . . is because he doesn't want to.*

My heart turned to stone in my chest. I'd grown used to having Kai around. He was reliable. He made me laugh. Despite a rocky start, we'd become good friends. But it was a friendship based on necessity and near-death experiences. Maybe he'd been missing his home the whole time he'd been with me in the Mortal Realm, and I'd been too preoccupied or self-centered to notice.

But not this time, I told myself. *If this is where Kai wants to be, where he feels most at home, this is where he should stay.*

That assertion burned in my mind, and a heavy pressure built behind my eyes, but I reaffixed my smile and said, "So this is where you live? It's beautiful."

"Yeah," Kai said distractedly. "Um, let's go inside."

He strode past me, under the horse-topped arch, and through the weatherworn wooden door beyond.

I shot a questioning look to Hortense, but she merely shrugged and followed him, seeming not to care that he'd completely ignored her presence during that whole exchange.

The inside of Kai's house was as lofty as the outside, with exposed beams supporting a vaulted ceiling. The stone walls were smooth on the interior, polished to display an impressive array of intricate veins running through the dark foundation—everything from gold and copper to silver and quartz. Seams of mortar between the stones gave an impression of shattered glass, except where actual glass provided a view of the opal sea through panoramic windows. I could still hear the endless crash of waves, but fainter. Not a single wisp of wind found its way inside.

Heavy tapestries covered wide sections of wall and cascaded in artful drapes of fabric along ceiling joists to prevent the large room from becoming an echo chamber. A universe of tiny glass lanterns hovered in the vaulted space above my head, casting colorful, uneven light. Below the artificial stars sat a large oval table and a dozen high-backed chairs, all made of wood, but no two alike. The floor was covered with the same springy moss as the forest, and the organic curves of the dining set made me suspect the room's furniture had been grown in place.

The scent of fresh herbs drew my attention to a kitchen area on my right, where several bunches of plants were strung upside down from small hooks in the wall. An enormous stone basin rested on a wooden pedestal below a copper faucet, and a cold hearth protruded from the polished stone. In front of the hearth, a collection of branches supported a freestanding piece of marble at waist height, upon which Kai placed his basket.

Cargo deposited, he nodded to Hortense, finally acknowledging her presence. "Well met, Hortense."

She inclined her head. "And you."

Turning to me, he eagerly asked, "I don't suppose you brought any candy?"

"Uh, no."

His expression turned to one of resignation. "Too bad." He glanced mournfully at the colorful fruits and vegetables in his basket. "So, what brings you to Enchantment and, more specifically, to my hometown?"

"I'm in Enchantment to talk to Bael." I glanced at Hortense. "Lord Bael. But I wanted to check in with you first and let you know that we may have a way for you to legally come back to the Mortal Realm . . . if you want."

He looked down, tracing a golden vein through the surface of the counter with his finger. "I suppose you're wondering why I've stayed away?"

I lifted one shoulder in a shrug, feigning a casual air I didn't feel. "The Mortal Realm is a dangerous place for fae right now, and I totally get wanting to spend time with your family."

Kai's bark of laughter caught me off guard.

"Sorry." He waved a hand, smothering another laugh. "That's not it at all. I was actually counting the days until I could go back before—" His face fell. Shifting his weight, he rubbed a hand over the back of his neck.

I opened my mouth to ask why he was acting so squirrely, but before I could form the question, the front door swung open with enough force to bounce against the stone wall.

"You wouldn't believe what Rhys just said to—" The woman who'd pushed into the house froze mid-step and mid-sentence. The salty sea breeze snuck in behind her, making the long strands of her golden hair dance where they weren't tied into braids or tucked behind her sharply tapered ears. She stood about five and a half feet tall and had the unblemished complexion of someone with a rigorous beauty regime. Her sharp features and high cheekbones were common among the sidhe, but I'd only seen the galaxy gaze through which she studied us in Kai, marking her as a relative.

Smoothing the front of a dress that looked to be made from a hundred layers of gauzy cobwebs, she lifted her chin, squared her shoulders, and said, "I didn't realize we had company."

"Allow me to introduce Lady Alex Blackwood and Court Tutor Hortense." Kai gestured in our direction, voice and posture both strained with tension, then he swept his arm to the new arrival. "This is Lady Tabita Kairn. My mother."

Tabita's eyes narrowed, hooding the galaxies beneath her long, pale lashes. Her mouth became a thin line. "So, this is the mortal mongrel you've been running around with."

I stiffened. It wasn't uncommon for people, both fae and human, to have a less than flattering opinion of my heritage, but they didn't usually come out and say it straight to my face.

Hortense pulled herself to her full height and glowered at Kai's mother. "I would remind you, Tabita, that while you may be a minor noble of this backwater town, Lady Alyssandra is kin to the Lord of Enchantment himself. You would do well to watch your tongue."

Tabita *tsk*ed. "I can only say what's true, as can all our kind. Mingled with the Lord's or not, mortal blood runs in her veins, and she's led my boy astray."

"Astray?" I asked, caught off guard by the accusation.

Tabita's gaze swung to me. She placed her fists against her hips and leaned forward, enunciating each syllable as she repeated the word. "Astray. As in, away from his true path. My son held a place of honor at court, trusted by Lord Bael himself despite his youth, and then *you* came along." She jutted a finger in my direction.

"That's enough, Mother."

Tabita turned her glare on her son. "You were well on your way to becoming captain someday, and you threw it all away. For what? *Her?*" Again the slender finger shot in my direction.

I winced, feeling as though the jab had made physical contact. It was true that Kai had resigned his commission as a knight, but that hadn't been *my* fault... had it?

"It's not too late, you know. You could still—"

"Enough!" Frustration tinged Kai's tone, and I wondered how many times he and his mother had had this conversation.

"Think about it." Tabita lifted her chin and sauntered past us. She paused on the lowest step of a staircase at the back of the room and added, "For Rhys's sake, if not your own."

Rhys? I wondered. *Did Kai find a girlfriend when he came home? Is that why he didn't return?* The thought of Kai falling in love created an odd sensation in my chest that made me want to rub my sternum—part joy, part fear. I wanted Kai to be happy, of course, but a new relationship would change his priorities.

Silence hung heavily over the room for a full minute after Tabita's quiet footsteps vanished into the upper levels of the manor.

When I couldn't stand the awkward tension any longer, I said, "She's ... charming."

Kai laughed, and it became easier to breathe.

"Oh, to be able to lie," Hortense said wistfully.

"Sorry about her," Kai said. "As you can probably tell, she's not thrilled that I renounced my knighthood."

"It was quite a blow to your family's status at court," Hortense said.

"What did she mean about it not being too late?" I asked.

He shook his head. "Forget about it."

"And who's Rhys?" I pressed.

Kai opened his mouth, closed it, shuffled his feet, and finally said, "Perhaps it's best if I just show you."

Chapter 3

KAI TOOK A moment to sort the contents of his basket, setting some items on the counter while leaving others in place. I was tapping my foot by the time he picked up the half-full basket again.

We backtracked through the town with Kai in the lead, winding along several smaller paths rather than following the main roads. The surge and crash of the waves faded as an increasing number of hills, buildings, and trees came between us and the ocean. Then the buildings, too, became few and far between. I held my tongue all through town and into the denser forest as my thoughts chased one another like cats trying to catch their own tails. Kai's mother clearly blamed me for Kai losing his status as a Knight of the Realm. The question was, did Kai? Was he having second thoughts about his earlier choices?

We stopped at the edge of a small clearing of calf-high grass that swayed in the breeze, which still carried the hint of salt despite our distance from the water. Kai cupped a hand in front of his mouth and made a bird call, though not of any species I recognized. An answering call came from the branches of an enormous oak whose snaking roots stretched the entire width of the clearing on the far side. The oak's silver leaves shimmered as something larger than a bird dropped through its branches and landed at the base of its trunk with only the smallest of sounds.

A fae with light-purple skin and wild green hair that matched the bright intensity of his eyes straightened from the crouch in which he'd landed. By human standards, he looked like a child, perhaps ten years old. Among the fae, such appearances didn't mean much, but his bearing made me think the representation was accurate. He wore short brown pants that stopped well above his ankles and a loose, cream shirt with laces at the collar and puffy sleeves—a combination that made my human brain immediately think *pirate*. A short sword strapped to his waist completed the effect.

Kai cleared his throat and gestured to the boy. "Alex, Hortense, this is Rhys."

Rhys walked over to our group. He eyed Hortense and me warily as he approached, sidling closer to Kai. "Who are they?"

"Friends." Kai handed his basket to the boy. "Let's show them what you've been working on."

Rhys gave us another assessing look, then bowed to Kai. He carried the basket back to the tree from which he'd descended, set it near the base, then drew his sword and started running through forms. His silver blade glinted in the sunlight, and I could hear the powerful exhales that accompanied each of his well-controlled strikes. I recognized several of the patterns from my own lessons in how to handle a blade, but for all his apparent youth Rhys seemed to be further along in his training than I'd ever gotten.

"I've taken Rhys on as my squire," Kai said quietly.

I glanced at his profile. He watched the boy's techniques with a mixture of guilt and pride.

"You're no longer a knight," Hortense pointed out.

"Not officially," Kai conceded, "but I know the training."

"You hope to make him a knight?" she asked.

"He hopes to become one."

I looked back and forth between them and out to Rhys. "I don't understand. Who is he?"

"He's the son of a friend," Kai said quietly. "A dead friend."

I swallowed and shifted my weight. "I'm sorry."

"His father was a Knight of the Realm. Flynn. He . . . took an interest in me when I was first elevated. Showed me the ins and outs. Kept me out of trouble." The corner of his mouth quirked up. "Or tried to."

I set my hand against his arm. "What happened to him?"

Kai's half smile became a frown. He took a shuddering breath. "He died in the battle against Shedraziel at Hoover Dam."

I stiffened, jerking my hand away. I'd been the one to insist Bael send his knights to help fight the murderous siren Shedraziel when she attacked the Mortal Realm. She was, after all, his general and therefore his responsibility. Many people lost their lives in that battle. Fae. Humans. Werewolves. It could have been so much worse, but that was little consolation to those left to grieve.

I watched Rhys as he moved smoothly from one stance to the next with perfect focus, remembering the mess I'd been when my mother and I received the notice that my father had died in action during the Faerie Wars. That had been a lie to conceal the truth of what he'd become, but I didn't know that at the time. I'd been so angry. I'd hated magic for taking my father away, but I didn't become a Purist. That had been my father's path. A path that, I'd thought, had gotten him killed. I chose instead the path of avoidance, doing my best to pretend magic didn't exist.

I snorted. *Fat lot of good that did me.*

Watching Rhys move through his forms, I wondered where he would direct his anger.

"Where's his mother?" I whispered, afraid I already knew the answer.

"She was in the Mortal Realm during the first sweep when humans started rounding up fae, before the war truly began. She died in one of the internment camps."

"He's an orphan?"

Kai nodded.

"By mortal terms, perhaps," Hortense said. "Fae do not abandon our young. We are not nearly so prolific as humans." She looked at Kai. "Surely the child has someone?"

Kai nodded again. "A great uncle in Nusquam. He's a tree whisperer and wants to teach Rhys the trade."

"What's a tree whisperer?" I asked.

"Someone who can coax plants to grow as they wish," Hortense said. "Usually a wood nymph or dryad."

I frowned. "Rhys looks like a sidhe."

"His father was," said Kai. "His mother was a dryad, and Rhys does have some talent for whispering." Kai pointed into the limbs of the oak.

Following his finger, I spotted what looked like an elaborate tree house among the branches. It seemed so natural there that I would have missed it entirely if Kai hadn't pointed it out. I dropped my gaze back to the base, where Rhys was working up a sweat. "But Rhys wants to be a knight."

"Exactly," Kai said. "He doesn't want to go to his uncle, but he's too young to be completely unsupervised."

"So, you've what, adopted him?"

"In a manner of speaking." Kai exhaled. "Flynn helped me when I was struggling to find my place in the world. I owe him a debt." He gestured to Rhys. "Now I can repay it."

I chewed my lower lip. Debts among the fae were serious matters, especially for someone as duty-bound as Kai.

"You won't be able to take him all the way to knighthood," Hortense said. "Not with your current status."

"I know."

A light bulb flashed on in my mind. "Is that what your mother was talking about? Are you thinking of requesting to be a knight again so you can train Rhys properly?"

Kai's chest expanded as he took a deep breath and let it out slowly. A muscle twitched in the side of his clenched jaw. "My mother only laments the lost honor of my post. She spoke out of place."

"She's a mother," Hortense said, "and you're little more than a child yourself. Too young to take on the role of mentor."

As I understood it, at eighty-seven years old, Kai would be about twenty by human standards. Younger than myself, but hardly a child.

"I know I can't officially apprentice him," Kai said, "But I can get him started. I can teach him the basics and, eventually, connect him with a full knight. Someone who can finish his education."

"So that's why you didn't come back," I said. "You're staying here to train Rhys." My throat clogged as the pressure in my chest tried to force its way up my throat. *I'm going to miss him so much.* But I could hardly fault his choice. It was, after all, the honorable thing to do. Honorable. Selfless. That was Kai to a T, and I would miss having that stalwart reassurance at my side. But more than that, I'd miss his easy smile and the way he made me laugh.

"Since things seemed relatively calm for the moment, I wanted to get some of Rhys's preliminary training done before heading back, at least give him a decent heads up about dealing with life in the Mortal Realm before he has to face it."

Hortense's eyes widened. "You plan to bring him with you?"

Kai looked away. "Not ideal, I know. But if I leave him here, he'll be shipped off to his uncle."

"Perhaps that would be for the best," Hortense said. "The Mortal Realm is no place for a child."

I shot her a scathing glare, feeling defensive on Maggie's behalf. "As if the fae realms are any safer. You have plants that eat people and shoes that make you dance until your feet fall off."

"The dangers are different," Hortense said, "not fewer. It all comes down to what a person knows."

No wonder Maggie wants to write that book, I thought. *What better way to protect her child than with knowledge?*

"Taking Rhys to the Mortal Realm would be risky," Kai said, "but if you need me . . ." He trailed off, his gaze asking a silent question.

Need . . . or want? I wondered. Kai had been the first person to tell me I had magic. He helped me get a handle on my powers and come to terms with my new status as a fae halfer. I'd grown so used to having him by my side through thick and thin that the thought of not having him around hadn't even occurred to me until days slid by without a word from him. *I guess a part of me believed he'd stay with me forever, but that's not fair. He's his own person with his own life. He has friends and responsibilities beyond just me.*

The familiar sense of abandonment that I'd carried since my father left to wage war against magic and never returned, amplified by every friend I'd made and lost when my mother moved us to a new town, rose within me. I'd tried keeping my distance from those around me, protecting myself from the scars I knew deep connections would inevitably leave, but a few people wriggled their way inside, and others had flooded through that breach. Now tethers connected me to so many people, and I'd allowed myself to believe, or at least to hope, that this time the results would be different. But Aiden was dead. James had been taken away by the council. Chase had returned to his family. Kai had taken on an apprentice. It felt as if all the connections I'd allowed to take hold in my heart were snapping one by one, and I was desperately gathering up the loose ends.

But I can't ask him to come back now. I looked at the boy diligently performing the forms Kai had taught him in the shade of the old oak, his shaggy green hair falling over one eye as he performed a dynamic thrust. *Rhys needs him more than I do.* I took a deep breath and blinked to hold back the pressure building behind my eyes. "You should stay here with Rhys."

Kai frowned. "Are you sure?"

I nodded. "Things are relatively calm right now. Negotiations between the fae and mortals are moving forward. With any luck, there will be a new treaty in place by the time Rhys is ready to visit. Then you can both come."

Kai searched my face. "What are you going to see Lord Bael about?"

I waved the question away. "A personal matter. Nothing to worry about."

"Although, if we're done here, we really should get going," said Hortense. "We'll be hard pressed to get back to the portal before nightfall as it is."

Kai opened his mouth, but he was interrupted by Rhys's shout as the boy performed the final technique of his form, a forceful overhead slash.

Rhys made a little flourish with his blade, sheathed his sword, then jogged to our group. Sweat glistened on his skin and dampened his shirt. He stared up at Kai with a serious expression. "How did I do?"

"Excellent," Kai said.

"Your weight is too much on your back foot when you parry," said Hortense.

Rhys tipped his head, considering.

Kai glared at the tutor.

"Your forms looked perfect to me," I said. "You're clearly a much better student than I was."

Hortense snorted.

"You studied the sword?" Rhys asked.

I nodded. "With Kai, in fact." I shot Hortense a narrow-eyed scowl. "And Hortense. They both taught me a lot." *Like how sore you get when you're dropped on your ass a hundred times in a row.* I leaned down so that I was closer to eye level. "I hear you're training to become a knight."

Rhys puffed out his chest. "Just like my father."

I swallowed the lump in my throat. "I never met your father myself, but from what Kai's told me, he sounds like a wonderful person."

"He was," Rhys said. "Brave and true. He did his duty and protected the realm."

And he died. My chest constricted.

We wouldn't have been able to defeat Shedraziel if Bael's knights hadn't held the bridge as long as they did—long enough for the Undine and their water dragon to arrive. We'd saved hundreds, maybe thousands of lives, but as I stared into Rhys's grass-green eyes, I wondered if Flynn's sacrifice had been worth it.

"We couldn't have done it without him," I said, my voice hitching on the last syllable.

Rhys's eyes grew wide. "You were there?"

I nodded.

"Rhys, this is Alex Blackwood," Kai said, "kin to Lord Bael." He gestured to Hortense. "Hortense is a respected scholar and tutor of the court, and she was right about your parry."

Rhys's cheeks flushed a deep violet.

"Speaking of Lord Bael," I said, "we really should get going. But I do hope we can get to know each other better in the future." I straightened and wrapped my arms around Kai's neck, pulling him into a hug. With his hair tickling the tip of my nose I whispered, "Take care of him . . . and yourself."

He squeezed my ribs, releasing me when I stepped away.

"Next time I visit, I'll bring candy." I waved to them both, then turned my back and strode into the forest, fighting to keep my breath even and my cheeks dry.

Hortense paced me like a wraith, drifting soundlessly over the sticks, leaves, and rocks that snagged at or crunched under my boots.

"Do you think Bael would let Kai be a knight again?" I asked when I was sure my voice wouldn't crack.

"Do you think Malakai wants that?" Hortense replied.

I watched light filter through the shifting leaves around us. Kai had loved being a knight. Honor. Duty. Loyalty. Those were hallmarks of his personality. I wasn't sure if he regretted resigning his commission, but I felt certain he'd earn it back someday.

We walked in silence until the town came into view, then turned north toward the field where our mounts waited. The sun had passed its zenith while we were in Kai's seaside town and begun its descent toward the western mountains, highlighting our next destination. Our gaala were right where we'd left them, munching clover under the watchful gaze of the hawk woman, who preened on a nearby branch. She let out a shrill squawk and flapped one wing at us, as though waving farewell. I shuddered and mounted.

The sea came into view once more as we climbed into the sky, and I strained to hear the pounding of the opal waves against the crimson shores until the rush of the wind stole all other sound. The salty scent and the tang on my lips faded as we rode toward the white cliffs that wrapped the expansive forest below in a cradle of granite and marble. With every surge of the gaala beneath me, I felt the tether connecting me to Kai grow thinner.

This isn't goodbye, I told myself. *Change is just a part of life.* But it was hard to ignore the hollow ache that whispered of all the people who hadn't come back.

I shaded my eyes from the sun as it dropped toward the massive peaks ahead, which seemed to grow taller with every pump of the gaala's legs. The sound of rushing water mixed with the wind. Subtle at first, the sound grew until it overtook its airy counterpart. The source of the sound was a massive waterfall that plummeted from a plateau carved into the face of the mountain for a thousand feet before striking the forest floor. The plume of mist caused by the crash of all that water obscured the ground for a mile around the base of the waterfall, but we weren't headed for the bottom.

My gaala climbed higher, following the path Hortense blazed, until the shining spires of Abonaille Malmür, the capital city of Enchantment, sparkled in the afternoon sunlight. A wide swath of deep indigo cut the city in half where the river ran through it before dropping off the edge. Marble walkways bridged the two sides at regular intervals. Higher on the cliff face, looking almost like a natural part of the mountain, Bael's keep loomed over the city. We angled toward the tallest tower, circling to gain the necessary altitude to reach the stone landing platform where airborne traffic was received.

The stone courtyard appeared empty, save for Hortense and myself, as our gaala settled back to solid ground. My ears popped in the sudden silence. I pressed tingling fingers to my numb cheeks and rubbed my arms to get my sluggish blood flowing again. "I need to remember to bring a coat when I come here," I said through chattering teeth. But even as I spoke, the sapping cold of our flight faded. Despite its location high atop a mountain, the city of Abonaille Malmür enjoyed balmy springtime temperatures year-round, thanks to the abundance of magic woven into its construction.

"Greetings, Lady Alyssandra." I startled as Rhoana, the captain of Bael's personal guard, stepped out from under the shadow of a twenty-foot arch at the edge of the open space in which we'd landed. Her long red hair stood in stark contrast to the forest green cape that draped her broad shoulders. Her eyes were flecks of silver caught in an indigo whirlpool that made it difficult to pinpoint the focus of her gaze. "We expected you a good deal sooner."

"Of course you did," I mumbled, considering the sleeve on my right arm, which covered the spiraling tattoo Bael had branded me with. The magical markings had a variety of uses, including boosting my natural fae abilities, warning me when I was being targeted by magic, marking me as Bael's kin, and alerting Bael whenever I entered or exited his realm. I couldn't exactly blame Bael for wanting to keep tabs on my comings and goings since we weren't always on the same page about the best course of action, but I hated feeling like a cat with a bell on its collar.

Two stable hands—both hobs with white hair, wrinkled faces, and long drooping ears—detached from the shadows and shuffled forward to take the reins of our mounts.

I twisted onto my stomach and slid down the gaala's side. My knees buckled slightly when they took my weight, causing me to stumble. I patted my gaala's pale neck and looked it in the eye. "Have a good rest now, you deserve it."

Shaking out my no-longer-numb limbs, I walked across the pale cobblestones and raised a hand in greeting. "Hello, Rhoana."

Rhoana bowed to precisely the correct degree for a high-level servant addressing a Lady of the Court, then she straightened and nodded respectfully to Hortense, who'd drifted up beside me as silently as a ghost. "Well met, Tutor."

Hortense returned the gesture. "And you, Captain." Turning to me, Hortense said, "Come to my rooms when you are done with your meeting. I will be ready."

I opened my mouth, but Hortense was already walking away. She passed under the arch and out of sight.

"Shall we?" Rhoana gestured for me to precede her.

Taking a breath to settle myself, I stepped beneath the towering stones that led into the palace proper. There was no sign of Hortense on the winding steps that wrapped the tower; it was as if she'd simply vanished after passing beneath the arch. Casting one appreciative glance over the expansive vista that stretched away across the keep, the city, and the valley that cradled the vast forest beyond, I began my descent. Rhoana matched my pace. Soldiers in the first guardhouse snapped to attention when we passed. We traded stone walkways and a cool breeze for carpeted halls and crystal stairs as we wound through the labyrinth of the palace's interior. Portraits that seemed to move and meticulously carved doors dotted the walls, guideposts for those more familiar with the space. I occasionally caught sight of something familiar, but around the next corner I would once more become hopelessly lost.

Rhoana stopped abruptly and gestured to a door halfway down a hall carpeted in lush, emerald moss. "The lord is within."

I studied the door. I wouldn't have been able to pick it out from the dozens of others along this hall, each carved with a blazing flame.

"I'll be glad of your escort after this meeting, as well." The words felt awkwardly formal, but it was as close as I could get to the taboo "thank you" or the equally dangerous maneuver of asking for a favor. Even small debts could be dangerous among the fae.

She nodded. "I shall remain here." She lowered her hand and stepped to the side of the door, taking up a stance that seemed simultaneously relaxed and ready to pounce.

I lifted my hand, rapped my knuckles against the wooden relief, and pushed the heavy door inward on well-oiled copper hinges.

"Hello?" I poked my head into the room.

The burble of water over rocks greeted me, each splash matched in perfect harmony to the thrum of an invisible harp that wove a melody through the cascade. A multitude of plants, ranging from towering fronds and silver ferns to fluffy pink bushes that resembled cotton candy, obstructed my view past the first bend in the sunken stone path, but I didn't need to see to know what lay beyond that living veil. I'd been in this garden before, when Bael offered me an impossible deal. A deal that I'd refused.

An anxious knot twisted my gut and my skin grew clammy. *He must know I've come to ask for something. He's reminding me what he wants. What he's always wanted.*

"Hello?" I called, louder this time.

"Back here." Bael's voice came from somewhere beyond the foliage.

I stepped fully into the room and let the door swing shut behind me.

Bael lounged on a low bench piled high with silk pillows in every garish color imaginable, which clashed terribly with his loose crimson shirt and forest-green trousers. The gangly limbs of Bael's teenage body and the smooth contours of his high cheekbones and hairless chin made him appear not much older than Rhys, but there could be no mistaking the weight of age behind the smoldering embers in his abyssal eyes. Complex braids and silver clips held long purple-black hair back from his pale face. He braced a paperback book propped open on one knee and held a half-eaten golden apple in his free hand—except it was no apple.

He took a bite, and the sickly sweet smell of goblin fruit overwhelmed my senses, drowning out the organic smells of the more innocuous plants around me. My mouth began to water. I closed my fists, digging my nails into my palms until my vision cleared. I'd taken a step closer without meaning to.

"It's good to see you, Alex." Bael wiped a trickle of golden juice off his lip with the back of his wrist. "Although I expected you hours ago. Did you get lost?" He peered at me over the top of his book. I couldn't help picturing a hunting lion about to pounce.

"A detour."

The corner of his mouth lifted. "And how is Malakai?"

He knew exactly where I was; he just wanted to see what I would tell him. Does he know about Rhys? Does he think I'm here to get Kai reinstated as a knight?

"He's fine."

Bael took another bite, and again the intoxicating smell washed over me, but the memory of the wasted bodies and screaming need of the kids Hortense and Maggie had only recently freed of the deadly addiction steadied my resolve. This time, my feet didn't move. I gestured to the fruit. "Do you mind?"

Bael glanced at the shiny goblin fruit as though surprised to find it in his hand—as if every action he took, every prop he placed, wasn't calculated to give him an advantage.

"Of course." He tossed the fruit over his shoulder. It disappeared into the vegetation. "Apologies. I'm not used to catering to the frailties of mortals."

I forced myself to hold my tongue. *I'm here to ask a favor. Getting in a fight would be a terrible way to start.*

Bael straightened, folding his long legs like a spider drawing back. He gestured to the now open section of bench beside him. "Please, sit." He tossed the paperback he'd been reading, or at least holding, onto the ground. A half-clad woman with windswept hair stared out of the tattered cover.

"You read romance novels?" I asked as I settled onto the pillows as far from Bael as I could get while sharing his bench.

"You're surprised?"

I shrugged. "It seems like an odd genre choice for an ancient fae lord."

"You don't think fae can be romantics?"

"My experience is that most fae value practicality above emotional sentiment."

He smiled. "A person can be practical in their life choices and still have a romantic soul." He brushed away a lock of purple hair that had fallen over one eye and twisted to face me square on, looking like the eager teen he most certainly wasn't. "What sorts of books do you like to read?"

Don't be fooled, I reminded myself. *He's trying to keep you off balance.*

"Mysteries mostly, but I'm not here to discuss reading habits."

He sighed and shook his head as though disappointed. "Straight to business, then."

I folded my hands on my lap and raised my chin. "I've been trying to recreate the daywalking amulet you made for James."

"Why?" Bael's expression was all predator. "From what I've been told, he no longer needs it."

So I didn't get here ahead of the rumors. It had been a slim hope. Bael had dozens of spies in the Mortal Realm; all the fae lords did. But even if they knew James had overcome the vampires' weakness to sunlight, even if they suspected I might have had something to do with it, none of them knew for certain what had happened or the extent of the phenomena. While the fae hatred of vampires ran deep, and vice versa, the immortal races were nothing if not patient. The fae wouldn't make a move until they understood exactly what they were facing. And I was one of the few people who could provide that information.

Giving Bael the details of James's transformation was a calculated risk, but the secret would likely come out eventually no matter what I did. The smart move was to get in front of it, to get Bael on my side before shit really hit the fan, and, with any luck, to remove James from the line of fire before the summit.

I swallowed, choking on an obstruction in my throat. What I was about to admit was going to make a lot of fae very angry. Hopefully Bael wasn't one of them.

"The amulets aren't for James."

He raised an eyebrow. "Amulets? Plural?"

"I need seven. One for each seat of the vampire ruling council."

Bael's eyes widened. I'd managed to surprise him. He shifted his weight. "You know their identities?"

"No," I lied. "I only dealt with their human servants."

"And you promised them daywalking amulets? Why?"

I forced myself to meet his gaze. "The vampire council recently became acutely aware of James's immunity to sunlight. Not surprisingly, they want it for themselves. As long as James is the only vampire capable of surviving daylight, he is, and will remain, a prisoner of the council. I want you to provide me with seven daywalking amulets in order to buy his freedom."

"You expect me to fund his rescue?"

"You know I love him," I said.

"And you know I don't approve," he replied. "You must be offering something significant if you plan to convince me that James being gone is a bad thing." He perked up. "Have your views changed on providing me with a child?"

My mouth went dry. I glanced at the clearing where, the last time I'd been in this garden, Bael had basically set me up on a blind date and told me to procreate for the good of the bloodline. "They have not," I said stiffly. "Children are not tools, they are not toys, and they are not bargaining chips."

"Pity." He settled back on his pillows. "Then what do you offer in exchange for my help?"

I licked my lips. Deals with the fae were dangerous, but if I wanted Bael to act against his nature, I had to give him something of value. Something I really, really, *really* hoped wouldn't come back to bite me in the ass. "James's daywalking amulet was destroyed during the battle at Arlington."

Bael nodded. "I suspected as much."

"So aren't you curious how he can walk shirtless under the midday sun without burning?"

He sat, impassive, waiting.

"I was able to imbue an immunity to sunlight directly into his core."

"That's impossible."

"Yet I did it," I said. "And I'm willing to tell you how."

Bael's expression remained smooth, but I could see the hunger in his eyes as he considered my words. During our first training session together, Bael had told me that overriding a living person's core was one aspect of imbuing that had persistently eluded him despite centuries of experimentation. He said it couldn't be done . . . but James was living, breathing proof that I—a mere halfer, new to magic—had succeeded where the Lord of Enchantment had failed. That had to sting his pride.

"If you can do that, you shouldn't need my amulets to secure James's release. Simply repeat the procedure for as many of the bloodsuckers as necessary."

Sweat prickled over my palms and along my spine. *He's trying to call my bluff.* This was the trickiest part of the negotiation. If Bael realized I couldn't repeat the process, or worse, that the information I intended to trade him was practically useless, I'd lose every ounce of leverage.

I thought back to a piece of advice my adoptive guardian, Sol, had given me when I was a teenager.

"The trick to any successful negotiation is to make your opponent think you're holding all the aces—that the best thing they can do is fold early to minimize their losses."

"Even if I have nothing in my hand?"

"Especially when you have nothing."

"So, lie my ass off."

"Exactly. But you have to make it believable."

I'd already confirmed that I imbued James to protect him from sunlight. I just needed Bael to believe I could do it again . . . and that I would if he didn't give me what I wanted.

Feigning disinterest I said, "I thought providing the vampires with limited-use trinkets would be a better choice than giving them permanent immunity to sunlight, but if you disagree . . ." I shrugged and started to rise.

"Handing daywalking amulets to vampires—*powerful* vampires, no less—would have serious ramifications."

Gotcha.

"You've done it before," I pointed out, dropping back into my seat.

"That was in payment of a debt." He held up a finger. "One amulet for one vampire who'd proven useful. You're asking me to outfit the leaders of my enemies with a way to overcome their greatest weakness."

"Vampires and fae don't have to remain enemies," I said. "Why not let this vendetta die?"

He chuckled. "You think they'd forgive centuries of slaughter?"

"You won't know unless you ask."

He waved a hand as though shooing a fly. "Vampires and fae will never see eye to eye." His expression brightened. He leaned forward, bracing his elbows on his knees and interlacing his fingers. "I propose a different solution. You've made contact, however indirectly, with the vampire council. We can set a trap to uncover their identities, then I'll kill them. James will have his freedom, and I won't have to betray my morals."

The fact that butchering people simply for being what they were didn't conflict with Bael's moral code, while the idea of compromising with those same people did, made me want to gag, though it came as no surprise. Bael had orchestrated the massacre of an entire realm, pushing dragons to the brink of extinction. He wouldn't lose a wink of sleep over killing vampires. He'd probably throw a party to congratulate himself.

"A fae attack in the Mortal Realm right now would derail the upcoming peace talks."

Bael shrugged. "Only if the humans found out. They don't even know vampires are real."

"Which would make an unsanctioned fae presence all the harder to explain." I shook my head. "I can't take that risk." *And I wouldn't even if I could,* I added silently. Despite my dislike of the vampire council for what they'd put me through, I had no intention of murdering them.

I drummed my fingers against my knee. *Time for Plan B.* "If you won't give me the amulets, teach me how to make them. It will be a simple exchange of knowledge between two people in a similar field. You show me how you made James's amulet, and I'll tell you how I made James immune to sunlight. What either of us does with the information beyond that is up to us. Your hands stay clean, and we both get something we want."

Bael exhaled and glanced up. I followed his gaze. The sky looked bruised beyond the leafy canopy, slashed by fading rays of light as the sun sank behind the city's mountainous cradle. "All right."

A ripple of confusion ran through me as my mind skipped a beat. I'd been ready for another round, or five, of arguments. Bael was clearly opposed to the vampire council gaining daywalking amulets. Despite my proposal, I hadn't expected where those amulets came from to make a significant difference to him. And yet . . . he'd agreed. *Why?*

Bael caught my gaze and narrowed his eyes. "But I have a caveat."

I tensed, growing suddenly cold. *There's the other shoe.* "What do you want?"

"I will show you exactly how I made James's amulet in exchange for all the information you possess about imbuing living beings. To that end, you will remain here in Enchantment and train with me for the next thirty days."

"What?!" I surged to my feet. "With the time dilation, that would be, like, *three months* in the Mortal Realm!"

He shrugged. "If you want to learn, that's the deal."

"Three days, maybe, but thirty? No way. The first time I came here, you taught me how to imbue in less than a day!"

"Mere basics. You're asking for something infinitely more complex. Besides, I want you to see how amazing this place can truly be." He smiled. "I fear your previous visits to my realm have left you with a rather unfavorable impression."

I suppressed an eye roll. *There's an understatement.*

"I'd intended to invite you to the upcoming solstice celebration regardless. Your timely visit has saved me a messenger. You can attend the celebration, explore the city, get to know the people, all while learning more about your powers."

I shuddered, recalling the last fae celebration I attended. It was not an experience I had any desire to repeat. "I didn't come here to sightsee."

"Perhaps not, but maybe, once you've gotten comfortable, you'll find you like this place."

I snorted. *As if I could ever be comfortable here.* Folding my arms, I began to pace. "Three months is a long time."

"It's hardly a blink," Bael said. "And you'll only experience one third of that."

I might experience less time passing in Enchantment, but that wouldn't change all the things I'd be missing on the other side—preparations for the peace talks, Emma's birthday, Maggie's baby being born. I'd have less than a week to fulfill my promise to the vampires when I got back.

"I have obligations in the Mortal Realm."

"Like your obligation to save James?"

My breath hitched. My thumb traced the knotted-fabric ring on my finger.

Bael spread his hands. "You have my answer. The choice is yours. Leave, if you wish. Otherwise, your training begins tomorrow at dawn."

He lifted his book from the ground and opened it, a clear dismissal.

I turned and stumbled out of the garden, unsure where I was headed but desperate to get away. All the cards were on the table now . . . and I was going to be sick.

Chapter 4

I SHUFFLED AFTER Rhoana in a daze, hypnotized by the fluttering edge of her green cape. My feet dragged with each step, delaying the decision I had to make.

Negotiating with Bael had gone more smoothly than I'd expected. I could learn to make the amulets that would free James from his role as the council's lap dog. I just had to give Bael thirty days—three months by Earth reckoning. It was a high price, but not one I *couldn't* pay. And weighed against James's freedom . . .

Three months. I repeated the phase over and over in my head. *Three months away from my home, away from my studio, away from my friends, away from my life.*

It wouldn't feel that long, I reminded myself, trying to find a bright side.

But I'll miss Maggie's baby being born, retorted my pessimism. *I won't be there to help David and Director Harris prepare for the summit. I won't be able to console Emma if things go badly with her family. And with Kai staying in Enchantment, too. . . .* Emma was perfectly capable of taking care of herself despite the loss of her eyesight, but my house was in the middle of nowhere. She couldn't exactly drive into town, and three months was a long time to be isolated.

I shook my head. *I'm a terrible, self-centered friend.* My earlier admission to Hortense rang in my ears. *But I'm the only one who can do this. If I leave now, James is stuck playing puppet for eternity . . . or until one of the other factions assassinates him.*

"The tutor's chambers," Rhoana announced.

I jerked to a stop and looked around the unfamiliar hallway. I hadn't registered any of the paths Rhoana led me down, any of the intersections or landmarks that might have given me some clue as to where I was currently standing. I thought there might have been stairs at one point, but a heavy fog seemed to have settled over my senses as I pondered my choice, blotting out the details of the world through which I'd walked.

Rhoana knocked on a heavy wooden door carved with twisting vines and five-pointed flowers.

"Come." Hortense's voice was muffled by the wood.

Rhoana opened the door but didn't enter. Instead, she stepped back, leaving the path clear for me. I walked into Hortense's world.

The smell of leather, paper, and dry herbs filled the air. The space before me was filled with tables, each stacked high with journals, papers, inkwells, maps, drawings, and silver instruments the purpose of which I couldn't begin to guess. Glass lanterns sat at the center of each table, glowing with a soft white light that seemed to lack any flame or heat. Wooden shelves lined with old books and coiled scrolls covered every wall, stretching from the polished oak on which I stood to the vaulted ceiling far above. Suspended from that ceiling were more of the shining glass globes. Halfway up, a narrow walkway ringed the room, accessible from a spiral staircase in one corner. Ladders attached to the shelves on rails, granting access to higher tomes, and it was upon one of these that I found Hortense perched, twenty feet off the ground, running her finger along book spines.

"One moment. You were faster than expected." Her voice still seemed dampened despite the lack of door between us.

The air felt heavy, or perhaps that was just my mood. I rubbed my hands together, noting the dryness of my skin. "Take your time."

My voice, too, fell flat, as if the room had swallowed the sounds. I traced a finger along the surface of the nearest table. Not one mote of dust dared mar the wood. Leaning over, I studied an open map. It depicted the city of Abonaille Malmür. That anxious, sick feeling welled up again as my gaze roved over the streets and canals, turning the unfamiliar names over in my mind.

It would only be thirty days, I told myself, but part of me wondered, *could I ever be comfortable here?*

"There you are," Hortense shouted in triumph. She pulled a book from the top shelf then slid down the ladder as deftly as an acrobat, book in hand. She waved her trophy. "*A Botanical Guide to Poisons and Potions.*" Tucking the book into a wide carpet bag that sat open on one of the back tables, she snapped the bag closed. "*Now* I'm ready to go."

She lifted the bag, no doubt packed to the brim with reading material, as if it weighed nothing at all and glided toward me over the polished wood.

"You live in a library," I said, desperate to delay the coming conversation. "That seems appropriate."

"Technically, I live *behind* a library." Hortense gestured to an alcove near the back through which I spotted something that looked like a nest.

"It's quite impressive."

"If you're impressed by this, we should stop by the *real* library," Hortense said. "This is just my personal collection."

"I'd like that."

Hortense frowned. Her dark eyebrows drew together. Her red eyes narrowed. "What's wrong?"

I opened my mouth, but rather than words, all that came out was a noisy sigh. I ran a hand over my hair, snagging on my ponytail. "I . . . won't be going back with you."

The words rang like a deadbolt slamming into place, locking me into my decision.

Hortense arched an eyebrow but otherwise held statue still.

"Bael has agreed to show me how to make what I need."

She continued to stare impassively.

I swallowed. "It's going to take a while."

She pursed her lips. "Please tell me you set a specific time frame."

"I'm not stupid." I thought of the hawk-woman in Kai's village and shuddered, wondering what kind of deal she'd made to end up there, and if she still believed it was worth the price she was currently paying. "I'll be gone for three mortal months. I need you to let Maggie, Emma, and David know." I hesitated. "David can probably arrange transportation for you when you get back to the reservation."

Hortense waved a hand. "I can take care of myself. The Mortal Realm may not be my home, but I'm familiar enough with it to get by. I'm more worried about you remaining at court without a chaperone. Perhaps I should postpone my return until your studies with Lord Bael are concluded."

Giddy hope swelled in my chest, followed by embarrassment. *I'm a grown woman. I shouldn't need someone to hold my hand, and Hortense has her own obligations, just like Kai. I can't expect her to put her plans on hold simply because I'm stuck here.*

I licked my lips, trying to work enough moisture into my mouth to smooth the rasp in my voice. "As much as I appreciate the offer, I'll be spending most of my time training with Bael. I doubt he'll want company."

"Indeed. Bael is rather secretive about his imbuing. His workshop is off limits to all save himself and, it would seem, you."

"Besides," I said, "I need you to tell my friends what's going on. I can't just disappear for three months without a word, and my phone plan doesn't exactly cover cross-realm roaming." I shook my head. *See you in a few days.* That's what I'd told them when I left.

I can't believe I'm going to miss the baby being born.

"Tell them all I'm sorry, okay? Especially Maggie. Tell her I promise she'll be my very first stop once I get back."

I sagged against the table with the map on it, staring at the city where I'd be spending the next thirty days. Last month, I'd been held captive by the vampire council in a secluded compound in Canada, completely cut off from all communication, with no idea how long my captivity would last or even if I'd survive. Somehow, this felt worse.

It's because Bael let me choose, I thought. *There's no one else to blame this time. No one to fight or get away from. If I stay . . . it's on me.* But this was my last chance to get James clear of the council before the summit. *My friends will understand.* I gripped the edge of the table. *Please, let Maggie understand.*

"It's getting late," Hortense said. "I should be on my way, and you should get some rest. It seems you have some trying days ahead."

I hesitated, not wanting to lose this last reasonably friendly face, but there was no reason to drag out this goodbye. Not when the people I really wanted to explain myself to weren't here.

Rhoana was standing right where I'd left her when Hortense and I emerged. She inclined her head. "Shall I take you to the gaala pad or to your bedchamber?"

Struggling with an intense desire to race Hortense to the roof and fly away from this place, I gave the tutor a farewell nod, took a deep breath, and said, "I'm staying here."

* * *

DESPITE HORTENSE'S ADVICE to rest, I stood for long hours on the balcony of the apartment I'd been assigned—alone, wrapped in silence and my own thoughts. I hugged myself as unfamiliar constellations winked from the black above, and the glittering lights of the city below glowed like a conflagration beyond the palace walls. The wind whistled past, but any voices it carried were too faint to reach me. Once upon a time, I'd craved silence and coveted solitude, but I'd grown accustomed to the noise and chaos of having other people around. Now the empty quiet prickled against my skin and made my hairs stand on end.

Exhaustion eventually called me to bed, but a few hours of fitful sleep found me back on my feet. I filled the enormous tub in the bathroom with scalding water and soaked until my muscles turned to jelly, then I snuggled into a plush, purple robe that had been set out for me. The mouthwatering aroma of fried sausage and fresh rolls enveloped me when I stepped into the main room. At some point during my bath, a silver tray had appeared on the dark wood dining table that shared the main room with a sitting area and a large fireplace. I hated the idea of anyone walking through my space, borrowed though it was, while I was unaware and vulnerable, but I'd learned on my first visit that trying to prevent the husvaettir—servants bound to the keep and responsible for its smooth operation—from conducting their tasks only led to frustration. Best just to let them do their jobs without fuss.

I lifted a buttermilk biscuit slathered in luscious blackberry jam off the tray and headed back to the balcony, pushing aside the gauzy lavender curtains that covered its wide arches. The polished marble was cool against my bare feet, and slightly slippery since I was damp from my bath. Despite the season and the magic cocooning the city, the morning air made my lungs ache when I inhaled. My breath hung like a cloud for a moment before blowing away. I munched my biscuit as the first blush of dawn chased back the indigo sky and set the frozen peaks behind Bael's keep ablaze in molten gold. Bracing my hands against the rail, I tipped my face to the light of the rising sun. Heat kissed my skin. The promise of a new day.

Day one.

Licking sticky jam off my fingers, I went back inside and slipped out of my robe. Since I hadn't planned on staying in Enchantment, I had exactly one outfit with me—the one I'd worn yesterday. Opening the wardrobe in the bedroom revealed a selection of clothes, all in my size, but none in my style. Not one pair of jeans or simple T-shirt graced the racks. Instead, I faced a sea of silk, lace, and satin. I glanced longingly at my dirty clothes, then pulled out a blue shirt with translucent sleeves and an asymmetrical hem. The closest thing I found to a normal pair of pants consisted of woven swaths of shimmering blue and violet fabric. Together, the articles gave me a distinctly nautical appearance.

Pulling my hair into a tight ponytail that would hopefully keep it out of my way, I snatched a second biscuit as I passed the table and opened the door to my room. Rhoana stood in the corridor beyond.

"These are for you, courtesy of Lord Bael." She held out a leather belt with a sheathed sword, a six-inch hunting knife, and a small satchel.

"How long have you been standing there?" I asked.

She jangled the items, reiterating that I should take them.

Gently pinching my biscuit between my teeth, I cinched the sword belt around my waist and secured the knife to my thigh.

Weapons were just part of the wardrobe in fae realms, especially at court, but the blades were a healthy reminder that being kin to the Lord of Enchantment was no guarantee of safety. There were plenty of fae who felt the same about mixed-race beings like myself as the human Purists back home. I checked the balance of my new sword. It was beautifully crafted, double-edged with an upswept guard and delicate scroll work etched around the ricasso. The hilt fit my hand perfectly, but holding it made me miss the familiar feel of the sword waiting on my dresser back home. The knife had a subtly curved blade with a clip point, serrated back, and a bone handle. Having the blades made me both more nervous and more comfortable. I hated the need for them and the threat they represented, but their weight was a solid reassurance. I might be out of my element, but I was not defenseless.

Inside the satchel I found a small, leather-bound notebook of rough paper and several sticks of charcoal wrapped in a chamois cloth. I smiled. As different as we were, Bael was an artist at heart; he understood the need to have a creative outlet close at hand. Other than a smidgen of genetic code, that was the one thing we shared. I tucked the satchel at my waist, feeling instantly more at home.

This time, I paid attention as Rhoana led me through the halls of the keep, mapping doors, intersections, alcoves, sculptures—anything that would help me navigate on my own. I recognized the sweeping curve of the main entrance room as we descended one of two staircases that spiraled down its outer wall, held aloft by thin strands of woven marble that created elegant archways large enough for a giant to pass through. Polished stone steps gave way to a springy carpet of moss dotted with tiny snow-white flowers that smelled of honeysuckle when I inevitably stepped on them. The greenery dampened the voices drifting out from the rooms beyond the delicate arches as servants, guests, and courtiers went about their business in this most trafficked section of the keep.

I held my breath and kept my gaze trained on my feet as I crossed the open space. Not that anyone was likely to shove a knife in my back in the entrance hall with the Captain of the Guard walking at my side, but I could feel a hundred curious stares like needles driving into my skin. No matter that I was wearing local fashion, accompanied by a familiar face, or had crossed this room a dozen times before, I still felt as if every fae stopped what they were doing to stare at me as I passed, their attention drawn by some elusive quality of otherness that clung to me like a toxic cloud and marked me as an outsider.

Rhoana passed under one of the lacy arches and stopped before a wide, white door with Bael's coat of arms—a sword and hammer crossed over a flame—carved into the pale wood. This was one of several side doors that accessed Bael's throne room, beyond which lay his private workshop.

"I shall collect you after your lesson," Rhoana said.

Nodding, I wiped a slick layer of sweat off my palms and reached for the door's golden handle.

Bael sat at the far end of a lake of smooth marble that glistened like diamonds in the dawn light streaming through the domed glass four stories above. I stepped inside and pulled the door shut behind me. The ambient noise of life in the keep broke off like a snapped thread. All I could hear was my own breath and the pounding of my heart. I took a step, and the soft scuff of my leather boots echoed like a thunderclap.

This room is meant to intimidate, I reminded myself as I strode forward, closing the distance to the dais at the far end as quickly as possible, short of breaking into a run. Ghostly shapes crowded my imagination as I hustled across the room—memories of partygoers pointing at the mortal in their midst with looks of disgust, amusement, disappointment, pity. An itch prickled between my shoulder blades. I glanced up to confirm the second-story balcony that wrapped three sides of the room was empty of any leering audience hungry for entertainment. The only soul present, save myself, was Bael.

I slowed as I approached the raised dais. At its center, Bael sat upon the iron throne that resided at the heart of this realm—a symbol of power for the man who claimed it . . . and a promise of pain to those who coveted that power. Only three fae could sit on that mass of toxic metal without burning alive. Bael, his crazy niece Marron . . . and me, though whether or not I technically qualified as fae was a matter of some debate.

"I'm pleased to see you this morning." Bael smiled down at me like the doting grandfather I once imagined he might be, the expression disturbingly incongruous on his teenage features. He wore no visible weapons, but that didn't mean he couldn't kill me faster than I could blink. The collar of his crimson silk shirt hung open, exposing a smooth, pale chest. Dark leather pants, worn at the knees, molded to his legs and disappeared into the tops of even darker boots. A cascade of purple-black hair draped his shoulders, decorated with twists of golden wire, pins, and shimmering jewels. Other than his youth, Bael might have been posing for the cover of one of his unlikely romance novels. "Do you accept my terms?"

"I'm here, aren't I?" I exhaled, forcing my hands to relax at my sides to keep them from balling into fists. "Thirty days. Not a moment more. During that time, promise me that you'll—"

Bael placed his right hand over his heart. "I swear to show you how I created the amulet that I gave to James all those years ago."

"And explain the process, so I can understand how it was done," I added.

He nodded. "And you will tell me everything you know about imbuing living beings."

I swallowed, trying to work moisture into my suddenly dry mouth. "Agreed."

"Then the deal is struck." A self-satisfied smile curved Bael's lips, making me wonder what I might have missed. "Let's get to work."

* * *

BAEL'S WORKSHOP WAS like an overgrown version of my own. Where my studio had three tables, his had nine. Where I had one cabinet set aside for projects in progress, he had an entire shelf-lined wall. And where my tools were stored carefully in one tidy corner of my workspace, Bael's were cast about like the haphazard casualties of a passing tornado. Still, the smell of wood, fire, sweat, and metal, the sense that this was a place of creation and dreams, put me at ease. I might be a stranger in a foreign land facing an uncertain future, but in this space, I was home. I took a deep breath, tipped my face into the natural light streaming from the floor-to-ceiling windows that looked out over the mountainous cliff beyond the keep, and smiled.

"A deal's a deal." Bael closed the door behind me and strode toward a collection of wooden bins that held scraps and supplies—blocks and planks of wood; tubes, wires, and sheets of various metals; gems; beads; clay; even panels of glass. My fingers itched to dig through those treasures as my brain started processing project ideas. "Take a seat."

I brushed a thin coating of silver dust off the surface of a tall stool and rested my elbows on the workbench in front of me.

Bael rummaged through his bins for a moment before joining me at the table I'd chosen. Lifting one hand, he displayed a large, yellow, gem-cut stone.

I sat up a little straighter. The jewel pinched between Bael's fingers looked very much like the yellow gem that had hung at the center of James's amulet before it was destroyed. I licked my lips. *After months of struggling to figure this stupid spell out on my own, I'm finally going to see how it's made.* My mounting anticipation made it hard to sit still, so I bounced my leg, but my gaze never wavered from what I hoped would be James's salvation.

Bael set the stone on the scarred and stained surface of the table, where it split the morning light streaming through the windows into dozens of tiny rainbows. "This will be the focal point for our spell."

"Is that a citrine?"

He shook his head. "This is chrysoberyl."

"Does the type of stone you use matter?"

He tipped his head side to side, as though unsure how to answer. "Any spell can be tied to any focus, but certain materials make achieving certain results easier."

"So why chrysoberyl?" I prompted, eager for every detail that might point to why my experiments had failed.

"The clarity of the stone and the way its facets are cut to catch light makes it ideal for a spell designed to collect sunlight, and the gem's refraction patterns create a perfect cage to contain that light. Be quiet now, and watch. I'm only going to do this part once."

"Why only once?" I asked, panicked. As Hortense and any of my college professors could attest, I wasn't the greatest student, even when I was trying my best.

"Because that's all I agreed to," Bael said.

"You also promised to help me understand the process."

"And I shall," he said, "but this will be the only demonstration. If you pay attention, once should be sufficient." He lifted his hands, cupping them in the air on either side of the glittering gem. "First, we locate the object's core."

My potential inadequacy filled me with doubts. I'd had months to examine the original amulet before James destroyed it in order to cut down my father's undead army. Clearly that hadn't been long enough. Could I absorb all the necessary information from a single demonstration? What if I missed something crucial?

Shaking my head to clear the unhelpful thoughts threatening to distract me, I settled my attention on the space between Bael's hands and shifted my awareness. *Pay attention*, I scolded myself. *You can't afford to let your mind wander right now.*

Exhaling, I relaxed my eyes as though I were trying to find the shape hidden within a 3D puzzle painting. I opened myself to the flow of magic in the world around me. A gray-blue haze rolled across my vision like fog over a moor, blurring the workshop to blunted shapes and smears of washed-out color beyond the table where Bael and I sat. I tightened my focus. Threads of energy, fine as hairs and glowing with vibrant ruby light, trailed from the tips of Bael's fingers. The fiery light trickled from a vast pool that shone within Bael, almost too bright to look at. The ends of those energy strands sank into the stone between his palms, burrowing until they were anchored at its heart.

I let my awareness follow those threads into the stone, trailing the ruby glow through a sea of prismatic yellow. The stone's core was a web of energy reaching into every atom, every molecule of the chrysoberyl. The threads hummed with purpose, and their song filled me with a sense of stability, order, and strength.

"As you can see, this stone already possesses many of the traits we need." Bael's voice drifted into my awareness as if from a great distance, yet his words were as clear as if he'd spoken them directly into my mind. "We can turn the stone into a cage with only a few minor adjustments."

He twitched a finger, and the trailing ruby thread attached to it tugged one of the gem's natural energy strands into a new orientation. The song resonating from the gem's core changed. Energy rippled across the crystalline structure in the walls of the stone, turning them to mirrors. I blinked, forcing my physical self to see the gem as it lay on the tabletop. It shone with the same golden clarity as before.

"We now have a prison that can hold sunlight," Bael said, sounding almost bored.

I gritted my teeth as envy snaked through me. I could alter the nature of an object, but not without a great deal of concentration and energy. Bael looked half-asleep. Still, at least he was showing me. I might have to work harder, but I had the same gift for imbuing that he did. I could do this. For James's sake, I had to.

"The next step is to forge a spell that will collect sunlight and funnel it into the prison we've prepared." His fingers moved, tickling out a silent aria on invisible keys. Threads of magic wove together, looping, twisting, tying, splitting, faster than my eyes could follow.

"Wait, what are you doing?"

"Laying the groundwork for the spell," he said. "Any lasting enchantment requires a solid foundation."

I recalled the way the first enchantment I'd ever created—a simple glowing ball of clay—winked out as soon as I lost my concentration. That, and the clay had made a terrific splat on the floor when it fell from my trembling hands.

"Now we add the details." His fingers danced through the air. "Define the desired area of affect . . ."

I tracked the movement of his hands, the flow of energy as strand after strand was added to the complex pattern of the spell, but I was falling behind. Every time I blinked, connections seemed to suddenly exist where there'd been none before. "Wait."

". . . create channels through which the light can flow safely to its destination . . ."

"You're going too fast." My head ached as I spread my awareness, trying not to miss anything.

". . . and anchor the spell to a trigger so it's not constantly active." Bael looped a cord of magic through the center of his shimmering creation and trailed the thread to the rhythmic pulse of his heart. "Tie it off . . ." He pulled a ruby string, and the whole complex web tightened, shrinking into a single knot at the center of the gem's core. ". . . and we're done." He relaxed his hands, which no longer glowed with the ruby light of his magic. "Easy."

I closed my mouth with a click of my teeth. The tightly woven bundle of magic he'd created was a perfect copy of what I'd seen when I'd examined James's original pendant—a dense puzzle of interwoven power that I had no hope of unraveling. Using my own power, I plucked at the outer layer of threads, each finer than a single strand of hair. In order to understand the spell, I'd need to untangle and examine every one—and I'd tried, back in my studio. Now I'd have another chance, but rather than feeling hopeful, my heart sank at the prospect. After seeing the spell's creation, I realized for the first time just how many layers of complexity were waiting behind that first, impenetrable shell. *I'd need a machete to get through this. Instead, I have to do it with tweezers.*

Blinking, I shifted my focus from the tangled knot to the physical stone lying innocuously on the table. It looked exactly as it had before Bael poured a massive amount of energy into it.

"Now that you've observed how the artifact was made, let's see you replicate the process."

I crossed my arms and glared accusingly across the table. "You said it would take a month for me to learn how to do this."

"We need to know where you're starting from." He reached one hand toward the gem, pinching the air above it. I adjusted my focus to see the shimmering thread of magic he'd taken hold of. With a single tug, the masterpiece he'd built unraveled. Strands of severed magic fell like confetti from the gem's core, dissolving as they drifted away.

I slammed my palms to the table. The stone jumped from the impact. "Why did you undo the spell?"

"Something like this is too dangerous to leave lying around," Bael said.

I snorted, glancing at the silver box on his shelf that held a world-devouring magical void. "I need to study it to learn how it works."

"The best way to learn is by doing, not watching," Bael said. "You had months to study the original amulet, yet here you are."

I curled my fingers, scratching my nails over the wooden surface, but I couldn't deny the truth. Studying the amulet hadn't gotten me anywhere.

He sat back and gestured to the golden gem in invitation. "Let's see what you've got."

Settling first my body, then my breathing, I opened myself to the magic at the center of my being. Unlike my practitioner magic, which came from the world around me, I had to dig deep to access the paltry reservoir of my fae magic. As the rosy energy washed over me, it riled my emotions, as this type of magic always did. I couldn't affect the core of something else without first embracing my own, including all the muddled thoughts and emotions I pushed aside on a regular basis in order to remain functional.

Excitement and anticipation about Maggie's coming child swelled and ebbed, turning to guilt and regret that I wouldn't be with her. Worry over James's indenture to the vampire council edged toward anger, then loneliness. That loneliness compounded as I pictured Kai standing beside Rhys, Chase choosing to stay with his sister, and the faces of the friends I'd lost. Walls of isolation seemed to close in around me. So many of us had come together to do what was necessary over the past few months, but time marched forward, circumstances changed, and people were moving on with their lives. Would I be left behind? The familiar sense of abandonment settled over me like a voice from the past calling me home.

Taking a shuddering breath, I let my fears and doubts, my hopes and dreams, wash over and through me, acknowledging each before letting it drift away. Once I was centered in my core, I reached my power out to the gem on the table, placing my palms a few inches away on either side, just as Bael had done. I pictured the change Bael had made, and undone—the refractive surface of the gem becoming a one-way mirror that would trap light inside. Where Bael had tugged one strand, I nudged dozens, coaxing them into new alignments, observing the changes, and making another small change. Sweat beaded on my forehead and chilled my skin. I was dimly aware of the physical world around me, of Bael watching from the other side of the table. What would he think of my clumsy technique?

I sifted through strands in the gem's core, pouring energy and intent where the gem resisted my change, fighting to remain what it was. Finally, the gem accepted my instructions. The ripple Bael had achieved after only a few seconds of coaxing spread from the stone's core, turning the facets to mirrors.

I slumped, letting my hands flop flat on the table as I released both my concentration and my magic. "There. One shiny rock prison." I wiped the back of my wrist across my damp forehead.

Bael looked at the stone. He looked at me. "And? Are you done?"

"With the prison part," I said. "Do you agree that it should hold light?"

He looked again at the gem. "This container is an adequate starting point."

"Very encouraging," I grumbled.

With step one out of the way, I lifted my hands back into place, called my magic, and set about building the foundation for the spell I'd watched Bael make. The first few elements seemed to go well enough, but as I moved to the second and third layers of the spell, the complexity grew exponentially. I had to focus some of my energy on binding the light, while another aspect of the spell required a network of invisible highways for the deadly substance to travel along. Then there was the self-sustaining element, the beating heart of the spell that would keep it running once tied off, not to mention the trigger and destination anchors. If I concentrated too long on any one aspect, the others started to unravel.

Time dragged on. My energy flagged. My concentration stuttered. I was trying to weave a braid with thousands of strands in the middle of a hurricane. Threads of energy kept slipping away, mingling where I didn't want them, tangling in some places, vanishing in others. Despite the fact that I was working on a level beyond physical limitations, I didn't have enough hands. Another cluster of threads broke loose. I twisted to collect them, and half the framework collapsed. The remaining strands snapped as my magic wavered, and the entire spell disintegrated around me.

I pushed away from the table and paced the room, exhausted but too anxious to hold still. "It's too big," I said, running a hand over my hair, "too complex." My stomach growled. My knees wobbled. I grabbed the edge of another table as a wave of dizziness nearly toppled me. Using my fae magic really drained me.

"You need to replenish your energy," Bael said. "Sit."

I returned to my seat as he poked his head out the workshop door and exchanged a few words with someone in the room beyond. The yellow stone sat, innocuous, on the wooden tabletop. I glared at its faceted surface. Here in the physical world, it was impossible to see that I'd made any change to its structure. Sunlight glinted off the gem, winking in mockery of my latest attempt to tame it. Frustration from every failed experiment I'd conducted in my pursuit of making this damned amulet overwhelmed me. "What good is making a prison to hold light if I can't catch any?"

"None at all," Bael said, returning to the table. "Food is on the way."

My stomach clenched and let out another low rumble. Food would help replenish my spent energy, but it couldn't shift the weight of my disappointment. It was foolish to believe watching Bael create the amulet in person would miraculously make all the pieces click into place for me . . . and yet I had. I'd been wrong.

Bael said this was a difficult spell, I reminded myself. *It'll take time and practice. That's why I'm staying here.*

"I'll try again once I'm rested," I said. *As many times as it takes.*

"In the meantime," Bael said, settling on his stool, "tell me everything you know about imbuing living beings, starting with how you changed your vampire lover."

Chapter 5

I TRUDGED ALONG the keep's hallways, dead on my feet as I reversed the path I'd taken with Rhoana that morning. My stomach growled despite having eaten the equivalent of three days' worth of meals in the past six hours. Nothing kicked my metabolism into overdrive like casting magic, and I'd pushed myself to my limits. Not that my efforts had produced anything close to success.

I took comfort in the fact that Bael seemed equally stymied. True to my word, I'd relayed everything I'd learned from imbuing James to walk in sunlight, including the fact that a change couldn't take hold unless both parties were in complete agreement about what they were trying to accomplish. Anything less would result in the subject's death if the caster tried to force the matter.

I'd expected Bael to be furious when the information he'd traded for turned out to be useless, but he simply *hmm*ed and muttered about similar results during his previous research.

Amber light slanted through window slits, slicing the marble into ribbons of light and dark that had a strobe-like effect as I drifted along. My muscles felt watery, and fluff seemed to fill my skull. A sharp, sweet smell tickled my nose. Rounding the final corner to my room, I came to an abrupt stop. Farther along, two men waited in front of my door.

Mica, the almost-heir to Enchantment with whom Bael had once demanded I produce a baby, sat with his back against a wall, ankles crossed, and hands folded behind his head. His relaxed posture gave the impression that he was lounging in the comfort of his own room rather than a public hallway. Blue-and-silver robes with wide sleeves and a tapered hem draped his trim figure, cinched with a leather belt that held two sheathed daggers and an ornate rapier. Silver embroidery traced the heavy fabric of ultramarine boots that laced to his knees. The tips of his sharply tapered ears peeked through a cascade of long hair the color of pale champagne, and silver flecks drifted on a marbled sea of blue and green in Mica's distant gaze. His lips pulled into a warm smile. "We heard you were visiting and thought we'd pay our respects."

"Though you certainly kept us waiting." Across from Mica, his lover, Haru, pushed away from the wall he'd been leaning against.

I'd seen Haru take the form of a human as well as a massive flying fox, but he stood now in his in-between state. While he wore the body of a man, large triangular ears tufted with red fur parted his snowy hair, and seven fluffy white tails tipped with crimson waved behind him, marking the gruff kitsune's age at just over six hundred years. His chest was bare save for a white vest embroidered with iridescent crimson thread, and he wore pleated white pants that I would have taken for a skirt if not for the seam when he moved.

"Now, now," Mica said as he stretched and straightened, "we can hardly blame her for being late if she didn't know we were coming."

Haru snorted and crossed his arms, though his lips maintained the sardonic smile that seemed to be their resting position.

Turning to face me fully, Mica offered a courtly bow. "If you're amenable, we would like to take you into the city for dinner. Perhaps show you the sights?"

I glanced back the way I'd come. "I'm not sure I'm allowed to leave the keep."

"You're not a prisoner," Mica said. "You're a guest. Surely you don't intend to stay cooped up in your room the entire time?"

I shifted my weight. That's exactly what I'd pictured doing. Though I had to admit, spending another night alone in my room didn't hold much appeal. I appreciated Mica reminding me that even here, cut off from my home and my friends, I wasn't entirely isolated. While neither Mica nor Haru were friends exactly, they were familiar. Both had proven useful allies when our goals aligned in the past, and if anyone could commiserate with my current situation, it would be Mica. He'd spent most of his life under Bael's thumb.

Mica offered me his arm. "Shall we?"

Casting another nervous look around the hallway, I hooked my elbow with his. "Lead on."

Haru took up a position on my other side, the hallway being wide enough for six average-sized people, or a single giant, to walk abreast. He didn't offer his arm, but his tails occasionally brushed my side distractingly as we walked.

Two guards—a towering troll with weathered stone skin holding a massive spiked club and an eloko wielding a spear—blocked the open gate. I stiffened. Would Bael really let me leave? Maybe he'd set some kind of magic barrier around the estate. I licked my lips and tightened my grip on Mica's arm as we approached the gate.

Mica glanced at me but didn't slow. When we were within speaking distance of the guards, he raised his free hand in greeting. "Evening Dorset, Vaughneg."

The eloko waved back, white teeth shining from his leafy beard.

I held my breath as I walked under the sharpened spikes of the raised portcullis. Nothing happened. I flexed the fingers on my right hand, checking for even the slightest tingle in the tattoo that spiraled up that arm, hunting for any indication that magic was being used against me. Nothing. Both guards bowed as we passed between them. I exhaled.

We continued across the courtyard beyond the gate, headed for the widest lane leading away from the keep. Lampposts of carved marble suspending globes of clear glass illuminated every corner like tiny novas, casting wide arcs of yellow light over the glistening cobblestone streets and ornately carved buildings. There was no distinction between road and sidewalk, perhaps because cars didn't exist in this realm, so we strolled directly down the center of the street.

I glanced over my shoulder, unable to believe I'd been allowed to simply walk out of the keep, yet no one seemed to be following.

The surrounding estates towered over us, making even the wide road seem narrow under their looming shapes. Wood and marble mixed seamlessly to create ornate archways, lofty towers, sweeping balconies, and elevated walkways. Plants clung to walls and cascaded from planters at every level, softening the stark stone and bringing life to the cold mountain peak that cradled the city.

"I guess no one in this town is afraid of heights," I muttered, craning my neck to find the line where the glittering windows of a particularly tall tower gave way to the stars above.

"There's a limited amount of space on the plateau that cradles Abonaille Malmür, so the city is forced to build up rather than out," Mica said.

For all its grandeur, the neighborhood seemed deserted. Only we three walked the street, and for every building with its windows lit, six others stood dark. "Where is everyone?" I asked. "The sun set less than an hour ago. Surely they're not all asleep already?"

Haru laughed. "Certainly not." He indicated the opulent buildings around us. "These are homes away from homes for members of Lord Bael's court, only occupied when their owners deign to visit."

"My parents have an estate two streets over." Mica's voice remained cheerful, but it carried a hollow note. "They're hardly ever there."

He reached into the breast of his shirt and pulled out a small, silver snuffbox. Flipping the lid with the ease of familiarity, he dipped one finger into the box's glittering contents and lifted it to his lips. As soon as the pixie dust touched his tongue, every hint of tension eased from his expression. His gaze grew unfocused. The box went back in his pocket.

I frowned but held my peace. Mica had basically been sold to Bael as an infant then cast aside for not living up to the lord's expectations. He was a prisoner in his own life. How he chose to deal with that trauma was none of my business.

"The servants, merchants, and other folk who actually keep this city running all live on the other side of the river," Haru said.

I raised an eyebrow. "You have a limited amount of space here, but you leave half the city empty? That seems stupid."

Mica shook his head. "The buildings aren't 'empty,' they're waiting. You'll see once the courtiers arrive for the Solstice Festival; most of these buildings will be occupied."

"Why can't the courtiers stay in the keep?" I asked. "There are plenty of rooms."

"Some do," Mica admitted. "Lesser ones, mostly. Maintaining an estate in the city is a status symbol, used or not."

"Waste of space if you ask me," muttered Haru.

I agreed—and the deserted streets were creepy as hell.

Something moved at the edge of my vision. The hairs on the back of my neck rose. I scanned the shadows. Nothing stirred.

Mica turned down a smaller street. He and Haru seemed relaxed, but the unsettling pressure at my back remained. Sweat prickled on my skin.

I slowed as I rounded the corner, falling back from the others. Dropping my hand to the hilt of my sword, I drew the blade and spun, slicing the air where we'd just passed.

Metal rang against metal as my blade connected with another. Rhoana met my gaze over our crossed swords. "Nice to see Kai's lessons weren't wasted."

"Are you here to take me back to my room?"

"No," Rhoana said, sheathing her sword.

I did likewise. "Then what are you doing here?"

"My job. Upon Bael's orders, I'm sworn to protect you for the duration of your stay. You're welcome to explore, but wherever you go, I go."

There it is. A sense of self-satisfaction flowed through me. I wasn't just being paranoid. Bael *had* given orders to monitor my movements, though I appreciated being given a leash rather than a cage.

"If you're going to follow me, I'd prefer you stay where I can see you," I said.

Mica swept an arm around my waist, turning me about and ushering me once more along the road. "Don't worry. In a few days you won't even notice her hovering."

Had he known she was there all along?

"The trick to ignoring bodyguards," Haru said, keeping pace at my side, "is to pretend they're part of the furniture—easy to overlook, but handy when you need them."

Rhoana made an exasperated sound as she trailed behind us.

Six blocks from the keep's main gate, we came to the banks of the river that divided the city. A smooth wall ran at waist height as far as I could see in either direction. Light danced over azure water as the river rushed along its trough. Recalling the size of the waterfall plummeting from the cliffside, I'd expected the roar this close to the river to be deafening, but it was hardly a whisper as it raced with frictionless ease through the polished chute.

"The river Algana," Mica said. "This river feeds the lakes and waterways throughout the forest below, all the way to the eastern marshes."

A grand bridge that looked to be spun from spider silk arced over the thirty-foot span of water. Fine white threads that seemed to glow with an inner light wove an intricate pattern that extended from both banks and twisted into ornate spires along either side of the paper-thin walkway. I paused with my foot on the lowest of three concentric half-circle steps that led onto the bridge, marveling at the sheer impossibility of the construction.

"Don't worry," Mica said. "It may look fragile, but a clan of cave trolls could dance a jig on this bridge and it wouldn't so much as wobble."

I wasn't worried the bridge would break. I'd witnessed enough magical miracles to know better than to judge strength by appearance alone. What gave me pause was the sheer alienness of the city through which I was walking, where even something as simple as the physics of a bridge or the way water sounded was different from anything I was used to.

A flood of homesickness overwhelmed me. I hugged myself, trying to ease the ache in my chest as I crossed the river. *I want to go home.*

Beyond the bridge, other pedestrians appeared on the streets. Just a few at first, but more and more as we continued on. Soon the crowd became a river that swept us up in its current, their voices creating the din I'd expected from the Algana. Sidhe seemed to make up the majority of the city's population, easily identifiable by their elvish features, though their skin came in every shade from moonlight white to deepest indigo. Likewise, their fashions ranged from medieval suits of armor and courtly dress to Bermuda shorts and Hawaiian shirts. But sidhe weren't the only race in attendance.

A green-skinned creature who stood barely as tall as my knee barreled past in what looked like a poncho made of couch upholstery. I twisted to avoid the little fellow and bumped into someone else. When I turned to apologize, I found myself looking up and up into the face of a ten-foot walking tree wearing a three-piece, pinstripe suit. A two-person rickshaw clattered by, pulled by a being who seemed to be made entirely out of bundled twigs, and a gnome cruised past on a bright red bike modified with gears and pulleys so the three-foot woman could work the petals.

As the crowds became more colorful and cluttered, so too did the scenery. The elegant manors of the elite gave way to smaller buildings, still four and five stories high, but narrower and packed close together. Wooden stalls and carts lined the streets. Some looked as if they moved from place to place, while others gave the impression of long-standing structures despite their slapdash appearances. Artisans and merchants shouted to the passing horde, offering their wares. Billboards made of paper, wood, or in some cases floating lights advertised everything from wishes granted to musical recordings from the Mortal Realm. Buskers walked the crowd or staked out intersections, trading entertainment for shiny baubles.

Haru danced a few steps ahead, did a little twirl and spread his arms wide, narrowly avoiding slapping a pink-skinned woman in a translucent bathrobe who fluttered by on iridescent wings. "Welcome to Abonaille's night market," he said with a sharp-toothed grin. "Where you can get nearly anything your heart desires."

"For a price," added Mica, as if I needed the reminder not to make impulsive deals with fae.

A dozen different aromas mingled in a gluttony of smells—some sweet, some savory, some rancid. The noise of a hundred conversations, the chime of bells, the holler of the vendors, and a dozen different songs being played on a dozen different instruments bombarded me. I locked my knees to keep from stumbling under the onslaught and turned my attention every which way, gaze jumping from oddity to oddity, trying to take it all in. Traffic split and swirled around us like water flowing around a rock. I found myself gripping the sword at my hip hard enough to turn my knuckles white.

I don't belong here. The statement echoed through my head, beating in time to my racing pulse. I'd gotten used to seeing strange things, accepting that people came in all shapes, sizes, and talents . . . but those had mostly been in small doses on my own turf. This was everything all at once. There was nothing familiar here at all. It was too much.

"Come on, I promised you dinner." Mica tugged my arm, pulling me toward the market stalls. Stopping in front of an open grill, he traded a handful of what looked like shards of colored glass for three wooden skewers, each piercing four dark spheres. He handed one to me. "They're called crasta."

I examined my spheres. Steam wafted off of them, carrying a smell like pie crust mixed with curry.

Mica bit one off his skewer. Haru pulled all four off his stick, tossed them in the air one at a time, and caught them in his open mouth. I took a tentative bite. Flavor exploded on my tongue—tangy and savory, with a texture like fried dough. It tasted like nothing I'd ever eaten before.

I continued to nibble as we waded through the market. Nearly naked people draped in gauzy scarves promised a good time from the upper stories of what I could only assume was a brothel. Haru nudged Mica and directed him toward a vendor whose cart was piled with bolts of cloth in everything from pressed flowers to woven gold. Beside the cloth merchant, a flicker of motion caught my eye. Colored lights darted around the insides of small glass globes suspended on strings. For some reason, looking at the flashing lights made me incredibly sad.

"Looking to trade?" A goblin behind the cart rubbed his knobby-knuckled hands. He wore a Grateful Dead T-shirt crossed with a beauty pageant sash and a diamond tiara.

"What are they?" I leaned forward, extending a finger to touch one of the dangling globes.

Rhoana was suddenly there, gripping my wrist. She gave a small shake of her head, and I withdrew my hand. I had no idea what might have happened if I'd touched the glass, but I was suddenly very glad Rhoana had insisted on following me.

"He's a memory merchant," she said. "I assume you don't want to lose any of yours."

All the warmth seemed to drain out of me. I looked again at the trapped lights. Those were people's memories?

Mica slapped me on the back. "See anything you like?"

I licked my lips. My fried dumpling wasn't sitting so well. "Actually, I think I'd like to head back now."

His smile faltered. "Is something wrong?"

"No, I just . . ." I hugged myself, rubbing my arms. "It's been a long day."

"We haven't even visited the pleasure district yet." Haru molded himself to Mica's back, reaching around to trace a talon-tipped finger along his neck and down his chest. "We could make you forget all your woes."

I backed up a step. "Um, no thanks."

"I'll take her back to the keep," Rhoana said. "You boys enjoy the rest of your night."

Mica studied me, his gaze full of concern. "Are you sure?"

I nodded.

"All right," he said. "We'll finish the tour another day."

I hurried out of the night market, thinking I would breathe easier with every step away from the crowds, but as Bael's keep loomed before me, I realized the sight brought me no comfort. What I wanted was my own home, my own bed. I wanted not to feel like I was drowning.

One day down, twenty-nine to go. Setting my jaw, I marched back through the gate of Bael's keep. *This is going to be the longest month of my life.*

Chapter 6

"YESTERDAY PROVED THAT, be it mentally or magically, you aren't capable of maintaining all the elements of this spell long enough to bring it into existence." Bael stood with his back to me, bathed in the rosy, dawn light streaming through the workshop windows. Today he wore a brown robe-style shirt that crossed low over his chest, billowing pants the color of sea foam, and white slippers. A loose bun decorated with a golden ornament held his long, dark hair away from his face.

I trapped my tongue behind clenched teeth, fully aware of my shortcomings and equally aware that defending my failures would serve no purpose other than to make me look childish. *But he doesn't have to make me sound like an idiot. He said himself this spell would take time to master.*

I crossed my arms and joined him at the window, staring over the craggy cliffs behind the keep. Beyond the edge of the city's plateau, a strip of the multicolored forest that blanketed the valley below was just visible when I stood close to the glass. I took a deep breath, glad I'd ignored the corseted options in my closet in favor of a less constricting calf-length dress in a gradient of pink at the collar to yellowish-green at the hem.

"I'm here to learn," I said, pleased with how even my voice sounded despite my irritation. "So, what do you suggest?"

"Begin with something smaller, something simple." He pursed his lips, pondering. "When Malakai first tested you for imbuing, he used a simple light test, did he not?"

I nodded, recalling the lump of clay I'd made glow just by closing my eyes and thinking about sunshine, and the wet slap of that clay hitting the floor when I looked down and freaked out at the sight of what I'd done. That was the first time I'd ever consciously used magic . . . sitting in my living room, denying what I was. *How far I've come.*

"We'll use that to begin, except instead of creating the light, you'll simply collect it. Once you're proficient at that, you can move on to the next step, and so on. Eventually—"

"I can put all the individual components together to make the amulet," I finished.

Bael moved to the drawer from which he'd pulled the chrysoberyl the day before. Instead of retrieving a single stone, he brought the entire drawer to the table nearest the windows and poured the contents onto the wood. A fortune of cut gems tumbled out—emeralds, diamonds, sapphires, garnets, and a number I had no names for.

"We'll start with storage capacity," Bael said. "Don't worry about blocking the light's visibility yet; we want to see it. Just collect as much as you can in each stone." He waved a hand, and a thick piece of folded fabric jumped off a shelf, shook itself out, and stretched from floor to ceiling in a far corner of the room. "Once you've stored as much light as you think you can in a single stone, take it behind the curtain to see how brightly it glows. That will be a good indication of how much light you've collected. For reference, if you'd looked at the gem in James's amulet without its mirrored shielding in place, you would have gone blind."

I swallowed, recalling the nova created when that amulet shattered, and the searing light that tore through my father's undead army. "If it's that bright, I'm not sure I should—"

"Don't worry," Bael cut me off. "Judging by yesterday's performance, you've a long way to go before you're competent enough to be dangerous. We'll perfect your containment technique long before the quantities you're channeling become an issue."

I swallowed the insult and tried to take comfort in the fact that Bael seemed confident I wouldn't accidentally melt my eyeballs.

Licking my lips, I picked up a weighty topaz and held it up to the light streaming through the windows, then I cleared my mind and reached for my magic. Familiar waves of doubt and frustration washed over me, along with a sense of dissociation that I had a feeling would be a constant companion for the next month. Once I was settled in myself, I pushed my magic into the topaz. I could sense the way the sun's light struck the gem's surface and bent, changing direction as it bounced off the facets. Following the hum of purpose in the topaz's core, I found the threads of energy that dictated the gem's physical properties.

Let the light pass through. I nudged a strand here, another there, using my magic to coax the stone into a new state of being until the beams of sunlight passed through the surface of the topaz as if it were clear glass.

Now for the cage.

I made the same adjustments to the topaz as I had to yesterday's chrysoberyl and swelled with pride when my efforts sent a ripple of change across its surface, but my self-satisfaction was short-lived. In mirroring the surface, I'd undone my earlier work. The sunlight was simply bouncing off the gem.

"View the two sides of the stone's boundary as separate objects," Bael said. He seemed distracted, as though his mind were elsewhere.

Huffing a frustrated breath, I returned the gem's exterior to its glass-like state, then focused my awareness on the threads of energy that connected specifically to the inner surfaces, avoiding those that passed all the way to the exterior. Half a dozen tugs on various strands of the gem's core, and another change rippled through the stone. This time, only the interior of the topaz became a mirror.

"I did it!" I shouted in triumph.

"Now see how much light you can put inside."

I tried not to let my irritation show, reminding myself that I was an adult. I knew my own worth. A pat on the head might have been nice, metaphorically speaking, but Bael was hardly going to be impressed by the equivalent of my playing chopsticks when he was trying to teach me Beethoven's Ninth.

Returning my attention to the topaz, I tried to create a feeling of drawing in, encouraging the stone to pull the light inside. When the gem felt full to bursting with light, I tied off my magic and withdrew. I blinked. The stone in my hand was a shimmering amber in the sunlight. I smiled.

Bael nodded. He didn't smile. "Take it behind the curtain."

When the heavy cloth fell closed at my back, not a scrap of natural light leaked into the corner. I opened my hand. The topaz was warm on my palm, but the dim amber light it cast barely illuminated my fingers—more a glow-in-the-dark sticker than the light bulb experience I'd been expecting.

My throat constricted. The triumph I'd felt a moment before turned to ash. *I've still got a* very *long way to go.* Suddenly, thirty days didn't seem like enough time.

Dejected, I lifted the curtain and stepped out. Bael remained by the window. He'd known what I would see, or rather wouldn't see, behind the curtain.

"The stone felt full," I said. It sounded like an excuse. Clearing my throat, I tried again. What mattered wasn't my failure but how I moved forward. "How can I make it hold more light?"

The corner of Bael's mouth quirked up. I'd finally said something he approved of. "How can a single canister of helium fill fifty balloons?"

"It's stored under pressure." The light bulb went on, flickered, then winked out. I frowned, thinking back to my high school physics class. "But light isn't like air. It doesn't have mass, so it can't be pressurized."

"Not in the traditional sense, perhaps," Bael conceded. "But magic makes a great many things possible."

While that was true, "it's magic" wouldn't help me learn. I opened my mouth to ask for a clearer explanation, but a knock sounded against the workshop door.

Now Bael smiled fully. "Finally."

Setting the lackluster topaz on a table, I watched him open the door. Three fae strode into the room. A panotti with long, leathery ears like those of a large, furless rabbit; an indigo-skinned sidhe with yellow eyes; and a short, blond hob. They each wore the green-and-leather livery of Bael's servants, and they each carried two silver cages. A smell of cut grass and wet earth followed them into the workshop.

"Set them over here." Bael indicated a long bench near one wall.

The servants set down their cargo and hurried out of the room without so much as a glance at their surroundings, seeming almost afraid to set eyes on anything in Bael's private workspace.

I wandered closer. Each of the six cages contained a small brown-furred creature, about the size of a guinea pig, with large, round ears that swiveled toward every sound. They crouched on two legs that seemed built for jumping, while two smaller legs tipped with black-fingered paws were tucked against their chests. Thick, whip-like tails lashed in agitation. I leaned closer to one of the cages, and the creature inside turned quicksilver eyes that took up most of its face in my direction. The pink nose at the end of its whiskered snout wiggled.

"What are they?"

"We call them droust."

"They're cute." I frowned, crossing my arms over a sick, twisting sensation in my gut. "Why are they here?"

"Their presence here has nothing to do with your training. Pay them no mind."

"But—"

"You have your tasks, I have mine. I suggest you concentrate on your studies." He pointed toward the windows and the waiting pile of glittering gems. "You have a long way to go."

I reluctantly walked away, but the scuffing noises coming from the droust in their cages followed me, along with a choking certainty that their presence in the workshop was my fault. I'd told Bael everything I knew about how I'd permanently altered James's core, including the fact that it was impossible without the subject's soul-deep consent and cooperation. But I'd seen the wheels turning behind his eyes. I didn't think he was willing to take my word for it. I glanced over my shoulder. *What is he planning to do with them?*

Settling with my back to Bael and his distracting menagerie, I picked up an aquamarine and repeated my experiment. I set the properties of the two-way mirror in about half the time I'd taken with the topaz. I let as much light as seemed naturally possible flow into the gem, then I turned my attention to the daunting task of forcing more into the prison.

Magic makes a great many things possible.

If I, or at least my awareness, could fit inside the gem, then surely physical space was no limitation to what the gem could contain. Twisting the stone's core, I tried to compress the existing light, to make room for more . . . and it seemed to work. The balance of light inside and outside the gem shifted; more flowed into my trap. When I once again felt as if not a single photon more could be added, I withdrew my magic and hurried to the curtained corner to see the results.

A quick glance as I passed showed Bael bent over one of the cages. He seemed to be whispering to the creature within.

As soon as the curtain fell into place behind me, I opened my hand. A faint blue glow illuminated my fingers and forearm—the same result as I'd gotten with the topaz.

"What the hell," I muttered. "I know I got more in there this time, so why—"

A terrible sound rent the air, part scream, part snarl. I dropped the stone in my haste to pull back the curtain. Bael was where I'd last seen him, leaning over a caged droust, but the creature wasn't alone in its cage. A flat board the exact length and width of the cage pressed against the struggling creature's back, crushing it under the weight of half a dozen stones that now filled the top half of the cage. The droust let out another soul-scraping scream. The other cages rattled as the struggling creature's companions jerked and chittered in agitation, perhaps realizing they were likely to be next.

"Stop!" I ran across the workshop as the pitiful creature struggled to inhale. "You're killing it!"

"Only if it doesn't cooperate," Bael said evenly, his attention fixed on the whimpering droust.

I slammed into the table and flipped the cage. A rock smashed against my fingers where I'd grabbed the metal bars for purchase. Rocks, board, and droust all inverted, so the tiny creature lay on top, paws twitching and sides heaving. I saw my reflection in its large, silver eyes.

"Why did you do that?" Bael demanded. Lines of irritation marred his seemingly youthful face.

"You were killing it," I shot back, cradling my battered knuckles.

"I was motivating it. You said a subject needed to *want* to change in order for imbuing to take hold."

My mouth dropped open. "You were torturing it so that it would want to change?"

"Of course," he said matter-of-factly. "I was attempting to strengthen its body the entire time. All the fool thing had to do was let me."

"It doesn't work that way," I shouted. "You can't *force* someone to want something."

"We can't know that yet," he accused. "You interrupted the experiment before we reached the critical stage."

"Because you were *torturing* a helpless creature!" I flapped my arms. Couldn't he see what he was doing was wrong? "You could have killed it!"

"That's why I have extras." He indicated the other five cages. The droust had quieted when their companion stopped screaming, but they were all huddled to the farthest corners of their cages, shivering. The pungent stench of fear wafted off them. These animals knew they were about to die.

"And there are plenty more where these came from," he said. "Droust breed at a rate that puts even humans to shame. You can't walk in the surrounding woods without tripping over one."

"I don't care how many of them there are," I said. "You can't just go around killing things to satisfy your curiosity."

His expression darkened. "That is the second time you've dared issue me a command." The temperature in the room seemed to drop. The droust stilled in their cages, hardly daring to breathe, and the sudden absence of those small, ambient noises made the pounding of my heart disturbingly loud. "I've shown you a great deal of lenience, granddaughter. I'm beginning to think that may have been a mistake."

Between the familiar atmosphere of the workshop and Bael's childlike countenance, I'd let myself relax, let myself forget what the being before me truly was. He stood perfectly still, but that stillness carried the promise of a threat—if he wanted, I'd be dead before I ever saw him move. Power radiated from him like heat waves under a desert sun. The ancient depth of Bael's inferno eyes was enough to drown me. My knees threatened to buckle as some animal instinct urged me to run despite the knowledge that fleeing would be useless.

"I apologize." I struggled to force the words past the pressure choking me. My voice shook. "I meant no disrespect."

The oppressive weight of his glare lifted, and just like that I knew exactly how the droust felt when I flipped its cage to relieve the pressure of the stones. I took a deep, shuddering breath.

"Apology accepted," Bael said in the slightly bored tone he'd used that morning. "Let's get back to work."

"Um . . ."

He glanced at me, seemingly surprised I'd opened my mouth again.

"While I don't presume to imply what *you* can or can't do," I said carefully, painfully aware of the paralyzing pressure I'd just escaped, "*I* can't just go about my business while this is happening." I gestured to the rescued droust. It had recovered enough to roll onto its stomach, but the wet wheezing sound accompanying its rapid breaths made me worry I hadn't been fast enough to reach it before something inside gave way.

He frowned. "Why? What happens to them doesn't affect you."

I took a deep breath and let it out slowly, allowing my emotions to slide through me as I did when I called my magic. If I wanted to make Bael understand where I was coming from, not to mention keep my hide intact, I needed to control my temper.

Fae judged the value of life differently than humans, and Bael wasn't just any fae. He'd decimated an entire civilization without batting an eye, and he only held off invading my own realm because I'd blackmailed him into delaying for a year—a deadline that was fast approaching. He would lose no sleep over the suffering of what he considered lesser lifeforms—a category that many fae believed humans fit into as well. I imagined my friends in place of the droust and shuddered.

"Witnessing the suffering of another living being *does* affect me, even if the abuse isn't directed at me personally." I looked down at my palms. "Ignoring mistreatment is the same as condoning it. If I'd stayed silent, I might as well have inflicted the damage with my own hands."

"You have empathy for these creatures," Bael said.

I nodded.

"And you are passionate in upholding your beliefs." He gave me a considered look. "I can respect that."

I exhaled. "So, you'll stop experimenting on them?"

"No."

"But—"

"While I respect your opinion on the matter, this line of inquiry is too important to abandon in deference to your mortal sensibilities. I regret any discomfort my decision may cause you, but you'll just have to bear it."

I gritted my teeth. "I can't just go on practicing my imbuing while you torture and murder these droust right next to me."

"Then I fear you will make very little progress toward your goal," Bael said with a frown. "If you should choose to spend the next twenty-nine days glaring at me in silent protest rather than advancing your skills, I will understand, but this experiment will proceed regardless. I will not allow you to interfere again."

The quiet threat thrummed through me. Sweat broke out on my palms. If I interrupted his experiments again, I wouldn't get off with just a talking to.

Defeated, I returned to my side of the workshop, dragging my feet over dusty stone. The waiting gems twinkled in the sunlight, inviting me to lose myself in my work. I slumped onto a stool and stared at the glittering pile.

There was nothing I could do to stop Bael. He was one of the strongest fae alive. I couldn't even dream of that kind of power. Yet I felt like a coward for backing down. I might have struck some compromise, done my work in another room where I wouldn't have to listen to the cries of Bael's victims, but I wouldn't hide from the consequences of my actions. I was the reason Bael had reopened this can of worms. I was the reason he had hope. Bearing witness to the pain he inflicted was the least I could do as penance for my shortsighted selfishness.

I lifted an amethyst to a soundtrack of anxious squeaks and hisses as Bael reset his experiment.

* * *

TEARS BLURRED THE pinkish light cast by the glowing tourmaline on my palm. It illuminated perhaps an inch farther than the topaz from that morning. Wiping my cheeks, I slipped past the curtain, tossed the stone on a pile with its companions, and gazed at the orange twilight beyond the workshop windows.

"Any progress?" Bael asked from across the room. Four exhausted droust cowered in their cages. Two hadn't survived.

Staring at the small, motionless bodies, I balled my fists. "No."

"Ah, well. Let's call it a day."

I bolted for the door, eager to escape the echoes of pain and the smell of wet fur and fried skin that permeated the workshop. Bael had been exceedingly thorough in his experiments.

The silence and blessedly clear air of the vast throne room was a balm to my senses, and I nearly collapsed from relief as I slammed the workshop door and leaned against it.

"Um, is everything okay?"

My gaze snapped to the familiar voice. "Kai!" I rushed forward and threw my arms around him, burying my face against his neck. "What are you doing here?"

Kai hugged me back, then stepped to the side, revealing Rhoana standing at attention a short distance away. "The Captain sent word about your extended stay and suggested I join you for dinner tonight."

"I thought you might appreciate seeing a friend," Rhoana said, "though it seems I underestimated how much."

I wiped tears from my damp cheeks. "That was considerate of you." Taking Kai's hand I said, "Come on. We can talk over dinner."

Rhoana shadowed us out of the throne room and up the main staircase. I glanced over my shoulder. "Are you planning to follow us all the way to my room?"

Rhoana nodded. "Malakai is no longer a knight. He has lost the right to roam the keep unaccompanied."

I shot a worried glance at Kai. Resigning his knighthood had been his own choice, but having Rhoana throw the consequences in his face had to hurt. "*I'm* accompanying him," I said. "Besides, after all his service, you can't possibly think he—"

"Alex," Kai broke in, "it's okay. She's just doing her job."

I grumbled but relented. The rest of our walk through the keep was marked only by the scuff of my boots—the others made no sound—and an occasional glimpse of servants scurrying through the halls.

"Ring when you're ready to leave," Rhoana said to Kai as she stopped outside my door. At least she didn't insist on overseeing our entire visit.

The scent of rosemary and hot fat struck me first when I opened the door, followed by a medley of more subtle flavors. The dining table was set for two with golden plates and crystal goblets. A rack of lamb, or some fae equivalent of lamb, rested in the center surrounded by silver trays of mouthwatering sides—a basket of fresh rolls, caramelized carrots, a hot, creamy soup, fingerling potatoes in a variety of colors, mini tarts, and wilted greens. Judging by the steam wafting off the food, it couldn't have been set out more than five minutes before we arrived. How had the servants guessed when Bael would release me from my training with such accuracy? And how had they known I'd have company tonight? I shook my head, astonished at the efficiency with which the inconspicuous husvaettir were able to run the keep.

Kai took the miraculous appearance of the meal in stride, settling into a chair without hesitation. "So, what happened?" he asked as he loaded his plate. "How'd you end up staying in Enchantment, and why were you so upset when you came out of Lord Bael's workshop?"

I lowered myself into the chair across from him and stared at the food. My stomach growled. My mouth watered. Despite the extra energy I'd been burning with my magic, I'd barely choked down three bites of lunch under the accusing quicksilver stares of the droust.

"I promised Bael thirty days and some information in exchange for teaching me how he made James's amulet." I carved off a piece of meat and moved it to my plate. "I might have made a mistake."

I told Kai everything as I heaped piles of each of the sides around my piece of meat, starting with James's imprisonment by the vampire council and their offer to trade his freedom for daywalking amulets. I explained the dangers of James representing vampires in the impending interspecies negotiations, my failure to recreate the amulet on my own, and the deal I'd made with Bael. Finally, I told him about today, and the true cost of the information I'd given Bael.

"I hadn't thought he could do anything with what I told him," I said. My chest tightened. "I *told* him imbuing wouldn't work without consent and a soul-deep connection to the subject. I never imagined he would . . ." I shook my head, staring at the spoonful of soup sloshing in my shaking hand. "How could he be so cruel?"

"To be fair," Kai said, "droust really are a nuisance. Fae kill them all the time in the same way humans kill mice or fruit flies."

"We don't torture them first!"

He lifted a placating hand. "I'm sorry you had to witness that."

But Kai's comparison had brought to mind a mouse that hadn't died instantly when it got caught in one of the traps my mom had set around our apartment. The metal bar had snapped closed over its lower half instead of its neck, and it had dragged itself, and the trap, halfway across our kitchen before dying. I set my fork down, the savory scent of the meat suddenly turning my stomach.

"I'm also sorry for the time you'll lose back home," Kai continued. "If you'd like, I can come back tomorrow, and every night until you leave."

"Won't that interfere with Rhys's training?" I asked.

"I'll work with him during the days, come to the keep just before sunset, and fly back in the morning."

I bit my lip. Knowing I'd have a friend to talk to at the end of each training session would make the next twenty-eight days much more bearable, but the same guilt that had prevented me from asking Kai to return to the Mortal Realm made me hesitate. Having him visit every day would certainly make *me* feel better, but what was best for him?

As the silence stretched between us, he gave me a conspiratorial look. "You'll be giving me an excuse to avoid my mother."

I couldn't help but laugh. "Well, in that case, how can I refuse?" I reached across the table and set my hand over his. His fingers were warm. The contact made me feel instantly more at ease, and knowing his dopey smile would greet me at the end of every training session made this alien world feel a little less scary—I could almost trick myself into believing we were roommates back home again, with him lounging on my couch when I finally dragged myself out of the studio. "But let's see if we can convince Rhoana to give you a proper visitor's pass."

Chapter 7

A TWO-INCH CHUNK of quartz glowed faintly between my pinched fingers. If I didn't know how much magic had gone into that stone, I might have dismissed the glimmer as a trick of the morning light, but Bael had stored over an hour's worth of sunlight into the white rock for me to practice with. I might have stored that light myself, but the process would have left me too tired to do much else. It had taken nearly a week for me to advance to the point where I could store a half-hour's worth of light in a gem with any level of consistency. Fortunately, Bael had given up experimenting on droust by the end of day four. Not having to listen to the poor creatures suffer had done wonders for my concentration.

The following week I'd moved on to expanding the functional surface area of my spell, drawing light from a wider range. Unfortunately, Bael found a new avenue of inquiry as well—his theory being that the droust didn't have enough cognitive ability to save themselves. To that end, the trials began again, this time with "willing volunteers." None of the servants who came one by one to the workshop died, but their screams were enough to give me nightmares. I hadn't made much progress on my training during the three days it took for Bael to admit defeat.

Two days ago, Bael had declared me ready to work on solidifying my containment. I just hoped he'd finally accepted what I'd told him about the impossibility of imbuing a living being without first building a bond of absolute trust. I wasn't sure I could take whatever next step he might dream up otherwise.

"Again," Bael said.

Exhaling in frustration, I released the spell I'd woven to turn the inner core of the quartz into a mirrored prison. The stone turned to a star in my hand, blinding to look at. Squinting, I began my spell again, imbuing the quartz's core to reflect the collected sunlight back on itself. The light winked out like an electric bulb when its switch was flicked. I blinked, clearing my vision. The quartz was dim, but it once again held that faint glow. *Damn.*

Bael shook his head. "There are too many flaws. If you can't seal those cracks, the light will not only escape, but eventually it will tear the spell apart. You can't leave seams."

"I know," I growled. "I'm trying."

He waved his hand. "That's enough for today. Go to the festival."

I froze. The light slanting through the windows put the time at slightly past mid-morning, well before the day's festivities were scheduled to begin. "Are you sure?"

He nodded. "Two hours is enough to fulfill your promise of daily training." He smiled. "It is a holiday, after all. Go. Enjoy yourself."

Eager to take advantage of Bael's generosity, I handed him the quartz. Bael always insisted on putting the materials I used away himself. Apparently, he was as particular about his workspace as I was about mine, despite the seeming chaos.

I waved as I trotted to the door and called over my shoulder, "See you tomorrow."

The throne room was a riot of color as servants decorated for the coming fete. I'd been beyond relieved when Bael informed me the previous day that I was free to attend the public festivities in the city rather than the official court party. I still had nightmares about the Winter Festival and the beautiful, terrible courtiers who had attended. I wasn't entirely sure what to expect from the public celebration, but at least I should be able to enjoy the day with a measure of anonymity that would have been impossible if I'd been forced to stand at Bael's side.

"Your friends are waiting at the main gate," Rhoana stated as she fell into step beside me, unfazed by my early release.

"Already?"

I hurried past the bustling servants and through the vast entry hall, which had been hung with thick garlands of delphiniums, amaranth, bougainvilleas, dahlias, asters, peonies, and a number of more exotic flowers that I had no names for. A stream of visitors trickled through the main gates—courtiers too poor to afford their own estates in town heading to guest rooms in the keep in time to spruce up before the party. Even the guards were decked out, wearing colorful ribbons from bands on their arms in deference to the day.

Kai stood with Mica and Haru at the edge of the courtyard beyond the main gate. He wore a billowing shirt of pale green tucked into a pair of khaki shorts. His galaxy eyes crinkled as he laughed at something Mica was saying.

True to his word, Kai had spent every evening with me since that second day, usually joined by Mica and Haru, who'd extended their role as welcome committee. Sometimes we shared a quiet dinner in my room, though more often the four of us explored the city. Slowly but surely, I'd grown used to the sights, sounds, and flavors of Abonaille Malmür. Now, I found the chaos of the night market almost comfortable, though I always wore my sword, and I never complained about Rhoana's hovering.

Mica slapped Kai on the back and tucked a strand of hair behind his tapered ear as a wisp of wind pulled it across his face. Colored ribbons were braided into the long, blond strands to create a fluttering rainbow. His teal shirt rippled in the breeze, giving an impression of ocean waves. Dark, form-fitting leather wrapped his thighs, tucking into knee-high, tan boots. Beside him, Haru wore only a necklace of morning glories, their vibrant blue standing in stark contrast to his pale chest, and a pair of translucent harem pants that left very little to the imagination.

The three seemed to have become fast friends during our weeks of evening escapades, and seeing them together brought a smile to my lips.

Haru noticed me first. He glanced skyward, smirked, and nudged Kai. "She's here. Pay up."

"Already?" Kai's swirling gaze found me. He sighed, pulled a red feather out of his pocket, and handed it to Haru. "I thought for sure Lord Bael would keep her for at least another hour."

"You were betting on when I'd get out?" I asked as I walked up.

"Just a friendly wager to pass the time," Haru said, tying his prize into his hair so it flashed just in front of his left ear.

"You look amazing," Mica said.

I did a little pirouette in appreciation of the compliment. I'd Frankensteined several garments together to create my festival outfit—a tunic-style dress in a gradient from desert rose to sunset orange with a coral-pink silk scarf, lime-green leggings, and my favorite leather boots. Vess, the husvaettir who I'd discovered was assigned to handle my day-to-day needs, had styled my hair in a series of pinned curls and braids woven with colored beads. Overall, I looked like a walking, talking flower, which meant I blended perfectly with the celebratory décor.

"Shall we?" I hooked arms with Kai and Mica, who snagged Haru, and I found myself humming "We're Off to See the Wizard" as the four of us ambled toward the city center. The ghost town of courtly estates beyond Bael's keep was livelier than I'd ever seen it. Messengers and servants darted through the streets at the whims of their masters, while lords and ladies reacquainted themselves with their city holdings or promenaded along the river making polite conversation in the never-ending game of courtly alliances. Flowers and ribbons draped every balcony, arch, and entryway, and the fae were decked out in their festive best, but the atmosphere remained cautiously reserved until we crossed the gossamer bridge over the Algana.

I suppose hundreds of years of expecting someone to stick a knife in your back makes it hard to relax, even at a party.

On the far side of the river, every inhibition that seemed to keep the courtly fae in check was let loose. Wine flowed freely from carts parked at every street corner, along with every fae delicacy I'd learned to love in the past two weeks. The mildly risqué outfits worn in the upper estates gave way to a kaleidoscope of colors and a clash of styles that made my eyes hurt. While Haru's immodest pants were enough to make my cheeks burn, many fae had foregone clothing altogether, and I found myself in contact with an unsettling amount of bare flesh as the foot traffic pressed in around me. This solstice festival was all about the bounty and freedom of summer, and these lower-caste fae seemed determined to live that theme to its fullest.

The buskers were out in full force, as were the theatre troupes. We paused at one intersection where several actors in glittering costumes reenacted Bael's historic defeat of the Mad God that had earned him his title as Lord of Enchantment all those centuries ago. Another group performed a parody of the Faerie Wars in which the mortal troops tripped over themselves and coaxed the audience to take part in their general buffoonery. The streets became so densely packed that our progress slowed to a crawl, and it wasn't just the streets that were crowded. Fae with wings or flying steeds zipped overhead, weaving between aerial acrobats who wowed the traffic below by dancing on gossamer threads strung between the buildings. I was glad Bael had released me early. With the shoulder-to-shoulder traffic and so much to see, it would take those extra hours to reach the market district at the center of town before the main feature began.

"I wish Maggie and Emma were here to see all this," I said wistfully.

"Not James?" Kai asked.

I laughed. "This kind of thing isn't really James's style." But even as I said it, I recalled some of the memories I'd seen in his core—parties from centuries past that swirled with gilt and gluttony . . . often culminating in feasts of the flesh and more than a few deaths.

Shuddering the thought away, I wandered toward one of a dozen stalls offering revelers additional ways to adorn themselves and traded four of the beads from my hair for two crowns of lavender and sunflowers. I set one on top of my own head, then turned and plopped the second over Rhoana's red hair.

"There," I said in satisfaction. "Now you look like you're enjoying yourself."

"I'm here to protect you," she said, "not enjoy the festival."

I shrugged. "There's no reason you can't do both."

She lifted the crown off her head with seeming reluctance. "I can't accept this."

I pursed my lips. Fae were weird about gifts, and gifts from different social classes even more so. I crossed my arms, refusing to take the crown back. She'd been assigned to guard me, but she'd become as much a part of my daily life as the boys, if a very quiet and somewhat distant part. "Consider it payment for a job well done." I offered her a lopsided smile. "You make an excellent babysitter."

She looked away, but she set the floral crown back on her head. A soft smile curved her lips.

"Why, Rhoana, you look almost approachable!" Haru crowed. He spread his arms as if to embrace her.

Rhoana narrowed her eyes. "Don't make me cut you, fox."

Haru laughed and pressed his hands over his heart. "You already have."

Mica shoved the kitsune, ushering him along. "Leave her be, Haru, or she really might give you a scar to remember."

We meandered until we reached the central plaza of the market district. A circle had been cleared, marked off by colored ribbons strung between decorative blown-glass stands.

Mica pushed his way to the front, towing me along until I was right behind the ribbon. "You won't want to miss this."

A few fae grumbled at our intrusion, but one look at Rhoana's guard uniform and they miraculously found space for our little group. No one wanted to tussle with the lord's guard.

I shifted my weight, easing a sore spot on my heel, but every movement brushed me up against a neighbor. My skin itched with the closeness of so many bodies. I glanced at the sky, shielding my eyes. The sun was directly overhead. "When does the show start?"

"Right now." Mica pointed to a shimmer of air in the center of the plaza. It could have been a trick of the heat, but the distortion hadn't been there a moment before.

A comically thin fae stepped out of the shimmer, unfolding and unfolding until he stood at well over eight feet tall. He wore a purple-and-green striped suit that clung to his spindly limbs. A poison-green scarf bloomed at his collar, and a purple, satin top hat with a lopsided kink that made me think of the Mad Hatter perched atop his head. He swept the hat off and bowed to our side of the crowd. He straightened, then bowed in the opposite direction without turning. Only then did I realize the hollow features of his pale-brown face were present on both sides of his head, separated by a thin strip of wild white that stretched from ear to ear across the middle. All his joints seemed to bend smoothly in either direction.

"Fair and fearsome folk of the realm, I bid you greetings on this festive occasion." The man's voice boomed across the plaza and filtered up the streets. "Today we celebrate the gifts of light, fertility, and the bounty and beauty of nature." He set his hat atop his head and gestured to the shimmer through which he'd come as he backed away. "But we cannot truly appreciate the dawn until we've experience the dark."

The next fae to emerge was four feet tall and dressed in streamers of deepest blues and purples that obscured any glimpse of the creature beneath. Once clear of the portal, the new arrival raised their arms. Rippling ribbons shot out from their body, soaring well above the tallest buildings, before arcing outward. The fabric spread as it fell, overlapping to create a shell of darkness that completely blocked out the sky.

For one terrifying moment, the space beneath the dome plunged into pitch black. I couldn't tell if my eyes were open or closed. My pulse raced. The scuff of feet, the rustle of fabric, a soft cough—every sound became deafening. Every brush against me felt like a threat. Then tiny pinpricks of light winked into existence like stars above, casting a pale blue glow that was barely enough to make out the shapes around me.

I licked my lips and eased my grip off my sword hilt. Mica and Kai were at my shoulders. Rhoana had my back. I was safe . . . relatively speaking.

An eerie music filled the darkness. More players had emerged from the portal during the moments I was blind. Six people dressed head-to-toe in black had joined the spindly fae I thought of as the ringmaster. They were nearly invisible except for the instruments they played—a silver flute, a golden horn, a lap harp, a wooden frame with hammered strings, something like a guitar with only three strings and a wooden paddle, and a wide, deep drum. The fae who'd blacked out the sky moved slowly around the plaza, singing of the dangers that lurked in the dark. Her voice brought tears to my eyes, and the tingle of the tattoo on my arm let me know she was casting a spell over the crowd so we would feel the biting cold she sang of, the physical and emotional emptiness that crept into a person in the depth of winter. I shivered. The air in my lungs turned to ice.

Just when I felt I couldn't stand the ache in my chest any longer, the music changed. A new singer stepped into the night, and she brought with her a blinding light that charred the entrapping ribbons, burning them away to reveal the sky beyond. The newcomer was six feet tall with well-padded curves swathed in generous silks displaying a multitude of pinks, reds, and golds. She sang of friendship and love, hearth and home. My breathing eased.

Embers and ash drifted down around us. The first singer, the one who represented the night, shrank back. The music took on a livelier rhythm that filled me with an urge to dance. The bone-weary cold of the moment before vanished, fading to a distant memory as heat and happiness flooded me. I turned my face upward and noticed those around me doing likewise. My stomach and heart both felt full. My skin warmed and the nose-to-toes flush of lust filled me. I breathed deep.

When my gaze dropped once more to street level, I found the plaza full. Day and Night stood on a wheeled platform with two tiers. The Night actress crouched on the lower section, which was decorated in blue and dripped with icicles. The upper tier was a floral explosion on which the Day actress stood proud, waving to the crowd. The ringmaster took long strides up the main street, calling to one and all to join in the revelry as the wagon rolled behind him, seemingly of its own accord.

A dozen other floats came through the portal, each portraying some aspect of bounty, and each making a circuit of the plaza before joining the parade. The wind carried the scent of spices from a wagon where a three-foot, brown-skinned woman wearing a dress that looked to be sewn from thousands of butterfly wings tossed tiny paper packages into the crowd. Kai caught one and handed it to me. I sniffed the envelope but didn't open it. My nose tickled with the scents of clove, cinnamon, ginger, cardamom, and nutmeg.

A green man in a bark vest tossed packets of seeds from a cart decorated to look like a giant gourd. A group of pixies flitting in formation showered the audience in glittering dust. Many of the attendees, including Mica, opened their mouths to catch the offering like snowflakes on their tongues. I looked at the ground for that one, holding my breath until the flitting sprites had gone.

Float after float rolled, rode, or fluttered by, tossing samples of everything from polished stones to steamed buns. Not everyone got everything, but no one would go home empty handed. The final wagon to roll by bore a dozen scantily clad fae who, rather than throwing anything to the crowd, beckoned them to follow with promises of love. The shimmering portal winked out and the ribbons that had been holding back the audience snapped simultaneously. The audience surged forward, trailing after the parade and the calling nymphs.

I held my ground as the eager partygoers raced past. When I was no longer in danger of being trampled, I turned to Mica and tipped my chin toward the departing parade. "Are you two running off, then?"

Mica shook his head and looped an arm around Haru's waist. "I have everything I need right here."

Haru kissed Mica then leered at me. "Unless you're interested in the orgy?"

I waved the invitation away. "Pass."

"Besides," Mica said, "there's plenty more to see and do here. This party will go on until sunset."

"Plenty of time to change your mind," Haru added.

Glancing around the market, I realized Mica was right. Only about one third of the audience had followed the parade, and more people were already flooding in to take their place. The smaller players, bands, and dancers that had paused during the main production started up again. Merchants called out their wares, trying to be heard over the din of the crowd. The lingering scents of the spice wagon were overwhelmed as the restaurants stoked their fires and set out their aromatic goods. My mouth watered. The song of the sun may have tricked me into feeling full, but now my stomach wanted the real thing.

"Let's head to The Pines."

The Pines had become one of my favorite haunts in the city, not only because the food there was amazing but because its atmosphere reminded me of home. As we passed under the hydrangea-festooned arch that marked its entrance, I was transported to an alpine meadow. The walls were enchanted to portray breathtaking vistas real enough to make you want to walk into them—which I'd actually done my first time there, much to my embarrassment and the amusement of my friends. Fans hanging from the vaulted ceiling circulated the scents of fresh pine sap and dry grass, which mingled pleasantly with the pit-fired fare.

Every table was packed, but Mica had a word with the owner, and a few minutes later we were settled on benches around the polished cross section of a massive redwood. There were definite perks to everyone knowing you were related to the lord of the realm, though I imagined it stung Mica's pride to be such a famous failure—the would-be heir who hadn't made the cut. I tugged the sleeve of my dress, ensuring it obscured my tattoo and my own relationship to Bael. Not that my identity would be hard to surmise in company with Mica and the captain of Bael's knights.

I motioned for Rhoana to take a seat beside me. She just gave a small shake of her head and continued to scrutinize the restaurant's other patrons, as she had every time I'd encouraged her to join us. At least I'd gotten her to keep the floral crown.

Three musicians circulated around the room, playing a merry tune on a tin whistle, fiddle, and small drum. Seated customers, and those left standing at the counter for lack of seats, sang along to what I assumed was a familiar song from the number of voices pitching in. The melody had the rhythm of a sea shanty, and the bawdy lyrics belted out by the boisterous crowd maintained that impression.

I shouted my order to a hovering pixie over a verse about a satyr who got lost between the thighs of a succubus for nigh on three weeks.

The next time the chorus repeated, Haru and Kai joined in with gusto, pulling me along with their enthusiasm. Shoulder-to-shoulder, the three of us belted out the lyrics, swaying in time to the music, and I was reminded of my carefree college days with David, Maggie, and my lost friend Aiden.

That thought sobered me up like a dunk in cold water.

I'd adapted quickly to life in Enchantment—faster than I'd thought possible—and that realization came with a surprising amount of guilt. Between my training with Bael and nights out with my friends, the worries I'd had about what I might be missing in the Mortal Realm had faded into the background. It was a bit of a shock to realize that in two short weeks I'd already missed more than a month of life back home.

Maggie's probably had her baby by now. On the tail end of that thought came a flood of other concerns: Emma living alone in the mountains, David drowning under piles of paperwork, the crew at Crossroads being targeted by Purity activists, the vampire council growing impatient and forcing James into the spotlight.

I glanced at the revelers around me and willed the levity I'd felt a moment ago to return, but I couldn't shake the melancholy that clung to me. Was it right for me to be relaxing, enjoying myself as though I were on vacation, when my real life was passing by without me? I had *one* goal to accomplish here in Enchantment, and my time was nearly up.

I twisted the ring on my finger, and memories of James flooded my thoughts. If I didn't manage to free James from his indenture to the vampire council, what would have been the point of coming here? Yet beating myself up wouldn't accomplish anything either. I'd made my choice. All I could do now was live with it.

I forced myself to keep smiling. Tonight, I would enjoy all that Enchantment's Summer Festival had to offer. Tomorrow, I'd attack my studies with renewed focus.

Chapter 8

I GLARED AT the pale tally marks carved into my headboard. A twinge of guilt pricked my conscience for defacing such a fancy piece of furniture, but I'd been so frustrated that first night that I hadn't cared and, after that, what difference did it make? The damage was done. Twenty-nine lines marched in a ragged row along the reddish wood just above the mattress. I ran my thumb over the freshest cut.

Twenty-nine days away from home. Twenty-nine days of dawn-to-dusk magic practice. Twenty-nine days . . . and still no amulet.

I'd learned to expand a spell's area of affect, create a near-perfect light prison, and enhance a gem's containment capacity . . . but I hadn't yet managed to put it all together.

I pulled out my knife and gouged a final line into the wood.

Thirty. I have to do it today.

Hiding the marks with my pillow, I headed to my final lesson.

Bael didn't turn when I entered the workshop. He stood bathed in the morning light that streaked through the windows, surveying the icy peaks surrounding his keep.

"This is the final day of our agreement," he said.

I closed the door and inhaled the familiar scents of wood, metal, stone, and resin that filled the room. "I know."

"Are you eager to leave?"

I frowned. I was eager to get back, but I wasn't actually eager to *leave*. While I wanted desperately to sleep in my own bed and check in on my friends in the Mortal Realm, I'd miss my evening escapades in the night market. I'd miss watching Mica tease Kai, and Haru's seemingly involuntary need to flirt. I'd miss the smells and flavors I'd grown accustomed to that didn't exist anywhere else. I'd even miss these training sessions and the comfortable familiarity of this workshop.

"Enchantment's not so bad," I admitted.

He finally turned to face me. "I'm pleased to hear you say that."

"But it's time for me to go home."

He gestured to a large yellow stone waiting on a workbench. "Let's see what you've learned."

I wiped my palms as I approached the table. The stone looked to be the same chrysoberyl Bael had used to demonstrate the spell on my first day of training. Bracing my palms against the table on either side of the gem, I took a slow, steady breath to center myself and called up my magic. The first rush of energy carried undertones of worry, anticipation, and anxiety. I needed this to go well. Thoughts of seeing my human friends again twined with regret at having to say goodbye to Kai. My desire to save James tangled with doubt about my ability to do so. The snippets of news I'd heard from the Mortal Realm filled me with dread even as the impending negotiations gave me hope. I let it all wash over me, then I exhaled.

Once my mind was clear of everything save the task before me, I shifted my perception and found the chrysoberyl's core. Bael had laid the foundation for his spell in a matter of seconds. Long minutes dragged by as I created the necessary anchors for my magic. Once those were in place, I formed the first layer of the spell. A tug here, a twist there. The interior of the gem became a near-perfect mirror. Next, I created a web that spread from the stone and expanded to cover an area roughly the size of the table on which it sat. Sweat beaded my brow, threatening to drip into my eyes, but I dared not move to wipe it. My breath shook, growing more shallow as my muscles strained against the invisible weight of forcing my magic into place. I imagined my will as a hammer, striking the ribbons of energy that made up the spell I was forging as I would a piece of annealed steel on my anvil back home. Slowly, the spell took shape.

I continued to build layer upon layer of the amulet, tying together all the components I'd practiced over the past thirty days—the cage, the tunnels, the anchor, the expanded field, the magical compression. A giddy thrill bubbled through me as the spell came together. *I can do this.*

I dug my fingernails against the wood of the workbench as my energy flagged. An aching hollowness swelled within me as I pulled on my reserves. The cables of my spell wobbled. Threads snapped. I rushed to patch the fraying magic, trying to hold this massive Cat's Cradle together as I wove in yet more strings. Cracks appeared in the mirrored surface I'd created, and I dove back toward the gem's core to shore them up. One of the anchors of my foundation tore loose. The spell collapsed around me in a chain reaction of snapped magic that battered me like an avalanche as the lost energy tore free from the form I'd tried to bind it to.

Gasping, I stumbled back. My legs, already shaking like leaves in a stiff breeze, collapsed under me, dropping me painfully on my butt. Panting, trying to catch my breath, I balled my fists. I was tired, exhausted even. I'd poured everything I had into forging that spell, but it hadn't been enough. The tremors that shook me were as much from frustration as fatigue.

I gritted my teeth and climbed back to my feet, using the table for support. The chrysoberyl glinted on the tabletop, taunting me. I resisted the urge to chuck it through the window and watch it plummet into the icy chasm beyond.

"Let me try again."

It was a stupid suggestion. I'd been well-rested, well-fed, and relatively confident for my first attempt, and that had been an utter failure. Now my muscles sagged, my head ached, and my stomach grumbled like an ancient god demanding sacrifice. The voice that had been quietly cheering me on during my previous attempt had fallen silent, replaced by a far less friendly, but more familiar, litany of doubt and resignation.

I'd put everything into that failed attempt. The results could only go downhill now that the conditions were worse . . . yet I couldn't just give up. I'd try again and again, until I'd wrung every drop of magic from my body and the sun had set on my final day in Enchantment. I refused to have come this far only to fail.

Bael, his face an impassive mask, studied me for a quiet moment then said, "Let us try something different." He walked to the workshop door, opened it, and waited.

Casting a defiant glare at the loathsome stone on the workbench, I shuffled after him.

Bael stepped onto the dais at the near end of the vast chamber, in the center of which sat his iron throne, the symbol of his lordship over this realm. He gestured to the dull metal. "Sit down."

I stopped at the edge of the dais and wrapped my arms tightly around myself. "Why?"

I'd perched on that seat before, briefly. I'd also stood with my hand resting on its back as Bael greeted guests at the Winter Festival. Iron didn't burn me the way it did most fae, but something about that throne made my skin crawl.

"Sitting here may grant you power."

I frowned, looking askance at the throne. "Sitting there will give me enough power to create an amulet?"

He gestured again to the throne, then took a step back, leaving my path clear. His unwavering gaze followed me onto the dais and toward the throne.

I bit my lower lip, worrying it between my teeth. Bael couldn't lie, so there was a chance sitting down would give me enough juice to accomplish my goal. The question was, what else might it do?

"Sitting here won't, like, bind my soul to your will or anything freaky like that, right?"

"I will have no more sway over you after you sit than I do right now."

"And it won't trap me here in Enchantment?"

"You've attended me for thirty days, as per our agreement. You are free to leave at any time."

If there's any chance sitting in this stupid chair for a moment can give me what I need to succeed . . .

I lifted my chin. I'd come too far, sacrificed too much, to give up without pursuing every possible option. I marched to the iron throne, pivoted, and sat down.

The cold metal chilled my skin, even through the fabric of my pants. I shifted my weight, trying to warm the seat, but my heat was no match for its frozen mass.

"What now?"

"Be calm," Bael said. "Open yourself to your magic. Seek the core of the throne."

Frowning, I closed my eyes and focused on the small pool of ruby power deep within me. Calling it forth, I let the magic potential fill me, then I sought the center of the throne upon which I sat. The cold weight of the metal pushed against me, threatening to crush me as I sank deeper. My body tingled. The throne's core seemed to be hidden beyond a veil of darkness unlike any I'd encountered in an inanimate object—a defense system to keep out intruders. The barest whisper caught my attention, as if someone were calling to me from beyond that wall.

Wrapped in my magic, I pushed against the boundary.

The darkness shattered. Light flooded my senses as I tumbled into the throne's core . . . except it wasn't a throne. Millions of threads of connectivity branched around me, stretching beyond my perception. The sheer magnitude of the magic set my nerves on fire.

"Welcome." That single word pushed into my mind on an airy voice that shook my bones and turned my muscles to jelly.

Surging back to the shelter of my physical body, I tumbled off the throne, falling to my knees. Curling into a ball, I clutched the sides of my head. My skull felt as if it had been split open with a hatchet. That *definitely* hadn't happened the last time I sat there.

Bael knelt beside me. "Well done, Alex." He gripped my arm just above my elbow and helped me sit up. "I knew you could do it."

"Do what?" I glared at Bael, blinking to clear my white-washed vision. The magic at the throne's core had seared my senses, like staring into the sun. "What exactly just happened? And whose voice was that?"

"She can be a bit intense, but the fact that she spoke to you at all means you've made great strides as an imbuer. You have potential."

I closed and opened my hands, working feeling into them. My whole body was filled with a tingling numbness.

"I'll be able to make the amulet now?" I asked dubiously.

Bael pursed his lips and took my hastily vacated seat. Watching him sit there made me shudder. What the hell was living in that chair?

"I'm afraid you aren't capable of recreating the amulet I made for James, nor even a pale imitation of it."

I stared at him in confusion. I was having trouble concentrating through the constant buzz that seemed to have taken up residence in my brain. "Then what was the point of making me sit on your stupid, possessed chair?"

He shrugged. "To see if you could."

I shook my head and immediately regretted it as my brain sloshed around the inside of my skull. "I don't have time for your games, Bael. You said you'd help me make an amulet."

He *tsk*ed. "I said that I would show you how I made James's amulet, which I did."

"And understand how it was made," I said.

"Which I also did." He raised an eyebrow. "Or is there some aspect of the spell that you don't comprehend?"

I opened my mouth, but the truth was I did *understand* the spell. I just hadn't been able to recreate it. Bael, in true fae fashion, had upheld the letter of our agreement while completely circumventing the spirit. Swallowing my initial argument along with my pride, I asked, "Then why couldn't I make one?"

Bael's fiery gaze bore into me. "You don't possess enough experience or power to hold an enchantment of that magnitude together. It's possible you never will."

Realization dawned like a lightning strike. "You knew from the very beginning that I wouldn't be able to produce an amulet on my own." I climbed slowly to my feet, leveling my gaze at Bael. "That's why you agreed to teach me even though you refused to make the amulets yourself. You knew I'd fail. You tricked me."

"No more than you tricked me," Bael said. "The information you offered in exchange for your lessons did not allow me to imbue living beings."

"That didn't stop you from trying," I ground out.

"Any more than repeated failures stopped you. We're left with the same result."

"Except you stole three months of my life in the process! You kept me here under the pretense of training even though you knew the lessons were pointless."

"The lessons may not have culminated the way you intended; that doesn't make them pointless."

"Then what was the point?" I demanded. "Why trap me here for thirty days and train me for a task I could never complete?"

"Not all destinations are obvious from the beginning of a trail."

"Enough cryptic bullshit. Useless or not, this could have been a simple exchange of information. Why did you insist I stay in Enchantment?"

He traced his finger along the armrest of his throne. "To prove that you could belong here."

Looking at the placid expression on Bael's face, devoid of either gloating or malice, a sense of inevitability settled over me. Complaining that a fae had manipulated me was like scolding a caterpillar for turning into a butterfly when what I'd really wanted was a bird. I couldn't fault him for being true to his nature. I'd known the game when I agreed to play, and he'd won this round. I didn't doubt there would be others. I exhaled and shook my head in exasperation. "I belong in the Mortal Realm." I turned my back on him. "Goodbye, Bael."

"I'll see you in a few days, Alex. Assuming the negotiations take place as planned."

I strode from the room without a backward glance.

The entrance hall beyond the throne room was nearly empty, which made Mica's presence all the more notable. He sat at the base of one of the slender pillars that supported the double stairs spiraling into the vaulted space above. When I stepped through the doorway, he sprang to his feet.

"You're done?"

I moved to join him. "Did you think I'd leave without saying goodbye?"

He studied my face as if expecting to find some secret tattooed across my forehead. "Did you sit on the throne?"

I froze and frowned. "*That's* your question? Not, 'Did you succeed at what you've been training for these past thirty days?' "

"You did, didn't you?"

"No, I damn well did not. Apparently, I never had a chance of producing the necessary level of magic," I snapped.

"Not your project," Mica clarified, "the throne. Did you hear a voice?"

87

"That's none of your concern, Mica." Rhoana emerged from a nearby arch, glaring daggers at Mica.

I scowled at both of them. "What's the deal with that throne, anyway? It felt almost . . . alive." I shuddered.

Mica looked away, his gaze growing distant. "I'm sorry you weren't able to achieve the results you hoped for. Safe travels on your journey home." Turning, he strode across the entry hall.

"Mica," I called after him, confused by his sudden coolness and equally sudden departure. When he didn't respond, or even pause in his retreat, I turned to Rhoana and asked, "What's his problem?"

"Disappointed potential," she replied.

I looked after Mica. When he was young, everyone expected him to become Bael's heir. No one ever explained to me how or why he'd failed to live up to that title, but from his questions just now and the sadness in his expression, I got the feeling it had something to do with the voice in Bael's throne. A voice I hoped never to hear again.

"You finished earlier than expected. Do you still intend to wait for Malakai, or shall we leave now?"

Now that I knew I'd failed, there was no reason to spend another second in Enchantment, but Kai had promised to come to the keep this afternoon and escort me back to the portal. As much as I hated the idea of hanging around for a few extra hours, I couldn't leave without seeing him. With our lives heading in different directions, who knew when I would get another chance?

* * *

WHY DID YOU insist I stay in Enchantment?

To prove that you could belong here.

Bael's answer rang in my head as I flipped through the sketchbook he'd given me—every page now filled with scenes from my nightly exploits. I paused on a drawing from the solstice festival—Haru, Mica, and Kai singing, tankards in hand, while Rhoana scowled under her floral crown. A twinge of sadness pinched my chest. Despite the fact that I'd been duped by Bael and failed my primary mission, I had enjoyed my time in Enchantment.

Opening the bag Rhoana had given me to hold the handful of possessions I'd accumulated over the past thirty days, I tucked the sketchbook beside a porcelain mask Mica had presented me with after the solstice celebration. A golden sun shone from one of the mask's temples, spreading stylized rays across its forehead, cheeks, and empty eyes toward a sliver of silver moon on the opposite side. I sighed. I'd thought Mica befriended me because he was similarly caged, but considering the way he'd acted earlier . . . *Maybe Bael ordered him to keep me company. Or maybe he was playing his own game this entire time.*

Shaking my head, I cinched the bag closed. Whatever I'd experienced in Enchantment, this farce was over. It was time to face the music. I'd failed to create a daywalking amulet. What was more, I'd learned that the magic to do so was beyond me, which meant I had no way of buying James's freedom. He was stuck being the face of vampire representation at the interspecies negotiations, which were now right around the corner. All I could do at this point was return to the Mortal Realm and support the proceedings as best I could. And that's exactly what I intended to do.

A knock sounded at the outer door to my apartment. A moment later, Rhoana strode into my bedroom.

"They're here," she said. "Are you ready?"

I unbuckled the belts that held my sword and knife, resting the weapons on the neatly tucked covers of the bed. Aside from that first night, I'd never drawn them, for which I was grateful. I'd witnessed three duels during my stay in Enchantment, two of which ended in someone's death, but my friends and Rhoana had managed to keep me out of trouble. Knowing a challenge to me would result in fighting the captain of the lord's personal guard had proven an effective deterrent.

Casting one last look at the pillow covering the tally marks carved into my headboard, I slung the pack over my shoulder and nodded. "Lead the way."

After a month of wandering Bael's keep, the walk to the upper tower was a familiar one. I nodded to the guards I passed, and many of them nodded back. Kai and Rhys waited on the landing at the top of the stairs. Kai wore the livery of Bael's court, despite resigning his knighthood. Rhys stood stiffly at his side with the comically awed expression of someone who was overwhelmed but trying, and failing, not to show it.

When I reached them, I stepped forward and wrapped my arms around Kai in lieu of a greeting.

He jerked, then returned my hug, patting my back. "Rough day?"

"I couldn't make the amulet," I whispered against his shoulder.

Rhoana cleared her throat and nudged Rhys's shoulder. "Come help me prepare the gaala."

As Rhys and Rhoana moved away, I released Kai and stepped back. "It seems that level of enchantment was impossible for me from the beginning. Bael played me."

Kai exhaled and turned to look over the landscape. "I can't say I'm surprised."

A barb of anger pinched my heart. "Did you know I couldn't do it?"

Kai shook his head. "No. But then, I don't know much about imbuing."

I rested my elbows against the banister. "From what Bael said, I don't think it was my imbuing that was the problem. It was the enchantment I was trying to anchor into the stone. I just didn't have enough juice." I cast Kai a sidelong glance. "Do you think you could do it? Create the spell and hand it off for me to imbue like we did with my light-imbued knife?"

Kai frowned. "I doubt it." His shoulders hunched. "I'm not a very powerful enchanter. Mica could probably do it. You might try asking him."

"Hmm." I looked away.

"What's the matter?"

"Mica was waiting for me outside the throne room today."

"To say goodbye?"

"That's what I thought, but all he wanted to talk about was Bael making me sit on his creepy ass throne."

Kai twisted to face me. "You sat on the iron throne?"

I shrugged. "It's not the first time. Although, this was the first time I heard it talk."

"You . . . what?"

"I heard it talk. At least, I think I did. Now I'm not so sure. What do you know about Bael's throne?"

"Only that it's cast from pure iron and is a symbol of his status as Lord of Enchantment. But if it's knowledge you seek, perhaps ask Hortense when you see her. Few know the history of the realm as well as the court tutor."

"I'll do that." I turned toward the plaza where we would take off. Rhoana seemed to be giving Rhys a lecture on proper gaala handling. "It's nice that you brought Rhys with you, but he looks like he might need a rescue."

The corner of Kai's mouth quirked up. "Escort duty will be a good experience for him, and it was an excellent excuse for Rhoana to meet him. Normally, the unofficial apprentice of a defunct knight would never get an introduction to the captain of the court guards, but I'm hoping she'll see his potential. Eventually, I'd like her to take over his official training."

I smiled. "You're a good mentor."

"We'll see." He shook his head as Rhys seemed to shrink under the pressure of Rhoana's attention. "He still has a long way to go."

Six harnessed gaala stood in the courtyard, along with Rhoana, Rhys, and two extra guards. The guards bowed when I approached. Rhoana lowered her head then glanced at Rhys.

Kai's apprentice folded nearly in half, as if he were trying to kiss his own knees. "Your escort is ready for departure, Lady Alex."

I nodded, fighting not to laugh at his earnest expression. He clearly thought escorting me was some kind of great honor, so I would do my best to play my part. "Then let us go before we lose the light."

The knights all mounted their gaala smoothly. Rhys and I had a little more trouble, but we managed. One by one we launched into the air, with Rhoana leading the exodus.

The keep fell away quickly as I soared over the streets of Abonaille Malmür. Pedestrians of a dozen different shapes, sizes, and colors jostled along the paths I'd walked for the past month. I drifted over the river and the plaza where the solstice parade had begun. I spotted The Pines at the edge of the bustling market and the bakery that served the best honey rolls I'd ever tasted. Then the ground fell away as we left the plateau behind and struck out over the valley. Within moments, the capital city was barely a glimmer atop the massive waterfall. Then it was gone.

I faced forward. My heart sang with the knowledge that I was heading home, yet I felt as if I were leaving a piece of myself behind as well.

Bael's voice drifted on the wind. *You could belong here.*

A month ago, I would have said that was impossible.

My gaala skimmed over the tops of trees whose leaves turned the valley floor into a patchwork of bright colors. We landed in a clearing carpeted with wildflowers that filled the air with a sweet and heady perfume. I dismounted as gracefully as I could, trying not to crush the flowers but unable to avoid them all.

"Fair winds and safe travels, Alex," Rhoana said.

I nodded to the guard captain. "I appreciate you looking after me during my stay. You made an excellent babysitter."

One side of her mouth quirked up. I took that as a win.

I turned to Rhys and offered my hand to shake. "Keep up with your training. I expect great things from you."

A flush stained the squire's cheeks boysenberry purple as his fingers closed over mine. "I'll do my best."

Rhys, Rhoana, and the two remaining guards stayed with the gaala. Only Kai accompanied me to the entwined oak and ash that marked the portal back to the Mortal Realm. I shifted the weight of my bag and looked at the azure sky.

"I'm going to miss you."

"I'll miss you, too," he said. "But this isn't goodbye, just a temporary parting of ways."

I nodded but didn't say anything. This *felt* like goodbye, and I had a lot of experience to judge by. In every school I'd left behind as a kid, when I'd told my schoolmates I was moving, someone inevitably promised they'd keep in touch, that we'd stay friends despite the distance. That never happened. Then again, Kai was more like a brother than a friend, so maybe this time would be different. *I guess we'll see.*

"Next time you visit Enchantment, bring some sweets with you."

I laughed, and Kai gave me a hug.

"If you ever need me," he said, "just send word. I'll be there in a heartbeat."

"Same to you," I said, "and you're always welcome at my place, visa or no." I gave Kai one last hug and turned away. He had his path to walk, and I had mine. I took a deep breath and stepped through the portal.

Magic twisted through me, wringing me out for one impossibly long moment of pain, then I stumbled breathlessly onto solid ground. I didn't throw up or collapse, as I had in the past, but experience with cross-realm portals didn't make them any more comfortable. I filled my lungs with air from the Mortal Realm, and even here in the woods, I caught the scent of industry that had been notably absent in Enchantment. A distant rumble drew my attention to a plane flying overhead. It left a bright-white line across the cloudless sky.

I smiled. "I'm home."

"Finally." The whispered word came from the underbrush to my right.

Before I could so much as lower my gaze, cold fingers clamped around my wrist, and I was pulled off my feet. The thorns of a gooseberry bush snatched at my hair and clothes as I tumbled through its branches, heading face first toward the base of a thick spruce. An involuntary shout left my lips as I raised my free arm to protect my face from the whipping underbrush and my impending collision, but rather than making contact with the tree, I passed through it. The world vanished, and I fell into darkness.

Chapter 9

MY KNEE CAME down on something solid. The pressure around my wrist pulled me forward, and I surged to my feet to keep from being dragged. My breath grew shallow as ice froze my lungs and throat. My stumbling steps came down on nothing, and nothing surrounded me, but I'd experienced this "nothing" before. I was on a shadow road, a path opened by a shadow-walker that could cross great distances in the blink of an eye. Unfortunately, only a shadow-walker could navigate such a path; anyone else would be lost in the darkness forever. So, as much as I wanted to pull away from the hand clamped around my wrist, I dared not fight my captor.

After a dozen stumbling steps, light burst around me. Still shuffling forward, drawn on by my aching arm, I blinked twice and rubbed my eyes with my free hand, trying to clear my vision. The gray fingers around my wrist belonged to a woman in a black lace dress and black boots. Dark hair cascaded over her back. She glanced over her shoulder.

With a flood of relief, I recognized the amber eyes and doll-like features looking back at me. "Morgan? What are you—"

She gave my arm another tug, and we sank into the deep shadow of a rocky, moss-covered cave. The scent of mildew filled my nostrils for a moment, then the twisting ache of crossing realms bombarded my senses yet again.

The pain flared and faded in one eternal instant, and my feet sank into fine, white sand. The cave behind me was sandstone rather than granite and dry instead of damp. Overhead, three enormous moons filled an indigo sky.

"Where—"

Another tug at my wrist cut my question short. I was back in the nothing of the shadow roads. How many jumps did this make? My brain was struggling to parse the flood of disjointed details. What in the name of Zeus's holy butthole was going on here?

When I stumbled once more out of the shadows, a gauzy piece of fabric brushed my face. The pressure constricting my wrist abruptly released. I stumbled over plush red carpet and slammed my shoulder into a wooden bookcase.

"I was beginning to worry you might never come out of Enchantment." Morgan turned to face me, flipping her long black hair over her shoulder as she spoke. She leaned against a writing table and crossed her arms. "You certainly took your time."

I twisted to glare at my kidnapper, rubbing my bruised wrist and bracing against the bookcase for support. "Maybe if I'd *known* you were looking for me," I snapped. "What's the big idea dragging me to . . ." I stalled, glancing around what seemed to be a small library from the seventeenth century containing two large desks covered in loose papers and haphazard stacks of books, wall-to-wall bookshelves, a velvet couch, and several reading chairs. Behind me stood a curtained alcove and a black door with heavy brass hinges. A gothic-style chandelier hung from the ornately carved ceiling panels, illuminating the room with clouds of glittering light trapped in glass orbs. The slightly nutty scent of linseed oil filled the dry air. "Where exactly have you brought me?"

Morgan smiled, though it was more a pinching of features devoid of mirth. "My home." She moved to a thick black curtain and pushed it aside, revealing a sea of gray-shingled rooftops beyond a wide, curving window. "Welcome to the Realm of Shadows."

Mouth open, I walked to the window. Those three glowing moons I'd caught a glimpse of earlier hung overhead, bathing the city beyond the glass in pale light. Deep shadows filled the spaces between tightly packed buildings. Ribbons of smoke rose from hundreds of chimneys. Beyond the city, white dunes stretched to the horizon.

I swallowed. Hortense had once warned me not to come here. Something about an old rivalry between Shadow and Enchantment. I cast Morgan a sidelong glance. Her father, Dimitri, was the Lord of Shadows. "Why exactly did you bring me here?"

"Not to feed you to Lord Dimitri, if that's what you're worried about." She settled against her desk again. "No one else knows you're here. I need to speak with you."

"And you couldn't do that at the reservation, why?"

"Too many spies," she said. "It's a matter of some . . . delicacy. Unfortunately, you've already wasted a lot of time. I've been staking out that portal for nearly a month. Why were you away so long?"

The reminder that the realms experienced time differently froze my blood. I'd never been to Shadow before. For all I knew, years could have passed since I arrived. "Dammit! I can't afford to lose any more time to mismatched realms."

"And don't I know it," she said. "Don't worry. Dimitri isn't a big fan of change. We could chat for a year and barely five minutes will have passed in the Mortal Realm. I'll have you home a few seconds after we left."

I exhaled, turning my back on the foreign landscape to give her my full attention. "Fine. What did you want to talk about?"

"First, you must swear not to reveal the source of any of the information I'm about to share with you. If you do, my life will be forfeit." She met and held my gaze. "I am walking a very thin line by speaking to you at all."

I frowned. "Okay. I promise not to tell anyone you talked to me."

She nodded. "Dimitri is planning to pull Shadow out of the upcoming negotiations."

I stiffened. "Why?"

"You know about the attacks, right?"

"Um . . . I've been a little out of the loop recently," I admitted.

She huffed. "Since the PTF rescinded all fae visas, and with them any semblance of PTF protection, hundreds of fae and halfers have gone missing from the Mortal Realm. We know from the ones who've escaped that the culprits are humans amped up on the drug Fantasia. I assume you know where that comes from?"

I sat down on a padded bench in front of the open window. Fantasia was a drug designed by human Purists to mimic magical abilities in regular humans. I'd seen what Fantasia-users could do firsthand. I'd also seen one of the facilities where it was developed. Fantasia was distilled from captured fae.

I shook my head. "Even without a treaty in effect, I can't believe the PTF would turn a blind eye to widespread Fantasia distribution. Setting aside where it comes from, a high percentage of users have dangerously adverse reactions to that drug. When it first hit the streets, there were dozens of accounts of people having psychotic breaks and going on rampages, slaughtering civilians before eventually killing themselves."

"There have been more cases of Fantasia users going berserk in the past month than the last year put together," Morgan said. "Whoever is making Fantasia, they're ramping up production."

"So that's why Dimitri is pulling out of the Mortal Realm?" I asked. "To prevent his people from being abducted?"

"He's already closed our borders," she confirmed. "That's why I had to catch you before you left the reservation. No one from Shadow is allowed on Mortal soil. Even the reservations are pushing it."

"I'm sure the PTF is looking into the matter," I said with conviction. "They'll find whoever is making the Fantasia and shut them down."

Morgan shrugged. "Maybe, maybe not. Either way, until a new treaty is signed, fae in the Mortal Realm are fair game."

"All the more reason for the fae realms to participate in the negotiations. The sooner there's a new treaty, the safer the fae in the Mortal Realm will be."

"Except Lord Dimitri isn't so sure there will be a new treaty."

I frowned. "What do you mean? Almost all the realms have agreed to participate. Certainly all the major ones. And we have the human leadership and Earth paranaturals on board."

She nodded. "And you're going to bring all those very important people to the same place at the same time. Perfect time for an attack, don't you think?"

"Of course," I said. "That's why the summit committee spent so much time and energy designing safety precautions to keep everyone safe, and I'm sure they came up with even more protocols and procedures while I was away. Besides, we're talking about a gathering of some of the most powerful fae alive. Crashing that party would be suicide."

"No doubt, but the attackers may not be the only ones to lose their lives." She sighed. "Shadow's intel network found evidence that the increase in Fantasia is connected to an impending Purity attack. If that's the case, the upcoming negotiations would be the most likely target."

"Meaning Purity's planning to fight magic with magic," I said.

"And for every Fantasia user who's lost control, there could be dozens who haven't. Even with half a dozen fae lords, it's possible not everyone would make it out alive."

I braced my hands on my thighs. "So we move the talks. We change the dates. Now that we know an attack is coming, we can counter it." I looked at Morgan. "What evidence did your spies find, exactly?"

She shook her head. "Only Dimitri knows."

"Ask him," I said. "The more information we have, the better our chances of stopping the attack."

"He isn't trying to stop the attack."

I stilled, replaying the conversation in my head. If the Lord of Shadows wanted to warn the negotiation attendees about a possible threat, he could have simply shared his concerns with the PTF or the other lords. His daughter wouldn't have snatched me off the reservation and spirited me to her room in secret. Then there was the promise not to tell anyone we'd spoken. At last I said, "He doesn't want anyone else to know."

She tapped the tip of her nose with her index finger. "My father believes that, with Fantasia, the Purists may be able to injure the fae in attendance. One in particular."

I set my jaw. "Bael."

"Bael has no heir, and he's too proud to allow a proxy to speak for him. He'll attend the negotiations himself."

I had to remind myself that just because the fae presented a united front when facing humanity, the different realms were not necessarily friendly toward each other, much like the various factions of Earth.

"Right now, Shadow is considered the second strongest among the fae realms. Even if Bael survives, he may be weakened. That could shift the balance of power. Dimitri plans to stand back until the dust settles, then assess his options."

"But if he backs out of the negotiations, won't the other lords know something's up?"

"Which is why he has no intention of telling anyone. He wasn't going to attend the talks personally in any case. He's much too paranoid for that. But he doesn't plan to risk Galen either. Shadow will simply fail to arrive at the appointed time."

"And your brother's okay with that?" Morgan's twin brother, Galen, was the designated spokesperson for the Realm of Shadows. I'd had dealings with him in the past, and he'd always struck me as a fair man.

"He cannot disobey a direct order from his lord." She looked away. "None of us can."

I studied her frown. "Then how are you sharing this news with me? I can't imagine you got Dimitri's permission, especially considering my relationship to Bael."

She gave a short, sharp laugh. "Not remotely. As I said, he doesn't even know you're here, and it needs to stay that way if I'm to keep my head attached to my shoulders." She stared at the carved wooden panels on the ceiling. "Like any loyal citizen of the realm, I would never dream of sharing information that my lord had specifically ordered me to keep secret. That doesn't mean I can't discuss the odd bit of news I just happened to overhear."

I considered Morgan's predicament, trapped between her oaths and doing what she believed was right. "I see what you mean about walking a thin line. Deciding to tell me must have been difficult."

She shrugged. "While Bael may be your kin, I know he's not your lord, and I believe you care more about the well-being of the Mortal Realm than helping the Lord of Enchantment win a contest of one-upmanship against my father." She sighed. "I don't agree with the direction Dimitri is taking this realm—locking our borders, trying to keep us frozen in time." She crossed her arms and shook her head. "Honestly, I wish he'd just die so Galen could take over."

I jerked, shocked by her candid pronouncement. "He's your father!"

"He's *old*." She glared at me, a fierce anger burning in her amber eyes. "You don't understand what eternity does to a mind. There's a reason none of the firstborn fae are around anymore."

"Fair enough," I said placatingly, "but surely there's some middle ground. Have you tried talking to him? Explaining your concerns? Maybe you could convince him a new treaty will serve your realm better in the long run than weakening Bael."

"My father has gotten more and more reclusive as his paranoia grows. Galen handles all the practical matters of running the realm at this point. All Dimitri does is hand down orders and hide in his rooms with his own twisted thoughts. He barely listens to Galen. He hasn't welcomed *my* advice in decades. But I refuse to spend the next few centuries stagnating in this prison because he let his rivalry with Bael overshadow our realm's need to stay connected to current events. If he won't listen to reason, I'll use a less direct method to set Shadow on the right path."

"You want me to soup up security at the meeting to thwart the Purist attack without letting anyone know about Dimitri's intentions?"

"No," Morgan said. "I want you to ensure Shadow is represented at that meeting."

I gave her a flat stare. "I can't *make* your brother attend."

"If you neutralize the threat to the meeting beforehand, with enough publicity that everyone both learns of the plot and knows the danger has been dealt with, Dimitri's pride will take care of the rest. Not only would the chances of harm coming to the other lords be negligible at that point, but if he were to miss the meeting under those circumstances, it would be taken as a sign of fear and weakness. He may be a stubborn old fool, but he's still a lord. He won't want to lose face."

I frowned. "You want me to uncover the details of the plot, without access to whatever evidence convinced Dimitri there was a plot in the first place, and neutralize the threat in a dramatically public way, all before the negotiations are scheduled to take place?"

She nodded. "Without letting anyone know that I tipped you off."

I let out a long whistle. "You don't ask for much, do you?"

"I assumed you'd want to protect the negotiations regardless of my motives."

"I do," I agreed, "and I'm glad you brought this to my attention. It's nice to know there are fae who see the value of cooperation. I'm just not sure a preemptive strike will be possible within the time frame. There are only a few days before the summit."

"I *had* intended to inform you earlier."

I nodded, ignoring the subtle probe for information about my extended stay in Enchantment. "I'll do what I can."

"Then I shall return you to the reservation, so you can get started." She held out her hand, and when I took it, she led me toward the fabric-covered alcove.

I cast a glance over my shoulder at the city silhouetted by three moons beyond the window, then I followed her into the shadows. Maybe I'd get the chance to visit properly someday.

* * *

LATE AFTERNOON SUNLIGHT cast long shadows as I stepped out of the forest and cleared my throat. The two PTF guards on the far side of the iron fence jumped and drew their weapons.

"Mind opening the gate?" I asked. "I'd like to get home before dark."

The guards looked at each other. Finally, the shorter of the two men holstered his gun and held out his hand. "You got an ID?"

I fished in my pocket, pulled out my driver's license, and reached through the iron bars to hand it over.

He took the ID, watching to see if my skin burned when I brushed the metal, then retreated to the guard building to check my credentials against the list of reservation visitors. Two minutes later, he came back with a disbelieving look on his face. He handed back my ID. "You were in there for three months?"

"Yep."

The second guard took a step away from me. "What were you doing?" he asked incredulously.

"That's none of your business. Now please open the gate." I put my ID away while the guards unlocked and opened the iron gate just wide enough for me to slip through. Ignoring their stares, I brushed a layer of dust, leaves, and twigs off the windshield of my blue Jeep, which was right where I'd left it, and climbed behind the wheel. My shoulders relaxed. I exhaled. I was on my way home.

Well . . . not *straight* home. I'd promised Maggie she'd be my first stop when I got back to town, and I was eager to meet her baby in person, but Morgan's visit had shifted my priorities. Maggie would understand. She'd complain, but she'd understand. I needed to swing by the PTF first. The sooner I made Director Harris aware of the Fantasia threat, the sooner she could start working on a solution. And now that I knew there was no chance of replacing James as the council's spokesperson, I needed to get the vampires folded into the Paranatural Alliance as quickly as possible.

Even speeding, it would take me three hours to reach Denver. David and Everly were both workaholics, so they'd probably still be in the office, but best to call ahead if I wanted to catch Sarah and Garrett, who headed the Paranatural Alliance, before they left for the day.

Turning my phone on for the first time in a month, I checked the battery and plugged in the charging cord I kept in my dash. When I was sure the phone wouldn't die during my call, I dialed David's number. Five rings. I was preparing a terse message for his voicemail when he finally answered.

"You're back!" David sounded tired and relieved.

"Fresh off the reservation," I said with a smile he couldn't see.

"And I'm your first call? I'm flattered."

Guilt wilted my smile. "While I *did* miss you, I'm actually calling because I have some information regarding the summit that we need to discuss. Can you set up a meeting between you, me, Everly, Sarah, and Garrett for six o'clock tonight?"

"Way to make a guy feel special," he grumbled. "Sarah, Garrett, and I are no problem. Director Harris is in D.C. right now, but we can probably get her on a video call."

I winced. "This is more of a face-to-face chat."

"She'll be back tomorrow morning," he said. "Or we could call Assistant Director Weatherly. He's here."

I considered the pompous bureaucrat who'd done his best to make my time with the PTF a living hell when I first started working for them and shook my head. A short delay was infinitely preferable to trying to convince Weatherly to allocate PTF resources on behalf of the fae. Hell, he might even sink so low as to slip info about the plot to his pal Governor Anderson to strengthen the Purist position on moving the summit out of Colorado. "I'll wait for Harris, but let her know I want to talk to her first thing tomorrow morning."

"Will do," he said. "Did you still want to talk to the rest of us, or is this an all-at-once sort of discussion?"

I started to say that I wanted to speak with everyone together, but the words died in my throat. Technically, Harris didn't need to be present when I told Sarah and Garrett about the vampires wanting to join the Paranatural Alliance. I'd planned to include her in the conversation out of respect and because I trusted her, but in some ways it might be simpler if she wasn't there for this initial conversation. I only needed the practitioners and werewolves to agree to let the vampires join the alliance, which would probably go faster without complicating the matter with a PTF perspective. I could sort out the vampires' status with the alliance tonight then present the facts to Everly when I met with her in the morning.

"Go ahead and set up the meeting with everyone else," I said.

"You got it," he said. "And Alex?"

"Hm?"

"Welcome home."

I smiled as the line went dead.

* * *

THANKS TO A seemingly endless number of road construction sites, it was after six when I finally pulled into the parking lot in front of the Denver PTF facility. I cut the engine, stared through the windshield, and wished there was a back entrance. Protesters were a common sight in front of this building, but the number of shouting, sign-wielding activists trampling the lawns seemed to have doubled since I'd left. Yellow caution tape marked the edges of the main pathway that led to the glass atrium of the front entrance, and uniformed security guards held the line, but the people on either side shouted insults, threats, and arguments across the open space like armies facing off before a skirmish. Signs shaken overhead on the left spouted Purity rhetoric about the evils of magic, comparisons between paranaturals and beasts, and endorsements for Governor Anderson's anti-fae policies. On the right were signs highlighting historical struggles for equality, enumerating the benefits of diversity, and calling people to remember and not repeat the tragedies of war. Curiously enough, both sides included signs that quoted various passages of scripture. It seemed religion could justify either opinion.

Taking a deep breath, I stepped out of my Jeep. The shouting, which had been a muffled rumble when my door was closed, rose to a fevered pitch that pounded my eardrums and made my head throb. The odor of sweaty bodies pressed together tickled my nose as I made my way between the flimsy strips of caution tape. The pressure of unwanted attention slammed into me as both sides found a new target, and I was finally able to make out some individual voices.

"Protect our children; send the freaks away!"

"Magic cured my son's cancer; imagine the advancements we could make together!"

"The only good fae is a dead fae!"

"People with magic are still people!"

The numbers appeared fairly even on either side of the no-man's-land through which I walked. I was glad the Purists weren't able to make a clean sweep of the debate, that the One Earthers were pushing back, standing up for the rights of magic-users, but the scene wrenched my heart. I'd spent the past year doing everything I could to prevent another war between regular humans and paranaturals. Now I was wondering if the humans were headed for a civil war regardless of what was decided about magic and the rights of those who wielded it.

The groups on both sides pushed forward, straining the caution tape. For a moment, I feared the protesters would overwhelm the guards trying desperately to hold them back, and I would be crushed between them when they clashed. I hurried my pace. My palms were sweating and my pulse was racing, but I managed to pass through the glass doors without engaging any of the protesters. I glanced over my shoulder as the door closed, once more muffling the shouts outside. The guards had succeeded in forcing the protesters back behind the yellow line, and the crowds, deprived of a specific target, resumed their verbal volley.

"Hello, Ms. Blackwood."

I jumped and swung my attention to the sandy-haired man behind the desk who watched me through thick lenses.

"Hey Carl," I said as I approached the desk. I hooked a thumb over my shoulder to indicate the crowd out front. "It seems like we have more protesters than usual."

"Both sides have gotten more vocal with the summit so close. If you ask me, we'll be lucky to make it to that meeting without bloodshed." He shook his head. "Hopefully they'll all calm down once a new treaty is drafted."

I frowned, thinking about how the people outside were likely to react when they discovered that vampires wanted a slice of that treaty pie. Even the One Earth folks might hesitate to welcome beings who fed off the blood of humans into their community.

"Here's hoping," I muttered.

Passing through a door on the right that led to a hallway lined with offices, I walked to the door with a brass placard that read *David Nolan*, rapped my knuckles against the wood, and let myself in.

David looked up from some papers he'd been studying. He looked exhausted. Dark circles shadowed his eyes, his tousled curls stuck out in all directions, and deep furrows creased his brow and framed his frown. His brown gaze met mine, and the ghost of a smile tugged his lips. He stood, circled his desk, and embraced me.

I squeezed him back. "It's good to see you, David."

Releasing me, he took a step back and said, "You're late."

I frowned. "Don't tell me they've gone home."

He chuckled and shook his head. "No one who's known you for any length of time would expect you to be prompt. Even when you're the one who sets the terms."

I stuck my tongue out at his back as he returned to his seat.

"Case in point"—he spread his hands—"a few days. That's how long you were supposed to be gone."

I winced. "I know, and I'm sorry. Didn't Hortense explain?"

"She did," he said. "Didn't make these past three months suck any less."

"Sorry," I said again, "but I'm here now."

He nodded and lifted the receiver on his office phone. "I'll let the others know."

Five minutes later, two more bodies crowded into David's office. Sarah was a lean five-foot-six who moved like a gymnast and radiated an aura of "don't mess with me." She'd been a regular cop and a member of the local werewolf pack when I first met her. Now she was the alpha wolf of the PTF pack and acted as liaison between the PTF and the rest of the werewolf community. Fresh from the gym, Sarah wore a white tank top, black shorts, and white sneakers. Sweat glistened on her tight, bronze skin. She pinned me with her dark-brown gaze as she entered the room.

Garrett rolled in close on Sarah's heels, his wheelchair taking up pretty much all the remaining space. He wore a tan suit with a white shirt and paisley tie. Close-cropped black hair faded to dark-brown skin at his temples in a military cut, probably a holdover from his time with the sorcerer troops. As a practitioner who knew the dangers of magic firsthand thanks to a backlash that left him paralyzed from the waist down, Garrett had been chosen to represent the human practitioners who sought to break free from their enslavement by the Church and the PTF. Together, Sarah and Garrett were the public leaders of the Paranatural Alliance, although both ultimately answered to the people they represented, much like James would be the mouthpiece for the vampires. I'd spent most of the drive here considering how I could convince them to induct vampires into the alliance before the summit.

I leaned against David's desk, bracing my hands to either side of my hips. "Thanks for coming."

"Of course," Garrett said.

Sarah nodded. "What's up?"

I shifted my gaze to Garrett. Sarah and David both knew what James was. Garrett, like so many others, had been left in the dark to protect the vampires' secret. His reaction would be a good indication of how the rest of the practitioners, and humans in general, might respond to the revelation that there was yet another paranatural race sharing their world. I took a deep breath and exhaled slowly. "The vampires have decided to come out of hiding."

Sarah whistled. "Ballsy."

"The . . ." Garrett stalled out, frowning.

"Vampires," I repeated. "They're real, and they want to join the Paranatural Alliance." I glanced at David. "*Before* the interspecies negotiations take place. They want a seat at the table."

David shook his head in disbelief. "You want to add them *now*? Less than a week before the summit?"

"Whoa, hang on," Garrett said. He glared at David. "Sarah I can understand, but *you* knew about vampires?"

David shrugged. "I only found out recently, but yeah."

Garrett shook his head, processing. At least he wasn't totally freaking out. That was promising. Then again . . . as an ex-paladin, a magical backlash survivor, and a friend to social outcasts in general, maybe Garrett *wasn't* the best example of how an average human would react.

I turned to David. "Please tell me you kept a chair open for them."

"Adding a chair at the table is hardly the largest concern here," Sarah said. "The fae won't want vampires attending the summit."

"Why?" Garrett asked.

"Fae hate vampires," I said. "Given half a chance, they'd wipe them all off the face of the earth."

"That's terrible!"

"The fae are hypocritical bastards," said Sarah.

I smirked. Werewolves disliked fae almost as much as fae disliked vampires. My smile fell. With so many deep-rooted prejudices . . . was there really any chance for peace?

"I guess that explains why the vampires would want to join the alliance," Garrett said. "Safety in numbers and all."

"Safer for *them*, maybe." Sarah narrowed her eyes. "Sounds to me like the vampires intend to use werewolves and practitioners as a shield to protect them from the fae."

"The fae aren't the only ones who are going to have a problem with this," David said. "Most humans don't even know vampires are real, and what they do 'know' are horror stories told around campfires. *Maybe*, if we'd given them time to process ... but I doubt the political and religious leaders of the human race will be happy when you sit a vampire down across from them and say, 'Guess what, guys? Bloodsuckers are real. They've been killing people from the shadows for centuries.' "

I glowered at him. "I wasn't planning to phrase it quite like that."

"How would you phrase it?" Garrett asked. "What are vampires like? And while we're on the subject . . . are there any more paranatural races who might be looking to join our organization down the road?"

I studied Garrett. He seemed to be taking the news about vampires in stride. I hoped the rest of the practitioners could adapt as quickly, though I doubted the general human population would.

"None that I'm aware of," I said with a shrug. "As to what vampires are like . . ." I leaned back, looking at the ceiling as I sorted through everything I knew about vampires. Finally, I settled on the simplest answer, despite the way it made my heart ache. I met his gaze. "You've met James."

Garrett's brow furrowed, his frown growing deeper. James's status as a paranatural wasn't a secret, but he'd been labeled "uncategorized" when the PTF tested him. They'd had no reason to suspect "vampire" was even an option, and his ability to walk in daylight certainly wouldn't have brought stories of the night-dwelling monsters to mind.

"Vampires are just like humans," I continued, "if humans lived forever. Like the werewolves, they started out human and were changed into something else through magic. They can be kind or cruel, violent or peaceful, stoic or fun-loving. There are as many different kinds of vampires as there are personality types among humans."

"David's right, though," Sarah said. "Humans will hear the word *vampire* and immediately picture all the worst-case scenarios from scary movies. We werewolves are having a hell of a time convincing people we won't rip their throats out at the drop of a hat, even though that almost never happens. Vampires actually *need* to eat people. It's going to be a shit show."

"*Feed from*," I said, raising a finger to emphasize the point, "not *eat*."

She crossed her arms. "You think the humans will care about that distinction?"

"They will if we're able to control the narrative," I said. "That's why the vampires need to come out *before* the negotiations take place," I said. "Once a treaty is signed that defines the relationships between the humans, fae, and alliance members, the vampires will be the odd species out—the only ones not protected by the treaty. The fae won't hesitate to reveal them to humanity at that point, and in the worst possible light. They'll use their new allies to rout the vampires once and for all. If the vampires reveal *themselves*, they can show humans that peace is possible."

"But they *do* feed from humans?" Garrett asked. "They drink blood, like in the stories?"

I nodded. "As I understand it, the magic that keeps them alive is constantly eating away at their bodies. They absorb energy from other living things to hold themselves together. But they don't have to kill their donors. I've been fed on before, and I'm fine."

I rubbed my neck, recalling the feel of torn flesh under my fingers. Okay, maybe "fine" was an overstatement. I still woke up screaming sometimes. But I was alive—proof that vampires didn't *have to* kill to survive.

Sarah crossed her arms. "Whether or not they *need* to kill, they often do. It would take a lot to convince humans that vampires can be good neighbors, and the feud between fae and vampires has been going on for millennia." She shook her head. "Letting vampires join the alliance will put the rest of us even more at odds with both the humans and the fae. It'll weaken our position during the negotiations."

"I disagree," I said. "The Paranatural Alliance is already the weakest corner of this triangle. The fae have more magical power, and the humans outnumber you ten thousand to one. The human authorities are willing to let you attend the conference because they assume you'll help them keep the fae in check since Earth is your home. That doesn't mean they see you as equals. Given half a chance, they'd collar us all and force us to follow orders in exchange for minimal comforts and the safety of our families, like they did with practitioners during the Faerie Wars."

Garrett crossed his arms. "Surely they wouldn't try those heavy-handed tactics again? Not after all the casualties they suffered when the sorcerers rebelled."

I stiffened, momentarily unable to speak past the lump in my throat as I pictured the burned-out rubble and charred corpses my father—the leader of that rebellion—had left behind when he "freed" the Church's sorcerers . . . only to turn them into foot soldiers in his necromantic army.

"Lives are cheap to people like that," David mumbled, "but they'll probably stop short of actual enslavement this time to avoid a repeat of the massacre in Italy."

"That's why we plan to offer loyalty in exchange for rights," Sarah said. "We're willing to be humanity's shield against the fae so long as they treat us fairly."

I gave myself a mental shake, pushing aside memories of my father's rebellion . . . a rebellion that *I* had put a stop to. The past was the past. I had to protect the future.

"That's all well and good," I said, "but the demands you can make are limited by the value you can provide. Right now, the Paranatural Alliance might be enough to force another draw if the fae invaded in earnest. That should ensure you're granted basic human rights. But what about the segregated schools? What about the restrictions on which jobs you can hold?"

I met and held Sarah's gaze, feeding the frustration burning in her eyes. Sarah had never wanted to be anything other than a police officer, and she'd been a damn good one, but the moment her paranatural nature came to light that path had been closed to her. Doctors, teachers, politicians . . . those careers were all off-limits to paranaturals.

"They'll give you the minimum concessions they can to ensure your cooperation, but both sides know that the Earth paranaturals have nowhere to go. If push comes to shove, the humans could make life very uncomfortable for you, and the fae have no reason to intercede on your behalf, unless you're willing to trade one set of masters for another."

"And you think including the vampires in the alliance will make a difference?" Garrett asked.

"As Sarah pointed out, the fae are going to kick up a fuss about vampires being included in the new treaty. That's going to get the humans thinking about *why* the fae are so worried about vampires when they had no objection to treating with werewolves or practitioners. Obviously the fae don't care that vampires kill humans. Plenty of fae do that, too. The logical conclusion will be that the fae fear vampires." I felt like pacing as I spoke, but there was no room to move in the cramped office, so I settled for making exaggerated gestures with my hands.

"If the humans see that the fae are truly concerned about the power represented by the alliance, your value will go up in their eyes, and with it, the concessions they're willing to make to get you to cooperate. Knowing that the fae are wary of the vampires will also make the humans think twice about trying to force paranaturals into service like they did with the practitioners during the Faerie Wars. Having that extra intimidation factor could mean the difference between paranaturals being treated as valued partners versus exploited, second-class citizens."

Garrett looked back and forth between Sarah and me, finally settling his gaze on her. "I admit I'm out of my depth here. What Alex is saying does seem to make sense, but I don't know enough to weigh the risks and rewards. What do you think?"

Sarah pursed her lips. "Alex made some good points. It's always better to negotiate from a position of power. The more power the better. But the vampires are a double-edged blade. If the existence of vampires scares the humans enough, there's a chance they'll team up with the fae to wipe us *all* out." She shook her head and pinned me with a scrutinizing look. "The vampires are going to need one hell of a smooth talker representing them if they want to"—she quirked her fingers—" 'control the narrative.' "

I shifted my weight and looked away as the frustration of my failure to extract James from the council's control settled over me. "James will be the spokesperson for the vampires."

David shot me a sharp look which quickly softened with sympathy. He understood what that statement meant . . . that my trip to Enchantment had been a waste of time.

Sarah frowned. "I hadn't realized he was so high in their ranks."

I shrugged, unwilling to explain James's actual situation. "Like you said, the vampires need someone who can placate the humans. He personally saved the lives of the Church's delegates during Shedraziel's attack on this facility. That should earn him some good will."

Sarah nodded. "It'll also serve as an example of how strong vampires can be. He held off several werewolves and human soldiers entirely on his own during that battle." She sounded both annoyed and impressed by that fact.

"Isn't there anyone else?" David asked. "You stepped down from PTF assistant director to behind-the-scenes consultant to get out of the limelight. Your boyfriend announcing he's a vampire will make you tabloid fodder again."

"I stepped down because this role fits me better," I said, although part of that decision *had* been about staying out of the public eye—a place where I was not at all comfortable. I dug my nails into the desk as another pang of frustration twisted my heart. "As for James, it's not ideal, but once the term 'vampire' is on the board as a paranatural option, it wouldn't take the PTF long to guess what he is, whether he's representing them or not."

David shrugged. "I don't know. The whole 'walking in daylight' thing would probably throw them off."

"Speaking of which," Garrett said, "how much of the legends about vampires are true?"

"They can eat garlic, hang out in churches, and see their reflections," I said, "but they do drink blood, they heal super fast, and they're functionally immortal, though not indestructible. The stuff about burning in sunlight is true."

Garrett frowned. "Then how does James—"

"Long story," I cut him off.

"At least James's unique ability means we won't have to rearrange the summit meetings to take place at night," David said. "That would have been nearly impossible."

Shifting my focus to Sarah and Garrett, I asked, "So, are we agreed that the vampires would bring more positives than negatives to the alliance?"

"Based on what I've heard here, I'm inclined to let the vampires join," Garrett said. He looked at Sarah. "But I'm obviously ill-informed on this topic, so I'll follow your lead."

Sarah arched an eyebrow. "You sure you don't want to run this by your people first? They may have their own opinions about being lumped in with vampires."

"Oh, I'm sure they'll have lots of opinions," he said. "But I doubt they're any better informed than I was, and it would take too long for you to bring us all up to speed. The practitioners will abide by the werewolves' decision."

I shifted my attention to Sarah. "So? Are they in?"

She swiped a hand over her hair and exhaled. "A decision this big requires a vote. I'll need to run it past the other alphas." Her brown gaze settled on me. "I'll let you know when I have an answer."

Chapter 10

THE STREETS OF Boulder, which had always struck me as crowded before, seemed wide and empty compared to the avenues of Abonaille Malmür. Not that they were actually empty. Plenty of people zipped through the roads or strolled along the sidewalks in search of their favorite flavor of night life, but the people seemed to blend into the landscape, small and easy to overlook. As strange as I'd found the varied appearances of the fae at first, it now seemed equally strange to me how little variety there was among humans. Two eyes, two ears, two arms. All roughly the same size. All some shade of beige or brown. Where were the wings? Where were the tails? Where were the colors? Everyone seemed so *muted*. And it wasn't just the people. The blocky shapes of the buildings, the litter-strewn ground, even the green of the trees. They all seemed to lack the vibrancy I'd grown used to in Enchantment. The same vibrancy that had overwhelmed me at first.

I guess people really can get used to anything, given enough exposure.

I parked under one of the old-fashioned streetlamps illuminating Maggie's neighborhood as the sun sank behind the Front Range and plunged the town into twilight. Lights blazed in the windows of her narrow townhouse. Cutting the engine, I followed the walkway to Maggie's front door. Despite the darkness that had rolled in during my discussion with David and the others, the night was warm, and I found myself missing the even temperatures afforded by magical climate control as I flapped my shirt to cool the sweat on my back. The air was thick, cloying. It stirred memories of thunderstorms, campfires, and cut grass. I stepped onto the porch and reached for the doorbell, hesitating an inch from the button.

What if the baby is sleeping?

Changing tactics, I rapped lightly on the door. When no one answered, I knocked a little harder.

A wail erupted inside the house, and I fought the impulse to run for my car. Luckily, Charlie opened the door before my inner teenager could take over, and I was forced to swallow my guilt about waking the baby.

Charlie's ruddy cheeks lifted with a smile when he saw me, but deep shadows bruised his eyes. "Alex!" He pulled me into a hug, then twisted to call over his shoulder as he pulled me inside, "Honey, it's Alex!"

"Sorry I woke the baby," I mumbled. "I did *try* to be quiet."

Charlie shook his head and ran a hand through his messy red hair. "Don't worry about it. He's up every few hours anyway."

I frowned. No wonder Charlie looked so tired.

We found Maggie in the living room, bouncing, swaying, and singing the second verse of *Mary had a Little Lamb*. The cries coming from the blanketed bundle pinned against her shoulder quieted to a snuffle as she patted and danced. I stayed at the edge of the room, brushing my nose to clear a tickle caused by all the potent smells in the house—sour milk, lotion, laundry detergent, and some odors I didn't want to think about.

Maggie paused in her dance, opened one arm, and came in for a hug. "It's good to have you home, Alex."

I twisted so as not to crush the baby between us and gently squeezed her back. Like Charlie, purplish shadows circled Maggie's eyes, though hers weren't as obvious against her dark complexion. Her tight black curls were a crazy frizz exploding in every direction, and her eyes held the glassy sheen of sleep deprivation, but she was grinning when she stepped back.

My gaze dropped to the bundle, which had fallen quiet.

"Did he go back to sleep?" I whispered.

Maggie shook her head and shifted her grip, bringing the baby down to the cradle of her arms. Alexander's light-brown skin puckered around his wide open eyes. His lips fought for real estate with his plump cheeks, crowding out his chin. "Alex, meet Alex. Or, to be more precise, Alexander Kiran Rohne. He was born on the solstice."

"Eight pounds, two ounces," Charlie said. "All ten fingers, and all ten toes."

I leaned over and stared into Alexander's deep brown gaze. "He's perfect."

"Do you want to hold him?"

I straightened and took a step back. "Um, I don't think—"

"Don't be a chicken," Maggie said. "He's sturdier than he looks. Just make sure you support his head." She pushed the baby into my arms. The smells of milk and lotion grew stronger.

Alexander squirmed in my arms. He sniffed, and his squashed little nose sounded stuffy. One tiny hand emerged from the blanket, as if he were waving to me.

"Hello there," I whispered. "I'm your Auntie Alex." I pressed my finger against his grasping hand, and fingers too small to believe gripped my much larger one. I smiled.

Alexander's mouth pursed and puckered. His eyes closed. Then that god-awful sound that had filled the house when I first arrived came back.

"Aah!" I froze in place, torn between wanting to get away from the screaming child and not wanting to drop him. "What did I do?"

Maggie laughed. "Nothing, love. He's just hungry." Maggie scooped her son back into her arms, settled in a padded rocking chair, and arranged the baby so he could eat. Silence settled over the room as soon as Alexander's mouth closed on the source of his meal.

Charlie patted me on the shoulder. "Don't worry, Alex. I freaked out the first dozen or so times he started crying, too. You get used to it."

Shaking my head, I stared down at the tiny miracle in Maggie's arms. "He's so . . . small."

Maggie nodded. Her smile faltered. "I worry about him, Alex . . . about the future he's going to inherit. Drugs, hate, violence. The Purists and One Earth supporters seem pretty even in numbers, but the Purists are willing to go to such extremes." She shook her head. "If the negotiations don't go smoothly . . ."

"They will," I said. "The humans and fae will sign a new peace treaty, and the local paranaturals will have a voice this time, too." I sat in the chair nearest the rocker, leaned forward, and rested my hand on Maggie's knee. My chest ached at the thought of any harm coming to the precious bundle nestled in her arms. "We'll make a safe place for him, Mags," I said, sealing that promise in my heart. "For everyone. Whatever it takes."

Maggie patted my hand. "Thank you, love. I know we will."

Clearing my throat and blinking away the sudden pressure behind my eyes, I glanced around the room and asked, "How is Hortense handling life with a human baby?"

Charlie laughed, settling on the couch. "She ran away."

I stiffened. "What?"

"No, she didn't," Maggie chided. "She just found somewhere quieter to sleep. She comes over every morning to work on our project." Maggie shifted Alexander to her other side. "Emma stops by most days, too. We invited her to stay with us when Hortense first told us how long you'd be away, but she ended up moving in above her mom's bakery. I think she was chuffed to have an excuse to spend more time with her family. Especially May. They've lost so much already."

We all grew quiet. Like me, May had spent some time in a fae realm where time moved faster. Unlike me, she hadn't had any choice in the matter. She'd lost years of her childhood in a matter of days. By comparison, three months was hardly anything.

"And Emma's mom is okay with that arrangement?" I asked. "They haven't killed each other yet?"

"The cease fire seems to be holding," Maggie said. "May always was the glue that held the other two together. Now that she's back, at least they have a chance at reconciliation." Alexander finished his meal, and Maggie sat him up to burp him. "I need to get this little guy to bed," she said, "but Charlie can put a kettle on if you want to stay. You can tell us what happened in Enchantment."

I looked from the squirming baby to my friends' glazed expressions. I wanted to relax and sip tea on their couch. I wanted to vent about Bael's treachery and my frustrations and failures with imbuing. I wanted to share my fears about the upcoming summit and brainstorm solutions. Most of all, I wanted to talk and laugh with my friends until I felt like I'd truly come home, but I shook my head. I shouldn't cut in on what little sleep they could manage, and they had enough to fret about without me adding to their worries.

"It's been a long day. I'm glad I got to say hi and meet the baby, but I think I'll head home now."

Maggie nodded. Maybe she even looked a little relieved.

That was the right call, I thought as we stood. Kissing Alexander on the forehead I whispered, "Give your parents a break, okay? They look exhausted."

Maggie snorted. "You should have seen us the first month."

I knew she made the comment in good cheer, but the reminder that I'd missed so much, and for so little gain, stabbed like a dagger in my heart. Forcing a smile, I bid them goodnight and saw myself out.

Back behind the wheel of my Jeep, I hesitated to put the key in the ignition. My house was under an hour away. My own couch. My own bed. My own shower. Maybe it didn't possess all the luxuries of a lord's keep, but home was calling. Yet I hesitated. Sitting under the warm glow of the streetlamp, I imagined the dark road leading up to my house. I watched silhouettes move behind the lit curtains in Maggie's house and pictured the empty rooms waiting for me. Home had come to mean more to me than walls and a roof.

I twisted the ring on my finger and thought of James. A rush of heat spread through me along with a memory of hands running over my skin, but when I let go, I felt colder and more empty than before.

Chewing my lower lip, I pulled out my cell phone and found Emma's number. My thumb hovered over the call icon.

Am I being selfish?

Emma had patched up her relationship with her mother. She was making up for lost time with May. Maybe she wanted to stay where she was.

"I should at least let her know I'm back in town," I said to the phone in my hand. "She can make her own decision from there."

Emma picked up on the second ring. "Oh my god, Alex, is that you? Are you back?"

"Hey, Em. Yeah, I'm back."

"Back at the house, or are you still at the reservation?"

"Actually, I'm just leaving Maggie's."

"Perfect! You can swing by Mom's bakery and pick me up on your way out of town. I'll be ready in ten minutes." She hung up before I had a chance to respond.

I stared at the silent phone for a moment. Maybe things weren't going so smoothly at the Yamada household after all.

* * *

THE LIGHTS WERE dimmed in the glass storefront of Emma's family bakery, and the neon "open" sign in the door was off, but the windows in the apartment above shone with life. I pulled to the curb and reached for the keys to cut the engine. Emma was out the door before my hand crossed the distance. Frowning, I lowered my hand as she hurried across the short, shrub-lined walkway and sidewalk, purple suitcase in one hand, white paper bag clutched in the other. She wore a tie-dyed T-shirt, black cargo pants, and combat boots, but what really caught my attention was her hair. In a disturbing display of practicality, she'd buzzed it off after losing her sight. Even after regaining some semblance of "seeing" through her wonky magic, she'd left it her natural brown. But the woman walking down the path was a vision of the Emma of old. Parted slightly off center, half her hair was dyed a vibrant purple while the remainder bore a deep forest-green color. Seeing this return of flair made me smile.

Emma stashed her suitcase in the back of my Jeep, then she sank into the passenger seat with a sigh. The scents of yeast and icing sugar wafting off the white paper bag cradled on her lap made my mouth water.

"Whatcha got there?" I asked hopefully.

"Day-olds," she said. "I figured we could have them for breakfast tomorrow."

I inhaled deeply and licked my lips. *Those pastries might not make it to the morning.*

I glanced again at the apartment above the bakery, scanning the windows. Neither Loni nor May was anywhere in sight. Turning a worried look on Emma I asked, "You ready to get out of here?"

"Am I ever." She latched her seatbelt and said, "Let's go home."

I pulled away from the curb, wondering what had happened and how to broach the subject, but Emma saved me by speaking first.

"It was great spending time with May, and even my mom and I were getting on okay. If it had just been the short visit we originally planned, it would have been no problem. But three months?"

I cringed, feeling the accusation even though Emma's tone was blessedly free of blame.

She shook her head. "By week two I was remembering all the reasons I'd left home in the first place. Add to that the changes around here . . ." She shook her head again.

"Changes?" I asked.

Emma's distant gaze swung in my direction. She shifted on her seat. "Governor Anderson's been throwing his weight around here in Colorado. He's using the collapse of the original fae treaty, the rebellion that broke the Church's hold on practitioners, and the fact that no one knows where werewolves fit in yet as an excuse to declare open season on any paranaturals not directly under PTF control. He even published a list of suspected paranaturals and paranatural sympathizers for Purists to target."

"What?! That's like endorsing a hit list! He can't do that!"

"But he can, because there aren't any laws protecting paranaturals' rights." She hugged herself. "Hopefully that will change once the summit takes place."

I tightened my grip on the steering wheel, thinking of my promise to Morgan. *I have to protect that meeting.*

"That's why I was eager to leave," Emma continued. "Mom wasn't so bad, all things considered, but she has a business to protect. She made it *very* clear she wasn't a paranatural sympathizer despite her daughter's unfortunate status as a practitioner. There are iron curtains hanging in the bakery now, and a beaded curtain over the door. The tables and chairs are all steel, and she tells every customer who comes in about how magic broke both her daughters. She'd point at us behind the counter and say, 'See the damage magic has wrought? One child blinded, the other had her youth stolen away.' Then she'd talk about Dad dying in the Faerie Wars and how the world was going to hell, all because of magic."

I kept my hands on the wheel as I navigated the curving canyon road, but it took everything I had not to hug Emma right then. "I'm so sorry you had to go through that."

She shook her head. "Mom doesn't really feel that strongly," she said. "Don't get me wrong, she does blame magic for what happened to us, but she understands that magic itself isn't evil. Still, she has a business to run. If the bakery got shut down by Purists the way Maggie's bookstore did, she'd lose her livelihood."

"She's pretending to be a Purist to avoid being targeted?" I asked incredulously. "Doesn't she realize that's almost as bad as being the real thing?"

Emma grimaced. "That's what I said, but she's scared, and she has May to think of." Emma's voice dropped to a whisper. "Not everyone is brave enough to fight, Alex. Most people don't want to get involved."

I frowned. I hadn't wanted to fight. Less than a year ago I'd been happily oblivious to the paranatural community, living my life with my head in the sand. Part of me missed that ignorance, when all I'd known about magic was that it had nothing to do with me. A terrible thought struck me. *If I'd remained ignorant of my own paranatural nature, would I be like Loni right now, paying lip service to Purity just to stay out of their crosshairs?* But I wasn't ignorant, and I never could be again. I hadn't wanted to fight, but I'd been fighting for most of the past year, and I wasn't done yet. I had to make up for the Lonis of the world. I was in the unique position to be able to actually do something to help the paranatural community get the rights that all living beings deserved. I was going to make sure those negotiations went off without a hitch.

"So, how'd things go on your end?" Emma asked as we crested the ridge that revealed Barker Reservoir and the twinkling lights of Nederland beyond. "Did you get what you needed?"

I hadn't thought my mood could sink any lower after Emma's revelations about Purity's activities while I was away, but the reminder of my failure plunged me to new depths.

"Not so much," I muttered.

She twisted to face me, worry wrinkling her expression. "But the negotiations are right around the corner. What are you going to do?"

I strangled the steering wheel as I turned away from the lights of the city and wound into the forested hills that hid my home. "There's nothing I *can* do at this point. This might be our only chance to get vampires included in the interspecies treaty. Once the fae have a pact with the humans and current alliance members, there's no way they'll allow vampires to join the party. It would literally become vampires against the rest of the world. We can't endanger the future of an entire race of people just because I don't want my boyfriend to become a political target."

Emma sagged in her seat, crumpling the bag on her lap enough to release another mouth-watering waft of sweet, doughy goodness.

I exhaled. "Right now, I need to focus on getting the vampires admitted to the Paranatural Alliance and figuring out the best way to introduce them to the human population. They have to appear strong, but not scary."

Emma snorted. "Good luck with that."

Gravel crunched under my tires as we climbed the final hill to my house. I stopped short. A dark sedan was parked in my usual spot. The curtains were drawn in my living room, but light leaked around their edges.

"Someone's been sleeping in my bed," I mumbled, reciting a line from *Goldilocks and the Three Bears* as I ran through possibilities of who the mystery car might belong to. Chase might have come back if the repairs at Crossroads were done, but he couldn't drive a car. He could barely stand riding in one. Maggie said Hortense found quieter accommodations after the baby arrived. I'd never *seen* Hortense drive a car, but that didn't mean she couldn't.

Turning to Emma I said, "Can you tell who's inside?"

She frowned. Her brow furrowed. "Not anyone I recognize." Her frown deepened. "Definitely a paranatural. Fae, maybe? They look . . . weird."

A sinking feeling froze my limbs. "Weird how?"

She turned her frown on me. "Their energy signature looks kind of like yours."

All the comfort of coming home drained out of the world in an instant. Emma "saw" through the patterns of energy that made up the objects around her, both living and inanimate. Different objects had different patterns. Humans, for example, appeared as dense swirls of bluish energy, while something like a car or a building held only a hazy outline. People with magic were brighter, more defined, and colored by the source of their magic. According to Emma, fae and werewolves usually appeared in warm colors, while practitioners and vampires tended toward cooler hues, usually greens and blues. I was swirled, a muddle of mismatched magics. I'd only ever met one other person who fit that particular description.

I swallowed past the lump in my throat. "Ash."

"Who?"

While I did my best not to lie to my friends these days, some secrets came with a death sentence. No one could ever know the true identity of the person I'd met in the frozen fields of Canada.

As if summoned by my dread, my front door swung open, and the half-demon-half-fae progenitor of the vampire race stepped onto my porch wearing tight blue jeans and a short-sleeved, white blouse decorated with pink flowers. Ash's raven hair was pulled into a high ponytail except for asymmetrical bangs that hid one dark eye. The orange glow of my porch light illuminated delicate features in a narrow face that looked decidedly more feminine than the last time I'd seen it, due to some combination of magic and makeup. I knew from mucking about in Ash's core that they swapped personas, and genders, like clothes—a side effect of living so many different lives over the centuries.

"A friend of yours?" Emma asked nervously.

"Um . . . not exactly." I didn't want Emma, or any of my friends, anywhere near Ash. Especially since Emma could tell Ash wasn't human. Ash had made it very clear during the vampire conclave that they'd kill *anyone* who discovered their secret. If Ash found out Emma could see people's souls, she was as good as dead. If they thought I'd told Emma, they might kill everyone I knew for good measure, and I had no doubt they could.

I gripped the wheel until my knuckles ached. This was not the homecoming I'd been hoping for. *How had Ash known I'd be back tonight?*

Ash waved in greeting, then made a beckoning gesture, inviting us inside.

I glanced at Emma, at the curve of the driveway behind me, and back to the porch.

Ash smiled, turned, and went inside, leaving my front door open.

Shit. If I drove away now, Emma would know something was wrong. That might be reason enough for Ash to kill her. Even from inside the house, Ash could be on us before we reached the end of the driveway. There was no way to get Emma clear unless Ash *let* us leave, and the open front door suggested Ash had other plans.

Twisting to face Emma, I turned up the music on the radio to thwart any paranatural eavesdropping and said in the lowest whisper I thought she could hear, "Whatever you do, do *not* let on that you know Ash isn't human, okay?"

She frowned. "Why?"

I bit my lower lip. Telling Emma that Ash would kill her without a second thought would only make Emma afraid, which would in turn make her more likely to slip up and give herself away. "Just trust me on this, Em. There's a very good reason Ash is hiding, so promise me you won't say a word."

"I can keep a secret, but who exactly is this person?" She crossed her arms. "Are they an enemy? Should I call David?"

"Definitely not," I said. "I'll explain later. For now, let's just say they're someone I'd rather not piss off, so be your natural, friendly self and don't let on that you know anything is off about Ash."

She frowned. "If you say so."

Wincing, I added. "Best not to use your sixth sense around Ash at all. That might raise uncomfortable questions."

She glared. "Right, so, blind and ignorant. Anything else?"

"Sorry, Em." Wishing I'd left Emma at her mother's bakery, I cut the engine and circled the car. Slinging my bag over one shoulder, I lifted Emma's suitcase and offered her the elbow of my free arm. "Welcome home."

Lights blazed in my living room, trapped by curtains that blocked the outside world. Ash stood in the kitchen, rinsing salad at the sink. A pot of water boiled on the stove. "Good timing." Like their face, Ash's voice was slightly different than I remembered—higher, lighter—reinforcing the persona of a cheerful young woman. "I was just starting some pasta. If you haven't eaten yet, I'll throw in extra."

"I'm starving," Emma said before I could respond.

Ash smiled. "You must be Emma. I've heard a lot about you. Has Alex told you who I am?"

I stiffened. Ash was sussing out how much Emma knew—possibly to avoid contradicting any lies I might have told to explain their presence, but maybe to determine if Emma was a threat.

"Only that your name is Ash."

Ash dumped a handful of spaghetti noodles into the boiling water. Tucking the longer side of their bangs behind one ear to reveal both artfully painted eyes, Ash fixed their gaze on Emma. "Alex and I met a few months ago through a mutual friend. I believe you're acquainted with James Abernathy?"

My breath caught. I balled my fists, fighting to contain the rage and despair that filled me when James's name passed Ash's lips. They'd been the one, through their puppet council member, Esteban, who brokered the deal to imprison James until I provided the vampire council with daywalking amulets—a promise I now knew I'd never be able to fulfill.

"I know James," Emma said. I could practically see the gears turning in her brain, trying to piece together what she knew about James with what she'd perceived about Ash and how the two might relate.

"Well, when I saw what Alex could do, I commissioned a special project from her," Ash said.

So we were going with "James the art gallery owner" as our point of connection. Cool. I could roll with that. Much safer than "James the vampire council's hostage."

Emma frowned. "You're an art collector?"

"Indeed. My private collection is something to behold." Ash shifted their gaze to me. "I expected an update on my order before now. When I couldn't get hold of you, I came in person to check on your progress. Alas, I found the place deserted."

"I've been out of town," I said.

"So I gathered. I hope you don't mind that I made myself comfortable while I waited."

I frowned, glancing around the room again. There was a novel I'd never read on the end table beside an empty coffee mug, the afghan from the back of the couch was piled in one of the chairs, and I was pretty sure I'd left the curtains open when I left. Ash hadn't just shown up because I was coming back tonight.... "How long have you been living in my house?"

"Just over a week," Ash said with a shrug. "Like I said, I expected to hear from you much sooner." They tossed the salad in a glass mixing bowl.

Emma braced her hands on her hips. "Wait, so you just moved in, uninvited?"

"It's fine, Emma," I said, trying to placate her.

Emma gestured in the general direction of the kitchen. "But who does that?"

"I told Ash she could crash here if she came to visit," I lied, using the pronoun Ash seemed to be displaying. "Granted, I'd expected to be home at the time, but the invitation stands." I glared at Ash, then forced myself to smile in an effort to remove the irritation from my tone. "It's fine."

Emma frowned but let the matter drop.

"I'm going to get washed up before dinner," I said stiffly. "Emma, you should do the same."

She opened her mouth, but I gave her arm a tug, and she followed me silently down the hall. I needed a moment to gain my bearings and collect my thoughts before I fessed up to Ash that I'd come up short on our deal, and no way was I leaving Emma alone with Ash if I could help it.

After depositing Emma and her suitcase in her bedroom, I stepped into mine and closed the door. Everything was *almost* as I'd left it . . . but not quite. The bed was made, but the edges of the bedding were tucked in, something I never did because I didn't like feeling trapped. Like the living room, the window was covered . . . but not just with curtains. A blanket had been nailed to the wall, blocking out the entire window so that no light could leak into the room. A cold certainty settled over me. Ash really *had* been sleeping in my bed.

Struggling to hold my temper as the feeling of having my personal space violated washed over me, I opened my sock drawer and pushed fabric aside until my fingers closed around the rough wood of a knife handle. I drew the blade from its sheath, letting the faint glow of the metal soothe me. I'd forged this blade with Kai's help, and we imbued it with enough light to hurt a vampire. I wasn't foolish enough to believe the dimly glowing blade would save me if Ash wanted me dead, but having an ace up my sleeve made me feel better, if only marginally.

I sheathed the blade and tucked it into my waistband at the small of my back, taking care to cover it with my shirt. Then I splashed some water on my face in the attached bathroom, noting the presence of a hairbrush and toothbrush that didn't belong to me, as well as a faint trace of rose perfume.

Gritting my teeth, I twisted the band on my finger, bringing up a memory of the last night I'd spent with James. A flood of additional memories rose as well, reminding me why it was so important that I not do anything to piss Ash off. Somewhere, half a world away, James was at their mercy. And now that I knew I had no chance of delivering the daywalking amulets I'd promised, that situation wasn't likely to improve. I had to tread lightly.

I closed my eyes as I continued to twist the ring, feeling James's arms around me, his chest pressed to my back in comforting reassurance. His breath tickled the top of my head as he pressed his lips to my hair.

"I miss you," I whispered.

I opened my eyes and stared into the mirror. I was alone in the bathroom. Exhaling, I released the ring and let my hands fall to my sides.

"I *will* see James again," I promised my reflection. "We'll find a way out of this mess. It's just going to take longer than we'd hoped."

First things first. I had to make nice with the killer in my kitchen.

* * *

THREE PLACES WERE set at my dining table when I returned to the living room with Emma in tow. The scent of Italian herbs and warm garlic bread filled the air. Ash set out three serving bowls—one with noodles, one with sauce, and one with salad—and a basket of bread. They poured a generous serving of red wine into each of our glasses and settled at the head of the table.

"I'd have prepared something more celebratory if I realized you'd be back today," They said as Emma and I took our seats. "A cake maybe."

"This is fine." I sounded like a broken record. Maybe if I just kept saying that everything was fine, everything would be.

Emma felt along the tabletop until she found her glass, then raised it in a toast and said with a smile, "To coming home."

I lifted my glass and clinked it against hers. Despite Ash's unexpected presence, it did feel good to be back in my own house. "To coming home," I echoed.

I glanced at Ash. Their smile had vanished. They were watching Emma and me with something like envy. Eventually, Ash tapped their glass to ours and said, "Welcome home."

We all sipped and set our glasses down.

Ash studied Emma. "Would you like me to serve for you?"

Emma shook her head. "I can do it. Just tell me the order of the dishes." She slid her hands over the tabletop to the first bowl.

"That's sauce," I said. "Noodles are to your right, then salad, then bread."

Nodding, Emma shifted her hands to the second bowl and scooped a heap of noodles onto her plate. "So, what did you commission from Alex?"

I cringed, but Emma was only doing as I'd asked—being her usual friendly, inquisitive self. If she actually believed Ash was a client who'd commissioned a piece through James's art gallery, all the better.

"A collection of small sculptures representing a person's struggle for freedom." Ash glanced at me, then turned their attention to filling their plate. "I do hope the work is almost complete."

I grabbed a slice of bread and offered the basket to Ash. "Unfortunately, I've hit a bit of a snag."

Ash frowned. "That *is* unfortunate." They lifted a slice of bread from the basket, studying the buttered surface. "I know James was looking forward to seeing the completed piece."

A knot lodged in my throat.

"Alex has a tendency to take on too many projects at once," Emma said as she poured a spoonful of sauce over her noodles, hitting her target almost dead center. "I'm sure she'll get to yours soon."

"I certainly hope so. They were supposed to be a gift, and I'm afraid we're running out of time." Ash chomped down on a piece of garlic bread and smiled appreciatively. Where had those ancient stories come up with the idea that garlic was a deterrent to vampires?

"We can discuss business after dinner," I said. "For now, let's just enjoy our meal."

A few blessed moments of quiet descended as we all dug in, then Emma, apparently uncomfortable with the silence, asked, "Where are you from, Ash? You have an interesting accent."

Ash finished chewing and dabbed a napkin against their lips before saying, "I was born in Romania, but I've moved around a lot since then. I haven't been back in . . . a very long time."

I cast a surreptitious glance at Ash, but they caught me looking. Their smile grew.

I focused on my food.

I'd read *Dracula* in high school, and I was pretty sure it was set somewhere in Romania. Had Ash named that place as a joke? Or had the old stories really been on to something? I'd come to learn that most human myths were based on some real-world fae counterpart. Maybe Ash had been the source of the local legends Bram Stoker based his book on.

"Do you miss it?" Emma asked.

"I do."

"Then why don't you go home?"

Ash's fork stilled against their plate. They frowned. Their dark gaze grew distant, and they said softly, "Perhaps, someday, I will."

"I was born in Hawaii," Emma said. "My family moved to the States when I was three, but I can still remember the sound of the waves outside my window." She shrugged. "Of course, I could just be imagining that memory—it's not like I haven't heard waves since then—but believing it's real makes me happy."

"Home holds a special place in a person's heart," Ash said. "Even if it exists only in one's imagination."

Emma grinned.

"How about you, Alex?" Ash asked. "Where do you call home?"

I twisted noodles around my fork, dragging them through tomato sauce. "I moved around a lot."

"That's not an answer," Ash pointed out.

I shrugged, thinking of all the rooms I'd slept in as a child and as an adult. They'd been places, some more comfortable than others. They hadn't been homes. Then I looked across the table at Emma. I thought of Maggie and David, Kai and James. "Here, I guess. I consider this my home."

Ash nodded. "You're lucky to have found a place where you belong." They swirled the wine in their glass and took a sip. "I do hope you never lose it."

The thinly veiled threat soured my appetite. I set my fork down. Ash was playing nice so far, but what would they do once I explained that daywalking amulets were impossible? That the promise I'd made was nothing but hot air and pipe dreams?

Emma peppered Ash with questions while she ate. Everything from Ash's favorite music—Russian Folk—to the weirdest job they'd ever held—working a crabbing boat in Alaska. I doubted any of the answers Ash gave were true. Then again, they didn't have any reason to lie about such trivial things, so who knew? I spent the intervening time pushing noodles and salad around my plate and dreading the end of dinner.

When Emma finally pushed away from the table with a satisfied sigh, I stopped pretending to eat. "That was great," she said, patting her stomach, "but I'm ready to hit the hay. Getting up at four every morning to help in the bakery these past few months has been killing me. I plan to sleep until noon tomorrow." She grinned and stood.

"Night, Em," I said.

Ash set down their silverware. "It was a pleasure to meet you, Emma. I hope we can chat more tomorrow."

"I'd like that," said Emma. "You have such interesting stories."

Ash remained at the table while Emma shuffled down the hall and went through her bedtime routine. I cleared the table. Once the soft music Emma played while falling asleep drifted out from behind her closed door, I caught Ash's gaze and tipped my head toward the more comfortable seats in the living room. "Shall we get down to business?"

"Your roommate is lovely," Ash said as they settled on the couch.

"Yes, she is." I took a nearby chair—close enough to whisper but not as intimate as sharing a seat.

"So . . ." Ash's voice lost the airy lilt they'd adopted as they nattered with Emma through dinner. "Tell me about this 'snag' you've hit."

I swallowed, and the sound seemed to echo. Folding my hands in my lap, I said quietly, "I can't make daywalking amulets."

Ash tapped one finger against the back of the couch where their arm was draped. Eventually they said, "Well . . . that *is* disappointing."

They leaned forward, resting their elbows against their knees. Ash's feminine features—their *human* features—seemed to flicker, offering a glimpse of the creature beneath the glamour. Eyes like pools of liquid gold bore into me. A flash of sharp teeth in a black-lipped mouth grinned wickedly.

"Are you absolutely sure?"

I glanced nervously toward the hall and Emma's closed door. She'd be in bed, not quite asleep. At vampire speeds, she'd be dead before I got my ass off my chair. "I've been trying," I said. "That's where I was these past few months. Studying. Practicing. I even convinced Bael to show me the process up close." I shook my head again, meeting Ash's gaze. "I . . . I can't do it."

Ash continued to study me, though their mask of humanity was now firmly in place. When they finally moved, the slightest shift of weight, I jumped as if I'd received an electric shock. My senses were on high alert, nerves and muscles humming with anticipation.

Their mouth quirked to one side. "Did you expect me to eviscerate your friend when you delivered the bad news?"

I frowned. "The thought crossed my mind."

They smiled fully. "Good. I'd hate for you to think me harmless enough to try to trick."

"I know you're not harmless," I said, "and this is no trick. Believe me, if I could reproduce James's amulet, I would." My voice cracked as the weight of my failure crashed against me. "I did my best. It wasn't enough."

Ash settled back, lounging. They crossed one ankle over their opposite knee. "I believe you."

I exhaled, melting into my seat.

"Unfortunately, that means James's position with the council will be extended . . . indefinitely."

I balled my fists on my lap. "Isn't there any other way I can buy his freedom?"

"As the only daywalking vampire on Earth, his value to us is priceless." Ash shrugged. "On a more positive note, you'll see each other when he joins the other delegates for the interspecies peace negotiations. I know he misses you."

I ground my teeth, trying not to imagine what kind of prison the council had James stashed in these past few months. I hated that I'd failed to free him, but my heart thrilled at the prospect of seeing him again. So long as we were both alive, there was hope. And as Ash had just pointed out, James was far too precious for the council to kill. Someday, we'd find a path to freedom.

"Speaking of which," Ash said, "I believe the negotiations are only a few days away. You're certainly taking your sweet time confirming our membership in the Paranatural Alliance."

"I wanted to be certain about the amulets first," I said.

"And now that you are?"

"I delivered your proposal to the werewolf and practitioner liaisons this afternoon. We'll have their response soon."

Ash narrowed their eyes, which were once more inky black. "And what do you expect that response will be?"

I shrugged. "I honestly believe having all the Earth paranaturals united under a common banner will be a good thing, but vampires have a seriously negative image to overcome. I can understand why the others might not want to be tied to it. Garrett seemed on board with joining forces, but Sarah needs approval from the other werewolf alphas. They'll be the deciding factor."

Ash nodded. "Then it looks as if I'll be your guest for a while longer."

"Oh, joy," I muttered. Maybe I could convince Emma to move back in with her mother in the morning.

Chapter 11

I JERKED AWAKE to the sound of my cellphone alarm blaring and violently stabbed my finger against the too-bright screen until the noise subsided. With a heavy silence ringing in my ears, I scrubbed a hand over my face and tried to get my eyes to focus. The ceiling that greeted me wasn't the white marble of Bael's keep, or even the cracked drywall of my bedroom. I was staring at white popcorn. My living room. I groaned and draped my elbow over my face to hide the view.

I was back in the Mortal Realm, in my own home, but Ash had claimed my bed. And what could I do? Kick her out? Yeah, that'd go over well.

Lowering my arm, I glanced at the back of the couch, half expecting to find the gray tabby who'd claimed that spot for the past year, but Chase's favorite cushion was empty. *I wonder how things are going at Crossroads?*

Swinging my feet off the couch, I sat up and groaned again as a twinge shot through my stiff neck. I'd gotten this couch secondhand over a decade ago. The foam was worn, the springs creaked, and the smell of dust never quite came out of the upholstery. Pushing the afghan off my lap, I shuffled to the coffee maker. Fortunately, the machine had already done its job, and the slightly bitter scent of dark roast brought me back to life.

The lack of light leaking around my closed curtains meant the sun wasn't up yet. At least, not enough to shine on my mountainside. My house was cast in shades of gray that stole depth and blunted edges, yet I left the lights off as I surveyed my surroundings and tried to shift my brain into gear.

A soft snore brought my attention to Emma's closed door. I glanced across the hall to my commandeered bedroom.

Once the sun was fully up, I could safely extricate Emma by opening all the curtains to trap Ash in my bedroom. But sunrise was still an hour off, and I'd told David I'd be in "first thing," which meant leaving in the next twenty minutes. And simply moving Emma back to the bakery wouldn't ensure her safety. It might just piss Ash off. Maybe they'd retaliate on principal, just to put me in my place. All things considered, it might be safest for Emma if we all played house until the alliance gave the vampires their response. But the more time the two of them spent together, the greater the risk Emma would do or say something to tip Ash off that she knew they weren't human.

I bit my lip, weighing the risks.

My bedroom door opened. Ash stepped into the hall. They smiled, white teeth flashing in the darkness. A human wouldn't have been able to see that smile in the predawn gloom. But neither of us were human. "It would be best if Emma remains here today."

I shivered. *Ash can't read my thoughts*, I told myself. *We're not connected anymore.* Still, I cast an exploratory look into the center of my being to ensure the link that had briefly connected me to Ash during our time in Canada—a link it had taken every ounce of my magical power to burn away—hadn't somehow grown back. That link had allowed Ash to share my thoughts and feelings. It let Ash control me. I would never allow them to get that close to me again.

"We have errands to run in town." I poured two cups of coffee and pushed one toward Ash.

"I'm sure you can manage alone." They blew steam off the top of their mug and took a sip. "Sometimes things look different in the light of day. I'd hate for you to get any foolish ideas."

I stiffened. I'd only been thinking about protecting Emma, but Ash's words reminded me that the ancient vampire would be vulnerable during the day. Emma was insurance against me trying anything. "You don't trust me."

"I haven't survived this long by trusting people."

"Emma might get suspicious if you insist the curtains stay closed all day," I pointed out.

"Your roommate is blind. Why should she care if the room is dark?"

I hadn't considered that. When Emma was in the house alone, she often left the lights off. Would it occur to her to open the windows? Would she even realize they were closed?

"Okay," I said, "but if anything, and I mean *anything*, happens to her while I'm away, I will burn you."

Ash arched dark eyebrows. "Really, Alex, you're acting like I'm your enemy."

"Well, I'm hardly going to see you as a friend when you've got a gun to my boyfriend's head."

"A gun *you* put there," they said. "Or have you conveniently forgotten that it was you who brokered the terms of that deal? And you who failed to deliver the means of his freedom?"

I ground my teeth.

"Relax." Ash smiled. "We're on the same side here. So long as everyone plays nice, I'll be out of your hair in a few days."

* * *

PROTESTERS HAD ALREADY converged in front of the Denver PTF headquarters, even though the first rays of sunlight had barely cresting the horizon. The top floor of the building shone with reflected light, in bright contrast to the shadows lurking below. Dew coated the ground, sharpening the scents of gathered bodies and trampled grass. A whiff of earthy, slightly sweet smoke let me know at least one person on the picket line was probably high. I waved my thanks to the security guards holding the path open as I hurried through.

A woman I didn't know sat behind the reception desk. I flashed her my ID as I headed for the staff hallway. David's office was empty when I peeked inside. *He's probably already with Director Harris.* No doubt the two of them would be spending every available minute of the next few days double-checking and fine-tuning the complex security plans for the summit. Guilt constricted my chest. I was supposed to have helped with those plans. Instead, I'd vanished for three months. And the news I was about to deliver would make their jobs even harder.

"Alex!"

I spun at the call.

Sarah stepped out of her office and caught up to me.

I frowned. As a PTF liaison, of course Sarah *had* an office in the building . . . but I'd never seen her actually *use* it. She generally stayed in common areas like the cafeteria or the gym . . . or avoided the building altogether.

"You're in awfully early this morning," I noted.

"I wanted to catch you when you came in."

I glanced at the elevator. "I'm heading up to talk to Director Harris."

"I'll keep this short." She continued down the hall, and I followed. She pressed the call button for the elevator. "I ran your proposal past the alphas last night."

Sweat slicked my palms. The elevator doors slid open. We both stepped inside. I pressed the button for the top floor. The doors slid closed.

"And?" I asked.

Sarah shook her head.

The elevator lurched. My stomach cramped. I wasn't sure the two were connected.

"Why?" I demanded. "Because the fae don't like them? I told you, that's part of why you need them. Did you explain how having the vampires on board would prevent the humans from coercing the alliance into obedience?"

She raised her hands as if to ward off my words. "I gave them all the arguments you gave me, Alex. And it was a close vote, but the werewolves are already fighting a negative public image thanks to that video of Sophie attacking you. If we throw vampires in the mix, we might as well start handing out torches and pitchforks. It'll be too hard for humans to see vampires as anything but monsters, and the fae are going to exacerbate that."

"But—"

The elevator chimed, and the door slid open.

"I'm sorry, Alex. I wish I had better news for you, but the vampires are on their own. We can't risk being dragged down with them when the humans decide they're too scary to let live."

"You'd rather side with the fae?" I asked angrily.

She looked away. "We'll follow the path that keeps us alive."

I stepped out of the elevator, shaking my head. "You're making a mistake."

"You're not the only one who thinks that," she said.

The steel doors slid shut between us, and I was left glaring at my own reflection.

I slammed my palm against the polished metal, letting out an inarticulate shout. Without the vampires, the rest of the alliance would get backed into a corner at the negotiations, trapped between the larger forces of the fae and humans. *They'll have to pick a side and hope whoever comes out on top treats them kindly.* Too bad neither fae nor humans were known for their kindness.

I rested my forehead against the door. My breath fogged the metal. *And the vampires will be hunted.* Like the werewolves and practitioners, the vampires weren't strong enough to stand against both the human and fae factions on their own. Once the negotiations were over, they'd be the only unaligned race. Their secret wouldn't last long at that point. The fae would make sure of that.

"If only I hadn't wasted so much time," I whispered. "We could have found a way to convince them."

"Practicing your speech in the mirror?"

I turned and found David watching me from the open doorway of the director's office. He wore his PTF security uniform—woven with iron threads to repel fae magic. Too bad iron wouldn't protect anyone from Fantasia-fueled practitioners.

David took in my expression and stepped fully into the hall, pulling the door closed. "Rough night?"

I thought of Ash, back at my house, waiting for news about the vampires' inclusion in the alliance. What would they do when I delivered the verdict? Would they take my failure out on James? Or Emma?

"Hey." David snapped his fingers an inch from my nose. "Earth to Alex. Did you even sleep last night?"

I nodded, then winced as a sharp twinge in my neck reminded me where I'd spent the night. "The alphas said no," I whispered.

He stared at me. "Well, shit."

"Yeah. Is Everly in her office?"

David nodded. "Just waiting on you." He gestured for me to precede him down the hall, which I did.

Director Harris's office occupied a full quarter of the building's uppermost floor, and a bank of floor-to-ceiling windows presented a breathtaking view of the sunrise setting the eastern horizon aflame. Everly Harris was seated behind a modern white desk. Long, black braids fell over the shoulders of her pink blouse when she looked up. She studied me with her rich, brown gaze. "Good morning, Alex." She gestured to one of the seats in front of her desk. "David says you have news to share."

Ignoring the offered seat, I hugged myself and walked to the windows as David followed me in and closed the door. Far below, the protesters were a writhing mass of shadows at the building's base. Anger bubbled inside me. Fear of people like that had caused the werewolves to vote conservatively. Fear of what those haters would do when the people they saw as monsters asked for human rights.

"We're supposed to be the example of peaceful coexistence, yet I come home to find Purity lynch mobs and government sanctioned hit lists. Why haven't you done anything to curb Governor Anderson's rampant anti-paranatural policies?" I hadn't intended to accuse Harris of negligence, but the alliance's refusal to admit vampires into their ranks coupled with Emma's stories from the bakery, Maggie's concern for her child's future, and the hate seething around the base of this very building short-circuited my brain and hijacked my mouth.

"Technically, he hasn't done anything illegal," she said.

I balled my fists. "That doesn't make what he's doing right."

Everly gave me a level, if tired, stare. "No, it doesn't. But I'm a sworn representative of the PTF, which is a global *law enforcement* organization. I can't interfere in local politics, no matter what my personal opinions may be."

"But the PTF is supposed to keep the peace between humans and paranaturals. Turning a blind eye to rampant discrimination and targeted aggression *isn't* keeping the peace."

"The PTF upholds the laws that define acceptable interactions between the species. But the Fae Accords have fallen apart, and the werewolves and practitioners were never part of that deal to begin with. That's why the upcoming talks are so important. Until there are actual laws protecting the rights of paranaturals, the only people I can protect are the ones directly under PTF jurisdiction."

And there it was. The carrot and the stick rolled into one neat little package. Serve us, and we can protect you. If not . . . "This is bullshit."

"I agree," Harris said, "but my hands are tied until a new treaty is signed. Hopefully one that includes werewolves and practitioners as well as fae. If not . . ."

We both fell silent, contemplating the all-out war that was likely to ensue if the various factions couldn't find some common ground. And Harris didn't even know about the wrench the vampires had thrown in the works. I thought of all the different races I'd seen interacting in Abonaille Malmür, far more than the handful native to Earth. How had they managed that? Then again, Hortense's lessons taught me that fae history was littered with bloody battles. Perhaps war was the only path to peace.

I swallowed and shook my head. I couldn't accept that. "Sorry. I'm just frustrated."

"Join the club," she said. "Now what did you want to discuss that you couldn't say over the phone?"

I took the empty seat next to David, who watched me with quiet concern. "What do you know about the drug Fantasia?"

Harris sighed and pinched the bridge of her nose. "I just spent two whole days discussing that very topic with my fellow directors." She sat back and crossed her arms. "Violent crimes involving Fantasia have more than doubled in the past month, and not just here. PTF directors have reported an increase in distribution worldwide, although the U.S. seems to be the epicenter."

"Do you know who's behind it? Specifically, I mean. Not just Purity."

She pursed her lips. "Purity representatives have denied any knowledge of current Fantasia production, insisting that the program was shut down after their test during the sorcerer rebellion backfired."

"Well, that's a crock," I muttered.

"You said you had information about the summit," David said. "Why are we talking about Fantasia?"

I ran a hand through my hair. "I have a source who says the increase in Fantasia is related to a planned attack against the upcoming meeting, that Purity is creating an army of magically enhanced soldiers to kill the attending delegates. As a result, some fae are considering pulling out of the peace talks."

"Which fae?" David asked. "Who's your source?"

I shook my head. "I'm not at liberty to say. But I trust their intel."

"Shit." Harris slumped in her chair and braced one hand against her forehead. "If we lose even *one* of the major realms, it could derail the whole negotiation."

"Not to mention the fallout if any of the attending delegates get hurt," David pointed out. "That would totally undermine the PTF's authority and call into question our ability to enforce a treaty even if we could get one signed."

"Purity's objective is, and always has been, to isolate and eliminate magic," I said. "Even if they have to use magic to do it. Whether Fantasia soldiers kill the delegates, the fae abandon the negotiations, or the PTF calls off the meeting, the end result will be the same. Purity wins. It would mean the current open season on any paranaturals not under direct PTF supervision will continue. And without the prospect of a treaty, the paranaturals won't take that lying down. Our only option is to neutralize the threat *before* the negotiations are scheduled to take place."

"Easier said than done." Harris folded her hands on her desk. "As you know, Fantasia is distilled from living fae. The PTF believes it was originally developed by a woman named Calliope Hayes—a Greek national who holds advanced degrees in biology, genetics, and pathology. She was the lead scientist in one of the European fae detention camps during the Faerie Wars, specializing in research and development."

"Aka, torture," I said.

Harris tipped her head, ceding the point. "Hayes was convinced fae biology held the secrets to untold medical advancements for the human race, but when the Fae Accords were signed, the camps were emptied and she was forced to abandon her research. Hayes petitioned the PTF to continue her funding, but her methods would have been a direct violation of the accords. She was shut down and only narrowly avoided being charged as a war criminal.

"We know she went back to Greece for a while. The PTF kept tabs on her research to make sure she wasn't stepping over any lines. She moved to Oxford, where she taught genomic medicine for two years. After that, she bounced between research labs here in the U.S. Her last known employer was a genetics lab in California, but they say she was laid off three years ago due to 'questionable practices.' No one has seen her since, but Fantasia is in line with the research and development she was doing during the war. Our best guess is that she found a Purity backer to fund her research and went off the grid to continue her project in secret."

I frowned. "So how do we find her?"

"That's where we've hit a wall," Harris said. "We know captured fae are being sold to labs through the black market, and based on distribution patterns, we're fairly certain Fantasia is primarily coming out of the Midwest. Specifically, the Chicago region. Unfortunately, we haven't had any luck infiltrating, or even locating, any black markets in that area. By the time we catch a whisper of a deal going down, the poachers and buyers are already in the wind."

"Then send more people," I said. "Overrun the streets of Chicago if you have to. Fantasia just became the number one threat to peace on this planet. You need to throw every agent you have at finding Calliope Hayes, shutting down her operation, and neutralizing the Fantasia-juiced magic-users she's created."

Harris shook her head. "While I applaud your enthusiasm, this isn't something we can just throw more people at. These markets are run by highly paranoid, well-funded, morally corrupt individuals. More agents on the streets would just drive any potential leads further underground."

"Infiltrating the criminal underworld takes connections," David said. "Connections we don't currently have, and don't have time to cultivate."

Highly paranoid . . . morally corrupt . . . well connected . . . The beginnings of an idea percolated through my thoughts.

"I might be able to find the Chicago black market," I said.

David snorted. "No offense, Alex, but these guys are professional-level ghosts. How do you expect to find them when the PTF, DEA, FBI, and who knows how many local cops can't?"

I lifted my chin. "With help. No one knows hiding from humans better than the paranaturals whose lives have historically depended on it."

Harris shook her head. "Chicago is outside my jurisdiction, and way beyond the borders that limit the activity of your Paranatural Alliance."

"The people I have in mind aren't members of the alliance." *Yet,* I added silently. *But just maybe, if I can make them look like heroes . . .*

A look of realization spread across David's face. "You can't mean—"

"You have a better idea?" I cut him off.

"You really think they'll help save a bunch of kidnapped fae?" he countered.

"If it gets them what they want."

"Hey," shouted Harris. "Someone want to fill me in here?"

I glared at David, hoping he'd take the hint and keep his damn mouth shut, then I shifted my attention to the director. "I know a group of paranaturals who have, thus far, chosen not to reveal themselves to the human population. If anyone can find your elusive black market, my money's on them."

Harris frowned. "What sort of paranaturals?"

"Not werewolves or practitioners, and therefore not bound by the agreement that prevents those groups from operating outside Colorado."

"Unclassifieds," she guessed. "Like your friend James."

I nodded.

Harris glanced at David. "You know who she's talking about?"

"A bit," he said.

"You don't think they'll help?"

David cut his gaze to me. "Like Alex said, they might help if they get something out of it."

Harris leaned back and exhaled. "What do they want?"

"Representation," I said. "They'd like to join the Paranatural Alliance."

"Alliance membership isn't up to the PTF."

"That doesn't mean you can't influence the decision," I countered. "Right now, the werewolves and paranaturals are reluctant to include more members for fear of fanning Purist hate against the alliance as a whole. But if the PTF were to endorse this new species, the rest of the humans would be more likely to accept them. That, in turn, would significantly reduce the alliance's reservations about teaming up with them."

Harris drummed her fingers against the desk. "If the werewolves are worried about these newcomers hurting *their* reputation, I assume we're not talking about fluffy bunnies who hand out kisses and lollipops."

I grimaced at that mental image. "Decidedly not."

"But *you* trust them?"

I hesitated. I trusted James . . . but vampires in general? Not so much. Still, they weren't any more conniving than the fae. They *could* be reasoned with. "I think the world needs them to maintain any semblance of balance."

Harris nodded. "Okay. If your unclassified paranaturals prove themselves helpful, and they show that they're willing to work with the PTF, I'll try to convince the board to endorse, or at least not actively oppose, their membership in the alliance."

"Deal," I said.

"Just to be clear, no species included in the Paranatural Alliance can participate in any mission or military conflict outside of Colorado without voiding their deal with the PTF. That means no practitioner or werewolf backup if things go south."

"I understand."

"And until a new treaty is signed, *any* paranatural—be they fae, practitioner, or other—without a specific PTF contract will have no legal protection. Whoever you send to Chicago will be entirely on their own."

"These guys are used to looking after themselves."

"Okay. Once your contacts pinpoint the black market in Chicago, report back to me. If the lead proves actionable, I'll send the full force of the PTF to shut down Hayes and her Fantasia operation."

"Great." *Now all I have to do is get Ash on board.*

* * *

THE CURTAINS WERE closed when I parked in front of my house. No surprise there. Muffled music drifted across the mountainside—something with a fast tempo and angry-sounding lyrics. Emma's music. The morning dew had dried, and the temperature was creeping up, even at this altitude. Taking a deep breath, I swung open the front door.

Ash and Emma sat facing each other on the couch. Neither looked up when I entered. The lights were on, though they weren't needed. Even with the curtains drawn, enough sunlight leaked around the edges to cast the room in an ambient glow. Ash had likely turned the lamps on out of habit—a side effect of spending centuries pretending to be human, in hiding from humans, fae, and even their own kind. A sharp, chemical smell filled the air. I closed the door and circled the couch. Ash brushed a layer of neon pink nail polish over Emma's thumbnail. Ash's nails were glossy black.

"Care to join us?" Ash asked, gaze fixed on Emma's hand as they applied a second coat. "Emma has an impressive variety of colors. I'm sure we could find something to suit your complexion."

"Ash noticed my collection on the shelf and asked if I wanted her to paint my nails," Emma said. "It's nice to get to use them before they dry out."

Irritation stirred inside me. Not at Ash, but at myself. Emma loved color. Before going blind, she'd dressed in crazy colors, dyed her hair constantly, and painted patterns on her nails. After her accident, she'd become rather . . . drab. The change had worried me, but I thought it was inevitable as Emma adapted to her new normal. It hadn't occurred to me to offer to paint her nails or dye her hair—things I never did myself—so that she didn't have to give up those colors.

I really am a shitty friend.

"Sure," I said. "What color do you think I should do?"

"Red," Emma and Ash said in unison. They both smiled, as if sharing some private joke.

Suppressing the urge to ask if they'd rehearsed that, I went to Emma's bedroom and found the shelf with her nail polish collection. *What had Ash been doing in here?*

I snatched a bottle of deep maroon and returned to the living room, dropping into a chair rather than trying to crowd onto the couch.

"So, what have you two been up to this morning?" I asked as I drew out the paintbrush. The chemical smell grew stronger, irritating my throat and making my eyes water.

"I haven't been awake long," Emma confessed. "You have no idea how glorious it is to sleep in after three months of getting up before the sun every morning. Not that I mind mornings in general—I've always been an early riser—but to start every day with my taskmaster of a mother assigning me some horrible, monotonous task like mixing the glaze for seven hundred cinnamon rolls was just . . . ugh!"

I smiled. I knew exactly how Emma felt. Granted the past three months had only been one for me, but my daily trainings with Bael had started at dawn and usually consisted of doing a single task a thousand times in a row.

"Anyway, Ash made eggs and sausages for breakfast. Then we mostly just sat around and talked."

I glanced at Ash. "Talked about what, exactly?"

The corner of Ash's mouth quirked up. "Oh, you know. This and that."

Emma looked in my direction, but her eyes remained unfocused. "Did you know Ash once dated the Prince of Luxembourg?"

"I didn't," I said.

"She's traveled all over the world."

"That part I *did* know."

"And how about you?" Ash asked. "Were your morning activities equally as educational?"

I hesitated, considering how to discuss my plans with Ash while Emma was around. Ash had set up a believable pretense of us having an artist-patron relationship during last night's dinner, so perhaps I could run with that? While I considered, a too-large glob of polish dripped onto my nail. Glossy red liquid flowed over my cuticle. "Educational is one word for it." I attempted to transfer the excess pigment to another nail, smearing some on the side of my finger in the process. It was sloppy work. "I think I've figured out how to get your project unstuck."

Emma frowned. "I thought you were meeting with David and Director Harris this morning?"

"I was," I said, "but it's a long drive. Plenty of time to think."

"I'm glad to hear that," Ash said, calmly drawing the brush over Emma's middle fingernail with a steady hand. "What brilliant idea have you come up with to 'unstick' my project?"

I swallowed, glancing once more at Emma. "Well, you know how I submitted a proposal to that new gallery to see if they'd be interested in exhibiting the work you commissioned?"

Emma frowned. "You're going to show in a new gallery? What about James's Souled Art in Boulder? Won't he be upset?"

"This new gallery is international," I said. "Getting included would mean a lot for my future. James's, too. He's totally on board. Anyway, the jury that decides which works to include is very aware of public opinion. They're worried these new designs might be a little too avant-garde for their audience."

Ash frowned. "They've rejected the work?"

"For the moment."

Ash's expression darkened.

I raised a hand to forestall them. "But like I said, I have an idea to get the project unstuck. Since the issue is public opinion, we should do a highly visible pop-up installation that garners a lot of positive attention. If we can attract the right kind of audience, then the gallery is sure to want us in their collection."

"Kind of like giving away free samples to get people buzzing about your product," Emma said.

"Exactly." I put the last shaky stroke on my right pinky, closed the bottle, and inspected my work. My brushstrokes weren't nearly as precise as Ash's. Then again, I hadn't had centuries to perfect my technique.

"Mom does that at the bakery," Emma continued. "She's always sending out gift boxes to local businesses and stuff. She's landed quite a few catering contracts that way. Once, a lady who sampled one of our mille-feuilles at work ended up hiring Mom to do her whole wedding."

"So we show the gallery there's a demand for what we offer, then renegotiate our participation." Ash blew lightly on Emma's nails. "You're all done, dear."

Emma beamed, holding her hands up, fingers splayed. "What do you think, Alex?"

"I think that color is totally you, Em. They look great."

Ash twisted the cap back on the bottle of pink polish and turned her attention fully on me. "Not a bad plan. But we don't have much time before the exhibit opens. What sort of pop-up can we arrange on such short notice?"

"Actually," I said. "I have an idea about that, too." I turned to Emma, who flapped her hands like a lazy bird to help her nails dry. "This part's going to get kinda technical and boring, Em. How about you put on an audiobook or something while Ash and I discuss the details?"

Please, please, please don't argue!

Emma hesitated for two thunderous beats of my heart, then she nodded. "Sure. I'll be in my room if you need me."

I exhaled. *Thank the stars.*

Ash watched me while Emma shuffled slowly to her room and closed the door.

I opened my mouth, but Ash held up one finger. A moment later they said, "Emma is now listening to her story. Tell me your plan."

Pitching my voice low I asked, "What do you know about the drug Fantasia?"

"Derived from living fae, developed by Purity, and semi-successfully weaponized during the recent sorcerer rebellion. There have been significantly more overdose cases in the past few months, which implies the number of overall users has also increased." Ash laced their fingers. "Why?"

I opened my mouth to tell Ash about the threat to the summit, but I hesitated. There was no love lost between fae and vampires, and Ash in particular. If they knew there was a chance to spoil the relationship between humans and fae, would they be able to set their prejudices aside and see the bigger picture? Or would they side with the Purists to take the fae down a notch? Maybe, after the alliance's rejection, they'd rather watch it all burn than keep begging for scraps.

Changing tactics I said, "The PTF has been trying to track down and eliminate the source of the drug, but they've hit a dead end. They think the scientist behind it is trafficking fae through a black market in Chicago, but they're not having any luck finding the market, or the people running it."

"And you think I can get that information?"

"Vampires have their fingers on the pulse of every major city in the world," I said. "I'm sure there's a nest in Chicago, and no master vampire would fail to keep tabs on the economics of their region."

Ash made a noncommittal gesture. "Say you're right. How would identifying the location of this market, should it exist, secure our place in the alliance?"

"The alphas who voted against accepting you did so because they fear pushback from the humans. Director Harris has promised to endorse your inclusion in the alliance if you assist the PTF in this matter. That'll carry a lot of weight in human society."

Ash stiffened. "You told a PTF director about us?"

I shook my head. "*Unclassified.* That's what James's official designation is in the paranatural registry. I just reminded her that he wasn't alone."

They nodded. "Assuming we locate this black market where fae are being sold, then what?"

"We tell Harris, and she sends in the troops."

Ash pursed their lips. "In your earlier analogy, you said we had to do something 'highly visible.' Something that would 'garner lots of positive attention.'"

I nodded.

"And you think calling in an anonymous tip fits that description?"

I shrugged. "Maybe not the most dramatic entrance ever, but the goal is to get the vampires admitted to the alliance and prove to the humans that you can work alongside them for the greater good of the Mortal Realm."

"I see." Ash stood up. "Let me make a call."

When Ash spoke into the phone, their voice changed, not only growing deeper but taking on a distinctly European accent. "*Privet, syn moy.*"

I frowned. I recognized that voice, though I didn't know the language Ash was speaking. Russian, maybe? The last time I'd heard that particular tone, it had come from the mouth of Esteban, Ash's puppet on the vampire council. Were they pretending to be him? Then again, he was basically just a magical extension of Ash, so why shouldn't Ash speak with Esteban's voice? They controlled the rest of him.

Ash laughed at something I assumed the other person had said—a deep belly laugh that didn't match their slender form. Then they launched into what I hoped was a request for information.

I drummed my fingers against my armrest and tried to follow the conversation, but I could only catch a few English words that slipped into the foreign flow. Ash mentioned Chicago and the PTF. Beyond that, I was lost.

Ash paced while they spoke, the green fabric of their skirt swishing around their legs with each pivot. They paused at the end of a circuit and said, "*Do svidaniya.*"

Definitely Russian.

Tucking the phone away, Ash turned and met my gaze.

I sat up straighter, anxious for a translation. "Well?"

"My contact in Chicago is aware of the black market there." Ash spoke once more in what I considered their normal voice. "The next one is happening tomorrow night. He's willing to provide us with an introduction."

"Introduction?" I frowned. "We just need the location."

Ash made a *tsk-tsk* sound. "The market moves. Different days, different locations, different hosts. In order to find it, you need an invitation that comes in the form of a telephone number. Call that number, and you'll be given an address. You show up at the address to get vetted for attendance. If"—they raised a finger—"and only if you pass that interview, you're then taken to the market's secure location. There's no way to get the information ahead of time."

I exhaled, deflating into my seat. "So, we're screwed."

"Not at all." Ash spread their hands as they returned to their seat on the couch. "My contact has the phone number, and as I said, he's willing to make an introduction. We'll fly some vampires in from another region to pose as poachers looking to sell a captured fae. They'll be taken to the black market, where they can learn the location of your scientist's lab from whoever purchases the fae. Then we bring down the scientist and her entire distribution network."

"Whoa, whoa, *whoa*. The goal is to pass the market's location on to the PTF, not go all gangbusters on the lab yourself."

"We're establishing the position of vampires in society moving forward, no? We will show the PTF that we can be useful allies, but we will not be subservient." Ash smiled, a predatory expression. "Besides, if the goal is to create a positive image, better to make the front page than settle for a footnote that the PTF might quietly sweep under a rug at their convenience. When the general populace sees that vampires have solved this problem that stumped both the PTF and the fae, that will make quite the impression, don't you think?"

I opened my mouth, closed it, and nodded. Succeeding where the fae and PTF had failed *would* make quite an impression. And ending the Fantasia drug trade would create exactly the kind of positive social image the vampires needed to counterbalance their other less-wholesome traits.

"Now all we need is a fae to sell," Ash said matter-of-factly. "I trust you can provide one?"

I startled. "Wait, what?"

"A fae," Ash repeated, speaking slowly, as if I might be too stupid to understand. "We need one to sell at the market."

I shook my head. "I'm not selling a fae to a Purity drug lab!"

Ash sighed and, still speaking as if to a particularly slow child, said, "Selling a fae is the only way to *find* the lab, and while my people could probably capture one, that would take time. Better to use your connections. I assume you can convince one of your fae acquaintances to play the part of bait."

"Who in their right mind would agree to be locked in a cage and sold to Purists?"

"Someone who wants to end the illegal trafficking, torture, and murder of their species?" Ash shrugged. "Or maybe just someone who owes you a favor. Fae debts can be a bitch."

That's for sure. But I'd called in all my favors. If I wanted a fae to participate in this crazy scheme, I'd have to find someone willing to risk their life for a price I was willing to pay. Since Morgan had dumped this problem in my lap in the first place, it seemed fair to ask her to provide the bait, but she'd made it clear that she wouldn't be leaving the reservation until this mess was sorted. Besides, endangering the daughter of the Shadow Lord probably wasn't the best political move.

Kai would volunteer, but that would mean taking him away from Rhys's training, plus another trip to Enchantment that would eat precious time and might lead to awkward questions if Bael caught wind of my abrupt return. Hortense was already in town, which was convenient, but I couldn't see her agreeing to put her life in the hands of vampires, even if I vouched for them.

That left Chase. He was reckless enough that he might agree to risk his life, and unlike Hortense, he wasn't entirely averse to interacting with vampires. He was also mercurial enough that he might say no just to piss me off, depending on his mood, but he was still my best bet.

"I have someone I can ask," I said.

"Good. I'll begin making the necessary arrangements. How soon can your fae—"

"I'm going, too," I blurted.

Ash hesitated then said, "Excuse me?"

"I'm not going to just hand one of my friends over to a group of vampires I've never met and trust that they'll keep him safe. I'm going with him."

Ash frowned. "Your fae friend will be rescued when we bring down the lab. No harm will come to him."

"What if something goes wrong and your people have to choose between completing the mission and saving the life of one fae? Do you still think he'd come home intact?"

"You'd save your friend even if it meant jeopardizing the mission?"

I frowned. "I'm not sure, but I want someone on site who will keep my friend's interests in mind if a decision like that needs to be made."

Ash crossed their arms. "How are humans supposed to learn to trust vampires if even *you* can't manage it?"

"This isn't because you're vampires," I said. "Or, at least, not *only* because you're vampires. I wouldn't trust a bunch of humans I didn't know either, and I doubt my friend will agree to put his life in the hands of people who'd happily count him as an acceptable loss if it meant a quicker path to get what they wanted."

Ash held my gaze for a long moment, then sighed. "Fine. Go collect your friend. I'll make our travel arrangements. We leave tonight."

"We?"

They gave me a condescending look as they pulled out their phone. "You are currently the only point of contact between the vampire council and the

Paranatural Alliance. You insist on going to Chicago to ensure your friend comes back unharmed. I'm going to ensure that you do as well."

I snorted. "You don't trust the Chicago vampires, either."

Ash rolled their eyes. "I don't trust *anyone*."

Chapter 12

MY CHEST CONSTRICTED as I surveyed the toppled bricks and twisted beams that had once housed the fae bar Crossroads. The roof was gone. A few sections of ruined wall remained around the perimeter, topping out at four feet or less and covered with anti-fae graffiti and Purity stickers. My mind tried to reconcile the scene before me with the space as I'd last seen it—the night of the PTF raid—decked to the nines for Jynx and Ava's wedding, and full of fae seeking refuge from Anderson's patrols. I'd gone to Crossroads seeking help and had accidentally brought hell down on all our heads.

I hugged myself, suddenly cold despite the blazing summer sun overhead.

Here I was, looking for help again. Only there was no one here. Chase had told me he was helping Targe rebuild the bar, but that was over three months ago. There was no sign of reconstruction in the wreckage before me. Just a pervasive sense of hopelessness and fear that made my stomach turn.

"They must have moved," I mumbled. I'd assumed that, since Targe legally owned this land, he would rebuild in the same location. But everyone now knew this building had housed a fae bar, and judging by the colorful decorations on the crumbling walls, a lot of people were glad to see it gone. Now that all the general visas had been revoked, Targe had no legal protection. He might still, technically, own this parcel of land, but that wouldn't protect him from a Purist mob knocking down his door and dragging him, or his halfer niece Ava, to their deaths. With all the poachers cashing in on fae hides lately, I was relieved they'd chosen somewhere less conspicuous to set up shop.

Bracing my hands on my hips, I squinted up at the cobalt sky. "Maybe Hortense will have some idea how to find them."

Something bumped against my ankle and slid away.

I looked down. A gray tabby trotted toward the rubble, hopped onto a chunk of cracked concrete, and looked back at me with luminous green eyes.

"Chase!" I started forward, and the cat darted into the cored-out remains of Crossroads.

I hesitated at what had once been a doorway, frowning. The tabby was nowhere to be seen. Maybe the cat had only *looked* like Chase. Maybe my mind had provided what it thought I wanted to see. I scratched an itch on my arm and surveyed the destruction. Again, I felt that wash of hopelessness and fear that made me want to turn away.

I took a step back . . . then froze. I looked down at where I'd been scratching. Despite the heat of the day, I wore a light jacket over my T-shirt to hide the tattoo on my right arm—a tattoo that had a tendency to itch when I was being targeted by magic.

Gritting my teeth, I forced myself to step through the ruined doorway.

The world vanished. My entire body felt as if it were being simultaneously turned inside out and ripped into teeny tiny pieces. I snapped back together before I had time to scream. My boots rested on a smooth, stone floor. My stomach heaved with the lingering effects of the unexpected portal travel, and I reached out to steady myself against the doorframe—a completely intact, intricately carved, oak doorframe. I inhaled deeply, trying to keep my breakfast down.

"I was wondering when you'd show up."

My gaze snapped up. My head swam, and I took another deep breath—in through the nose, out through the mouth.

Chase leaned against a black-painted wall, arms crossed over his bare chest. His long, silver hair cascaded around his shoulders and trailed all the way to his washboard abs. I jerked my eyes back to his face before they could travel any further down his naked body.

The same luminous green eyes that had gazed at me from the gray tabby I'd followed crinkled with a smile as Chase showed off his perfect incisors.

I crossed the distance between us in two steps and wrapped my arms around his neck, pulling him into a hug. "It's good to see you, Chase."

He moved to return the hug, but I stepped back before he could get a good enough grip to trap me and smacked him on the arm. "Why didn't you stick around in the alley? You were there and gone so fast, I'd almost convinced myself I dreamed you."

He rubbed his arm, scowling. "You're lucky I noticed you out there at all. We're not exactly advertising our whereabouts these days."

I looked around the wide corridor with its black walls and ceiling that seemed to absorb the light provided by a single bulb overhead. The air was cool and slightly damp, especially compared to the dry heat I'd just left. A single door, also black, blocked the far end, and the carved wooden doorway I'd apparently stepped through led to a solid stone wall. "About that . . . where exactly are we?"

Chase's Cheshire Cat grin returned, and he pushed open the black door, beckoning me to follow. "May I present the new, and improved, Crossroads." He swept his arms wide to encompass the enormous space.

I walked down a set of long, shallow steps to a polished dance floor and turned a slow circle. The room was almost a perfect recreation of the fae establishment I remembered, before it had been turned to rubble. A full-service bar sat at the center, wrapped in a polished black counter and padded stools, complete with a sidhe and a gnome deep in their drinks. Semi-private booths with vinyl, U-shaped benches lined half the room. The back wall held a raised stage framed by six-foot speakers and theatre lights. I inhaled and caught a heady mix of cinnamon, honey, and alcohol.

"Alex!" A young woman with short white hair and an equally short black skirt erupted from the office door to my left, bounded across the room, and launched herself fully into the air from three feet away.

Jynx slammed into me, wrapping both her arms and legs around me on impact.

I stumbled, limbs pinned. Only Chase's body check from the opposite side prevented his sister's momentum from knocking me over. I gasped, sandwiched between the two shifter siblings.

"Welcome home." Jynx dropped to her feet with all the grace of the snow leopard that was her other form.

I stumbled as my center of balance shifted once more. "Uh, good to be here." I glanced around the bar again. "Wherever 'here' is."

"Underground," Jynx said. "Beneath what's left of the old bar. Targe set up a permanent portal above that brings customers down." She turned and waved at the seven-foot, barrel-chested leprechaun behind the bar and called, "Targe, look who's here."

The establishment's owner looked up from pouring a drink and met my gaze. He nodded once, lips pressed tight, then handed the frothy mug to the gnome at the bar.

Probably wondering what kind of trouble I've brought to his door this time, I thought guiltily.

"I'm sure he's happy to see you," Jynx said, frowning at the big bartender. "He's just tired. It's been a beast to get this place up and running again without anybody noticing. Especially with all the Purity patrols lately."

"About that... If the portal I came through is permanent, aren't you worried a patrol or one of the vandals spraying Purity propaganda on the ruins of the old bar might stumble in here and find you?"

"Let them," Chase said with a predatory grin.

Jynx rolled her eyes. "They can't. Not only did we place a strong aversion spell around the property to dissuade uninvited guests, but the portal is keyed so only beings possessing magic can pass through. A regular human stubborn enough to cross the threshold would find themselves standing in nothing more than the pile of broken bricks and cracked concrete they saw from the other side."

I frowned, thinking of how portals to fae realms were targeted to exclude vampires. Of course, those did more than ignore. If a vampire were foolish enough to walk through one, the magic would rip them to pieces, like walking through a person-sized paper shredder. "Isn't keying a portal really hard? I thought it took a top-level caster."

"And we've got two," Jynx said. "Speaking of which, come on. Ava's gonna flip when she sees you." She grabbed my sleeve and dragged me toward the office out of which she'd emerged.

The room was small compared to the vast chamber we left, but still large enough to house a desk, four chairs, a couch, a coffee table, a filing cabinet, and a glass display case filled with all sorts of odd little knickknacks.

A petite woman sat behind the desk, hands pressed to either side of her head as she studied the pages of an open ledger. A deep furrow wrinkled her brow, and she muttered to herself, seemingly oblivious to our arrival.

Jynx circled the desk and wrapped her arms around her wife, kissing the mess of orange hair piled on top of her head. "Look who's here."

Ava glanced up, did a double take, and sat back from whatever she'd been studying. "Alex! You're back." Her frown turned into a smile, but there was still a lot of tension in her expression.

I sank into one of the chairs facing the desk. "Hey, Ava. Everything okay? You look stressed."

"She's overworked," Jynx said, squeezing Ava's shoulders.

"We've reopened the bar, but patronage has been abysmal. Hopefully that will change once the peace summit takes place, assuming that brings a modicum of stability to this realm." Ava closed the ledger. "Anyway, I'm sure you didn't come here to talk about our financial situation."

"And knowing you, I doubt this is a strictly social visit." Chase stretched out on the office couch, arms tucked behind his head. "What do you want?"

"For starters, I'd like for you to put some pants on," I said, staring pointedly at the ceiling.

He chuckled, but out of the corner of my eye I saw him grab a piece of frayed green fabric off the armrest and drape it over his lap. "Happy?"

I glanced at the well-placed hoodie and nodded.

"Are you on another quest?" Jynx asked, her words tumbling over themselves. "It's got something to do with the peace talks, doesn't it? You're always in the thick of things. Do you need us to do some undercover work again?" She bounced on her toes. "Oooh, are we going to spy on the delegates for the summit? Do you want us to dig up some dirt on the humans to make the negotiations easier? Or is this about the fae?" She crossed her arms. "We can't spy on the Shifter Lord, obviously, but the others are fair game. They'll be tricky to get close to, though. Everyone coming will be uber powerful, so they'll probably see right through our glamours."

She braced her palms on the desk and leaned forward, pinning me with her wide, blue gaze. "So, what's the mission?"

"Maybe she'd tell you," Chase said, "if you ever gave her a chance to speak."

Jynx stuck her tongue out at her brother, but she settled back on her heels and crossed her arms again.

I laughed. I'd missed the shifter siblings. Then I remembered why I was there and the danger I was about to put Chase in.

"It's great to see you guys," I said. "All of you. But you're right." I looked at Chase. "I'm not here just to say hello."

He sighed. "What's up?"

I considered telling them the whole story—they were my friends, after all—but knowing this plan would benefit the vampires and potentially allow them to stand on equal footing with the fae—at least from a human perspective—would make most fae balk. Even these ones. And while Chase didn't work directly for the Shifter Lord these days, he might feel obligated to report what the vampires were trying to do. I didn't want any of the fae moving to block this opportunity. Best to keep the motivations closer to home, at least for the time being.

"I assume you're aware of the fae that have gone missing and their correlation to the drug Fantasia?"

That sobered everyone up. Even Jynx stilled.

"We know," Ava said in a small voice. "It's why we're being so careful to stay out of sight, and why our customers are so sparse. Without any kind of legal protection, even those of us who've lived our whole lives here in the Mortal Realm and tried to abide by the PTF's regulations are fair game. In fact, the paranatural registry has turned into a hit list. Those of us who followed the rules were the first to be targeted."

"Which is why I always thought registering was a terrible idea," Chase said.

"Well, the PTF think they've tracked down the source of the drug," I said. "A scientist working out of Chicago, but they can't get close to her."

"You need us to find her," Jynx said, looking entirely too eager.

I shook my head. "We plan to reach her through a black market sale. The problem is, the only items these people are interested in purchasing are captured fae that they can use to fuel their drug production."

"You need bait," Chase said flatly. "Enough to attract the scientist's attention."

I nodded.

"Why not ask your knight to do it?" Chase asked. "He'd happily throw himself on a sword for you."

I shifted in my seat. "Kai is still in Enchantment."

Chase frowned and sat up. "Don't tell me the knight's afraid?"

I shook my head. "He has his reasons." I wasn't sure if Kai taking on an apprentice was a secret, but fae tended not to share personal information with people from different realms, even with those they considered friends, and they *definitely* didn't like to be gossiped about. "He'll be back when he's ready. In the meantime, I need someone *now*."

"And you figured, 'Hey, Chase won't mind being thrown to the wolves. I'll just bat my lashes and he'll jump through my hoop'?"

I glared at him. "I thought *maybe* you'd want to prevent any more fae from getting kidnapped and harvested for parts by destroying the Fantasia pipeline." I crossed my arms. "I guess I was wrong."

Jynx's hand shot into the air. "I'll do it."

"No." Chase and I said in unison.

Jynx deflated.

Ava patted her hand in sympathy, though she looked relieved. Jynx was kind and brave. She was also young by fae standards—basically a headstrong teenager who'd run away from home to be with the lover her parents forbade her from seeing.

"What's in it for me?" Chase asked.

"Other than being a hero to your people?" I frowned. "What do you want?"

Chase's gaze slid to his sister and her wife, then drifted toward the office door. "I want a PTF special commission."

I raised my eyebrows, surprised. Chase had steadfastly refused to register with the PTF, preferring his chances of staying one step ahead if they ever caught on to what he was. Taking a commission would basically make him a contracted employee. Maybe even he was tired of hiding.

"I might be able to arrange that with Director Harris, but you'll have to be fully registered with the PTF to get a commission. Are you sure you want to do that?"

"The commission isn't for me." He leaned forward, bracing his elbows on his knees and lacing his fingers. "I want the PTF to sanction Crossroads as a safe haven for anyone who seeks refuge here, and I want guaranteed protection for Targe and his entire family, so they can operate said safe haven in peace."

My mouth fell open. "You want the PTF to authorize the operation of a fae bar?"

He met and held my gaze. "Targe bought this land. He paid his taxes. He registered with the PTF and secured a legal resident's visa. He put his entire life into this place. Then the PTF took it all away with the flip of a switch. And he's not the only one. Assuming the humans and local paras are serious about signing a new peace treaty, they're going to need places like this where fae can relax and blow off steam." He spread his hands. "Consider it an investment in the future."

"If this place gets publicized as a fae hangout, it'll become a target for Purity nut jobs with sniper rifles and pipe bombs."

"We can handle the zealots so long as we don't also have to watch our backs with the PTF," Ava said. "And we can establish new protocols to protect the identities of our clientele."

I pinched the bridge of my nose. "Okay, so you want a commission for Targe and his family to run Crossroads."

"In exchange, I'll let you shove me in a cage and sell my ass to a crazy scientist who juices fae for drugs," Chase said.

"Temporarily," Jynx specified, raising one manicured finger. "I assume you have a plan for getting him out unharmed."

"Of course," I said. "Once we verify the location of the scientist's lab, I'll call in the cavalry." *Never mind that the cavalry in this case will be a nest of vampires.* "How soon can you be ready?"

Chase shrugged. "Whenever you are."

"Great." I stood and nodded to the phone on Ava's desk. "Give me the number. I'll call you once I secure Targe's contract."

Ava jotted the phone number on a slip of paper and handed it to me.

I opened the office door and nearly ran face-first into Hortense, who raised one eyebrow and glowered in her usual disapproving fashion.

"Targe said you were here." She stepped to the side, allowing me to pass.

I glanced over my shoulder, registering Jynx's mischievous smile and Ava's look of tired concern, then I pulled the door closed behind me.

"What are you doing at Crossroads?" I asked.

Hortense gestured to a row of narrow balconies overhead. "The services here have expanded to include rentable rooms for fae in need of sanctuary."

I grimaced. It seemed Targe's commission would need to include both bar and boarding house. "Wait a minute, you have a PTF commission. Why do you need sanctuary?"

"Have you met Margaret's new child? More importantly, have you *heard* it?" She shook her head. "I couldn't reside in that home another night and hope to retain my sanity."

I chuckled. "Charlie mentioned you ran away."

She scowled. "It was a strategic retreat." Casting a surreptitious look at the bar's other patrons, she pitched her voice low and asked, "How fared your training with Lord Bael?"

My laughter died. "Not as well as I would have liked."

"I'm sorry to hear that."

I sighed. "It seems I was never strong enough to do what I'd hoped, and Bael knew that from the very beginning."

Hortense pursed her lips but didn't respond. She didn't look surprised.

"Did you know I would fail?"

"I am not familiar with imbuing. I could not have predicted your success or failure."

"But Bael could."

She shrugged.

I ran a hand through my hair. "Anyway, I have other concerns now that I'm back. I'll see you later." I turned toward the exit. Then, recalling Kai's advice about seeking knowledge, I turned back. "Hey, Hortense, what can you tell me about Bael's throne?"

"His throne is formed of pure iron. Only an imbuer may sit upon it without being terribly burned. It is both the literal and figurative seat of power that symbolizes lordship over the Realm of Enchantment."

"Is it *alive*?"

Hortense frowned. "Why do you ask?"

"Bael had me sit on it and . . . well, I thought I heard a voice."

She stared at me impassively. She would clean up at a poker tournament.

"Do you know anything about that?" I prompted.

"I will look into the matter," she said. "For now, I must collect some materials for Margaret, and I'm sure you have other places to be." She strode past me and entered a door farther down the wall that, I assumed, led to the rentable rooms above.

Pushing my frustration with Hortense's less-than-satisfying answer aside, I turned once more toward the exit. She was right. I did have other places to be.

* * *

I PASSED THE protesters, security staff, and reception desk at the PTF building in a blur, my mind focused on what I would say to Everly when I reached her office. I was glad my plan seemed to be meeting with success, but I couldn't shake the feeling that the situation was spiraling out of my control. Ash had agreed to bring the vampires on board but changed the terms of the mission. Chase had agreed to act as bait, but his price had sent me to conduct yet another negotiation. And what if Director Harris didn't approve the special commission? Or if she did, would she make a demand of her own? I sighed and rode the elevator to the top floor.

Voices drifted from Everly's office, muffled by her closed door. I rapped my knuckles against the wood. The voices cut off.

The door swung open, and it was David's face that greeted me. The tired lines around his eyes, coupled with his burgeoning beard, gave him a haggard appearance, more so even than when I'd seen him earlier that morning. What had happened in those scant few hours to so visibly wear him out?

David's mouth arced up, but the smile didn't reach his eyes. He rubbed a hand over his face. "Hey, Alex. This isn't a good time."

"Sorry, but I need to talk to Director Harris." I held his gaze. "It's important."

"Let her in." Everly's voice came from somewhere behind David.

He stepped back, opening a path.

Everly stood in front of her office windows with her arms crossed and her back to the room. Her posture reminded me of Bael and the pose I found him in nearly every morning of my training, drenched in sunlight as he surveyed his kingdom through the lofty workshop windows. Except Everly wasn't alone.

Deputy Director Peter Weatherly sat in a squat, brown leather chair. His dark-blue suit was tailored to fit his tall frame, and I could probably see my reflection in his perfectly polished shoes if I got close enough. He appraised me as I entered, his mouth turning down at the corners. Weatherly and I had spent a short stretch as co-directors of this facility, until I declared that the life of a bureaucrat wasn't for me. I was happy not to have to see his smug mug every day anymore.

Across from Weatherly sat a stocky man with olive skin and dark, close-cropped hair. Black eyes studied me from behind rectangular glasses.

David gestured to the stranger. "Alex, this is Mr. Barlowe. He's providing the summit's venue and some onsite staff."

"Nice to meet you, Mr. Barlowe. I'm Alex Blackwood." I extended my hand.

Mr. Barlowe stood. "Cole, please." He took my offered hand and kissed the back. "It's a pleasure to meet you, Ms. Blackwood. Your contributions to the equal rights movement are an inspiration."

"Uh ... thanks." I pulled my hand back, wiping it surreptitiously on my pants. "As I understand it, you're quite an advocate for paranatural rights yourself."

He waved the comment away. "That makes me sound entirely too altruistic." He smiled. "I'm a pragmatist. Like many people, I lost loved ones during the Faerie Wars. I just want to make sure history doesn't repeat itself."

"That's very enlightened of you. Plenty of people who lost loved ones became Purists."

He shrugged. "Humanity's strength lies in our ability to learn from our failures and adapt. If the war taught us anything, it's that humans can't conquer magic with numbers alone. We must evolve if we intend to survive. It's time for us to forge a different path. This summit will mark a turning point in history, and I'm honored to be a part of it."

Weatherly snorted.

I glanced at him. A black planner, several olive-green folders, and a few scattered papers lay on the glass coffee table in front of him. I caught a glimpse of satellite photos marked with circles and arrows and a few portraits that looked as if they'd been taken from a distance without the subject's knowledge. Weatherly followed my gaze and swept the contents into a pile beneath his planner.

"Sorry to interrupt your security meeting," I said to Everly's back, "but I have a time-sensitive matter to discuss with you. A follow-up to our earlier conversation."

She nodded, not turning to face me. "Thank you for your reports, gentlemen. We'll continue this discussion later."

"Not too much later, I hope," Weatherly said. He picked up his stack of documents and stood. "The Governor is not going to back down on this matter, and relations between the local government and this office are already strained."

Everly nodded. "I understand the situation, Weatherly."

He hesitated a moment longer, staring at the director's reflection in the window until that reflection's gaze met his in the glass. He exhaled noisily, shot a glare in my direction, and let himself out.

"Right, well ..." Barlowe lifted a shiny silver laptop off the table and tucked it under his arm. "Pleasure meeting you, Ms. Blackwood." He followed Weatherly out of the room.

Director Harris finally turned away from the window. She massaged her fingers against her forehead as if trying to ease a headache.

"Everything all right?" I asked, taking Weatherly's seat.

"Almost nothing," Everly said. "And Weatherly is making sure I remember that."

I shuddered, recalling the way Weatherly had pointed out every mistake I made, no matter how small, during my time working with him. I was convinced he'd even orchestrated a few situations specifically to trip me up just so he could demonstrate how incompetent I was. It didn't help that he was a Purist and I was a product of mixed magics—considered an abomination by humans and fae alike. But Everly wasn't me; she wasn't stuck with him. "You're his boss. Why don't you just fire him?"

"On what grounds?"

"Being an asshole?"

She chuckled. "If that were grounds for dismissal, Capitol Hill would be a ghost town." Her expression sobered. "Seriously though, he may be a Purist and a spy for Governor Anderson, but he's also a competent assistant who respects and upholds the role of the PTF. If what we're doing can't hold up to even *his* scrutiny, perhaps we shouldn't be doing it."

"Scrutiny is one thing, prejudice is another."

"I'm happy to have people like Weatherly on board. Unlike Purity, I have no intention of silencing dissonant voices. It's acknowledging those differences in opinion that keeps us honest."

I frowned. "So, you actually *like* working with him?"

She shrugged. "Liking someone is not a prerequisite for respecting them. He's a useful window into a different perspective. Something we all need from time to time."

I shook my head. "I get needing to consider multiple perspectives, but I couldn't stand listening to him harp on about the evils of magic all day."

"When we stop listening to the voices that don't agree with us, we risk missing something important," she said. "Besides, aren't we trying to make a future for *all*? Surely that umbrella includes the Purists."

I sighed. "I guess that's true."

"And it wasn't so long ago that you yourself hated magic," David said as he took a seat opposite me.

"I was never a Purist," I said, irked by his reminder. "I was . . . an ignorist. I just wanted magic to leave me alone."

David laughed. "That's not a word."

"And ignoring a problem doesn't solve it," Everly added. "Sticking our heads in the sand is not a viable option."

I spread my arms. "I'm here, aren't I?"

"Sooner than expected." Everly took the third of the four seats around the coffee table. "Have your mysterious friends located Chicago's black market already?"

I grimaced. "Yes and no."

"Well, that clears the situation right up," David muttered.

"Apparently the black market is a two-stage . . . maybe three-stage? . . . infiltration. It's invite-only and moves constantly. There's a special phone number to call if you're interested in attending."

David glanced at Everly. "That tracks."

"Do your friends have this phone number?" Everly asked.

"They do," I said, "but that's only the first step. The phone number gets you an interview where someone checks your credentials and goods. If you pass that checkpoint, they take you to the market."

David frowned. "If your friends set up an interview, we can ambush whoever shows up and try to get the market's current location out of them. But if it takes more than a few minutes to break them, probably there's some kind of alert in place, and the market would scatter."

"Exactly," I said.

"Do your friends have enough connections to get past the checkpoint and into the market proper?" Everly asked.

"The black market is just another checkpoint," I said. "The real goal is the Fantasia lab. We need to identify the people buying kidnapped fae and hit them directly at the source. And the only way we've come up with to do that . . . is to sell them a fae."

David stiffened. "You wanna do *what* now?"

"No fae is going to agree to play bait for the PTF," Everly said incredulously.

"Actually, I know someone who will." I waited until I had their undivided attention. "But in return, he wants a PTF special commission." I glanced at David. "Like the one you provided Hortense in exchange for access to Maggie's research project."

Everly crossed her arms. "Who is he?"

"The potential bait prefers to remain anonymous."

She frowned. "Then how does he expect the PTF to protect him?"

"He doesn't. He wants the PTF to endorse and protect a fae sanctuary in the Mortal Realm." I met and held her gaze. "I believe you're familiar with the fae bar Crossroads?"

She looked away. As the regional director of the Western United States, Everly had signed the orders that sent the PTF raid into Crossroads to find me, destroying the structure and arresting dozens of fae—including Targe—who'd then been shipped to a concentration camp on charges of harboring a fugitive.

"The commission is to protect the proprietor, Targe, and his entire family, and grant them permission to legally own and operate the bar as a safe haven for paranaturals."

Harris shook her head. "One or two fae I could probably swing, but licensing an establishment like that in this climate is just asking for trouble. It would require round-the-clock patrols to prevent Purist attacks on such a tempting target."

"No, it would require the PTF having Targe's back when he dealt with threats to his business and customers."

"That could work," David said. "The fae are hardly helpless. If the PTF designates the property the same way they would an embassy or reservation, then the owner would have legal grounds to defend it from aggressors."

I nodded.

"Embassies have diplomatic immunity," said Everly. "What if a fae commits a crime, then seeks sanctuary at Crossroads? Do you expect us to just let them go?"

"Of course not," I said. "You can phrase the terms of the commission to include some kind of extradition for specific cases or something. They're not trying to be unreasonable; they're just trying to find a way to live here legally. Think of this as a dry run for the upcoming summit. Maybe you'll learn something useful about negotiating with fae. At the very least, you'll prove that the PTF is earnest about establishing peaceful relations."

Director Harris tapped a finger against her lips, considering. "In exchange, your nameless fae will let himself be sold to the drug ring?"

I nodded.

"The PTF couldn't make any guarantees about his safety in this situation. He'd be alone behind enemy lines until we tracked him to his final destination, with no idea how long it'll take us to get him out."

I nodded again. "That's why I'll be the one making the sale."

They stared at me in shock and confusion.

"No," David said. "No, no, for so many reasons, no."

"I agree with Mr. Nolan," said Everly. "That is a terrible idea. As I said before, no members of the Paranatural Alliance can participate in this operation."

"Well, *technically,* I'm not a member of the alliance."

"You've represented their interests in front of the PTF board."

"But the alliance currently only consists of two species," I reminded her. "Werewolves and human practitioners. Since I'm part fae, I don't fit into either of those classifications." Truthfully, with my mix of practitioner and fae magic, I didn't fit *any* classification. As near as I could tell, I was the only one of my kind.

Everly pursed her lips.

"Don't tell me you're actually considering this?" David said incredulously.

She shrugged. "If it ends Fantasia . . ."

"She's not a field agent," David persisted. "She's had no training for an undercover operation."

"I had no training as a diplomat or a soldier either," I pointed out defensively, "but I think I filled those roles pretty damn well when the situation demanded it. This is a good plan."

"I'm not saying we shouldn't follow your plan," David said. "Just that we should send a trained operative as the point of contact. Someone with combat and espionage training. That'll give your plan the best chance of success."

He wasn't wrong, exactly. Sending a trained agent probably would increase the odds of success . . . if we were talking about my original plan of alerting the PTF to the lab's location and letting them handle the cleanup. But Ash and the vampires now had plans of their own. Plans that didn't include PTF oversight. Besides, trusting Chase's life to some random PTF soldier would be almost as bad as leaving him alone with the vampires.

"You're not the most subtle person," David continued, "and you've made a lot of noise recently. You've been on TV more than once. Chances are someone at the market would recognize you."

Crap. I hadn't considered my recent fame-slash-infamy. That could complicate matters.

"You didn't even think of that, did you?" David shook his head. "It's not just full fae who've been taken. There are plenty of missing halfers." He pinned me with a worried look. "One slip and you could end up on a slab right beside your friend."

"He's not wrong," Everly said. "And while being a PTF consultant affords you some degree of protection—more than your friend the bait—flashing your pass would instantly blow your cover, and I doubt the people behind an illegal fae organ-harvesting ring are going to care much about who does and doesn't have PTF paperwork."

"This is too important and too dangerous a job for you, Alex. Let the professionals handle it."

"I wish I could," I said honestly, thinking about how much I didn't want to go undercover with only Ash and a bunch of vampires I'd never met as backup. "But it has to be me."

David opened his mouth, and I held up my hand to forestall him. "This *is* an important job. Important enough that we need to give it the best shot at succeeding. My contacts in Chicago are understandably wary of revealing themselves to the PTF, and my fae friend needs someone he knows will watch his back if he's going to put his life on the line. The PTF hasn't done much to earn the trust of any of the paranatural species. Hopefully that's changing, but right now, you all need a bridge to make this work. Like it or not, I'm that bridge."

David scowled, but he didn't argue.

Everly nodded. "Okay. I'll start the paperwork for legitimizing Crossroads and its proprietor. Keep me appraised of your time frame as the situation develops. I'll make sure there are agents ready to mobilize on your signal once the lab is located."

"Maybe I should go with you," David said, "as backup."

My heart soared at the prospect of having a friend by my side . . . but holding my hand wasn't the best use of David's talents, no matter how much better it might make me feel.

I walked over to his chair, leaned down, and gave him a hug. "I appreciate the offer, David, but you have too much to do here. The safety of the summit and its delegates takes top priority." I straightened and gave him a conspiratorial smile. "Unless you're okay letting Weatherly make the security decisions?"

He snorted. "Point taken. I'll hold down the fort. Just promise you'll come back safe."

I winked. "I'll do my best."

Chapter 13

I STUMBLED THROUGH the door, my arms weighed down by grocery bags. Ash and Emma were side by side on the couch, sharing a bowl of popcorn, while an animated Polynesian girl belted out a song about voyaging across the ocean on the TV.

"Welcome back." Emma waved a fistful of popcorn overhead, then shoved it in her mouth.

Ash glanced over the back of the couch, their focus dropping to my many shopping bags. "Stocking up?"

I nodded toward Emma, then jerked my head toward the back of the house. Kicking off my boots, I carried my haul into the kitchen and began sorting groceries.

Ash pushed the bowl of popcorn entirely onto Emma's lap. "Excuse me, I need to make a run to the bathroom."

"You want me to pause the movie?" Emma asked.

"No. I've seen it before." Ash glanced my way as they passed, then continued to my bedroom.

I waited a moment, tucking away the last of the refrigerated items, then followed.

"Did you find willing bait?" Ash whispered as soon as I closed the door behind me.

"Yes."

"Good. I've chartered a private flight out of the Boulder Municipal Airport for ten o'clock tonight. Have your bait meet us there. We can discuss the rest of the details once we're in the air." Ash patted me on the shoulder. "This will be fun. You and me, working as a team." They smiled. "Team Abomination."

"You and I have very different definitions of the word fun," I said.

They shrugged, slipped past me, and returned to the living room to watch the end of the movie.

I glared after Ash, then I pulled a backpack out of my closet and stuffed some clothes into it. Clothes that I hoped would give off "heartless poacher" vibes. I dumped some makeup into the bag as well, unsure what I'd need to make a convincing disguise. I also tucked my light-imbued knife into a pocket on the side. Hardly TSA-approved, but Ash had said this was a private flight, and vampires tended to handle their own security. I doubted I'd be walking through any metal detectors.

I opened the drawer in my nightstand and considered the Sig Sauer David had given me. *In for a penny, in for a pound.* I added the gun and a box of bullets to my bag. People probably weren't allowed into the market with weapons, but you never knew. These were criminals, after all. Maybe everyone would have a gun.

I tossed some toiletries into the bag. Clothes, toothbrush, weapons—just the bare essentials. I zipped it closed then pulled out my cell phone.

I called Crossroads first. Chase agreed to meet me by the plane at ten o'clock, along with Ava, who would collect Targe's contract. Everly was my second call. I let her know our time frame, and she promised to have the contract signed, sealed, and ready to pick up on my way to the airport. That just left Emma.

The credits were rolling when I came out of the bedroom. Emma hummed along to the soundtrack.

"Good movie?" I asked, taking a seat.

"Almost as good as the first time I saw it," Emma said.

"Listen, Em, I have to leave for a few days."

She turned her face toward me, her unfocused gaze disturbingly piercing. "Why?"

"That joint project that Ash and I are working on . . . we need to visit the gallery in person. Talk to the curator."

She continued to stare for a moment, then shrugged and leaned her head back against the cushions. "Okay."

"I've stocked the fridge, but call David if you need anything."

"I'm not a child, Alex. I'll be fine."

"I know," I said.

The final notes of the credit music ended. Emma sat forward, groped for the remote on the coffee table, and powered off the TV. She stretched her arms above her head with a groan, then said, "I could use some fresh air. Would either of you care to join me for a walk?"

I glanced at Ash. "Sure, Em. I'll join you."

"I'll pass," Ash said. "I need to pack for our trip."

Emma and I slipped on our shoes and left, with Emma gripping my elbow.

We walked slowly, allowing Emma time to find her footing with each step, heading along one of the many animal trails I'd widened in my time on the mountain. The sun, nearly directly overhead, warmed my skin, and I turned my face up to enjoy it. After strolling for ten minutes, Emma pulled me to a stop.

"What's going on, Alex?"

I turned to face her. "What do you mean?"

"Who is Ash, really? She seems nice enough, but I can tell you're afraid of her. Your voice gets tight every time you talk to her. And don't think I actually believe this whole art project cover you two are selling. You haven't taken a commission since James went missing. So if you met through James, it wasn't through the art world."

I shook my head and laughed. "Damn, Em. You should have been a detective."

"Yeah, well, there's still time." She crossed her arms. "Now what's *really* going on?"

I looked around, calmed by the scenery—the rustle of wind through leaves, the sharpness of the air, the scents of soil and growing things. "There are some rocks up ahead. Let's sit down for a bit."

Emma stepped around me and tromped toward the rocks. She perched on the largest boulder, flaking off some of the pale lichen clinging to its surface. I settled on a squat piece of granite.

"Is Ash a vampire?"

I stiffened and shot a concerned glance at the path back to the house, even though I knew Ash couldn't have followed us.

"I know you told me to pretend she's human, but she definitely isn't. Add to that that she keeps all the windows closed and never steps outside during the day, and I'm thinking vampire."

"How could you tell the windows were closed?"

She gave me a "don't be stupid" expression and spread her arms, pale skin practically glowing in the sunlight. "Sight isn't the only way we experience light."

I sighed and leaned back on my arms. I wished I could tell Emma the whole truth, but Ash's true identity was a burden I could never share. "Yes, Ash is a vampire." I spoke softly, even though we were far enough from the house that even paranatural hearing couldn't pick up my voice. "The 'project' we're working on together is getting the vampires added to the Paranatural Alliance so they can participate in the interspecies summit."

"Why didn't you just tell me?"

"Ash works directly with the vampire council. That makes her very dangerous and super-extra-paranoid. If Ash finds out that you know her secret . . . I'm not sure what she'll do."

Emma shook her head. "Fine. What's actually happening with this trip? Where are you two going?"

"Chicago. I'm actually working on a covert mission with the PTF to track down the source of Fantasia. Then the vampires are going to shut down the operation to earn some positive PR as a 'hello' to the human race."

A pair of starlings called out to each other as they wove aerials overhead.

"That's ..."

"Yeah."

"Why you?"

"Because the PTF can't find who they need to find, but the vampires can."

"Except the PTF doesn't know that vampires exist."

"Exactly."

"And eliminating Fantasia ... that's the 'free sample' you were talking about earlier?"

"Yep."

We sat in silence for a while, baking under the sun and listening to the rustle of leaves, then Emma's voice broke me out of my reverie. "I'll go with you."

I twisted to look at her. "What? No."

"You don't trust Ash, which is hardly surprising since she works for the people who are literally holding your boyfriend hostage. You need someone to have your back."

"Harris made it very clear: no practitioners or werewolves can be involved."

"*You're* a practitioner," she quipped.

"I have practitioner magic," I agreed, "but I'm something else." *Abomination.* The word whispered through my thoughts. "I'm not part of the alliance, so even if this shit goes sideways, the fallout can't land on them. Besides," I said, before she could point out that she wasn't technically a practitioner anymore either, "I won't be alone. Chase is going, too."

She frowned. "Why Chase?"

"We need a fae for our plan to work. He volunteered."

"He *volunteered*?" She dragged the word out.

"Well, he agreed, anyway. In exchange for a PTF commission for Targe so he can legally reopen Crossroads."

She crossed her arms. "I still think I should go."

"If you go, Ash will realize you know what she is. She'll erase your memory, or worse." My voice hitched. I would *not* let Ash kill Emma. "Please, Emma. Don't make this more complicated than it already is."

Emma thumped her heels against her rock. "Fine. But if you and Chase don't come home safe, I'm gonna hunt Ash down and chop off her head."

I leaned over, resting my cheek on Emma's shoulder. "Thanks, Em."

* * *

"ANY PROBLEMS?"

I jumped as a slim, stern-looking man stepped into a pool of light beside the pedestrian gate leading to the boarding area of Boulder Airfield. I took a step back, then I saw his eyes. I'd recognize those black holes anywhere. The underlying structure of Ash's face remained basically the same, but the angles appeared more severe without the softening effects of makeup or a frame of dark hair, which was now pulled into a loose bun. Their eyes were set deeper, the angle of their nose was steeper, and their skin seemed rougher, more weathered. Wearing black cargo pants with a crazy number of pockets, black combat boots, and a black tactical vest over a dark-gray, long-sleeved shirt, Ash looked exactly like what they were pretending to be—an ex-soldier turned faerie hunter.

"Good to go." I held up the manila envelope containing Targe's signed contract from Everly, then used it to indicate Ash's altered appearance. "That's quite the costume change. Should I be insulted that you felt the need to gender swap for this mission?"

Ash shrugged. "The people we'll be working with in Chicago are . . . traditional." Their voice was slightly lower, but not so low as when they pretended to be Esteban.

"You mean they're chauvinists," I guessed.

"Just let me do the talking."

I rolled my eyes. "Shall I grovel at your feet while I'm at it?"

"If you think it will help." They didn't so much as hint at a smile.

"Charming," I said flatly.

Ash led the way to a small Cessna waiting on the tarmac and climbed inside. Pinpricks of red, green, and white lights marked the vast darkness beyond the plane. I turned to watch the approach. Pools of overlapping light marked the walkway and nearby buildings. My hair snapped and tangled in the intermittent gusts tearing along the foothills as I paced in front of the plane.

"Alex."

I spun. Two backlit forms walked toward me, one tall with a long silver braid, the other short and capped with orange. From the angle of their approach, they might have circled around the side of the main building, but I knew better. Ava would have opened a portal directly from Crossroads, and she'd go back the same way when we were done.

"Nice night for a clandestine exchange," Chase said, stopping in front of me. He wore a loose, gray T-shirt and faded jeans. His feet, as usual, were bare.

I handed Ava the manila envelope I'd gotten from Everly. "There are three copies of the contract in there, already signed by Director Harris. Have Targe sign all three copies. Keep one and give the other two to David. He'll make sure they get properly filed."

Ava opened the envelope and skimmed the documents as I spoke.

"Well?" Chase asked.

"Protection for Targe and any relatives who reside with him, and full licensing for Crossroads." Ava nodded. "This all looks in order." She turned to me and wrapped her arms around my neck, papers in one hand, envelope in the other. "You did it, Alex."

"It was my pleasure," I said, squeezing her back. Honestly, I didn't entirely believe that a piece of paper could keep them safe . . . but the intent was there, and that was a start.

Ava withdrew and tucked the precious forms away.

Chase patted Ava on the head. "Try to keep my sister out of trouble while I'm away."

"Try not to get Alex killed."

He rolled his eyes. "What, no concern for your brother-in-law?"

"Eh." She shrugged, then she smiled. "Kidding. You'd better *both* come home safe." She slugged Chase on the arm.

"Ow." Chase rubbed the spot she'd hit. "What was that for?"

"That was from Jynx."

"She punched me before we left."

"This one's for later, when you think about doing something heroically stupid."

"Stupid, maybe," Chase said, "but heroism isn't in my nature. I'll leave the heavy lifting to the PTF."

I snorted. As a fae, Chase couldn't lie. That didn't mean everything he said was the truth. He honestly didn't think himself heroic, but he'd saved my life enough times that our opinions differed on that point.

Ava backed up, lifting her empty hand in farewell. "Fair winds and safe travels."

I waved back. "You, too."

She smiled, turned, and walked toward the place where I'd first noticed them. Ava made a circular gesture with her free hand as she walked. She vanished into a shimmer of darkness between one step and the next. I blinked, and the shimmer was gone.

Chase gestured to the plane behind me. "This our ride?"

I nodded, and he headed up the steps, but he stopped abruptly at the hatch. I bumped into his back.

"Alex," he said in a cold, tight whisper, "who is that?"

I peeked over his shoulder. Ash sat in one of six leather passenger seats.

"Chase, meet Ash. Ash, Chase. We'll be working together for this operation." I gave Chase a gentle shove to get him moving. He shuffled inside and sat facing Ash on the opposite side of the plane. Ash watched with a bored expression as Chase strapped in. I stowed my pack and sat directly across from Ash.

"All aboard?" The pilot asked from the cockpit.

"That's everyone," Ash said.

The pilot closed the hatch, then returned to the cockpit and pulled on a pair of large headphones. I raised my window shade to watch the runway speed by and drop away. We three passengers didn't speak again until the city lights below were indistinguishable from the starry sky around us.

Chase broke the silence first. "You're PTF?"

Ash looked at Chase, laced their fingers, and shook their head.

I twisted in my seat to face Chase. "There are a few details about this mission that we should clarify before we land."

Chase sniffed, attention still on Ash. "You smell of magic."

Ash didn't bat an eye. "My master's magic."

Chase's lips peeled back. "Thrall." He hissed the word between bared teeth.

It never ceased to amaze me how good Ash was at hiding in plain sight. Neither fae nor vampires seemed able to tell what Ash was, although strong ones could sometimes sense an aura of magic about them, as Chase had. *I wonder if a werewolf could sniff them out?*

Chase turned his glare on me. "What's going on here, Alex?"

"Remember how I told you we needed to sell you at a black market in Chicago?"

"Yeah."

"Well, the PTF couldn't *find* the black market, much less get an invitation to attend."

He glanced at Ash. "Let me guess. The vampires could?"

I nodded.

"And the PTF . . . ?"

"Doesn't know they're involved, just that I'm using a contact in Chicago who prefers to remain anonymous for the time being."

"So the cavalry you're going to call in to save my ass once I lead you to the Fantasia lab?"

"Vampires," Ash said.

Chase's gaze stayed fixed on my face. "And you waited until *now*—when I was a thousand feet up and speeding toward Chicago—to tell me I'd be working with vampires?"

I winced. Guilt warmed my cheeks and palms, but I choked down the urge to apologize. I hadn't lied. I'd just omitted certain facts in order to get the outcome I needed. *Geez, I really have been spending too much time around the fae.*

He shook his head and chuckled, finally looking away. "You're more conniving than I gave you credit for."

I exhaled. From a fae, "conniving" was a compliment, but it didn't make me feel any better about tricking my friend.

"Are you mad?"

He shrugged. "What would be the point? A deal was struck. You held up your end by delivering Targe's contract, for which I promised you could sell me at this market. It was my oversight not to identify all the players involved." He smiled. "Did you think I would whine about 'trust' and 'fairness' like some human?"

"Maybe a little," I admitted, thinking of how betrayed I'd felt by Bael's deception when he told me I'd never be able to recreate James's daywalking amulet.

"Done is done." Chase settled back at an angle where he could keep both Ash and me in view and crossed his arms. "Any other details you care to share?"

* * *

IT TOOK TWENTY minutes to get Chase up to speed with the plan . . . or, well, most of the plan. We left out the bit about vampires getting PTF endorsement to become members of the Paranatural Alliance and joining the summit if we succeeded.

Chase tapped his index finger rhythmically against the arm of his seat. He kept his gaze fixed on Ash. "Fae are being harvested. Humans are being attacked. It makes sense that those groups want to put an end to Fantasia." He narrowed his eyes. "Why do the vampires care?"

"Fantasia may be primarily a fae issue," Ash said smoothly, "but no one in the magical community wants the Purity activists to grow any stronger. A threat to one magical being is a threat to *all* magical beings."

"Satisfied?" I asked.

"Placated." He folded his hands on his lap, tipped his head back, and closed his eyes. "For now."

"Then I suggest we turn our attention to your appearance," Ash said to me. "It would be best to have your disguise in place before we land in Chicago since both your face and your status as a PTF contractor are fairly well known. We don't want to complicate the situation unnecessarily."

"Oh." I knew I'd need to mask my identity from the black market people; I hadn't realized I'd be hiding from my supposed allies as well. If Ash had kept quiet about the PTF's involvement, did that mean the locals didn't know that the ultimate goal of this operation was to reveal vampires to the world? I glanced at Chase. It seemed Ash was keeping their people in the dark as much as I was. When the call came to expose themselves, would they follow orders . . . or would they balk?

"I have my makeup with me," I said, "but I thought I'd have time to buy some hair dye when we got to town."

Ash pursed their lips. "I was thinking of something a little more . . . extensive."

I frowned. "Such as?"

"How good is your glamour?"

"My . . . glamour?"

"Fae talent for hiding what they look like." They gestured to Chase, who could easily pass as a twenty-something human male, albeit one with unique hair and prettier-than-average features. "Glamour."

"I know what it *is*." I crossed my arms. "What makes you think I can make one?"

Ash raised an eyebrow. "All fae can. It comes with the blood."

"Well, not all halfers can, and that's what I am."

They waved a hand dismissively. "Most halfers could; they just don't realize it."

"Fine. Put me in the 'didn't realize it' category." Excitement bubbled up inside me. No one had ever mentioned that I might be able to cast a glamour before. I guessed, since most fae used glamours to pass for human, and I already looked human, it just hadn't come up. "How does it work?"

"Glamours are extensions of the fae who cast them. Unlike illusions, they have substance, texture, functionality, and they don't rely on the perceptions of observers. In order to create one, you need to"—they paused, as if searching for the right words—"extend your magic outside of your body . . . like growing an exoskeleton."

"How do you know so much about glamours?" Chase had opened his eyes and was staring suspiciously at Ash.

Ash met his gaze. "Know thy enemy."

And know thyself, I thought.

"Let's start small," Ash said. "Concentrate on your fingernails. See if you can make them longer."

I placed my hands on my knees and stared at them. The white crescents of my nails were even with the tips of my fingers. I took a deep breath and reached for my fae magic. It opened to me on a surge of emotion—excitement, worry, pride, frustration. . . . I took another breath, let it out, and directed my magic toward my fingers, picturing what I wanted to have happen the way I did when I used my practitioner magic. In my mind's eye, I watched my nails extend and taper to pointed claws.

In reality, nothing happened.

I exhaled, shook out my hands, repositioned, and I tried again . . . and again . . . and again. My nails stubbornly remained white crescents at the tips of my fingers.

Ash watched with growing disappointment, while Chase pretended to sleep. After several dozen failed attempts, Ash said, "Okay, maybe altering physical shapes is too much for you. Let's change the color of your hair."

I took a moment to recenter, unlatching my seatbelt so I could get more comfortable. I closed my eyes and imagined magic flowing into my hair. I willed the hair to change color. I opened my eyes and tugged a lock forward for inspection. What I saw was the same dark auburn I'd had my entire life.

Next, I tried to mold my magic into a physical cover for my hair as a whole, like a veil. Then I created a sheath for each individual strand. When neither worked, I sought the inner workings of the hairs. Most fae didn't have access to imbuing magic; they created glamours that sat on the surface. But I could dig deeper. With enough energy, I could twist the truth at the heart of creation. Changing my hair color should be child's play.

I found the ebb and flow of energies that made up my physical presence and followed the lines back to my weblike core. From there, I could rewrite the threads that told my hair what color and texture to be . . . but imbuing my core would be like rewriting my DNA. And without any way to map what currently existed, there'd be no guarantee I could put it back the way I'd found it when I was done. *Probably best to keep the changes superficial.*

"You're trying too hard." Chase's voice jarred me out of my thoughts.

My awareness snapped back to my physical body. I rolled my neck, easing the stiffness there. "Are you suggesting I give up?"

"Glamours are instinctual," Chase said. "Fae children learn to hide like human children learn to walk. You're thinking about your magic as something separate from the rest of you, something you can boss around. Don't tell it what to do, just manifest what you want."

As hokey as that sounded, I knew exactly what he meant. Not long ago, when Ash had tried to enthrall me, I'd somehow merged with my magic. The barriers between it and me had vanished; the magic had become an extension of my will. Unfortunately, I'd been unable to reproduce that feeling. "I'm *trying*."

"That's the problem. Stop trying. Forget about the fingernails or the hair," he said. "The individual pieces don't matter. Glamours are intuitive, an innate defense mechanism. Just *feel* how you want to look."

I gritted my teeth and tried to *feel* different . . . with exactly the same result. Every failure resonated with the echo of my failures in Enchantment, building like a sonic wave that threatened to shatter me like a sheet of glass.

Who am I kidding? I exhaled and slouched against my seat.

"I guess you were right," Ash said.

I rolled my gaze to where they lounged across from me, where they'd watched me fail over and over with the same empty look Bael had worn as I pointlessly beat my head against the invisible wall of his training exercises. "About what?"

"Maybe you can't use glamours after all."

For some reason, Ash's acceptance of my failure made me angry, especially since they were the one who'd put the idea in my head all that wasted energy ago. I glared. "Maybe I need a better teacher."

"Or a mirror." Ash grabbed my wrist, pulling me out of my seat and into the tiny onboard bathroom. They barely managed to wedge the door closed behind us. Even with my ass pressed against the sink, Ash was standing far too close for comfort.

"This isn't going to work," Ash whispered, quiet enough that even Chase wouldn't be able to hear.

"You're the one who said halfers could make glamours," I pointed out, equally quiet.

"And you might be able to figure it out someday, but we don't have time for you to keep messing about and burning energy. Even if you *could* manage to construct a glamour at this point, I wouldn't trust it not to shatter the moment you got distracted. So I'm going to cast an illusion over you instead. We'll tell that shifter out there that you succeeded in creating a glamour."

"His name is Chase."

"I don't care."

"Will an illusion even work?" I asked. "What if there are security cameras?"

"*My* illusion will work," Ash said. "Trust me."

I stared into those dark eyes. As a vampire—*the* vampire—Ash had as much invested in the success of this operation as I did, if not more. I nodded.

"Good." Ash spun me to face the mirror and met my gaze in the reflection, hands braced on my shoulders. "Now, let's discuss your makeover."

Fifteen minutes later—we didn't want it to seem as if I'd immediately succeeded after all my earlier failures—Ash and I emerged from the bathroom. My skin was darker, my nose was wider, and my hair was a light brown that matched my new eye color.

"You two were in there for quite a while." Chase said, his eyes once more closed. "Did you join the mile high—" He opened his eyes, took one look at me, and closed his mouth.

I returned to my seat. "What do you think?"

He frowned, examining every inch of me.

"Not exactly a quick learner," Ash said, reclaiming their own seat, "but she got there in the end."

I schooled my expression. Like all halfers, Ash could lie. Unlike most of us, they'd had a hundred human lifetimes to perfect the art. I was an open book by comparison, and I didn't want Chase reading me.

"You did this on your own?" he asked.

I swallowed. "Do you like it?"

He glanced suspiciously at Ash, but all he said was, "It'll do."

Chapter 14

OUR PLANE TOUCHED down, jostling me out of a light doze. I yawned and rubbed my eyes. With the time difference, it was nearly two o'clock in the morning. Chase stared out his window, which he'd opened despite there not being much to see. Ash's attention was fixed on their phone. The plane taxied for a bit, then the pilot cut the engines and opened the hatch. Ash was up and out of the plane as soon as the stairs were down. The pilot followed. I stretched, grabbed my bag, and headed for fresh air.

A man in his thirties exited the driver's seat of a black limousine that was parked a little ways from the plane. He circled the car and opened the rear door. Another man, this one closer to fifty, stepped out. Dark hair with steel-gray wings, trimmed short on the sides and swept back on top, matched a manicured beard and mustache in the same palette. The man's skin was ruddy and weathered, with deep creases at the corners of his eyes. He tugged the lapels of his blue suit as he straightened, then he strode forward to greet us.

He froze on his third step, staring over my shoulder.

I turned and found Chase emerging from the plane.

"It's okay," I said, turning back. "He's with us."

The man resumed his forward progress, if a bit stiffly. "I had assumed the fae captured for this sale would be transported in chains."

"He's not a captive," I corrected. "He's a volunteer."

The man's frown deepened. "You are Sloth's representative?"

"That would be me," Ash said, tucking away their phone.

"Ah." The man turned away from me and shook Ash's hand, as if everything now made sense. He fired off a few sentences of what I was pretty sure was Russian. Ash responded in kind, leading the man back toward the limousine.

I started to follow, but Chase pulled me slightly aside and leaned close to my ear. "Sloth?"

"The title of one of the vampire council members," I whispered back.

"I know," he said. "You're working for the council?"

"Not directly," I hedged.

"A vampire's thrall is an extension of the vampire. If Ash belongs to Sloth, you're working with Sloth. How in the Rift did *that* happen?"

"It's a long story."

"Consider it a dying man's last request."

"You're not going to die."

"I might, once my people find out I inadvertently teamed up with one of the leaders of the most loathsome creatures in existence."

"Even if working with him ends the fae abductions?"

He shrugged. "That could help, but I'm betting that's not why Sloth is participating in this operation."

I glanced at Ash and the Russian as they moved away from us, then at the driver and pilot, who were conversing near the back of the plane. "A few months ago, James and I were approached by some vampire representatives who accused us of being a threat to their secrecy. We managed to get off the hook, mostly, but they took James as a hostage, saying they'd only release him if I created seven new daywalking amulets."

Chase grabbed me by the shoulders. "Tell me you didn't actually make those?"

I shoved him off. "I would if I could, but I can't. I spent the past three months in Enchantment learning exactly that," I said angrily. "Anyway, Ash came looking for an update. When I heard the PTF had hit a wall in their hunt for the source of Fantasia, I thought the vampires might have better luck and asked Ash to make a few inquiries. Turns out they have connections in the Chicago criminal scene, so here we are."

"Why do I get the feeling there's more you're not telling me?"

"I told you it was a long story. I had to leave some pieces out."

He tipped his head back, looking at the sky. "I leave you alone for a couple of months...." He snapped his gaze back to me. "Does Ash know you can't make the amulets?"

I nodded.

"But he still agreed to help with your mission?"

"We made a different deal," I said. "And before you ask...no, I won't go into the details right now."

He rubbed his jaw and chin in contemplation. "Did you actually *meet* Sloth? Could you identify them? Because that information would be worth a lot."

Chase's words chilled me. "Bael asked me the same thing." I shook my head. "The summit, what I'm doing here, everything I've done in the past year... I'm trying to foster *peace*. It's time the fae put down their feud."

Chase sighed. "I know you love James and all, but vampires aren't like the rest of us. You can't trust them. They're too dangerous."

"That's exactly what Purist humans say about the fae, but just because something *can* be dangerous, that doesn't mean it has to be, or even that it will be."

Chase frowned. "You've got a good heart, Alex." He exhaled and ran a hand over his forehead. "I just hope it doesn't get us all killed."

"Are you two coming?" Ash called from the open door of the limo.

I nudged Chase with my elbow and started forward.

"Hey, Alex?" Chase said softly.

"Yeah?"

"I'm sorry about James."

I nodded. *Better late than never.*

Ash and our escort were seated on a bench that ran parallel to the car. I slid into one of the seats that faced forward.

"Alex," Ash said, "this is Ivan, a local lieutenant. He'll be taking care of us while we're in town."

"Nice to meet you," I said.

Ivan nodded, then his expression turned sour as Chase joined us and pulled the door closed. Clearly trying, and failing, to hide his disgust, Ivan said, "As requested, we've prepared a safe house for you to spend the day in. We'll head there now."

Ash nodded. They'd likely used Chase's presence as an excuse for private accommodations, but Ash probably would have arranged to stay outside the nest regardless. From what I'd learned in my initial interactions with Ash, they didn't particularly enjoy the company of their own kind. The fact that every fae in existence wanted them dead wasn't the only reason Ash lived in hiding. They had no interest in playing either a devil or a god, having experienced quite enough of both.

"What can you tell us about getting into the market?" I asked.

Ivan looked at Ash, who nodded.

I gritted my teeth.

"A market representative will tell us where and when your interview will take place. Once on site, they'll verify that you're not a fae or werewolf by cutting you with an iron knife."

I stiffened. Iron wouldn't affect either Ash or me, despite our having fae blood. That didn't mean I liked the idea of getting sliced up.

"Nothing deep. Just a scratch. If you were fae, the iron would burn you. If you were a werewolf, you would heal before their eyes."

I frowned. "So would a vampire."

"True," Ivan said, "which is one reason we only attend markets through our thralls."

I shot a nervous look at Ash. They seemed calm. Did they have a plan for fooling the test? I itched to ask, but I couldn't with Ivan and Chase around.

"Since there isn't such a straightforward method for identifying practitioners unless you have a paladin on hand, the representative will then place magic-dampening collars around your necks."

"Wait, *everyone* wears a collar?" If all went to plan, I wouldn't need to use any magic on this mission, but the thought of being *unable* to use it shot a jolt of panic through me.

Ivan shook his head. "Just new attendees and registered practitioners. The only magic allowed in the market is either caged"—he glanced at Chase—"or controlled by the hosts."

I swallowed. I was *not* liking the sound of all this security.

"Then they'll check your goods and, assuming you pass your interview, you'll be blindfolded and driven to a new location. Vendors set up early in the night. Shoppers and people with items to auction"—again he indicated Chase—"are brought in later. The market runs for one full day. No one is allowed to leave until the host declares the market closed, at which point everyone is escorted off the premises and returned to their starting locations." He spread his hands. "That's it."

"What about physical weapons?" I asked.

Ivan shook his head. "You'll be searched. They'll take your phones as well."

So much for bringing my gun. I asked a few more questions, to which I received only grunts or nods, before giving up on conversation.

We hadn't flown into Chicago proper, but rather to a regional airport southeast of the city, so we endured half an hour of awkward silence before arriving at the three-story, red brick building where we'd be staying. Ivan led us to a small, two-bedroom apartment on the top floor. Dried-out, hardwood floors creaked underfoot. Yellowing paint peeled off the walls, while cardboard and blackout curtains provided safety for light-sensitive occupants. A round table with a green vinyl top and four mismatched chairs filled the space nearest the single row of cabinets, sink, fridge, and stove that comprised the kitchen. The other half of the room boasted a sunken brown couch, a wooden rocking chair, and a large television. Both bedrooms included a single queen-sized bed and a wardrobe. The bathroom fixtures were a sickly green color and plagued by rust, but they seemed operational.

"I apologize for the accommodations," Ivan said as he gave us a brief tour. "This was all we had available on short notice."

Ash nodded. "This will be adequate."

"Chase." I tipped my head toward the smaller of the two bedrooms. "You and I can share."

Chase slipped into the offered room, clearly eager to put a door between himself and Ivan.

Ivan said something in Russian, and the driver, who I gathered from Ivan's comment was named Tony, pulled out his cell phone and gestured to me. "Stand in front of this wall."

I glanced suspiciously at the blank wall he'd indicated. "Why?"

"So I may take your picture."

I continued to stare at him, uncomprehending.

"It's so he can make your false ID," Ash said.

"Ah." I posed in front of the wall and let Tony snap my picture. Once he was satisfied, he pulled a laptop and a small printer out of a bag and set up shop at the kitchen table.

Ash and Ivan stood in the living room, deep in conversation. Considering the hours vampires and their servants kept, all three would probably be up for hours.

I shook my head. "I'm going to bed now."

None of them reacted as I withdrew.

"Skin or fur?" Chase asked as I closed the bedroom door.

I dropped my pack on the floor and kicked off my boots. The idea of sharing a bed led my thoughts to James. I sat on the edge of the mattress and twisted the fabric ring on my finger. Memories flooded my senses. His palm cradled my cheek, soft and warm. The scent of blackberries and cloves swirled through the room. I closed my eyes and inhaled, then I released the breath . . . and the memory. I opened my eyes. "Fur, if you don't mind."

Chase nodded. Between one breath and the next, he shifted—a rippling effect that reminded me of a time lapse video of ice melting. A moment later, a gray tabby jumped onto the bed and curled up on the comforter. Before joining him, I dug in my bag and retrieved my light-imbued knife.

"Just in case," I whispered. I wasn't really worried about Ash double-crossing me, not as long as our goals remained aligned, but I'd sleep better with the blade under my pillow.

Chase purred his approval as I slipped off my pants and snuggled in beside him.

* * *

A VAMPIRE, A fae, a thrall, and two magical misfits hiding their identities from at least half the people present, all locked in a tiny apartment together. . . . It was no surprise when someone lost their temper. Especially since that someone was me.

"Oh, come on. Just a quick walk around the block to stretch my legs." I'd slept about four hours before waking to the unfamiliar sounds of city life—voices, cars, music, the elevated train—filtering through the single pane windows. Between the constant din, the artificial lights, and the warm, stale air in the apartment, I felt as if my senses were under attack. I needed to get out.

Tony shook his head. "Ivan said no one leaves."

I glared at the closed door to the second bedroom, which Ivan had apparently retreated to slightly after sunrise, leaving Tony and Ash—the two supposed thralls—to stand guard in the living room.

"I never agreed to those terms." I crossed my arms. "We have an entire day to kill before our meeting tonight. I'm not spending it cooped up in here."

"If you're going, I'm going," Chase said, looking apprehensively at the closed bedroom door. It was hardly surprising that he didn't want to be left alone with the vampires.

Tony glared at Ash. "I suppose you want to go, too?"

Ash shook their head. "But perhaps a short excursion is in order, if it will grant us some peace. Since you know this city, you should escort these two. I'll remain here to guard Ivan while he sleeps."

Tony's expression looked almost pained as he considered his options. Waking the boss was obviously a big no-no, as was disobeying an order, but he couldn't physically prevent us from leaving on his own. I almost felt sorry for him, except that I was tired, grumpy, and needed to stretch my legs.

"One hour," he said, casting a nervous glance at Ivan's door. "Not a second longer."

"I'll take it," I said.

The air was a cool, humid, slap in the face that helped me finally wake up as we stepped onto the sidewalk. I took a deep breath of industry mixed with way too many bodies. Diesel, sweat, oil, tobacco, sewage, rust, fresh foods, and old trash. . . . The smell wasn't entirely pleasant, but it was *alive*—the breath of the city—and I savored it. The sun, which I hadn't been able to track in the apartment, was still near the beginning of its journey, cutting long swaths of shadow across the narrow streets.

Tony led Chase and me on a walking tour of the neighborhood, pointing out notable sights, including one of his favorite sandwich shops, a bakery that boasted the best cannoli in town, and a stone church that had apparently survived the Great Chicago Fire of 1871. We also walked under one of the many bridges that supported the famous Chicago "L." As we traveled, one thing became abundantly clear: Purity had an even stronger foothold in this city than they did in Denver.

Not only did Purity logos dominate nearly every window, but the few stores who'd opted not to toe the company line were obviously being punished. Like Maggie's bookstore, they suffered broken windows, graffitied slurs, and people blowing iron dust into the faces of potential customers. On the sidewalks, pedestrians fell into three general categories: confident groups wearing Purity armbands, timid individuals who scurried from place to place with their heads down, and gawking tourists, like us, who were generally ignored. Walking down the street felt less like sightseeing and more like crossing a demilitarized zone under the oppressive feeling that conflict might break out at any moment, shattering the thin veneer of civility.

By the time we made it back to the apartment, I was actually glad to return to the enclosed space, cramped and acrid though it was. I didn't demand to be let out again, instead spending the next few hours watching reality TV, wedged on the couch between Chase and Ash. It was a surreal experience, but a nice reminder of what I was striving for, and why it was so important that this mission succeed.

I turned in shortly after lunch, determined to get what rest I could before we infiltrated the market.

No sooner had my head hit the pillow, it seemed, than rough hands shook me awake. Startled and disoriented, I groped for my light-imbued blade. My mind registered Ash's features looming over me in the gloom at the same moment my fingers found the knife handle. I forced myself to relax, but I kept my grip on the weapon.

"What's wrong?" I asked groggily.

"Nothing." Ash straightened and stepped away, gaze moving to my hidden hand. Did they know what was under my pillow? "We got the call. It's time to go."

I rubbed my eyes and sat up. Chase, in cat form, perched at the foot of my bed. He must have woken as soon as Ash stepped into the room.

"I'll be right out," I rasped.

Ash retreated, closing the door, and I fixed my gaze on Chase. "You ready for this?"

He cocked his head and meowed.

"Yeah," I said. "Me neither." I pulled on my "badass poacher" outfit of camo cargo pants, a black shirt, hiking boots, and a leather jacket, returned my knife to my backpack, and stepped out of the room.

An iron-framed, steel-mesh cage the size of a medium pet carrier sat on the kitchen table. It hadn't been there when I went to sleep. I stopped in my doorway, staring at the cage. "Um, where did that come from?"

"Ivan procured it for us," Ash said.

I didn't want to know why Ivan had a fae-proof cage on hand. "I thought we were just going to handcuff Chase. A cage like that will hurt him."

Ivan shot Ash a look that screamed, "Is she serious?"

Ash met my gaze. "We're poachers, Alex, not police."

"You won't be allowed into the market with an uncaged fae," Ivan added.

I bit my lower lip, looking from the cage to Chase. Another thought hit me. The cage was big enough for Chase in his current cat form, but not big enough for a human. "If he goes in there, surrounded by so much iron, his glamour will break and he'll revert to his natural state. That cage isn't big enough to hold him."

Ash frowned. "What makes you think your friend's humanoid shape is his natural state?"

"I . . ." I closed my mouth, embarrassed by my ignorance. Looking at Chase I asked, "Is this cat the real you?"

He gave me a condescending, and very feline, look.

"They are both the real him," Ash said. "While shifters *can* cast glamours, that is not how they change forms. Rest assured, our bait will not suddenly grow to human size when he enters the cage. In you go, kitty."

Chase's ears flattened. A low rumble reverberated in his chest.

Ash returned Chase's glare. "We don't have all night."

"At least let me cover the bottom so he doesn't burn his paws." I ran to the bathroom and snatched a towel off the rack, where a quick glance in the mirror reminded me—with a start—that my face was not currently my own.

"Poachers aren't known for their bleeding hearts," Ivan warned when I returned with the towel.

"But neither would they want to damage their goods," Ash said. "I don't think a towel will raise any red flags."

I spread the fabric over the base of the cage, then I stepped back and looked apologetically at Chase.

He leapt to the table and entered the cage, hesitating only briefly as he crossed the threshold. He circled, settled, and stared out through the opening.

I held his gaze as I closed and latched the cage. "Don't worry. You'll be out of there in no time. I promise."

He closed his eyes and lowered his chin to his paws.

"We must leave now if you want to make your meeting," Ivan said.

I wrapped my arms as far around the cage as I could and lifted it, careful not to jostle Chase into the sides.

"Would you like me to carry it?" Ash asked.

"I've got him."

Ash shrugged and opened the door for me. "As you wish."

* * *

TONY LET US out in front of the Chinese restaurant we'd been instructed to visit by Ivan's market contact. A red billboard painted with large gold characters advertising on-site dining, takeout, and delivery, as well as the store's phone number, spanned the length of the brick storefront. Blinds blocked any view through the front windows or glass door, which bore a white-and-red "closed" sign.

Ash stepped between a pair of stone lions positioned to either side of the entrance and tugged on the door. It swung open. They peeked inside then said, "It seems we're the first to arrive."

"Let's wait inside," I said.

Tony helped me maneuver Chase's cage out of the car.

"This is where we leave you," Ivan said. He nodded to Ash. "We'll be ready to move as soon as you send word."

Ash held the door open for me as I carried Chase's cage into the dark restaurant. The sound of the car's engine faded, then cut off as Ash let the door close. Dozens of round tables dotted the room, each draped with a white cloth and circled by red-and-gold-upholstered chairs. Large paper lanterns hung above each table. The walls were painted with floral murals, but the details were hard to make out in the dark.

I set Chase's cage on the nearest table and rolled my shoulders. Chase wasn't heavy, but all that metal was, and the bulky shape was awkward. I took a deep breath laced with sesame oil, oyster sauce, and garlic.

"How long do you think we have till the market representative shows up?" I asked.

Ash shrugged. "We have five minutes until our official interview time. Ivan indicated they were usually punctual."

"Are you worried about their security measures?" I glanced at Chase, wondering how to phrase my real question. "What if my glamour breaks when they cut me?"

"It won't." Ash walked a lazy circuit of the room, inspecting a golden dragon statue, a fish tank with only two fish in it, and the host podium near the door, which held a pile of menus and a laminated seating chart.

I leaned close to Chase's cage. It was difficult to see inside in the dim light that leaked through the blinds from the streetlights beyond, but Chase seemed to be curled up in the center. Burns weren't the only danger iron posed to the fae. Prolonged exposure to high concentrations could poison them.

"This will all be over soon," I whispered.

A swath of light cut across the room as the front door opened. The silhouette of a large man stepped into the restaurant. He glanced around the room, taking in Ash by the fish tank and me by the cage with a single look.

"Follow me." He crossed the dining room and ducked behind a wooden lattice near the back.

I lifted Chase's cage and hurried to follow, though I let Ash take the lead.

Behind the wooden lattice was a short hallway that ended in a set of restrooms to the left and opened into a large kitchen on the right. Lights flashed on as I followed our guide into the kitchen, and I had to stop as the sudden light blinded me. I blinked a few times, finally getting my eyes to focus.

The newcomer stood well over six feet tall. He was bald but had an impressive mustache with curled tips. He wore a denim jacket, brown slacks, and a gray patterned shirt.

"Set the merchandise there." He pointed to a long counter in the middle of the kitchen. Once I'd done as he asked, he said, "Ivan has vouched for you, but we have protocols for newcomers. This is for everyone's safety. You understand?"

"Of course," Ash said. "I'd expect no less."

The man nodded. "Show me your arm."

Ash rolled up their sleeve and extended their arm.

Mr. Mustache reached into a small backpack that I hadn't noticed before. From it he withdrew a sheathed knife, about six inches long. He freed the blade. The metal didn't glint as polished steel usually did. This blade was dark, almost black. It seemed to absorb light more than reflect it.

"Iron," the man explained. He set the blade against Ash's exposed skin, pressed until the edge sank in, and dragged it across.

Ash didn't blink. They stood statue still as blood welled from the slice, rolled to the underside of their arm, and dripped to the floor.

Mr. Mustache leaned close to inspect the wound.

I held my breath. While Ash was part fae, their fae blood had been twisted and changed by the Rift energy of their father. Like me, iron didn't affect them. I wasn't worried about Ash registering as fae. Ironically, it was the werewolf test they might not pass.

We all waited while Ash's blood continued to drip on the kitchen floor, long past the point where a werewolf . . . or a vampire . . . should have healed. Finally, Mr. Mustache pulled a towel out of his bag and wiped the wound. The blood smeared. The cut remained. The blood began to flow once more.

Mr. Mustache grunted, wiped the wound again, and applied a large, beige, bandage to cover the cut. Then he picked up his knife, wiped it clean, and turned to me.

I took a deep breath, shoved up my sleeve, and held out my arm. I was again caught off guard by the darkness of my skin. Ash hadn't made me as dark as Maggie, but the difference was still jarring compared to the pasty complexion granted by my Irish-German ancestry.

The iron blade seemed to draw the heat out of my skin. It reminded me of the deep cold of Bael's throne. Merciless. Unyielding.

Mr. Mustache pressed down, and I forced my arm to remain straight, though it may have shaken a little. Ash had managed to create and maintain an illusion of blood splattering against the floor during their own test. They should have no problem keeping my fake face intact for mine.

The blade slid away, and my flesh parted behind it. I hissed at the pain but managed not to move. Blood welled, dripped. Mr. Mustache followed the same procedure he had with Ash. Watch, wipe, bandage. He cleaned the blade, sheathed it, and stuffed it back in his bag. Then he wiped the blood off the floor with the same towel he'd used on both Ash and me and put that away as well.

"Are either of you practitioners?" Mr. Mustache asked.

"No." Ash responded immediately.

I shook my head and focused on pulling my sleeve down over my bandaged arm.

"Good. Then you won't mind wearing these." He dangled two thin metal rings from his fingers.

I swallowed and reminded myself that practitioner magic wasn't the only magic at my disposal. If push came to shove, I could still call on my fae magic. Right?

Then again, I didn't actually know how magic-dampening collars worked. . . .

The heavy smell of ginger and garlic that permeated the kitchen made my nose itch, but I forced myself to breathe steadily and hold still while Mr.

Mustache circled around behind me. My nerves crackled. Sweat prickled my scalp. My hair was lifted aside, the sensation making me shiver. Smooth steel touched the back of my neck, the sides. The ring completed, latching into place just over my collarbone with a magnetic snap.

Mr. Mustache moved to Ash.

My hands drifted up to the collar. The ring was less than an inch wide and about the thickness of a quarter. A five-knuckle hinge rested against the back of my neck, directly opposite a small box with rounded corners. That would be the locking mechanism.

I was tempted to call up my fae magic right then, to verify that I could still access it . . . but as I understood it, practitioners who tried to cast magic while wearing a collar ended up causing themselves immense pain as the magical energy completed a circuit that delivered an electric shock to the caster. The stronger the magic, the stronger the shock. Probably just touching my fae magic wouldn't shock me, but my magics tended to mix together. I might not be able to channel one without brushing up against the other, and I couldn't risk alerting Mr. Mustache that I had magic if I was wrong. So I lowered my hands to my sides and tried to act relaxed as Ash's collar was secured.

"Are we good to go now?" I asked.

"Almost," said Mr. Mustache. "I just need to verify the merchandise."

I gestured to Chase's cage. "See for yourself. He's in there."

Mr. Mustache peered through the front grate and whistled softly. "Shifter fae are hard to track. How'd you catch one?"

"Trade secret, I'm afraid," said Ash.

Mr. Mustache nodded, then he reached in his bag and pulled out a thin metal rod that telescoped to about two feet long.

I inched closer. "What are you doing?"

"I told you. Verifying." Mr. Mustache jammed the metal rod through the grate.

Chase let out a pained yowl and smacked against the back of the cage, trying to get away, but Mr. Mustache pinned him in place.

Ash's hands clamped around my upper arms, holding me fast. I hadn't even realized I'd moved, but every muscle in my body strained against their grip.

"Be calm," Ash whispered in my ear.

Mr. Mustache withdrew the iron rod.

Chase's scream tapered to a pitiful whimper. Seared meat might not have been out of place in the kitchen, but the smell of burnt fur made my stomach turn.

Ash gave my arms one last warning squeeze, then released me. When Mr. Mustache turned around, I had myself under control.

"He's the real deal." Mr. Mustache grinned at us, clearly impressed by our cargo.

I met his gaze as calmly as I could and forced myself to smile back, thinking, *You're going to pay for that.*

Mr. Mustache collapsed his rod and tucked it back in the bag, then he withdrew a handheld radio. Depressing a button on the side, he said, "Good to go."

A back door to the kitchen that blended almost perfectly with the white walls opened, and a second man stepped through. This one was shorter than Mr. Mustache—shorter than any of us, coming barely to my chin. He was stocky, with a bushy beard and frizzy brown hair that reached his shoulders. He reminded me of a dwarf from Lord of the Rings.

I frowned. *Could he actually* be *a dwarf?* Human lore about elves was based on a variety of fae species, including the sidhe. Stories about dwarves probably had a similar background. *I wonder which fae inspired them?*

The probably-not-a-real-dwarf held out a small tray that looked like a safety deposit box with a locking lid. "Cell phones and weapons." His voice was gruff but not unpleasant.

Ash dropped a phone and folding knife into the tray. These were both for show, since Ivan had warned us about the procedure. He'd supplied us each with burner phones and simple weapons, as would be expected. I placed my set of disposable possessions in the box as well. My actual phone was tucked alongside my gun and knife in my backpack at the safe house.

The new guy stepped back, and Mr. Mustache brought out a security wand. "Spread your arms and legs." He did a quick sweep with the wand to verify we didn't have any transmitting devices and gave us each a physical pat down to ensure we hadn't stashed any additional weapons. "Clear."

The second man closed and locked the metal box that held our props. He handed Ash a small silver key. "Don't lose this if you want your stuff back."

Ash nodded and tucked the key into their pocket.

"Follow me," said Mr. Mustache.

He slung his pack over one shoulder and led us out the back, into an alley that smelled of stale food and mildew. A silver SUV with tinted windows blocked most of the alley. He opened the back door and motioned us to climb inside. I slid through to the far seat and latched my seatbelt. We were almost there. This was going to work.

The second man carried Chase's cage to the back of the SUV and secured it in the trunk with bungee cords. When he was done, he circled the car and opened my door.

I looked at him curiously. "Forget something?"

"Last step," he said. He pointed, and I followed his finger to find Ash looking back at me. Mr. Mustache stood beside the other open door. A hypodermic needle glinted in his hand, moving toward Ash. Something sharp pierced the side of my neck.

I twisted, shoving the dwarf-like man away, but the cold pressure surging through my veins told me the damage was done. He closed my door, and the distant echo of a thud told me Ash's door had been closed as well. I turned to look, but the colors in the car streaked and ran together like paints in the rain.

What the hell was going on? Ivan hadn't mentioned anything about drugs.

I reached for the latch on my seatbelt, but my muscles turned to jelly. My fingers fumbled against the button. I couldn't depress it. Whatever he'd given me was very fast acting.

We passed all their stupid tests! But we must have done something to give ourselves away. Had Mr. Mustache noticed my reaction when he hurt Chase despite his back being turned? Had Ash's illusion wavered when their blood was wiped away?

I slumped in my seat. My shoulder bumped against Ash. My eyes closed. *It doesn't matter what tipped them off. We're screwed.*

Chapter 15

SWEAT, LEATHER, METAL, wood. . . . The scuff of a shoe. Someone clearing their throat. The brush of fingers against my wrist. I jerked awake with a gasp.

It took a moment for my eyes to adjust to the bright can lights recessed into the ceiling of the white-walled room in which I found myself. Half a dozen people slumped against the walls around me, including Ash immediately to my right. Their eyes were closed, but their hand rested next to mine. *Was it their touch that woke me?*

A woman in tight jeans, knee-high boots, and a black shirt that clung to her like a second skin stood in the middle of the room. She turned at my gasp, and her brown gaze found me. She strode forward. As she moved, light glinted from a silvery band around her neck, previously hidden by the chestnut hair cascading down her back. My hand rose of its own accord, fingers groping a matching collar.

Memories flooded back. The Chinese restaurant. Mr. Mustache and his stout companion. The tests. The collars. The needles.

I looked around the sterile room again. There was no sign of Chase or his cage. But the fact that there were other people present was a good sign . . . wasn't it?

"Good morning," said the woman who'd walked over.

Ash groaned and rubbed their eyes. Since most drugs didn't work on vampires, I assumed this groggy pantomime was an act put on for the woman looming over us.

"What happened?" Ash asked, looking as confused as I felt.

I glared at the woman. "They drugged us."

"A necessary precaution." She gestured to the room's other, still sleeping, occupants. "As you can see, it's standard operating procedure. Any lingering effects should wear off shortly."

"Where's my f—"

Ash nudged me.

"—fae?" I said instead of "friend." "The shifter I brought to auction."

"All auction goods are cataloged and secured in the staging area. Your ownership tag is there." She pointed to a red paper band—the kind you might get at a theme park or concert—looped around my wrist. It bore a six-digit number. Ash lifted their arm to show an identical band.

"We'll call the reference number on your band when your item goes up for auction."

I frowned, looking around the stark room. "And until then?"

"Eat. Drink. Shop." She gestured to the room's single exit. "Enjoy the market."

A rustle on the far side of the room brought our attentions to a pencil-thin young man in a blue suit who was holding his head as if nursing a hangover.

"If you'll excuse me," said the woman, and she walked toward the groaning man.

Ash was on their feet in an instant. They pulled me up as well, and we moved toward the door. The woman ignored us, repeating her greeting for the recently wakened man.

The door was plain. Not a single sound come from beyond it. Taking a deep breath, I reached out and twisted the handle.

Sounds and smells bombarded my senses. Amber light shone from thousands of small glass bulbs on crisscrossed cords overhead. A gentle breeze cooled my skin, circulated by massive fans set into the vaulted ceiling above the layer of lights. Gray acoustic foam lined the upper walls and ceiling, dampening echoes but failing to suppress the hundreds of conversations that filled the air with an endless, indistinct buzz.

Ash gripped my elbow, tugging me to the left. I reluctantly let the door to the sterile room swing closed.

We slunk along the near wall, behind stalls that opened toward a central aisle running lengthwise through the middle of the room. Red velvet cords marked the backs of booths and highlighted narrow paths that cut through to the main thoroughfare, but we kept to the back alley where the crowd was thin enough to navigate with only minimal weaving. We passed five doors identical to the one from which we'd emerged. Unlike the spiked foam that started just above the doorframes, the spaces between showed smooth concrete. I glanced again at the covered walls, strings of lights, and spinning fans. Despite this single room being many times larger than my entire house, there didn't appear to be any windows.

Are we in some kind of bunker?

Ash pulled me to a stop in a somewhat clear space, then glared at the nearest people until a circle of relative privacy opened around us.

Keeping their attention on the passersby, Ash leaned in and whispered, "We're a two-hour drive outside of town."

"I knew you were faking," I whispered back.

"I'd be insulted if you thought otherwise."

"Ivan never mentioned getting drugged." I crossed my arms, partly in anger at Ivan's oversight and partly to squash the anxiety that rippled through me at the memory of that needle plunging into my neck. "I thought we'd been discovered."

Ash shrugged. "It's been a few months since anyone from Ivan's nest attended the market. Maybe they changed the procedure."

"What about Chase?" I asked, even more quietly. "Is he really all right?"

"As 'all right' as a prisoner on an auction block can be." Ash lifted their wrist to show off our matching bracelets. "The goons who drove us here slapped one of these on your fae's cage before unloading us all, just like the lady in the white room said."

I nodded. "What now?"

They shrugged again. "We kill time until the auction."

* * *

I SLURPED BLENDED iced coffee out of a plastic cup in front of a booth set up as a café. I'd been surprised to find such a normal business operating at a "black market," but coffee wasn't the only comfort on hand in this subterranean superstore. Flames licked the sides of a massive wok two stalls down, and across the way, the aroma of garlic and chili wafted off a grill loaded with lightly charred, spiced corn. A quick lap of the perimeter had revealed more rooms opposite the ones from which waking guests continued to emerge and along one of the hall's shorter ends. These were labeled with colorful signs advertising short-term accommodations that ranged from private beds to exotic company. The other end was blocked by a red velvet curtain guarded by four people wearing green uniforms.

Now on my second tour down the central aisle, I took my time perusing the available merchandise. I had a persona to keep up, after all.

I jostled through the shoulder-to-shoulder crowd, trying not to spill my drink as tattooed thugs, jean-clad farmers, and businessmen in Armani suits all bumped against one another. Some shoppers wore black veils or ski masks that obscured their identities, and I found myself wondering if it was caution or shame that made them hide their faces. Some vendors shouted their wares while others just waited for shoppers to come, confident in the demand for their products. The overall effect reminded me of the fae market I'd visited each night in Enchantment, and I was surprised to realize how much I missed those outings.

I stopped at a table displaying finely engraved silver snuff boxes, like the one Mica so often pulled from his robes. A single, open box under a glass case showed a pile of shimmering pixie dust inside. The next booth was a three-sided stall lined top to bottom with weaponry. Swords, knives, and throwing stars hung alongside machine guns, pistols, and rifles. I took a moment to appreciate the craftsmanship on the blades before moving on. Iron curtains, chains, and leather pouches full of iron shavings shared a booth with a collection of warding charms that resembled wind chimes and promised to repel magical beings. I tapped one of the dangling items and recoiled—not because I was part fae, but because the suspended object turned out to be a small finger. The next display revealed equally gruesome jewelry. Bracelets and necklaces made of pointed teeth. Earrings with gossamer teardrops that might have been dragonfly wings but probably weren't.

I quickly moved on, but the next booth was even worse. Shocked, I hesitated long enough for the burly brunette behind the table to inquire if I was looking for anything in particular. The space behind her was packed with cages full of small, non-sapient fae creatures that bore shapes similar to frogs, hedgehogs, or, in one case, a golden retriever. I spotted three droust like the ones Bael had experimented on, and a single pyaku, though the red panda-like creature was much smaller than those I'd once ridden in Enchantment—probably a baby. The largest cage held something shaped like an oversize hyena with sleek black fur. White ridges that glinted like exposed bone curved below its eyes and traced its spine, tapering away to several whip-like tails. More cages hung from metal poles above, each containing one or more colorful birds. And suspended on individual stands on the table, tiny, blown-glass jars contained miniature people enveloped in crackling light.

"Spark sprites," the woman said. "Each one guaranteed to produce at least ten thousand joules before burnout."

Bile rose in the back of my throat.

"You interested?"

Shaking my head, I backed away from the tortured souls in their tiny prisons. Stepping into the current of shoppers, I bounced off a man wearing skin-tight leather pants and a biker jacket, spun around, and staggered to a stop in front of a stall selling an eclectic collection of what looked like totally mundane knickknacks. Frowning, I leaned in for a closer look. A tarnished mirror. An old coin. A silver spoon. A brass candlestick. My gaze settled on a jade marble the size of a penny. There was no reason such items would be for sale in a place like this, unless . . .

"You've got a keen eye," said a tall man with unkempt blond hair standing behind the display. "You won't find more powerful, or practical, artifacts anywhere."

I shivered. Fae artifacts were dangerous, illegal, and lucrative. Of course I would find some here.

"Take this little beaut, for example." He lifted the stone I'd been looking at. "Seems harmless enough. No circuitry. No metal. Easy to slip through security. But with the right command, this baby can petrify every living thing within ten thousand cubic feet."

I frowned at the man, appalled that such a device even existed, let alone that he thought I'd actually *want* such a thing. I swallowed, thinking of the small silver box I'd once held that had ended an entire world, and nearly done the same to mine. A box I'd last seen sitting on a shelf in Bael's workroom. A splitting ache drilled into my skull—a warning from the geas Bael had placed on me so that I could never share my knowledge of that terrible tool.

Shying away from those painful thoughts, my mind turned to the PTF agent who'd collected fae artifacts by tracking down and murdering their halfer guardians, including one of my best friends. "Where did you get these?" I couldn't keep the accusation out of my voice.

" 'Fraid I can't say." The merchant scratched his shaggy blond head, exposing the blue bracelet on his wrist.

Everyone at the market wore a bracelet—another tidbit Ivan had failed to mention. Near as I could figure, the bracelets were a classification system. Red bracelets, like mine, marked people with items in the auction and doubled as ownership tags. Vendors wore blue. People wearing yellow seemed to be exclusively shoppers with nothing to sell. I hadn't figured out what the green or black bands meant yet. Along with the colored bands, nearly one third of the attendees wore magic control collars like the one around my neck.

Thinking about the collar made me feel as if I were choking.

"How much for the marble?" Ash asked, leaning in at my shoulder.

I jumped. Ash had faded into the crowd shortly after our first circuit, mumbling about taking a closer look and slipping away before I could voice an objection. I hadn't spotted them since, so having them suddenly show up beside me was a bit disconcerting.

"Thirty thousand," said the man.

That *did* make me choke. That damned pebble cost more than my car! Then again, something like that could take out the entire peace summit I was here to protect in one deadly stroke if it made it past the door. I made a mental note to ask David what precautions were in place against artifacts getting smuggled in.

"Maybe later," I grabbed Ash's sleeve and pulled them down one of the side paths that connected the crowded central aisle with the slightly less crowded perimeter.

"Where have you been?" I hissed.

"Sightseeing. Though you're the one acting like a tourist. You need to control your expressions better. I could spot you as a bleeding heart from a mile away."

"Well, excuse me for having a soul."

Ash opened their mouth, but before they could speak the overhead lights flashed off and on twice. The milling shoppers stilled. The room hushed. I held my breath.

"Good afternoon, everyone." The voice, an airy soprano, blared from speakers set around the room at the same level as the lights. "If you'll please direct your attention to the main stage."

The red curtains that blocked off one end of the large room rose, revealing an elevated wooden platform with stairs on either side. A middle-aged woman with freckled skin and white-blond hair stood center stage with a microphone. Her low-slung, too-tight, gold dress sparkled under the lights. Four men and two women in green uniforms and control collars stood at attention behind her.

"Welcome to the market. Now that everyone's had a chance to refresh themselves and peruse the general wares, we're ready to kick off the main event. But first, I'll go over a few house rules so we can keep things moving smoothly." She sashayed back and forth on the stage as she spoke, high heels *click-clacking* against the boards, magnified by the microphone.

"If you have an item in the auction, please pay attention when your lot number is called. Once the final bid for an item is confirmed, I'll indicate one of the numbered rooms to the left of the stage." She gestured to the doors from which I, and the other unconscious guests, had emerged. Each now bore a glowing number above the door. "At least one representative and no more than three from both the selling party and the purchasing party will join a member of the market staff to finalize the details of the transaction. If you have multiple lots for auction, your items will be spaced accordingly to provide ample time between transactions." She stopped her pacing and faced the audience. "That said, we have a full docket today, so don't dawdle."

"What if an item comes up that we want to bid on while we're completing a transaction in one of the private rooms?" shouted a man from the audience.

"Enlist a partner to pick up the slack," the woman replied. "Otherwise, better luck next time." She barely paused before barreling on. "Lastly, I want to remind you all that the use of magic, of any type and from any source, is strictly prohibited. If you're caught using magic, and we *will* catch you, you'll be banned from participating in any future markets." She gave the crowd an intense side-eye through lowered lashes. "That's *if* you're still breathing. So keep those baubles you just bought in your pockets until tomorrow. Now, let's get this show on the road."

Many of the shoppers migrated toward the stage, though some took the opportunity to engage with the vendors now that the crowd had thinned a bit. Ash and I drifted toward the stage as well, but stayed near the back of the group; we weren't planning to bid on anything.

A set of two-way double doors—like those you might find in a restaurant's kitchen—opened to the right of the stage. A woman in the black outfit of a stagehand rolled a cloth-covered cart up a ramp and parked it under a blinding spotlight.

"First up," said the woman with the mic, "is lot three-seven-nine-two-A, a set of maps depicting the locations of three unregistered fae portals. Lucrative hunting grounds for those with the courage to make use of them."

The black-clad figure yanked the cloth off the cart to reveal a yellowed scroll on a wooden stand inside a glass case beside two more modern sheets of folded paper.

"We'll start the bidding at two thousand dollars."

The crowd, which had been perfectly still during the item's description, erupted as numbers—as well as a few threats and insults—were shouted back and forth. Hands shot into the air like popcorn, some only once, some over and over. When no new hands rose, the woman with the microphone pressed a button on a small device that created a loud chime. "Sold for fifty-seven hundred dollars to the serious-looking gentleman in the rawhide trench coat. Please make your way to room one."

The stagehand wheeled the cart with its merchandise down the opposite side of the stage and through a second set of double doors. Almost immediately, the first set of doors opened again, and a second covered cart—nearly twice the size of the first and accompanied by three stagehands—was brought out.

"Next is one of our big ticket items," the hostess declared. "Lot three-six-four-eight."

One of the helpers removed the cloth cover with a flourish.

My mouth went dry. Inside a four-foot-square cage knelt a human boy wearing an oversize T-shirt and loose jeans. He couldn't have been more than fifteen years old. Unkempt, mousy brown hair shaded his eyes, casting deep shadows under the spotlight. Modern handcuffs anchored his wrists to the cage between his knees, and a metal collar ringed his neck.

"Ever wish you had on-demand medical services? Maybe you've been injured in the field, far from help. Maybe you watched a friend die because they couldn't afford the ridiculous rates charged by registered healers. Maybe you just want a cut of that action. Whether you're looking to extend your life or line your pockets . . . here's your golden goose. An unregistered, undocumented practitioner with a talent for healing."

Murmurs echoed around the room, and even some of the shoppers who clearly weren't planning to participate in the auction drifted closer.

"The bidding starts at one-hundred-fifty thousand."

Again the popcorn hands shot up, and the shouts grew louder and more colorful as the numbers steadily rose. Eventually, the buzzer sounded, and the poor kid was sold for half a million dollars—a good deal considering what he could offer. Healers were rare, and expensive. Having a personal practitioner was unheard of . . . at least in any legal, moral society.

The slave was trundled offstage, while the people selling him went to room three to shake hands and transfer funds.

I wanted to puke.

"Lot three-two-oh-five. This little beauty has been causing quite a stir lately."

My attention swung back to the stage, where the cover had just been pulled off another small, one-man cart. The hostess gestured to a glass box with dozens of tiny vials suspended inside.

"One dose and you won't have to fear the fae anymore. Super strength, invisibility, telepathy . . . gain the perks of magic without giving up one ounce of your humanity. Or pad the price and make a fortune. Sixty doses of Fantasia, yours for the starting price of just fifteen hundred dollars."

The bidding war went faster this time, with the final price topping out at just over three thousand.

I watched the people bidding, doing my best to memorize faces so I could describe them to Everly when I got home. Maybe she could get to these dealers before more drugs hit the streets. But it was the seller that I was really interested in. When the hostess announced room five as the meet-up point for the Fantasia transaction, a petite woman with shoulder-length blond hair split off from the group she seemed to be a part of and made her way toward the private rooms. If Fantasia really was coming out of a lab near here, that would be the group that could lead me to the source.

I balled my fists.

"Lot three-nine-one-seven," announced the hostess. "A bona fide fae shifter."

I glanced at the bracelet on my wrist. *This is it.*

Two helpers wheeled the next cart out, and one whipped off the cover to reveal a small gray tabby hunkered in the middle of a mesh-lined cage. Tufts of singed fur and burned skin showed where he'd bumped against the cage or been prodded by iron rods like the one Mr. Mustache had used to test him, and I found myself silently repeating the promise that these people would pay.

Chase arched his back and hissed at the crowd, which responded with jeers and catcalls.

My heart twisted to see Chase looking so vulnerable. It was all I could do to stop myself running onto the stage to let him out.

The hostess lifted her hands, and the crowd fell silent.

"Break his spirit and keep him as a pet, or put him down and sell him for parts. The starting bid for this caged kitty is eight thousand dollars."

Hands shot up as the bids rose, but the contenders quickly whittled down to three real options. One was the group the absent blond belonged to. Their bids were being fielded by a tall man in a plaid dress shirt. The other bidders included two burly men who spoke German and might have been twins and a Korean man in a business suit.

I wish I had my phone so I could take pictures of all these assholes.

Blondie's companions placed the winning bid at just over fourteen thousand dollars, and the hostess directed us to room four. The man in plaid moved away from his group.

Between selling Fantasia and bidding on fae, these people have to be connected to Purity's drug lab. The knowledge that I was getting closer to my goal almost made me smile, but nothing could ease the pain I felt at watching Chase get wheeled offstage and through the auction doors.

Hang on, buddy. I'm coming.

I nudged Ash and headed for the private room where Mr. Plaid was about to shake hands with a devil and tell us everything we wanted to know.

* * *

A REDHEADED MAN in the green uniform of a market representative stood in front of the door to room four. Mr. Plaid waited beside him. Once we were inside, it would be my job to restrain the buyer while Ash neutralized the greater threat of the guard. Then we could take our time getting the information we needed.

"Are you the sellers?" the representative asked when we arrived.

Ash and I each raised our arms to show the matching numbers on our wristbands.

He nodded, opened the door, and gestured for us to precede him.

"I haven't seen you at the market before," said Mr. Plaid as he led the way.

"We don't usually work in this area," I said. From the way he moved, Mr. Plaid struck me as more of a clerk than a mercenary. Still, looks could be deceiving.

"Oh? Where's your normal stomping ground? Perhaps I could put you in touch with one of our sister organizations."

The dull hum of the main chamber cut off as the market representative closed the door.

I glanced behind me.

Ash blurred. In the span of a single heartbeat, Ash had their hands braced on either side of the guard's face. Ash was slightly shorter than the redhead, so they had to look up to maintain eye contact. I expected to see the representative's eyes glaze over as Ash's magic took hold. Instead, Ash frowned.

Mr. Plaid turned, noticed the odd tableau, and furrowed his brow. "What are you—"

I intercepted the arm he was raising to point at Ash and twisted it behind his back to lock out his shoulder. Then I drove my heel into the back of his knee, forcing him to the ground. The fight was over before it began. I'd been right about Mr. Plaid's combat skills.

"What the hell do you think you're doing?" bellowed my prisoner. "Let go of me!" He could shout all he wanted. These rooms were soundproofed for privacy.

"Shit." Ash's curse drew my attention.

As I looked up, the guard hit the floor with a heavy *thud*—neck snapped, eyes staring.

The man I was holding whimpered and tried to break free. I tightened my grip, eliciting a sharp gasp, but most of my attention stayed on the dead man.

Ash dropped to a knee in front of us, rustling my hair with the breeze of their movement.

"Why did you kill him?" I hissed. "That wasn't the plan. Now they'll know something is wrong as soon as we step out of this room."

"He had a mental ward in place to prevent tampering, and I don't think it was his, which means there are likely more guards on their way."

"Shit!" I echoed.

"You'll need to deal with whoever comes in while I get what we need." Ash reached out, tore the collar off my neck, and tossed the pieces away.

Bringing their wrist to their lips, Ash bit into their flesh, wiped the oozing blood onto two fingers, and shoved them into my prisoner's mouth. Mr. Plaid's eyes dilated and glazed over. Vampires could enthrall human minds without sharing blood, but this was faster and would grant Ash instant access to the man's thoughts. It might also break his psyche, but, considering the corpse by the door, we were past subtlety.

"How long will—"

The door slammed open, revealing a tall, thin man wearing a green market uniform and a newsboy cap over long blond hair. He lifted his arms, revealing a black band on his wrist.

I disentangled myself from Mr. Plaid and straightened.

The new man dropped his arms, a conductor marking the downbeat, and an invisible force slammed me to my hands and knees. Mr. Plaid grunted and coughed a spray of blood as he collapsed to the floor. Even Ash hunched under the pressure.

Of course they would send magic users to suppress a magical security breach, I chided myself. *That must be what the black wristbands denote.*

Shaking under the enormous weight trying to crush me, I called on the more offensively useful of my two magics, grateful to have the collar off. Blue-gray fog rolled at the edges of my vision as I connected to the energy of the Rift—the chaotic space between realms from which practitioners drew magic. Hazy faces peered through the veil as I called my power, but the filter of fae magic within me, thin though it was, dissuaded the demons who dwelled in the Rift from coming closer.

The blond man circled us like a shark, hands extended. Three more people came into the room, all in green uniforms. More magic-users? Or a cleanup crew to scrape us off the floor after the first guy turned us into pancakes?

The pressure on my back and shoulders multiplied. My elbows buckled, dropping me to my forearms. My forehead touched the floor. Sweat dripped down my face. My lungs labored to expand. Red tinged my vision.

I glanced at Ash. They were on their stomach beside the prone Mr. Plaid, but Ash's expression was calm, concentrated, as they stared into Mr. Plaid's eyes. How long would it take to rummage through the man's thoughts and find what we needed? I had to buy that time. Everly was counting on me to protect the peace talks, and Chase was counting on me to get him out of the cage I'd put him in. I couldn't afford to crumble here.

Gritting my teeth, I channeled magic through my muscles to keep from being completely overwhelmed. Then I focused on forming a ball of compressed air between my palms. My hands shook. When the pressure against my palms was greater than the pressure at my back, I surged upward with a wild cry and launched my magical projectile at the stick figure who'd dropped an invisible building on me.

The magic missile caught him in the chest, knocking him clear off his feet. The pressure vanished.

I gasped for breath.

The man's hat fluttered to the ground.

"Oh ho!" One of the three who'd followed the blond man inside—a slim woman with a buzzed head, purple lip gloss, and iridescent green eyeshadow that made her look like an insect—planted her hands on her hips. She grinned at me. "Looks like we might get a workout with this one."

The woman and her two remaining companions each wore a black wristband. Whether enslaved practitioners like the boy in the auction, or regular humans souped up on Fantasia, this lot was dangerous . . . and four against one were not good odds. Still, I had a job to do.

I climbed unsteadily to my feet and grinned back.

Chapter 16

THE WOMAN BLURRED and disappeared.

A fist slammed into the side of my face.

The world tipped as I staggered, but I regained my balance in time to pivot with the next attack, lessening the blow. The woman's hits weren't particularly hard, but she was fast. Maybe as fast as a vampire. Luckily, I'd had some experience fighting vampires.

I relaxed my vision, relying instead on my other senses. The scuff of a shoe. A waft of air. The scent of sweat and almonds. The slightest pressure against my skin.

I twisted as the next punch came in, scooping my arm under her extended shoulder and matching my hips to hers. The momentum of her attack carried her onto my back as I cut out her base and rotated.

She toppled over my shoulder and slammed to the ground. I grabbed her wrist for a follow-up, but a flash of light drew my attention to the remaining combatants. A man with dark skin and a weightlifter's body had both his arms extended toward me, fingers splayed. Half-a-dozen spinning blades that looked to be made of glass or ice flew toward me.

I jumped away, twisting to dodge as best I could, but the translucent knives were too close and clustered too densely to avoid them all. A gash opened on my upper arm, another on my thigh. I stumbled and dropped to one knee.

The final member of the market's magical suppression squad loped forward on long, muscular legs. She lifted one leg into a full vertical split and swung it down in a perfect ax kick.

I dove to the side.

The woman's boot hit the ground with a deafening *crack*. Concrete shattered. Earth compacted. The space where I'd been kneeling became a crater.

Holy shit! If that hit me, I'd be dead!

I rolled to my feet, putting as much distance between myself and the wrecking ball of a woman as I could.

The speedy girl's fist connected with my cheek. A kick slammed into the back of my knee, dropping me as I'd dropped Mr. Plaid.

Rather than immediately jumping up—an instinct drilled into me from hours of training with my werewolf sparring partner—I pressed my palms to the floor, exhaled, and focused on my magic. I found the core of the concrete beneath my hands, and I loosened the bonds between its component parts.

A yelp sounded to my left. The speedy woman's foot sank into my newly created sand trap. She stumbled, jerking to a stop with her foot buried to the ankle as I snapped the concrete back to its natural state and rolled out of reach.

The woman shrieked and railed, but these guards all seemed to be one-trick ponies—humans boosted on Fantasia. Real practitioners, like me, had a bigger bag of tricks.

I wiped sweat from my forehead to keep it out of my eyes as the slower, stronger woman closed on me.

Behind her, the first man I'd sent flying was back on his feet, and the guy with the magic knives sent a volley of daggers spinning toward Ash's exposed back.

I sent an arc of unrefined energy into the blades aimed at Ash, scattering them before they could hit their mark, then I ducked as the larger woman's fist sailed toward my head in a skull-crushing haymaker.

The wall behind me exploded on impact, showering me with debris and choking me with concrete dust.

A piece of rubble shifted under my foot as I tried to bolt, dropping me to my hands and knees. I looked up. My world shrank to the woman's interlaced fingers as they came down in a two-fisted follow-up guaranteed to obliterate me.

There was no time to dodge, no time to cast a spell. The world muted, drowned out by the rushing in my ears as I watch my impending death approach.

Pale arms wrapped around the woman's waist. She jerked backward, yanked off her feet. The barest brush of her knuckles skimmed past my nose.

The rest of the room flared back into existence.

Ash flung the burly woman across the room, where she slammed into the dark-skinned knife wielder who'd been preparing his next volley. The woman screamed as she became his inadvertent pin cushion before sandwiching him into the back wall.

I groped for purchase along the shattered concrete and stood up. Beyond the hole, an alarm flared to life, shrieking like a banshee. Red and white lights created a strobelike effect in the room beyond as vendors and guests ran in stop-motion flashes.

Ash took a step toward the last guard standing.

The man who'd tried to turn us into pancakes when he first walked in stepped back, his face a mask of panic. He raised his hands.

Pressure slammed into me, as did Ash, and we both flew backward through the hole in the wall.

Wood splintered, glass shattered, and fabric tore as we plowed through one vendor's stall, across the aisle, and into another, scattering people and products in our wake. Several cages burst open as they hit the floor. A small pyaku streamed over my legs and rushed up a wall, like some huge, furry insect, to dig at an overhead vent cover. Sprites and birds flitted like technicolor confetti through the air. I jerked away from a crablike creature that scurried over my hand.

Ash tore the locks off more prisons, freeing their occupants. The large, hyena-like creature I'd seen earlier stalked out of its cage, tails lashing like snakes. It bounded past me and tore into one of the fleeing vendors, clamping solid jaws around the woman's forearm and yanking her off her feet.

Gunshots cracked in clustered bursts from a line of soldiers standing along the front edge of the stage, rifles to shoulders, Mr. Mustache among them. A wall of translucent orange light blocked the stage area, fueled, it seemed, by a petite woman who stood off to one side with her arms raised and her eyes closed. She wore the same uniform as the other guards and a black wristband. The orange glow was more pronounced, almost opaque, around her. Frantic people looking to escape the freed creatures slammed their fists against the magical barrier, sending ripples over the surface. The light kept them out, but the guards' bullets didn't seem to have any trouble passing through.

The hyena-creature flinched and flailed as some of the shots found their mark. It shattered three more stalls before it barreled into the crowd, dragging its screaming human chew-toy with it.

Another burst of gunfire accompanied an explosion of concrete dust as I rolled to my feet, narrowly avoiding being turned into Swiss cheese. I bolted in a scrambling hunch for a nearby armor vendor's stall and vaulted the side. Bullets pinged off the shields, vests, and helmets on display.

Ash soared overhead, skidding to a stop beside me. They mumbled something, but their words were drowned out by the sirens, screams, and ricocheting bullets pounding in my ears.

I peeked around the side of my cover, examining the orange barrier. *Chase is back there somewhere.*

I turned to Ash and opened my mouth to ask what the plan was when the world went dark. Not dark as in the simple lack of light when you close your eyes. The light vanished, yes, but so did the sound, and the smells, and the very ground beneath my knees. I floated, formless, in an absolute void.

My heart pounded. At least I could still feel *that*. I reached out, groping for purchase. Something closed around my wrist, and I jerked in surprise, though even through the fear I felt a surge of relief at the contact.

Ash's face came into focus. Their grip on my arm was strong as steel. The darkness receded. People stumbled all around us, groping with their arms out, flopping on the ground as though trying to swim, rolling over each other as they flailed for purchase.

"We have to go." Ash pulled me toward the back of the room.

I pulled back, motioning toward the stage, where the line of soldiers stood statue still, guns raised but eyes unfocused. "Chase is this way."

"We can't get to him through that barrier."

"Then we bring it down," I said. "I'm the reason he's here, and I'm not leaving without him."

"He'll be fine," Ash said. "We, on the other hand, are in serious danger."

"They know we weren't real poachers. They'll kill him."

"No matter how he came into their care, he's still a valuable commodity. As long as he's caged, his position hasn't changed. Ours, however, has. If you want any chance at saving him, we need to get out of here, *now*."

A blazing flash of white washed out the world.

I blinked, rubbing tears from my eyes.

The people around us stopped moving as though blind and looked around.

"Well, shit," Ash swore. "They have Tamsin's Mirror."

I peeked over the shelter of our shields toward the source of the white light and spotted the market host holding what looked like a silver hand mirror over her head. "What's that?"

"A powerful fae artifact that shatters illusions." Ash gestured to my hand, resting against the glittering green scales of a dragon-hide shield. "Even mine."

I stared at my hand—pale and callused with a scattering of freckles across the back. I grabbed a lock of my hair and pulled it into view. Auburn. My disguise had vanished along with the darkness.

"Shit," I echoed. *So much for flying under the radar.*

"There are too many variables in this fight," Ash said. "We have what we need. We should get out."

I cast another look at the auction stage. Bursts of gunfire flashed as guards targeted the fae creatures we'd released from their cages. A magical shield, a platoon of soldiers, the host with her mirror, and who knew how many other practitioners and fae artifacts stood between me and the door through which Chase had been taken. A frontal assault would be suicide.

I nodded stiffly, feeling like I might throw up.

Ash yanked me to my feet. I swung the dragonscale shield around to guard my back as we burst from cover.

Gunshots rang out. Bullets pinged off the armored scales. A man to my left gripped his throat, blood oozing between his fingers, and collapsed. Something that looked like an elaborate dream catcher burst into a cloud of white feathers on my right.

Halfway down the aisle, Ash snatched something off the floor, whispered into their hand, and lobbed the jade stone the vendor had tried to sell me earlier into the air behind us. I glanced over my shoulder as I ran, tracking its course. Soft green light expanded from the stone as it soared toward the stage. A sprite who'd been buzzing overhead froze mid-flight. The electric blue of its skin turned dull gray. The petrified sprite shattered when it hit the ground.

Color drained out of the gravity mage, starting where the light touched his fingertips, until he was a statue standing amid the rubble of the broken wall with his hands raised, a look of rage chiseled on his features. People screamed as the green light expanded. The gunfire tapered off.

Ash pulled up short in front of an iron scissor gate and tore the locking mechanism out of the wall. Dropping my shield, I grabbed the bars and pulled the gate open until there was a gap large enough to slip through.

"Alex!" Ash wrapped around me, cocooning me with their body.

Glowing blades thudded into the wall on either side of the tunnel. Heat blazed across my upper arm, quickly turning damp with blood. Ash jerked against me then sagged to the side, flopping to the ground with a heavy *thump*. Their eyes stared blankly at the ceiling.

"Ash!"

I glanced behind me. The practitioner who'd thrown the knives was grinning wickedly. The burly woman who'd punched the hole in the wall barreled toward me like a charging bull.

I grabbed Ash's wrists and dragged them into the tunnel.

Even if I could lock the gate behind us, a few inches of metal wouldn't stop the locomotive of a woman bearing down on us.

"Come on, Ash," I said through gritted teeth as I pulled. "This is no time to play dead."

My foot slipped, and I landed hard on my ass.

The woman's face twisted with grim anticipation.

I glanced around the tunnel. Concrete floor, concrete walls, and a low, concrete ceiling with an electrical cable snaking along the center to power a string of overhead lights. A section of one wall had crumbled where Ash had ripped the latch free.

Focusing on that weak point, I pulled energy into my body and poured it into the wall. Cracks shot from the breach, shooting across the wall and up over the ceiling. Chunks of concrete broke loose. Sweat poured down my face and dripped into my eyes. My hand shook. I closed my fist. A sound like thunder cracked through the tunnel. The ceiling collapsed.

I tucked my hands under Ash's armpits and heaved, scooting us backward as the cave-in expanded.

The bull-like woman's raging face disappeared as the rubble snuffed her battle cry.

The light above flickered and died. Silence and darkness stole my senses as thoroughly as Ash's spell.

"Ash?" I whispered. Dust clogged my throat, making me cough.

I collapsed the tunnel. Fear gripped me as the reality of my situation sank in. *What if there's no other way out?*

The air suddenly felt thick and warm. My pulse raced.

"Ash," I said again. I shook the corpse in my arms. "Wake up."

I'd seen vampires recover from being impaled, slashed, smashed, and snapped. A knife or two should have been nothing. Why wasn't Ash moving?

The longest I'd seen a vampire take to recover from an injury—short of decapitation—had been when James snapped a vampire's neck . . . repeatedly.

I groped along Ash's shoulders to their neck. A knife protruded just below their hairline, right at the base of their skull. Anxiety and adrenaline spiked through my system. Had the blade severed Ash's spinal cord? Did that count as decapitation?

I thought of James, half a world away. If Ash died for real, would James feel it? Would all of Ash's immortal children shrivel away to nothing, ravaged by the effects of too much time on suddenly mortal bodies? That was the prevailing theory among the fae, the reason they'd hunted Ash so relentlessly over the millennia. A single blow to strike down every vampire on Earth.

"No," I gritted through clenched teeth. "Dammit, Ash, you wake the hell up!"

I yanked the knife out of Ash's neck.

Ash jerked on my lap, took a shuddering breath, and sat up.

I exhaled, letting the knife fall from my shaking fingers. Ash held the key to saving Chase, the promise of vampire cooperation, and James's life in their hands. Those were reason enough to be happy they'd survived, but I was surprised to find I was also just relieved that Ash was still alive. Well, as alive as a vampire could be. Maybe I just didn't want to be alone in the dark.

"Much appreciated," Ash said. Light bloomed, a faint bluish glow that danced above Ash's hand and made my skin crawl. I didn't have happy memories of dark places with blue lights. "What's the situation?"

I shook myself, pulling back from that memory so I could focus on the present.

"I thought you were dead."

"They got a lucky shot. What happened after I went down?"

"I dragged you into the tunnel and collapsed it behind us." I looked at the pile of rubble and settling dust. "I doubt it will take long for those magic users to get through. There's also a chance they'll circle around from the main exit and come at us from the other end."

"Then we'd best get moving." Ash stood, plucked a knife out of their arm, another out of their leg, and motioned toward their back. "Would you mind?"

I pulled out the final crystalline dagger, burrowed between Ash's shoulder blades. Blood spurted, slowed, and stopped. I considered keeping the weapon for when the bad guys caught up, but the blade was made from someone else's magic. I couldn't trust it, so I let it clatter to the floor. Staring at the pile of bloody blades that had been meant for me, I whispered, "I'm glad you're okay."

Ash flashed me a humorless smile. "Were you afraid you'd lost your map, or worried about your boyfriend?"

"Both," I admitted. "But I'm also just glad you're okay."

They gave me a strange look. "We'll be faster if I run for both of us."

I nodded, and Ash scooped me off my feet. Wind snapped at my hair as the gray uniformity of the tunnel slid past, illuminated by the bobbing blue light zipping along beside us.

"How did you know the trigger word for that fae artifact?" I asked breathlessly as I bumped against Ash's chest. Their hold on me wasn't as gentle as James's always was. Ash didn't seem used to carrying people, handling me more like a sack of potatoes than a passenger.

"I've been around a long time," Ash said quietly. "I've encountered that relic before."

Ahead, a set of stairs dead-ended at a pair of metal panels set into the ceiling. Ash shifted my weight to one arm, extended the other, and slammed into them. For a split second, Ash's hand was illuminated against bright steel as light poured into the tunnel. Then their skin began to sizzle.

I landed hard on the stairs as Ash dove away from the opening. The door slammed shut with a resounding *thud* that echoed through the tunnel. The smell of charred flesh assailed me.

Blinking away the afterimage of sunlight, I gingerly rose and crept back down the stairs.

Ash crouched near a wall a little way up the passage, rocking back and forth and cradling their hand. The watery blue light they'd summoned flickered near their shoulder, pushing back the darkness.

"Are you—"

"I'll be fine," Ash snapped.

I moved closer but froze when their gaze swung to me. The black of Ash's eyes had bled to the edges, and gold swirled through their centers. Even through that alien appearance, I recognized the hunger in them. Ash was a vampire—an injured vampire—and the fastest way for a vampire to heal . . . was to feed.

I swallowed. Sweat prickled my scalp. I took a step back. "I'm going to look around." My voice sounded oddly flat. I took another step backward, keeping my eyes on Ash. "Maybe I can find something to cover you with long enough to climb into a vehicle."

"Just remember," Ash said, "I know where your friend is being taken. Leave me here, and you'll never find the lab."

My anxiety gave way to anger. "You don't need to be an asshole. I wouldn't have left you regardless." Turning away, I went back to the stairs and carefully pushed open one of the overhead doors. Ash was far enough back that the warm, yellow glow couldn't reach them, but I slipped through quickly and closed the door, just in case. The hatch was set into a concrete cylinder that protruded about four feet above the ground. I straightened and looked around.

"Well . . . shit."

Towering corn fields stretched in every direction. Cicadas buzzed. A gentle breeze sent ripples across the sea of green stalks and tugged my hair, but the blazing sun already had me sweating, and there was no escape in sight. The nearest structure was a large wooden barn, at least two stories tall and three times as wide. Judging by the distance and direction, that was probably the main entrance to the market. It wouldn't take our pursuers long to reach us, even with the confusion below and the head start Ash's speed had bought. Slightly farther away to the left, a white, single-story farmhouse sat beside two silver silos. My heart sank. Even sprinting, I couldn't reach the farmhouse, let alone hotwire a car and get back to Ash, before our attackers came out of the barn.

"Think, Alex. Think!" I pressed my fists to my temples and turned around once more, searching for some bastion of hope amid the blazing daylight. Fields. Fields. More fields. A few scattered trees, and some groves in the distance that were probably planted around other farmhouses. Nothing close enough to be useful, and nothing to protect Ash from the sun.

"Damn it!" I dropped to a squat, bunching my fingers into my hair. I stared at the ground, steeling myself to deliver the bad news. Something glinted in the dirt.

Curious, I hopped down and pried a hefty piece of quartz out of the ground. It was cool against my palm but seemed to glow in the sunlight.

My heart skipped a beat.

Could I?

Clutching the stone to my chest, I slipped back into the tunnel. Maybe my time in Enchantment hadn't been such a waste after all.

Chapter 17

"YOU WANT ME to what?!" Ash stared at me incredulously. Now that we were alone, Ash had relaxed the stiffer posture and mannerisms they'd adopted during our trip to Chicago, falling somewhere between the two personas I'd witnessed since finding them in my home. Their hair had come down during our tussle in the market, the asymmetrical bangs covering one side of their face and softening the angle of their jaw.

"I want you to trust me," I said.

"Trust you . . ." Ash continued to stare at me, as if hoping what I'd said would suddenly make sense. They pointed at the cellar door. "By going out there?"

"You have a better idea?" I asked. "We're running out of time."

Ash shook their head. "I'd rather take my chances with whoever comes after us."

"At least let me test my theory."

Ash pursed their lips and lifted their injured hand, skin shiny pink and blistered. "Do you have any idea how much this hurts? It's like being burned, flayed, and frozen all at once."

"I can't imagine," I said quietly. "But I should be able to protect you."

"*Should* . . . using magic that, by your own admission, you failed to master in Enchantment."

I took a deep breath, pushing through my doubts. "I failed to make daywalking amulets, that's true, but I *was* able to funnel a significant amount of sunlight into a stone." I held up the quartz. "I can redirect the sun that would otherwise hit you into this . . . at least, for a little while. Long enough for us to get somewhere safe." I stared into those gold-streaked, abyssal eyes. "I *can* do this."

Ash rubbed a hand over their forehead and pushed to their feet. They looked incredibly tired. "What do you need me to do?"

"This spell takes a lot of focus," I said. "I won't be able to maintain it *and* run, so you'll have to carry me."

"Easy enough."

"And I'll need to tap into your core," I continued.

Ash frowned. "Like you did in Canada?"

I nodded.

They rubbed their uninjured hand against their chest. "I did *not* enjoy that."

"I can't promise you'll like it any better this time," I whispered. "If anything, I'll need to go even deeper to make sure the spell covers every inch of you."

Ash looked down the dark tunnel, up to the closed hatch, and back to me. Their lip curled. "Fine." They scooped me up and moved toward the exit, bracing their back against the shielding metal. "Tell me when you're ready."

Taking a deep breath, I called up my imbuing magic and let my awareness sink into the quartz cradled in my hands. My stomach grumbled. I'd already used a considerable amount of magic today, not to mention the blood I'd lost from all the cuts and scrapes I'd accumulated during the market fight; I needed fuel, and soon. Pushing past the discomforts of my physical body, I focused on the rough edges and clouded surfaces of the quartz. Not an ideal receptacle for trapping sunlight, but I had to make it work. I plucked the threads of the crystal's core, just as I had day after day in Bael's workshop, until I held a prison for the sunlight we were about to collect. Then I created the paths that would funnel light safely from the outer edges of the spell to the prison inside.

I exhaled, taking a moment to center myself. Next came the hard part—anchoring the spell. Harder still because of who I was anchoring it to.

Ash might have been one of the stone statues we'd left in the market if not for the sluggish beat of a pulse thudding against my shoulder and the occasional tickle of a breath across my forehead. Setting my hand against the black, blood-encrusted fabric over their chest, I trailed the tethers of my spell as my awareness sank toward the convoluted maze of Ash's core. The tunnel vanished. The aches of bruises, cuts, and hunger faded away. I floated in a forest of spider silk webs.

Sinking deeper, I found the thicker strands of Ash's core, solid enough to hold the anchors for my spell. I chose the strongest thread and set to work. My senses brushed the memory buried there as I tied off my spell.

The melodic strains of a song sung in a language I'd never heard, but could somehow understand, drifted to the nest of blankets where I lay.

"Saedeul suhong gajeseilo,

Nolae leul, bulemyo.

Naeyong elu jibelio,

Indohabinada."

The song is about a rainbow-tailed bird that makes its nest in crystal branches and calls souls home. I sing along with the familiar lullaby as Mother hangs our laundry to dry on the windowsill. Our voices harmonize. She turns her pastel-pink gaze to me and smiles. Moonlight dances over the fall of her white-blond hair, turning it silver.

Grief and anger slammed into me, pushing me out of the memory, but not before I placed my anchor. Ash's core writhed, protecting the precious thread they didn't want to share. That was fine. So long as the anchor remained in place, I had no need to pry further.

Avoiding the thrashing threads of the angry mass, I grappled another strand that seemed to feed deep into Ash's core and dropped onto the cobbled stones of an old bridge.

"What are you?" My friend stares at me, his gaze wide and frightened. His pulse drums in my ears, calling my hunger.

I shake my head. "I'm your friend."

"You're a freak! A monster!" He backs toward the edge of the bridge and the drop to the icy river below.

"Calm down."

"Leave."

"I only—"

"Get away from me!" He grabs a torch from its cradle and waves it in my face, but it's his look of absolute hatred that stops me in my tracks. "I said begone, demon!"

Swimming to the surface of the memory, I pulled myself free. I'd seen that one before, when I'd tried to uncover Ash's secrets in Canada. It was no less heartbreaking the second time.

Two down, one to go. Looking for my next target, I was struck by another pang of envy at how easy this whole process seemed to be for Bael. He didn't have to muck about in people's memories. He could make a transferable amulet as easily as breathing, while I had to hardwire the spell into a specific person, and even that was a gamble.

Huffing out a breath of frustration, I yanked my remaining spell tether closer and grabbed the next thickest thread I could find.

Wood creaks. Dry hay scratches my skin. Dust tickles my nose. I cover my mouth with both hands to stifle a sneeze, but I dare not come up for air. Light leaks through cracks between the warped slats of the barn walls. The doors rattle again. The townspeople have found me.

I tied off the final anchor and fled the memory, disturbed by the sense of fear and anticipation that clung to me. Ash had probably killed the people pounding at the barn door, but I got the feeling that victory had come at a steep price.

I gave myself a mental shake. While these glimpses into Ash's past were interesting, I had problems in the here and now that needed my attention. Grasping the foundational thread of my magic, I cinched the tethers connecting Ash's core to that of the quartz in my hands, and with that, the spell was set. Any sunlight that made contact with Ash would be funneled safely into the reflective prison inside the quartz . . . if I'd constructed the spell correctly.

Returning my awareness to my physical body, I licked my lips and whispered, "I think we're good to go."

"Are you sure?" Ash squeezed me tighter . . . uncomfortably so. "If I burst into flames, I'm taking you with me."

I swallowed my doubts, checked my magical bindings, and nodded. It was now or never.

Ash pressed their shoulder to the door until the thinnest possible sliver of light spilled through the crack, illuminating their banded wrist and the back of their hand. We both waited in tense silence, watching for the faintest trace of burning. As one, then five, then fifteen seconds passed, Ash's eyes grew wide with wonder.

It's actually working! Elation bubbled through me. Not that I hadn't thought this would work, I just . . . My confidence had taken a beating lately. After Bael's bombshell that I would never be able to create a daywalking amulet, I hadn't been entirely confident even of the parts of the spell that I'd mastered during my training. But Ash's skin remained smooth and unburned.

Ash inhaled and thrust the door fully open. Sunlight poured into the tunnel, bathing us both. Ash's pale, nearly translucent skin seemed to glow. Ash stepped out of our hiding spot and squinted into the light.

The rumble of an engine drew my focus beyond Ash's shoulder.

"Um, sorry to ruin the moment, but we've got company."

Ash turned and spotted two Jeeps barreling toward us over a dirt road that led from the barn above the market. They were nearly upon us. We'd burned through our lead.

"Hang on." Ash bent their knees, coiling like a snake, then launched forward in a spray of dirt and shredded leaves.

The corn field became a corridor of blurred green that parted like waves sliced by the prow of a boat. A boat on a very turbulent sea . . .

I bumped and bobbed in Ash's arms, clinging desperately to the quartz that was keeping them—keeping both of us—alive.

Gunfire popped like staccato beats on a snare drum, shattering the illusion of a lazy country afternoon.

I flinched as greenery, clods of dirt, and ears of corn exploded around us.

Ash pulled ahead, outpacing the Jeeps over the uneven ground. Then they hissed and stumbled, dropping to one knee.

"Are you hit?" I asked. Panic closed in with our pursuers.

Ash glared at me, and I recoiled. Smoke curled off their skin. A strip of charred flesh peeled off their cheek. "You said you could do this!"

"I—" Horror and shame stole my voice.

"Fix it!" Ash surged to their feet once more, barely avoiding being run over by the first of the open-top Jeeps. A young man standing in the back grabbed the roll bar for balance, nearly dropping his assault rifle, as the driver swerved to follow Ash's new course. A woman in denim jeans and a red crop top sighted down the barrel of a long rifle from the back of the second Jeep.

Ash darted to the side.

Thunder cracked. A bullet burst through Ash's shoulder in a spray of blood and bone.

Ash staggered but didn't fall. Bullets weren't a problem for a vampire. Sunlight was. The skin on Ash's forehead was starting to blister.

Shutting out the chaos of my physical surroundings as best I could, I examined my spell. The tethers I'd created were fraying. Even as I watched, one of the threads connecting Ash to the quartz snapped, whipping like a downed power line.

Ash screamed, but I didn't have time to inspect the damage. I grabbed the severed tether and dove into Ash's core.

I hate this country. There is no warmth in it despite the dry heat that rolls through the open walls of my palace and dances over the dunes of the desert beyond. Blinding white creeps along the edges of my world . . . threatening death, whispering of relief . . . but it cannot reach me at the heart of the shadow.

A man in a saffron robe clears his throat, dragging my attention back to the procession of nobles arrayed before me.

I glance at an open coffer. More gold. I flick my wrist, and the man prostrating himself behind the offering scurries away while one of the servants removes the gold.

The next man offers half a dozen bolts of silk. I look again at the vast desert beyond the beautiful arches of my daily prison. Perhaps I should hang some curtains.

When I look back, the silks have been replaced by four young women strung with golden chains. I meet each gaze, but I find only emptiness. Every girl resembles the next. Painted faces hiding broken souls. I wave them away, heavy with my own sense of futility.

The next offering causes a commotion. Three guards drag him forward and press him to his knees. His chains are not thin gold, but heavy iron. Long, matted hair obscures his sun-leathered face. He snarls like an animal, and when his gaze meets mine, I find a fire that momentarily batters back the cold of the abyss within me.

I sit up a little straighter. This one could be interesting . . .

White-hot pain scraped across my shoulder blade, shattering my concentration. I jolted back into my physical awareness. A third of Ash's face was blackened and peeling like layers of paper in a fire.

Ash stumbled and staggered as they ran, keeping pace with our pursuers but no longer pulling ahead. The sun's damage was slowing us down, and I doubted Ash could perform even a simple spell under these conditions. My heart sank. Bael had been right. I wasn't powerful enough to stabilize a spell of this size and complexity, even for a short time. I hadn't wanted to accept that truth. Now my pride was going to get Ash killed.

Blinding light flared between my fingers, searing a line of devastation across Ash's neck and chin. The smell of burning meat soured my stomach.

I clutched the quartz until the edges threatened to break my skin, trying to contain the light leaking from my imperfect prison. The deadly rays slipped through the cracks in my spell as hairline fractures became fissures, became chasms. I curled my body tight around the tiny nova cradled against my chest and frantically tried to build a new web around the crystal's core. The quartz wasn't as polished or pristine as the gems I'd practiced on. Its slightly clouded surface and irregular angles didn't lend themselves to lossless light refraction, and my magic wasn't advanced enough to make up the difference.

Despair strangled me as I frantically tied off the loose ends of my new spell, weaving them to patch sections of the quartz prison where the light had burned through. Cinching the new net into place, I turned toward the writhing mass of Ash's core. Golden streaks rippled across dark red strands as the convoluted knot twisted in agitation, straining my tethers. The spell needed more anchor points.

My physical body cramped. My thoughts were growing fuzzy. I didn't have much energy left to give. Pushing through my fatigue, I gathered the new threads of my patchwork spell and once more approached the angry mass of Ash's core.

Sparks dance along silver blades as they grind together, inches from my face. The man before me snarls. His features remind me so much of my mother.

"Why are you doing this?" I demand. "We're family."

"You're the reason my sister is dead. That you share my blood is all the more reason for me to kill you and put an end to this shame."

Seven hunters had found us this time. A small team, but effective. They'd gotten closer than any fae in a century. Now my uncle is all that remains. Those of my children who survived the initial attack stir anxiously near the edges of the room.

I do not want to fight my uncle. Part of me knows he is right. I am the reason my mother is dead. But the children, young and old, who watch our fight with anxious anticipation are also my family. Their lives—long though they may be—are such fragile things, still tied to my own. I cannot be the reason they die.

Shifting to the side, I relax my guard and allow my uncle's blade to bite deep into my collar, wedging in the bone. With my blade now free, I drive the tip between his ribs.

His eyes bulge. He clings to his hilt, trying to force his blade deeper even as his life ebbs.

"You will never . . . know peace." Blood bubbles past his lips. "Abomination."

One quick twist destroys his heart.

Wind whistled past, snarling my hair and drying the tears on my cheeks. I was weightless. Then I blinked, and the ground rushed toward me. Ash buckled when we hit, rolling to absorb the impact. Sky became dirt became sky again.

Shouts and a crunch of metal on stone drew my attention. Twenty feet away, one of the Jeeps had failed to stop before the bank of the river Ash had just vaulted. It rested nose down, hood crumpled and partially submerged in the rushing waters. The sniper in the red crop top had fallen clear and was being swept downstream.

The second Jeep skidded to a stop in a shower of gravel that rained over the driver from the wreck as he extricated himself from the Jeep's airbag and climbed the vehicle like a ladder back to solid ground. The remaining gunner lifted their rifle to take aim.

Ash lurched away from the bank under a hail of bullets. Scenery flashed by, but not at the blinding speed we'd had at the beginning of this race. Ash drooped under my weight. The flesh around the right side of their mouth crumbled, blowing away like their namesake to reveal a skeletal grin of inhumanly sharp teeth.

The Jeep peeled out, tearing down the opposite bank in search of a safe crossing.

We have to put enough distance between us and our pursuers that they lose our trail before they reach a bridge.

But even as I had that thought, Ash fell to one knee.

I turned my attention to the spell. Both the quartz prison and the anchors I'd set in Ash's core were holding, but the section between had thinned like Silly Putty stretched between two points. Sunlight leaked from the insufficient funnel, burning through the fragile web of my spell.

Ash's scream jolted my stunned mind to action.

My spell wouldn't hold. I didn't have time to build another, and even if I did, I couldn't create a spell stable enough to do the job. So, I did the only thing I could think of. I wrapped my magic around the quartz prison and tied it to the threads of my own soul. Then I thrust my consciousness into the thrashing black-and-gold vines at the center of Ash's core.

Chapter 18

FIRE CRACKLES IN the ring of rocks Mother arranged at the mouth of the cave. I don't need the warmth, or the light, but it makes her happy to have those things. I look beyond the drifting embers to rustling leaves that blot out the backdrop of the night sky.

"Tell me again, Mama, about the forest around your home."

"Our home," she corrects. She inhales deeply and gets a faraway look in her eyes. When she exhales, she says, "How about I show you."

I sit up straighter. Mother doesn't often use her magic. She's afraid of drawing attention. But we're deep in the forest and it's the middle of the night. No one will see. She slips past the fire and out of the cave.

I follow. The air is cold against my skin—made colder because of the lingering heat of the flames. Twigs and leaves crunch underfoot, stirring scents of dry wood and decay. The flickering light at my back makes my shadow dance.

"The forest at home is not like the forest here." Mother waves a hand and the trees glow white. They become transparent and seem to stretch all the way to the stars above. Each cellophane leaf is a perfect prism that scatters the firelight into a million shimmering rainbows. Burgundy vines draped with vermilion trumpets climb the crystal trunks and fill the forest with the scent of nutmeg.

"Two rivers flow through the forest." Mother strolls between the trees, and the dry ground becomes a riverbed. My feet sink into thick, green moss as I follow.

As we walk, the wind in the leaves becomes a million tinkling voices that sing my mother's lullaby.

"Where the rivers meet, you will find our home."

We step into a small clearing. A second stream trickles into existence from the far side, snaking over to join the water we walk beside. The land sloughs away at the junction point, becoming a short stone cliff veiled by a waterfall. Moonlight glints on a widening pool below.

Mother turns to the space above the waterfall. A building blooms from the ground, twisting and stretching like an unfurling frond. Four stories of balconies, cupolas, columns, and cornices surrounded by sprawling walkways that wind between towering trees. A few smaller houses emerge in a similar fashion, nestled among the trees, but my attention remains fixed on the first structure. This is the house where my mother was born. Where *she grew up. Where she lived for over three hundred years before I was born. This is the home she longs to return to . . . where she has promised, one day, to bring me.*

I follow a stone path to the front door. Relief images carved into the beams and lintel tell the story of my family's history. I reach for the handle.

The illusion shatters. Crystal glitter rains around me, swirling on a cold breeze before being swallowed by the dark forest. We've strayed far from the fire.

My mother sets her hand on my shoulder and whispers, "Someday, you will see it in person."

I let my tears fall.

Wood splintered.

Someone screamed.

A door slammed.

I tipped sideways. My head hit cold, hard tiles. My skin was on fire.

I opened my eyes, but I couldn't see a damn thing.

Ash groaned and shoved me from behind.

I rolled onto my stomach, bracing on my forearms. My shoulder bumped something hard. I caught a whiff of ammonia. Sweat soaked my clothes and slicked my hair, making me shiver, but my skin felt tight and hot. Every inch of me hurt. I panted as if I'd been the one to run that marathon through the fields.

Light spilled over me, illuminating the green tiles under my hands, the bathtub in front of me, and the toilet by my side.

I twisted to find an elderly man with a white beard silhouetted in the doorway. He hunched around an object in his hands. My focus shifted to the barrel of the shotgun pointed at my chest.

"Who are you?" Demanded the man in an airy, slightly cracked voice. White eyebrows furrowed over deep-set eyes half sealed by drooping lids. "What do you want?"

Ash stirred beside me, twisting to see the man in the doorway. The long strands of their dark hair parted.

I gasped. The lower quarter of Ash's face was missing on the right side. Blackened strands of muscle and severed tendons clung to the bones that made up their cheek and jaw. Their right hand was similarly skeletal from the wrist down.

My stomach heaved. They'd stepped into the sunlight because I said I would keep them safe. I'd done my best, but their injuries were proof of my shortcomings.

Ash moved. I couldn't register more than that. Wind whipped through the small room, throwing my hair across my face. The stench of charred meat rolled over me.

The shotgun hit the tiles.

Ash rode the old man to the floor, teeth buried in his neck.

A woman screamed.

Ash glanced to the side. The scream cut off. I heard a distant *thud*.

"Stop." I pushed to my knees. My skin cracked. Yellowish liquid oozed from a dozen ruptured blisters across my bright-red hands and arms. I winced. My face felt like plastic. Tears blurred my vision. By tying my own core into the spell, I'd managed to buffer Ash from the sunlight that would have consumed them like a spent match, but I'd taken the damage from that exposure.

Breathing through the pain, I crawled toward the doorway. Every movement flayed my nerves, but I forced myself to keep going. If my magic had been stronger, Ash wouldn't have needed to feed. I grabbed Ash's ankle. "Please," I gasped. "Don't kill him."

Ash twisted out of my grip, swinging their golden gaze in my direction. They snarled, a rabid dog mad with hunger. Blood coated their chin and teeth, but as I watched, muscle grew back and skin closed over those glistening fangs. The new skin wasn't perfect, however. A seam remained, marking the damaged area with a puffy scar. Ash would need more blood to heal fully. Possibly every drop in this house, mine included.

"We're here to prove that vampires are more than mindless monsters. If you kill an innocent person because you can't control yourself, you can kiss your seat at the peace talks goodbye."

Ash's teeth remained bared, but a glimmer of understanding flashed through those depthless, golden eyes.

A muffled voice said, "Nine-one-one dispatch, where is your emergency?"

Glancing to the side, I found an elderly woman with steel-gray curls and deep brown skin sitting on the floor. She wore a flower-patterned dress and thick glasses. She stared directly ahead with unseeing eyes. My gaze dropped to the phone in her hand. *Shit.* She'd called the police.

"Placate them and hang up." Ash's voice was low and rough.

The woman lifted the phone to her ear. "Sorry. I couldn't find my husband for a moment, so I worried he might have wandered off, but he was only in the garden. We're fine now. You have a nice day." She ended the call and set the phone down, continuing to stare ahead with that blank expression.

I swallowed a sour flavor at the back of my throat. Somehow, Ash had enthralled the woman without touching her, let alone sharing blood. I hadn't known they could do that.

Ash stood, wobbled. They seemed small. Frail. The points of tapered ears protruded from their dark hair—the first physical indication I'd ever seen of their fae ancestry. Their face seemed narrower than before, with thin lips and a pointed chin, both stained with blood.

Ambient light filtered in from two large windows behind Ash, but the slant of the shadows outside showed we were protected from any direct rays. The front door hung slightly ajar. Splintered wood protruded from the frame where Ash had kicked through the lock.

Ash quirked a finger at the woman. A single, skeletal fingertip protruded from a patchwork of pink skin and white scars that made Ash's hand resemble a lace glove. Turning, Ash shuffled slowly past a maroon sofa and matching recliner that framed a small stone fireplace and continued through a doorway in the far wall. I spotted a four-poster bed beyond.

The old lady rose and followed, passive as a shadow. She didn't even glance at the man with the bloody gash on his neck.

"Don't kill her!" I shouted.

Ash closed the door.

I turned my attention to the old man's chest. I couldn't tell if he was breathing.

I should check his pulse . . . but the thought of moving even the length of his body made me want to cry. Not only was my skin burned beyond the likes of anything I could remember, I also had dozens of lacerations, small and large, and more bruises than I could count. Beyond the physical beating I'd taken, I'd used a lot of magic, which filled me with a different sort of ache. I felt as if a hole had been carved out of my center.

I groped for the farmer's discarded shotgun, skin stretching uncomfortably over my knuckles as my fingers closed around the barrel, and pulled it into my lap. Then I watched the bedroom door to see what would emerge.

* * *

THUMP.

My eyes snapped open.

Another *thump* sounded as Ash forced the front door back into its frame despite its twisted hinges.

A smear of blood streaked the floorboards from the empty space beside me to the bedroom, where I now saw two sets of feet at the end of the bed.

I tightened my grip on the gun.

"Are they dead?" I asked quietly.

Ash stepped over my legs and into the bathroom. "They're doing better than you right now." Ash crouched beside me. "My blood can heal you."

I wanted to laugh, but just breathing took everything I had. "As if I'd fall for that."

"Fall for what?"

"Letting you get a foothold in my soul." I'd burned Ash out of my system once before. I could probably do it again. That didn't mean I was eager to try. I wasn't going to let them get their hooks in me again if I could avoid it. "I told you before. You will *never* control me."

They traced an X on their chest with one finger. "I promise not to try to enslave you should you accept my help."

I huffed, skeptical. "You're not a fae."

Gold flashed in Ash's once-more-black eyes as they looked away, and I was reminded of the anguish I'd felt in Ash's memory when they fought their uncle.

We're family.

All the more reason for me to kill you.

Despite the impurity of their blood, their ability to lie, and the fact that they'd been hunted since the day they were born, Ash still considered themself fae.

Talk about a complicated family relationship, I thought. I couldn't imagine having my own relatives want to kill me. I'd fought my father, but that had been *my* choice. In the end, it had been my father's love for me that ended the battle. Ash was more fae than I was, yet I'd been invited—commanded even—to visit my ancestral home in the Realm of Enchantment, while Ash had been exiled from theirs before they were even born. I'd felt the insatiable draw Ash felt toward their mother's homeland in those memories, and the despair of knowing that if they ever tried to reach it, their very essence would be unraveled by the traps woven into the portals between realms.

"Would you hesitate if I were human?" Ash asked.

A lump lodged in my throat. If Ash's offer had come from Luke or Emma, I would have allowed them to heal me without hesitation. Likewise, if Ash were a human doctor, I'd trust them to do whatever they thought necessary. A queasy coldness settled over me. After all I'd been through and everyone I'd met, I thought I had reached a point where I accepted all races equally. It seemed I wasn't as open-minded as I thought.

Just as Ash considered themself fae despite all evidence to the contrary, I still thought of myself as a human first and foremost . . . and humans were food for vampires. I'd rejected Ash's offer out of fear. A healthy, well-justified fear, but fear nonetheless. Here I was trying to convince the world that all species deserved equal treatment, but I was still struggling to master my own instincts. If I intended to practice what I preached, I needed to move past emotional reactions and make my decision based on the current evidence. The fact that Ash had refrained from killing the house's residents spoke volumes about their commitment to prove vampires could coexist with other races, and they'd stepped into the sunlight with only my word that I would keep them safe—a huge leap of faith on their part.

I lifted my hand off the gun and made a slow fist, staring at the cracked skin stretched tight over my knuckles. Every movement blazed like sticking my hand in a fire. I wouldn't be able to raid the Purity lab in this condition. Ash was offering a solution.

"You asked me to trust you. I'm only asking the same."

"Okay," I said. "Just a few drops. No strings."

Ash held my gaze. "This will create a temporary bond between us, but it'll fade in about a week. You have my word."

I nodded. James had said something similar when he first shared his blood with me, before I used my magic to twist the connection into something more permanent.

Ash slid their thumbnail across the inside of their wrist. Crimson liquid welled out. They extended their hand. The blood glistened on their skin an inch from my lips. It was up to me to meet them in the middle.

Wrinkling my nose in distaste, I leaned forward and licked Ash's wrist. The coppery taste of blood filled my mouth. I swallowed. My muscles seized. My nerves burst apart.

Fae and demons came from the same place, but while demons embraced the chaotic nature of the Rift, the fae rejected it. The fae magic in my blood raged against the demonic contamination I'd taken in, burning it out of my system in one overwhelmingly painful assault that was over almost as soon as it began.

I slumped sideways, bracing my forearms on the cool floor and gasping for breath. The sensation of being torn apart had lasted barely a moment, and I was glad to be rid of it. That suffering was a fact of life for vampires—a chronic ailment like arthritis or fibromyalgia. The symptoms could be eased for a time but never cured. After centuries of being constantly unraveled and stitched back together, I was amazed more of them hadn't lost their minds.

I blinked and found soft, pink flesh on the backs of my hands. The blisters were gone. I inhaled deeply and smiled. My skin no longer threatened to split apart. Those few seconds had been enough for Ash's blood to turn my third-degree burns into a light tan.

My stomach growled and cramped. Ash's blood had eased my pain, but it hadn't replaced the energy I'd burned using my magic. My eyelids drooped. I could barely lift my head. I needed food and rest, but first I needed to ensure Ash hadn't left any nasty surprises behind.

I shifted my focus, falling into myself. The pinkish-purple threads of my core twisted over and around one another, forming the foundation of my existence. A ribbon of shimmering silver snaked through the others. When I touched it, the distant comfort of James's presence settled over me. As far apart as we physically were at the moment, we were still connected. I held that lifeline for a moment, overwhelmed by how much I missed him. Reluctantly, I released the silver thread.

Another metallic flash drew my attention to a dark strand rippled with gold, so thin it was nearly invisible except where it glinted like firefly flashes through the tangled reeds of my core. I caught the discordant thread and realized that, while I certainly was tired and injured, not all of the pain and exhaustion I was feeling were mine.

Curious, I followed the golden thread. This strand didn't fade with distance as James's had. It ran in a short, straight line, bridging my core to Ash's. I traced it to the far end and found Ash treading water in a sea of sorrow, exhausted beyond belief, but determined not to drown.

I gasped. I wasn't prepared for the tsunami of despair that washed over me. I hadn't felt this the last time I'd been connected to Ash. Maybe it was because we'd both been willing participants this time, or something to do with the way I'd twined my core to theirs to patch my spell? Whatever the reason, I was finally seeing past all of Ash's masks to their core truth, and the truth was that they were *tired*. Tired of fighting. Tired of hiding. Tired of living. But unable to stop.

A steel door slammed in my face, thrusting me back to my physical body. Ash rose and turned their back to me, bracing their hands on the sink.

I opened my mouth, but words seemed too shallow to address what I'd glimpsed. Ash had the weight of an entire species on their shoulders, but that wasn't even the largest portion of their burden. Ash's mother had wanted her child to live despite the will of her family, despite being branded a traitor and an outcast, despite the dark nature of Ash's conception. She'd chosen to love Ash even though that love turned the whole world against her. Moreover, she'd promised that Ash would one day walk through the lands of their ancestors. Ash was tired beyond anything I could have imagined, but to stop treading water would be to let that promise and everything their mother had sacrificed sink beneath the waves. A dogged, if hollow, determination not to make their mother a liar was all that kept them going.

You don't understand what eternity does to a mind. There had been fear and frustration behind Morgan's words when she spoke of her father. How much worse must it be if that eternity was plagued by pain, loneliness, and the uncompromising judgment of the dead?

I wiped tears from my cheeks and took a deep breath. "How far are we from the market?"

"About sixteen miles," Ash answered. "I changed direction a few times since losing the jeeps at the river and passed dozens of viable hiding spots before stopping here. Hopefully they won't realize we've stopped at all."

"I should call Everly, have her send agents to the market."

Ash turned to face me. "The plan is to hit the lab, not the market."

"The *plan* was to get the lab's location discretely, without anyone realizing what we were up to, but that plan went to shit when we killed the first guard. Now they know we aren't who we said we were. They're probably evacuating the market as we speak, and who knows where Chase will end up." I leaned my head against the bathroom wall, staring at the water-stained ceiling. "I can't believe we just left him like that."

To my surprise, Ash sat down beside me, shoulder to shoulder with our backs against the wall. "I understand that you're worried about your friend, but don't let that concern blind you to the bigger picture. Right now, all anyone knows is that a couple of magic users slipped past security and made a mess at the black market. They don't know who we are or what we were after, but if the PTF suddenly raids that facility . . ."

"Everyone at the market will realize we were working with them." My thoughts felt slow, even after Ash's infusion healed my body.

"If you call the PTF, the market will be cleared out long before any agents arrive, and you'll have tipped off the organizers and attendees that today's disturbance was more than a couple of disgruntled practitioners working alone. Every bad guy within three states will be in the wind seconds after the PTF gets boots on the ground . . . including the Purity lab that bought your furry friend."

I thumped my head lightly against the wall, wondering what to do. Ash was right that the market would almost certainly be cleared before any PTF agents reached it, so the odds of intercepting Chase before he was taken away were pretty much nil. That meant my best shot at saving him was to hit the Purity lab Ash had learned the location of as we'd originally planned. But what if the disturbance at the market was enough to spook Dr. Hayes into evacuating even if she didn't know we were coming after her specifically? Ivan's nest was ready to attack, but they couldn't move until dark. Everly had PTF troops standing by. They might be able to reach the lab within the hour . . . but the vampires would lose their chance to look like heroes. They'd still get some credit as informants, but I doubted Ash would settle for that. The vampires were looking for a headline to mark their debut, not a footnote.

"What are the odds you'll give me the location of the lab right now and let the PTF take point?"

Ash's silence spoke volumes.

"Yeah." I sighed, letting my eyes drift closed. I was so tired. "That's what I thought."

"Our original plan is still the best path forward."

"Easy for you to say; you don't care what happens to Chase."

"True, but I *do* want this mission to succeed."

My stomach grumbled loud enough to wake the dead.

Ash snorted and stood. "You should eat something and get some rest. I'll call Ivan and make the necessary preparations for tonight."

"Mm," was all I could manage. Rest sounded good. Food sounded better. I rose with a groan and made a beeline for the fridge.

* * *

"TIME TO WAKE up, Alex." Ash jostled my shoulder.

My eyes felt gummy.

Hazy, amber light slipped through the gauze curtains of the farmhouse windows, turning Ash's pale skin orange. They still wore their fae face, complete with pointed ears and narrow features.

I sat up and stretched. I was stiff and sore, but not in any real pain, which was a minor miracle after the way I'd felt earlier. The six ham-and-cheese sandwiches and two glasses of whole milk I'd downed before passing out on the couch had done wonders for my energy levels, and the jump start Ash's blood had provided, coupled with my natural fae healing, meant I was feeling *almost* normal.

Ash settled beside me on the couch. The scars left from our sunlight flight seemed even more prominent than when I'd gone to sleep.

"I assume you don't want Ivan to see you like this," I noted, indicating their appearance.

"I'll recast my glamour once the sun sets. It will be easier then."

The sky was growing darker by the minute. Most of the vampires I'd met seemed able to function during the day, so long as no sunlight fell directly on them, but they did seem . . . less. Perhaps ambient sunlight affected vampires in the same way being near high concentrations of iron affected fae—not instantly devastating, but a slow poison that sapped their strength.

Ash exhaled, watching the fading light. "Despite the rather painful circumstances, it was nice to wear my own face for a while." A sad smile lifted their lips. "It's been a very, *very* long time."

"Speaking of masks . . ." I turned my hands over, inspecting the freckled backs and pink palms. "Will you recast your illusion on me?"

Ash shook their head. "Now that there's no danger of your identity alerting the black market operatives to our plan, it should be safe enough to wear your own face."

"Won't Ivan be angry that we lied to him?"

"Lies are a part of life." Ash waved their hand. My gaze caught on the patchwork scars. They, too, seemed worse. "I'll handle Ivan."

"I'd still prefer—"

"Look." Ash turned to face me. "Loath as I am to admit it, I don't have the strength to maintain a convincing illusion over you right now. I should have enough energy to hide myself and direct the raid on the Purity lab tonight, but your anonymity isn't a high enough priority to waste magic on."

Realization sank in. Unlike with humans, time didn't heal a vampire's wounds . . . it made them worse. I'd been able to gorge and sleep, but sipping from the elderly couple hadn't been enough to heal Ash fully. Without another food source, Ash had been slowly wasting away as they waited for the day to pass.

I studied the scars on Ash's face. *My fault. My failure.* Suddenly feeling better didn't feel so good. "Here." I extended my arm so the inside of my wrist was exposed and turned my face away. "Don't take too much."

Seconds passed.

"You must really want to hide your identity," Ash said quietly.

I shook my head. "I don't need your illusion. I just don't want you passing out halfway through the raid tonight."

"Feeding would strengthen the bond between us; it will take longer to dissipate."

I glared at them. "Do you want this meal, or not?"

"I don't want you claiming later that I tricked you."

I nodded. "Go ahead."

Ash cradled my wrist, gentle but firm. Their touch was ice against my skin.

I closed my eyes. I hated this. Merak. James. Ash. I would never get used to vampires taking my blood. But it was my fault Ash had gotten hurt, and they weren't *taking* my blood this time. I was giving it.

Ash's lips brushed the tender skin of my inner arm. I tensed, bracing for the pain I knew was coming.

A slight pinching sensation made me twitch, then a feeling of comfort washed over me. My muscles relaxed. The pressure in my chest eased. My worries faded to the background. Everything was going to be fine.

Ash lowered my limp hand to my lap.

I looked to the side. The seams where Ash's skin had regrown were barely visible.

"You're still not fully healed," I said.

"But I'm better." They gave me a sardonic look. "I promise not to pass out during the raid."

I looked at my wrist. A tiny nick marked my skin—no more than a paper cut. Nothing like the bite marks that had covered my body after my unwilling stay in Merak's nest. I rubbed my thumb over the small wound. "I expected it to hurt more."

"Vampires don't *have* to make feedings painful. That's a matter of taste." Ash shrugged. "Some donors even enjoy it."

James once told me that the people he drank from usually experienced something akin to a cocaine high, which made it easier to cultivate recurring donors. They were literally addicted to him. That hadn't been *my* experience, but Merak had been a sadistic bastard, and James had been half out of his mind when he fed from me.

I could feel Ash's lingering hunger through our connection, like an itch at the back of my mind. "I appreciate you showing restraint."

"Not monsters," Ash said. "That's what we're trying to prove, right?"

My thoughts drifted back to James. He'd hurt me, but I definitely didn't consider him a monster. I hoped we'd be able to convince the rest of the world to see vampires that way.

The sense of contentment Ash had instilled in me started to crack. Guilt twisted in my chest. Who knew what James had been through these past three months, and here I was getting all buddy-buddy with his captor. My mood soured.

"He's all right," Ash said.

"What?"

"James. You're thinking about him . . . worrying about him. Don't. He's a prisoner, but a valuable one. No dungeons. No torture."

Now that blood had gone both ways, the hair-thin thread that connected us had grown to a solid cord. I shored up my mental defenses and crossed my arms. "You're saying you didn't dig around in James's head looking for a way to control me?"

The scar around Ash's mouth puckered with their smirk. "I'm saying he's sitting comfortably in a beachside villa in Spain. He's the vampires' only option for global negotiations. So long as he cooperates, he'll be well treated."

"That's something, I guess." We lapsed into silence. Maybe James representing the vampires wasn't such a bad thing. Yes, it put him in added danger from the Purists, but it also gave him leverage. Maybe, once the initial negotiations were over and James was established as the vampires' mouthpiece, we could renegotiate the terms of his captivity. But first we needed to get the vampires admitted to those peace talks . . . and we needed to save Chase.

Chapter 19

THE WARM METAL hood of Ivan's SUV dented as I shifted my weight, trying to get a better view over the seemingly endless rows of corn in which we'd parked. Ivan and two dozen of his vampire brethren had rendezvoused with us shortly after sunset. He hadn't been thrilled to learn my true identity, but, as Ash predicted, he'd taken our deception in stride, simply handing over my backpack and moving on with the mission.

My arms ached from holding up the binoculars Ivan had lent me. I'd decimated the remaining contents of the farmhouse fridge after my nap, but I still felt lethargic, hollowed out. Hopefully this mission would go more smoothly than the last. I wasn't sure how much fight I had in me. Not that I planned to do any actual fighting tonight.

Figures the size of insects moved around the farmyard Ash had identified as the Purity lab; they were barely visible, even to my fae eyes, as full night set in. Corn rustled here and there as vampires closed in from the surrounding fields. I swung my binoculars from side to side, scanning the half dozen barns, silos, stables, and other buildings that dotted the secluded property. *Chase could be in any of them.*

Bright flashes drew my attention to the eastern perimeter, and a series of rapid *crack-crack-cracks* shattered the silence. The fight had begun.

The familiar buzz of adrenaline hummed in my veins. My palms grew slick. My muscles twitched with anticipation.

A second bout of gunfire broke out on the western edge of the property. Shouts went up, dampened by distance. A wall of flame split the farmyard in two, casting a wavering orange glow over the area. Lightning streaked out of the clear, star-studded sky. I squeezed the binoculars until I lost feeling in my fingers. We'd expected magic users, but dread and frustration bubbled through me as I scanned the distant battlefield, unable to discern friend from foe among the clashing figures. I wasn't used to sitting on the sidelines while others charged into danger—even when those people were faster, stronger, and generally better equipped than I was. I'd gotten used to being front and center in the action.

I should be there.

Ash touched my shoulder. I jumped at the contact and turned to look at them. With Ivan and the others on hand, Ash had donned their masculine mask and gone back to their strong, silent persona, erasing any trace of the vulnerability I'd seen earlier. All I could feel through our link was a hint of that bone-deep weariness that threatened to swallow me if I ventured too close. At least Ash's melancholy had the benefit of smothering my impatience.

They held my gaze. "We each have our role to play."

My role was to facilitate communication between the vampires and the PTF, not charge pointlessly into battle. I exhaled, relaxing my death grip on the binoculars.

A year ago, I wouldn't have imagined being even *this* close, let alone any closer. I would have handed this whole mess off to the authorities on day one and retreated to my solitude. Now, here I was, anxious to lead the charge. Part of that was wanting to make sure Chase was safe, but if I was being honest . . . I *liked* feeling important. I liked being right in the middle of unfolding events and having a hand in directing their outcome.

Gods, what am I becoming? I shook my head and returned my attention to the distant battle.

The flames had died down. Dark mounds dotted the open area. Nothing moved aside from smoke rising off the scorched earth.

I hope they remembered not to kill anyone. Ash had drilled our instructions into Ivan and his men—it still pissed me off that the infiltration force was entirely male—before they moved out. They had to move slowly enough to appear on camera; they weren't to kill anyone unless absolutely necessary for their survival; they were to confirm a debt from every fae present before opening the cages.

I wasn't thrilled about that last, but Ash had insisted. The vampires needed all the leverage they could get to convince the fae to lift their lifelong execution order against the vampire race, which meant making the freed fae believe the vampires had saved them of their own volition. Having a half-fae member of the PTF present would complicate matters, so I'd stayed behind.

Ash's phone buzzed. They glanced at it. "That's the all-clear."

I lowered the binoculars. The entire fight to secure the complex had taken less than two minutes. Vampires really were terrifying.

Ash and I climbed into one of the black SUVs Ivan and his team had driven. It would have been faster for Ash to run us to the farmyard, but they were back to pretending to be human, so we rolled along the dark, dusty road, anticipation gnawing at my nerves.

The battlefield was much as I expected when we stepped out—blackened ground, shattered doors, and a few smoking craters. I knelt beside the nearest prone figure, a woman with short brown hair and a gash over one eye. Her hands and feet were secured with zip ties. A steady pulse beat under my fingers when I pressed them to her neck.

"We followed your rules." Ivan stepped out of the shadows beside one of the larger barns.

"No casualties?" Ash asked.

"None."

"And the fae?"

Ivan tipped his head toward the barn. "In there."

Leaving the downed Purist, I raced to the barn and through a gaping hole littered with splintered wood that had once been a door. The smell hit me like a solid wall. Piss, sweat, blood. Stains soaked the sawdust ground in rusty tie-dye. Cages lined both walls, varying in size from eight-foot boxes that could hold a troll to cubes that would fit on the palm of my hand. They were all empty. Two vampires I recognized from our pre-raid briefing stood at the far end of the barn, securing the limbs of two unconscious humans who must have been stationed here as guards.

I ran over to them. "There should have been a gray cat in one of these cages. Where is he?"

The first vampire ignored me entirely. The second shot a confused look over my shoulder.

"All the fae scattered when we opened their cages," Ivan said, coming up behind me.

I shook my head. "Chase knew I was coming. He wouldn't have left."

Ivan shrugged. "Perhaps the bait you used to get into the market wasn't here."

Ice bloomed in my center, freezing me in place. "He had to be," I whispered.

I'd convinced Chase to come on this mission. I'd promised to keep him safe. I'd abandoned him in the black market and let Ash convince me not to call in the cavalry, because I believed that he would be *here*. So, where the hell was he?

"What about the scientist?" Ash asked. "Where is she?"

Ivan gestured toward the splintered exit. "We found her working in a lab in the western-most building."

"Let's go have a chat." Ash caught my gaze, a lifeline through my panic. "Maybe she knows where your friend is."

I shuffled after Ash and Ivan in a daze. We'd captured the scientist responsible for making Fantasia. That was good. We'd accomplished our mission. But all I could think about was that Chase hadn't been in that barn.

The westernmost building turned out to be a five-story, two-tiered, defunct grain elevator with cement walls and a tin roof. At least from the outside. The inside was a different story. Pristine white walls, glass doors, and banks of LED lights hid behind the peeling paint of the gutted exterior. A perfect disguise.

Half a dozen white lab coats hung from hooks just inside the entrance. A nearby table offered boxes of blue plastic booties, blue gloves, and paper masks. Long steel tables and packed shelves broke the workspace into distinct stations. Stacks of pipettes, petri dishes, beakers, burners, test tubes, scales, and safety gear covered the work surfaces alongside larger equipment. An ambient hum from all the devices and doodads spread across the counters filled the air—machines continuing experiments as their masters slept. Vials of liquid of various colors spun in a white box with a domed lid. Racks of slides sat beside a microscope. Glass bottles of who knows what soaked in a temperature-controlled sink, steam wafting off them in translucent curls. Several glass-fronted fridges, like you might find in a convenience store, displayed severed appendages, organs floating in murky liquid, and other horrors.

I covered my mouth and took several deep breaths through my nose to keep from being sick.

"Where's Dr. Hayes?" I asked once my stomach settled.

Ivan pointed up. "Top floor."

The second level was much like the first—cluttered but sterile. Two lab techs in white coats with blue accents sat under the watchful eye of a vampire guard. A thin man with a ponytail and a neatly trimmed beard glared at me through thick, round glasses. His companion, a plump woman with frizzy gray hair, slumped against him, a gash bleeding freely on her forehead. They must have been working late when the raid began.

The third and final floor was smaller, maybe half the size of those below. Two long tables held samples and processing devices similar to those in the labs we'd passed, but the walls were lined with books, and a window looked out onto the night. A woman with pale olive skin, hazel eyes, a long nose, and dark, curly hair pulled into a bun sat behind a large steel desk. She didn't appear frightened by the thuggish vampire standing beside her—more put out, as if we'd interrupted something that she was eager to get back to.

I stormed through the center of the room, stopping just short of the desk. "Where are the other fae?"

She frowned, a small wrinkle creasing her forehead. "What do you mean?"

"We found your prison barn, but there must be someplace else that you keep newer captives."

She shook her head. "If you want to know where test subjects are housed, speak with Jason. He handles facility operations."

"We'll do that." Ash set their hand on my shoulder. The fire of my frustration dampened to a smoldering ember. "You're Calliope Hayes?"

She lifted her chin.

"And you created Fantasia?"

Her frown became one of annoyance. "I'm a medical scientist, not a drug dealer."

I snorted, gesturing at the equipment behind me. "You're seriously going to deny that you've been kidnapping fae and harvesting their DNA despite the fact that we are literally standing in the middle of your lab right now?"

"Not at all," she said. "Do you have any idea how many humans die each year from heart disease? Cancer? Diabetes? Respiratory failure? Stroke? AIDS? Millions. Do you know how many *fae* die from those same diseases?" She set her elbows on the desk and interlaced her fingers. "None. The healing properties that they exhibit are beyond any medicine we currently possess. And we're not just talking about diseases. Did you know that most fae heal at more than double the rate of an average human? Some can even regrow limbs."

I surreptitiously rubbed a cut on my upper arm—one of the gashes I'd received from a crystal blade at the market. A normal human would have needed stitches. After half a day of rest, I barely needed a Band-Aid.

"That little extra boost could save most of the people who die on an operating table or on the way to an emergency room."

My mind jumped involuntarily to my mother, bleeding out in a hospital bed from her car crash injuries. Since Bael's charm had amplified my fae heritage last fall, I'd suffered far worse and survived. If he'd awakened the magic in her blood, as he had mine, would she still be alive? Could Dr. Hayes's research have saved her?

"Magic is just science we don't yet understand," Hayes continued. "By studying the regenerative properties of various fae species, I've already found what I believe may be a cure for Alzheimer's. Who knows what other conditions we could cure? If humans want to survive, we don't need to eliminate the fae; we must evolve beyond them."

I took a shaky breath, forcing words past the lump in my throat. "Even if that's true, it doesn't give you the right to torture and kill innocent people."

She made an offhand gesture. "Hardly innocent. Under the current laws, these fae weren't supposed to be here. They chose to endanger themselves by coming to a place where they don't belong. I won't apologize for taking advantage of that opportunity. This line of inquiry is too important not to follow just because it offends the moral sensibilities of a few short-sighted pacifists."

Her words reminded me of the argument I'd had with Bael back in his workshop, and the tiny droust whose lives he'd considered inconsequential. The calm confidence in the scientist's expression, the certainty that she was right, amplified that comparison.

Anger boiled within me. I shook my head. Bael might have been powerful enough to get away with playing God in Enchantment. This woman was not. "That's not your call to make. I won't let you and your Purist ideals endanger our chance of forging a lasting peace between the races, no matter your justifications. Tells us about the attack you have planned. Who did you send the Fantasia to?"

"I have no idea what you're talking about," Hayes replied.

I took a step forward, but Ash grabbed my arm, holding me back. A tide of suspicion rippled through our connection. "That makes two of us. What attack?"

I gritted my teeth. Right. I hadn't told Ash about the other reason for this raid. Well, the cat was out of the bag. "We received a credible tip that Purity was planning an attack against the summit using Fantasia-dosed soldiers. Finding the distribution source was our best bet at tracking them down. Since the vampires needed a way to boost their PR, having you assist seemed like a good opportunity to kill two birds with one stone."

"Am I a bird or a stone in this analogy?"

I shook off Ash's grip. "It's just a saying."

"You used me."

"And you used me," I replied. "That's the nature of our relationship. But my having an ulterior motive doesn't change anything. You still get your headline."

"So why not share the whole story from the start?"

I glanced at Ivan. "I couldn't take the chance that the vampire council might choose to let the attack happen rather than help me stop it."

Ash studied me. The corner of their mouth quirked up. "Fair enough."

"You deceived the council." Ivan stepped toward me with a growl.

Ash lifted their hand.

Ivan froze, but continued to glare at me.

"Motives aside," Ash said, "we're all in this together now." They gestured to Dr. Hayes. "Ivan and I will question the doctor while you find your furry friend."

I shot Ash an irritated look, but the memory of Chase on the auction block stopped me from arguing. I needed to make sure the threat to the summit was contained. I also needed to find Chase. I couldn't be in two places at once.

Can I trust you? I sent the question through the golden thread anchored in my core.

We're in this together, Ash repeated.

"Fine." I focused on Dr. Hayes. "Where can I find your operations manager?"

"Jason?" She looked at a gold watch on her wrist. "At this time of night, he's probably in the old machine shed we converted to living quarters for the staff."

I turned away from the remorseless woman and leaned close to Ash. "Get the information we need, but Dr. Hayes needs to be intact when we hand her over to the PTF, body *and* mind. People are going to put everything that happens here under a microscope." I glanced around the lab. "No pun intended."

"Dr. Hayes will be whole and healthy for her arrest," Ash assured me.

I hurried back through the lower labs and scanned the property, then I headed for a long, low building with metal sides and three bay doors. Vampires were rounding up the people who'd been trussed and dropped in the open—leading, carrying, or dragging them into the barn where I'd expected to find Chase. I shuddered at the thought of anyone being locked in those cages, but these people deserved it. If justice prevailed, everyone here would spend the rest of their lives in a cage. At least they wouldn't have to worry about being dissected or harvested for parts.

I glanced into an open shed as I passed and wished I hadn't. A long steel counter and a large steel sink with a flexible, shower-like attachment filled one wall. Steel hooks, a rack of knives, and two chest freezers lined the other. Butcher shop turned body disposal—again, the farm had provided a perfect cover for what was really happening here.

I hurried my steps, trying not to imagine what I'd find if I opened those freezers. Fae bodies disappeared after death. Halfers' didn't. We left meat and bones just like regular humans. Evidence that would need to be cleaned up.

A snort and snuffle drew my attention to a fenced area where a dozen large, pink pigs lay in a straw-strewn pen. One turned its snout in my direction as I passed, then it went back to munching on what looked like a piece of broken bone.

A small door on the narrow side of the machine shed led into a cozy living space complete with kitchen area, dining table, and several couches. Two dozen people sat with tied hands and ankles under the watchful gaze of three of Ivan's vampires. Some of the captives wore regular clothes. Others sported pajamas and sleep masks. One woman was wrapped in a green sheet.

"Which one of you is Jason?"

No one spoke up, but a few groggy gazes drifted toward a Hispanic man with a shaved head. Neck tattoos trailed under the collar of his pink button-up shirt.

I stood directly in front of him. "Where are the other fae? The new arrivals?"

He stared back in silence.

"I know you purchased new test subjects from the black market earlier today. Where are they?"

Jason's bored expression didn't waver.

Everyone on this farm was a Purist zealot willing to kill for their beliefs. Most were probably willing to die for them as well. The only other time I'd been in a Purity lab, a redheaded researcher shot herself after I told her she was going to turn into a werewolf. Purists might be okay utilizing manufactured magic in the form of drugs, but becoming a true paranatural was a different story.

I indicated the nearest vampire. "You've seen what these guys can do, right? You know what they are?"

"They're faerie freaks." Jason spat on the floor.

I grinned. "No. They're not." I braced my hands on the couch back on either side of Jason and leaned in until my lips brushed his ear. "They're vampires . . . and they're recruiting. One word from me, and they'll rip out your soul and turn you into a creature of the night."

Jason stiffened. "That's not—"

"What? Possible?" I chuckled softly, a little freaked out by how crazy it made me sound. "Say goodbye to your humanity."

I straightened, grabbed the front of Jason's shirt, and pulled him to his feet. Then I turned to the vampires. "Who's hungry?"

"Wait!"

Jason's shrill shout hurt my ears, but I kept my expression neutral as I faced him. "Something you want to say?"

"Our representatives aren't back yet, so whatever you're looking for . . . it isn't here."

I frowned. The guy Ash enthralled at the market might be dead, but there were at least five people in that group. *Someone* should have made it back. "It's been hours since the market closed."

Jason shook his head. "The market never closes before sunset."

"The market was attacked this morning. There's no way anyone's still there." I dragged him another step closer to the vampires.

"If security was compromised, the organizers would have enacted lockdown protocols," he said in a rush.

I glared at him. "Explain."

"All the goods and guests would've been taken via portal to a secure, undisclosed location."

"For how long?"

"Usually forty-eight hours. Sometimes longer, depending on how long it takes the organizers to find and plug the leak."

"What happens to the merchandise?"

"Returned to the people holding their claim bands."

"What if something isn't claimed?"

"It's donated to the organizers, usually sold off to fund future markets."

Shit. The market had been in lockdown for most of one day already. That left one more before Chase was moved. I had to find him before I lost the trail entirely.

"You said they moved the goods and guests via portal?"

Jason nodded. "At least, they did the last time I was in a lockdown. That was a few years ago."

I searched Jason's eyes for any hint of deception. Finding only fear and shame, I released his shirt and gave him a shove. He dropped heavily to the couch.

Stepping into the open yard, I took a deep breath of the humid night. I felt a little bad about casting the vampires as monsters in order to get Jason to talk when this whole operation was designed to improve their public image, but I doubted these bigoted Purists would have seen them as anything else regardless. Unfortunately, the answers Jason gave weren't what I wanted to hear. Chase wasn't coming to this Purity compound. He'd been portaled away . . . and I had no idea where.

I covered my face with my hands and tried to think. Chase was in danger because of me. There had to be *something* I could do.

"Portals." I lowered my hands and stared at the starry sky. "Portals can only take people a limited distance." I frowned. I had no idea how far a portal could carry someone, or what other limitations they might have . . . but I knew someone who would.

Pulling my phone out of the bag Ivan had returned to me, I dialed the number for Crossroads.

"Hey, Alex."

Jynx's carefree voice almost broke me.

"Alex? You there?"

"I'm here."

"What's the matter? You sound upset."

"I . . ." Guilt choked me.

"Okay, you're officially freaking me out now. What happened?"

"I lost Chase." The words stretched into the night, carrying my confession into the world.

"You. . . . What do you mean you *lost* him? Is he . . ."

"No! At least, I don't think so. But he was taken through a portal. I was hoping Ava might have some idea how to track him, or at least narrow down my search grid."

"Hang on."

Muffled noises filtered over the line as, I assumed, Jynx went in search of Ava.

"Alex?" Ava's voice was tight with concern. "Do you know what kind of fae opened the portal Chase was taken through?"

"No."

"How long ago was it opened?"

"About ten hours."

"Any idea how long it stayed open?"

"Long enough to evacuate a hundred plus people and several carloads of merchandise."

"Good. That's good. The longer it was open, the longer its ghost will last."

"Ghost?"

"Where are you?"

"The boonies west of Chicago."

"And that's where the portal was opened?"

"No. The portal was opened in an underground bunker a few miles from here."

"Can you get back there?"

I hesitated. The race from the market was all a blur, and Ash hadn't been in great condition either. "Maybe."

"This isn't a maybe situation, Alex. Can you get there or not?"

According to Ash, we'd traveled about sixteen miles south to reach the farmhouse. That would get me close. Ash might be able to pinpoint the location from there. If not... I'd drive through the countryside until I found the right field with the right barn if I had to. I set my jaw. "I'll get there."

"Then we have a chance, but time is a factor. Sooner is better if we're going to try this. Once you're where you need to be, call me back. I'll make the necessary preparations on my end."

Hanging up, I raced back across the farmyard, past the pigpen and butcher shack, past the prison barn, to the remodeled grain elevator. I burst into the top-floor lab and said breathlessly, "Ash, I need your help."

"Hello to you, too." Ash perched on the edge of one of the long steel tables, phone pressed to their ear. "I was just bringing your boyfriend up to speed. Want to say hello?" Ash lowered the phone so its screen was face up and pressed a button.

My pulse stuttered then sped up. Clutching the fabric ring on my finger, I hurried forward to lean over the blank screen. "James?"

"It's good to hear your voice, Alex."

Something loosened in my chest. "Yours, too. How are you?"

"Eager to see you," he said. "I landed in Denver half an hour ago, but it won't feel like home till you're here with me."

Confused, I strummed the silver cord tied to my soul and was shocked by the strength of its response. James was much closer than he had been the last time I touched that thread. I cast a questioning look at Ash.

They shrugged. "Call me an optimist. I put him on a plane before we left the safe house last night. Now you just need to call your PTF Director and arrange a meeting so we can coordinate the next stage of this plan."

I glanced at Dr. Hayes, who stared blankly ahead. Ivan stood behind her, one hand resting on the back of her chair. "You had Ivan enthrall her?"

"A temporary condition, I assure you," Ash said. "Her mind will be clear within the hour."

I nodded. "What did you learn about the attack?"

"It seems Dr. Hayes isn't a Purist herself. She only works with Purity as a means to an end. Fantasia was a side effect of her research, which she traded for funding, protection, and a continuous supply of test subjects. She never had any interest in disrupting the summit."

I braced one hand against the table and tried to get my thoughts in order. One definitive strike to end the immediate threat, break the Fantasia drug ring, and give the vampires a PR boost. That had been the plan, but . . . "She has no idea who's planning the attack on the summit?"

"It could be any of the Purity cells that received shipments of Fantasia. Luckily, we have a list." They pointed to Hayes's computer. "Thirty-seven targets, along with fourteen secondary labs around the world, that need to be shut down before word of Dr. Hayes's capture gets out lest her associates go to ground."

I swallowed. "That's . . . a lot of targets. Way more than the PTF can rout before the summit."

"Which is where we come in." Ash's teeth flashed in a feral smile. "What better way for the PTF to show their endorsement of vampire inclusion than to participate in a joint operation on a global scale? Rather than eliminating a single threat and putting a dent in Purity's drug trade, we can make a clean sweep of their Fantasia assets, including harvesting and distribution facilities. Talk about a headline! By the time this is over, the werewolves and practitioners will be begging us to join their alliance."

I rubbed my temples. An operation on this scale, on short notice, and Everly would already be pissed that we'd raided the lab on our own instead of calling it in as I'd originally promised . . . but the overall goal remained the same, just on a larger scale. Without knowing which facility was planning the attack, taking them all down simultaneously was the best—the *only*—way to protect the summit.

"I've already briefed James on the operation," Ash said. "Once we have your director on board, I'll contact the council and they'll start mobilizing nests near the nighttime targets. In the meantime, you and I will hop on a plane back to Denver with Dr. Hayes."

I shook my head. "Everly has PTF troops standing by to secure this facility. We don't need to take Dr. Hayes anywhere."

Ash gave me an impatient look. "You're not much for showmanship, are you? Which do you think will make the better impression: a quiet exchange in the middle of the night, or a public address at which James hands Dr. Hayes over to Director Harris under the afternoon sun and announces vampire participation in a joint operation that crippled the Fantasia network and saved the summit?"

"Okay, I take your point, but I can't go home yet."

"Why not?" James's voice came out of the phone sounding close to panic. A knife twisted in my heart.

Ash frowned. "I take it you didn't find your friend?"

I shook my head.

"What friend?" James asked. "What's happened?"

"Follow your orders," Ash said. "We'll see you in Denver." They hung up before James or I could respond. Tucking the phone away, Ash leveled their steady stare at me. "If the cat isn't here, there's nothing we can do."

"We can *look* for him," I said incredulously. "I may have a way to track where the market people took him, but I need to get back to that underground bunker."

"You *may* have?"

I couldn't hold their gaze. "There's no guarantee."

"Then the answer is no. We're on a clock to solidify our position before the summit. We don't have time for a wild goose chase."

I lifted my chin. "If not for Chase, this whole plan would have been dead in the water. You were only able to play the hero here and identify those other targets because Chase got us into the black market to begin with."

"And I appreciate that," Ash said. "Don't let his sacrifice be in vain."

"I can't abandon him again." I shook my head. "I should never have left him there in the first place."

"If you hadn't, you'd be dead, and he'd be no better off."

I crossed my arms. "I'm not leaving without him."

Ash compressed their lips to a tight, threatening line. They turned to Ivan. "Put Dr. Hayes in a car. We'll be along shortly."

Ivan gave me a long look, dripping with disdain, then he nudged the doctor's shoulder. "Let's go."

Ash and I waited in silence until the door closed behind them, plus enough time for them to reach the next floor. Then Ash pinned me with their dark gaze. "You'd risk the safety of the summit for a single fae?"

"Chase is family."

A twinge of . . . *something* drew my attention to the golden thread tied to my core. *Longing?*

"Please, Ash. I'll call Director Harris. I'll explain the situation and arrange her meeting with James. Just help me get to the market and save Chase."

Ash walked to a row of windows on the east wall and looked out over the dark countryside. They sighed. "I'll take you to the market location on my way to the airport and ensure Ivan provides enough muscle to save your friend, should you find him, but that's where I leave you. I can't afford to be drawn into another magical battle with the black market practitioners. I've stuck my neck out too far on this operation already." They crossed their arms and turned to face me. "You'll be missing a pivotal moment in history, and there's no guarantee you'll find your friend. Are you really okay with that?"

Recalling the way I'd felt sitting on the sidelines during the lab raid, I realized it *would* hurt to miss the moment when James delivered Dr. Hayes into PTF custody and announced the existence of vampires to the world, but not as much as it would hurt to lose Chase. I met Ash's curious gaze and let them feel my resolve. "We each have our role to play."

Ash smiled at the echo of their earlier words. "Then it's time to go."

Chapter 20

IT TOOK THE better part of an hour to backtrack to the field where Ash and I made our escape from the black market, and each second that ticked by struck me like a physical blow. Would enough of the portal remain? Would Chase have been moved already? Was he even still alive?

I shook my head. *I can't think like that. Not yet.*

Wind laced with the scent of a storm tore through the open windows of the SUV. I shivered and rubbed my arms for warmth. We were approaching the wee hours of the morning, and the memory of sunlight on my skin was a fading dream. Ash rode beside our vampire driver, since they were most likely to recognize something in the dark landscape sliding past, while I sat in back with Dr. Hayes and her vampire guard. The doctor's stupor dissipated as we drove, though a sense of sleepy relaxation clung to her. Hopefully, by the time she landed in Colorado, there'd be no evidence of Ivan's mental tampering.

I glanced over and found Dr. Hayes studying me as if I were a sample in one of her Petri dishes.

"You're the halfer who's immune to iron," she said. "The one who stormed the PTF board meeting on national television."

"So?"

"You want to save lives."

I nodded.

"So do I."

"You kill people," I said coldly.

"And you haven't?" she asked. "I saw the aftermath at Arlington."

I turned away, staring out my window.

"There." Ash pointed, and we rolled to a stop in front of a red barn that, I assumed, hid the market's main entrance. The structure was large enough to encase my entire house with room to spare.

Ash twisted in their seat. "Last chance. Are you sure you don't want to see this operation through to the end?"

"That *is* what I'm doing." I opened the door, grabbed my pack, and slipped out.

Hayes caught my gaze. "Humans must evolve to survive, as you have."

I closed the door.

"Happy hunting," Ash said through their open window. "And, Alex . . . try not to die."

Ash's SUV drove off, leaving me in a cloud of dust with the second vehicle and the five vampire goons Ivan had assigned to accompany me. Ivan himself would babysit the Purity lab until the agents Harris sent arrived to take custody of the facility. As predicted, the PTF director hadn't been thrilled to discover we'd taken action without alerting her, but my update had given her other things to worry about. We were all going to have a *very* busy night.

"Let's see what's inside," I said, pulling open the barn door. I didn't expect to find much, but I needed to verify that the market hosts hadn't done anything crazy, like collapse the bunker, that would thwart our rescue attempt.

A switch near the door flooded the interior with light from six wall-mounted lamps. All evidence of the Jeeps that had pursued us was gone save a tapestry of overlapping footprints and tire tracks crisscrossing the dirt floor. A mechanic's workbench and a stack of crates occupied one wall. The steel frame of a large cage elevator filled the northeast corner.

I dropped my pack and headed for the elevator. "There's our way down."

All six of us fit with room to spare, though I doubted I was the only one uncomfortable in the cage. Especially after seeing the lab.

Rather than a modern button panel, the elevator had a single lever that could be cranked to one side or the other. I scissored the cage door closed and swung the lever to the left. The cage dropped half an inch before catching—just enough to launch my stomach into my throat. Gears turned, chains clinked, and the cage descended into a concrete shaft.

Either the bunker where the market took place was deeper than I imagined, or the elevator was incredibly slow. Or maybe my anxiety was simply stretching my perception of time to drive me nuts. Whatever the case, a lifetime seemed to pass before the bottom of the shaft opened up. The dim light filtering in from above stretched just far enough to reveal a switch on the wall near the elevator. Everything beyond was a sea of shadows.

Opening the door, I flipped the switch. Strings of lights flared overhead, illuminating the auction's staging area. Scraps of paper, splinters of wood from broken pallets, and a single service cart with a bent wheel littered the abandoned space.

This is probably where the portal was opened.

The vampires spread out, securing the area. One opened a door and let out a low whistle. "Looks like quite the party."

The door led to the right of the main stage. From there, I could see the devastation caused by my escape—shattered cages, broken stalls, walls riddled with bullet holes. Empty spaces showed where intact booths had been evacuated in their entirety, but the area around the room where Ash and I had been attacked looked like a demolition site. The tunnel through which we'd escaped was a landslide.

Worst were the statues that ringed the stage . . . what was left of them. I stepped carefully amid rubble that had once been living beings. A hand here. Part of a face there. Either the petrification had made them so brittle they couldn't support their own weight, or the market hosts hadn't wanted to leave any identifiable bodies behind. I was betting on the latter.

Among the scattered remains were chunks of calcified scales, feathers, and faces from various fae critters who'd escaped their bonds during the fight only to be caught in the spell's blast radius. I walked through the wreckage, freezing when I recognized the long, stone mustache and lower jaw of the man from my pre-market interview. Picturing the way he'd hurt Chase, I wanted to celebrate Mr. Mustache's fate, but mostly I just felt sick.

"Serves you right," I muttered, prodding the loathsome piece of statue with the toe of my boot.

Something glinted in the rubble. I knelt and lifted a stone too smooth to have broken from the shattered soldiers—the jade pebble the merchant had tried to sell me that morning. I shuddered. *So much devastation caused by such a tiny thing.*

"What's that?" asked one of the vampires, peeking over my shoulder.

I shoved the artifact in my pocket. "Just a rock." Straightening, I pulled out my cell phone. No signal. "I'm going up to make a call."

Back in the barn, I dialed the number for Crossroads.

"I'm here," I said when Ava answered. "Well, technically, I'm in a barn on top of the bunker where the portal was most likely opened, but I had to come above ground to call you."

"That's perfect. It's actually better if you're not directly overlapping the portal's location for this part."

"Okay, what do I do now?"

"I'm sending you a picture."

My phone chimed. I opened Ava's email. She'd sent what looked like a mandala—a circle full of swooping patterns and flowing symbols.

"I need you to draw that on the ground *exactly* as it is in the photo. The outer circle should be at least four feet wide."

I glanced around the barn for anything I could use to draw on the floor. Tearing a greasy sheet off the crates near the workbench, I found a can of rust-preventative spray paint with a picture of a green tractor on the front. I shrugged. "Paint is paint, I guess." I shook the can and started spraying.

The spray can's nozzle didn't give great control, so I had to scuff out and redraw some of the finer lines several times before I was satisfied. Eventually, I snapped a picture of my masterpiece and emailed it to Ava. "Will that work?"

"Let's find out. Step back." The line went dead.

Unsure what was about to happen, I pressed my back to the barn wall and waited.

A dull hum filled the air as the symbols I'd painted started to glow. Arcs of energy crackled over the surface of my design. The hairs along my arms and the back of my neck stood on end. My ears popped, and the air above the sigil was filled with a shimmer that distorted my view of the far wall.

Jynx stepped out of the shimmering space—short white hair fanned like a static-charged mane around her face and an expression like a thundercloud. Her bare feet didn't seem to touch the ground as she stepped away from the portal. Her cerulean gaze locked onto me like lightning to a rod, sending tingles down my spine. Seeing her made me want to jump for joy and run and hide all at once.

I hadn't realized Ava's plan involved anyone physically coming here. A portal over that kind of distance was a massive undertaking. The only other time I'd seen it done, Targe and Ava had half-killed a few dozen fae and werewolves to power it. Even with enough juice, fae could only teleport to places they'd already seen, and I was pretty sure none of them had set foot in this barn before. I eyed the sigil, wondering what exactly those symbols I'd drawn had done . . . and who was paying the cost for this spell.

Ava was close on Jynx's heels, her usual waitress attire swapped for black leggings crossed with double thigh sheaths housing foot-long blades. The butt of another knife protruded above the edge of her left boot, and a bandolier of squat throwing daggers draped her fitted shirt from shoulder to waist like a Miss America sash.

I took a step forward to greet them, but I stopped short when a third person stepped through the still-visible distortion of the portal. Hortense wore her usual "old lady" glamour to mask the inhuman green of her hag complexion and the red of her eyes, but the Victorian-style dress she preferred was on full display. As was the thin, black scabbard of her rapier.

I frowned in confusion. Not that I wasn't happy to see my old tutor—her fighting skills put even Kai's to shame—but she had no stake in this that I could see, and fae did nothing for free.

A man I'd never seen before stepped through next. He wore a light-brown suit that was loose around his shoulders and tight around his gut. A mop of dark, unkempt hair topped a ruddy complexion with full cheeks, a large nose, and narrow, deep-set eyes. I squinted, focusing past the haze of magic that made this man appear human, and found green skin, a shade darker than Hortense's. His eyes took on a yellow sheen, and his craggy features now resembled a collection of mossy rocks along a riverbed. A long, curved blade hung from his waist, hidden along with his true appearance by his glamour.

Stunned by this unexpected parade, I simply stared as Targe stepped into being, wearing what looked like the hides of half a dozen animals, a circlet of bone, and a heavy leather belt from which twin axes the size of my torso hung at either hip. The shimmer of the portal snapped closed with a soft *pop* and a ripple of pressure that rocked me back on my heels.

I shook my head. "How. . . ?"

"You didn't expect me to just sit around twiddling my thumbs while my brother was in danger, did you?" Jynx grinned. "This is going to be great leverage the next time Chase gives me his 'don't be reckless' speech."

I turned to Ava. "But how did you open a portal all the way from Colorado to a place you'd never been before?"

She shrugged. "A pair of matched sigils solved the targeting problem. As for the power . . ."

"Chase is family," Targe said, "and he's the reason Crossroads is legal. I made it clear that anyone staying under my roof owed him. They were all too happy to pay that debt in the form of powering our spell."

"Though some of us chose to lend more direct assistance," Hortense said.

"Speaking of . . ." I turned to the stranger and offered my hand. "I don't think we've met. I'm Alex."

"Pete." He gave my hand one stiff shake that bruised my fingers.

"I figured we might need some decent fighters," Targe said. "Goblins are strong and sturdy. Good in a scrape."

"Happy to have you," I said with feeling. "Although, you all should know, I have some other helpers waiting downstairs, in the room where I think the portal was opened."

The fae went still as statues.

"PTF?" Hortense asked.

I took a deep breath. "Vampires."

Targe's expression darkened. "What are you doing working with vampires?"

I shrugged, not willing to dive into the whole convoluted tale of orchestrating a positive spin for the vampire's societal reveal and bid for membership in the Paranatural Alliance. "They were available."

"Well, now *we* are available," Targe said. "We can handle this on our own."

"I barely escaped the black market with my life last time," I said. "The people holding Chase have magic, guns, and a wide array of anti-fae paraphernalia. I'll take all the help I can get."

"I'm not working with no stinking bloodsuckers." Pete spat a reddish glob into the dirt.

And this is why I kept my project to get the vampires admitted to the summit a secret from the fae, I thought with a sigh. *But they can't avoid each other forever. This mission might make a good dry run for future interactions . . . assuming we all survive the introductions.*

I straightened my shoulders. "You've committed to rescuing Chase, as have the vampires downstairs. We have a common goal . . . unless you're planning to back out of your agreement with Targe?"

"Course not!" Pete said.

"Then I suggest you make peace with working alongside vampires." I held Pete's gaze until he looked away with a grumble, then I met the eyes of each of the others. Jynx and Ava took my pronouncement in stride. They were young and less steeped in the dogma of their people. Targe looked angry, but then, Targe usually looked angry. Hortense's expression was unreadable.

When no more objections were voiced, I gestured to the elevator. "Let's get going."

Hortense fell into step beside me at the back of the group and whispered, "You've chosen a dangerous path."

"This is the only path I see with a future." I cast her a sidelong glance. "I hope you'll walk it with me."

She frowned, watching Pete's back as he lumbered into the elevator. "We shall see."

Silence filled the shaft on the long, slow ride down. The fae crowded in the center, as far from the steel frame of the cage as they could get. When the elevator reached the bottom, Ivan's five vampire soldiers turned to face us. Five guns left their holsters. Fangs flashed.

The fae at my back bristled. Hands dropped to hilts and hafts. Jynx shrank. Her dress fluttered to the ground beside the snarling snow leopard she'd become.

"Stop!" I raised my hands, one palm facing the vampires, the other facing the fae. "Stand down."

Since I wasn't yet riddled with bullets, I opened the gate and stepped out of the elevator, though I kept myself carefully between the two groups. Facing the vampires, I said, "These are my friends. They've come to help."

"How did they get here?" asked the blond-haired, brown-eyed vampire who seemed to be the leader of their group.

"That doesn't matter right now. The important thing is that they're the ones who are going to get us where we need to go next."

No one moved.

I took a step forward, hands still up and open. "I know a lot of what you've been asked to do tonight has gone against your instincts, but you understand that there are larger plans in motion, right? Plans that Ivan has instructed you to help me with."

Blondie frowned.

"Right now, that means working with these fae to take down a black market stronghold."

I held my breath for another moment, then the blond vampire holstered his weapon and motioned for the others to do likewise. "We'll behave if they do."

I tipped my head in gratitude. Not that an unarmed vampire was any less of a threat, but the gesture mattered.

The fae shuffled out of the elevator but remained clumped together. The two groups faced off from either side of the room.

I looked at Ava. "What now?"

Ava cleared her throat, rubbed her hands together, and closed her eyes. "Now I search for your portal scar."

We all stood quietly, watching as Ava turned first one way, then the other, then slid one foot slowly along the floor and shifted her weight in a single laborious step. She repeated the process . . . again, and again, and again. Jynx moved the broken cart and other tripping hazards out of the way as Ava crept along in her strange, circular dance. I shifted my weight back and forth between the balls of my feet, wanting to ask what she was doing, but afraid to break her concentration.

"Here," she said softly. She opened her eyes.

"Can you tell where they took him?"

"Better than that," she said with a smile. "Portals tear the Rift, and those tears leave scars when they close. The longer a portal is open, the deeper the scar." She moved her fingers through the air as if tracing something I couldn't see. "Sometimes, if the scar hasn't completely healed, a fae with similar abilities can reopen the portal."

"So we can just . . . walk into their stronghold?"

Ava nodded. "With any luck, we'll catch Chase's captors off guard."

"Though we'll have no idea what we're walking into," added Hortense. "They may have set traps against pursuit."

"Either way, we don't have a better option," I said. "Chase is on the other side of this scar."

Ava looked at Targe, who joined her. He also traced his hands over the empty space Ava had identified as our entry point. Then he said in a gruff voice, "Everybody ready?"

The vampires took up sprinter's stances. Pete and Hortense drew their blades. Jynx coiled, ready to spring. I checked my gun in its holster and slipped my knife from its sheath.

"Ready."

Targe counted, "One, two, *three . . .*"

The two leprechauns grunted, and the air split open with a *pop.*

Jynx dove headfirst through the narrow space between Targe and Ava as the two of them strained away from each other. The vampires went through next, a blur of motion I could barely track.

"Hurry," Ava hissed through gritted teeth. Sweat sheened her forehead.

I charged through the shimmering air.

The world inverted, twisting my senses inside out. Then reality snapped into focus around me like a slap to the face. I stumbled forward and bumped into the blond vampire's back. Catching my balance, I looked at my surroundings. Three dozen workers in gray jumpsuits stared back at me, frozen at various stages of cataloging items spread across row after row of shelves in what looked like a massive distribution warehouse. Iron girders, iron shelves . . . just being in this building would weaken the fae.

Jynx launched herself at the nearest worker, sinking her teeth into a startled woman's forearm.

The woman screamed, and the tableau was broken. Shouts went up all around, echoing off the rafters. Workers dropped what they'd been handling and scattered.

So much for the element of surprise.

"Are these ones okay to kill?" Blondie shot the question over his shoulder.

"No," I said. I wasn't sure exactly where we'd landed, but there was a chance these workers didn't know what they were involved in. Even if they did, justice was a trial and a prison cell, not getting your throat ripped out because you worked for assholes. "Incapacitate only, just like before."

Blondie shouted something in Russian, and the vampires became streaks of darkness flowing through the aisles.

"Like before?"

I spun and found Hortense by my shoulder, staring at me with her inscrutable poker face. Pete was a few steps away, sword in hand, glaring in the direction the blond vampire had gone.

"It seems this lot were more than simply 'available'," she said.

An alarm sounded, splitting my ears with a screeching siren. Red and white lights flashed from the ceiling. I winced, squinting through the strobe effect as the vampires chased the workers deeper into the facility. Targe and Ava were the last to emerge from the portal. Ava clapped her hands over her ears as she emerged. Targe drew his weapons.

"Which way?" he shouted over the alarm.

The woman Jynx had mauled whimpered on the floor, curled around her shredded arm. She flinched when I crouched in front of her. "Where are the fae captives?"

The woman shook her head, continuing to whimper. Jynx hissed. Blood stained the white fur around her mouth.

"B-b-b-back room," the woman stammered. "Live storage."

"Where is the back room?" I demanded.

The woman curled tighter, scrunching her eyes closed. Tears drenched her cheeks. Jynx swiped her claws across the woman's leg, tearing fabric and skin alike.

"Back room," the woman bawled. "Back room! Back room!"

I shook my head and stood. "Let's spread out and look for this 'back room.'"

Targe nodded and headed down the aisle to my right with Ava and Jynx in tow. I turned left with Pete and Hortense. We passed three workers the vampires had dropped, all unconscious, before we reached the end of the aisle. Shouts, screams, and crashes loud enough to be heard over the alarm showed the vampires were clearing other areas. More shelves towered overhead at the end of the aisle, the first row of many running perpendicular to those behind us. This warehouse wasn't just storage; it was a maze.

A group of eight humans—all wearing uniforms that looked suspiciously like PTF riot gear—surged toward us from the right, each armed with a slender baton that crackled with faint blue light. Pete raised his sword and charged forward with a blood-curdling battle cry that stopped the humans in their tracks. Hortense shook her head, as if embarrassed to be seen in such uncouth company, but she followed him into battle. Gripping my knife, I brought up the rear, happy to let the others take the lead. The aisle was wide enough to drive a forklift through, which was an advantage for the fighters with longer blades. I, on the other hand, had to get up close and personal.

Pete bowled into the first guard, knocking him to the ground and swinging his sword in a downward slash that was clearly meant to do more than just incapacitate.

"Try not to kill them," I shouted as I closed with a lanky brunette with bushy sideburns.

Pete continued his slash, but before the strike could connect, another guard's baton slammed into Pete's ribs.

I expected the blow to leave a nasty burn, the usual fae reaction to iron touching their skin. Instead, Pete jerked and twitched. His eyes bulged.

Hortense's rapier whipped through the air, forcing the guard to withdraw his baton to block her attack.

Pete stumbled, panting, clutching his side with his free hand. A hand that now boasted knobbly green fingers and long black nails. The blow had shattered Pete's glamour, exposing him in all his green-skinned, yellow-eyed, goblin glory. The smell of charred flesh came a moment later. He *had* been burned, but that was no normal iron rod.

"Fae!" shouted one of the guards.

I hoped, seeing what they were up against, the guards might turn tail and run, but if anything, they seemed emboldened by this news.

The ring of metal on metal joined the blaring alarm as Hortense engaged the main force, pushing them back with speed, strength, and skill that more than made up for their superior numbers. Then I lost track of what was happening with the others, as the man in front of me swung one of those crackling blue rods at my head. I did *not* want to experience what had happened to Pete firsthand.

The baton whistled through the air as I ducked low and took a swing at my opponent's knee. Sparks jumped from my blade as it connected with the iron fibers woven into his clothes.

He skipped back, taking only a shallow graze. Not enough to slow him.

The baton came down in a chopping motion similar to Pete's. I raised my blade to block. The impact sent tingles through my bones, and my arms shook under the baton's continued pressure. This guy was stronger than he looked.

A flicker of movement drew my attention down. A quick snap of the wrist extended a second baton in what had been the guard's empty hand. The new threat whistled toward me, trailing crackling blue light that danced like lightning along its surface.

The overhead baton still threatened to split my skull if I dropped my block, so I twisted as the second rod made contact. Pain lanced through my side, exploding through my nervous system and seizing my muscles, but the momentum of the hit combined with my initial motion was enough to complete the turn. The baton above slipped down my back as I rolled off the second hit, and the two batons connected. A jolt of energy slammed against my torso, launching me away from my attacker.

I slid across the floor on my stomach, too stunned to break my fall. My muscles continued to twitch and spasm. My fingers cramped around my knife.

Rolling to my side, I found my attacker had been sent sprawling as well. Apparently, the batons did not like to touch.

Hortense screamed, drawing my attention to a cloud of glittering, gray dust. Iron shavings. Her "old lady" glamour melted away, along with several layers of exposed green skin, as she whipped her sword in blind fury and stumbled out of the toxic cloud. The humans surged forward, pressing their advantage as our best fighter gasped and coughed, spraying the ground with blood.

Pete sliced one of the three guards he was engaged with across the chest, then retreated as another pulled what looked like a grenade from her uniform.

Releasing my knife, I drew the gun from my holster, exhaled to steady my aim, and shot the woman with the grenade. She jerked backward with the bullet's impact. The object she was holding fell with her, bursting apart in a second shower of glittering dust.

I shifted my aim to the group closing on Hortense and fired until my magazine was empty. Several bullets pinged off armor, but four bodies dropped to a chorus of grunts and yelps. Maybe they'd survive. Maybe not. Using magic would have given me a less lethal option, but channeling took time. I wasn't willing to risk our lives to save theirs.

When the dust settled, two of the downed guards didn't move. One glared at me, gripping a wound on her arm. The fourth crawled toward his more fortunate companions, leaving a trail of blood through the iron shavings as he dragged legs that no longer worked.

"I thought we weren't supposed to kill anyone?"

I pointed my empty gun at Blondie before registering his voice. Seeing him standing over me, I holstered the pistol and retrieved my knife. "They didn't leave me much choice."

Footsteps pounded the concrete behind me. Another group of soldiers charged into view, probably drawn by the gunfire. Leading the newcomers was a woman I recognized—the petite speed demon from my fight at the market.

Spotting me, she raised her fists with a smile. Blue light crackled along her gloved knuckles.

Blondie whooshed past me in a gust of wind that tangled my hair.

"Be careful," I shouted. "She's fast!"

The speed demon became a smear of color imprinted on my vision as she zoomed forward to meet the vampire. Sparks flew, and for a moment, Blondie's startled face snapped into focus. He clearly hadn't expected a human to land a hit, let alone for that hit to *hurt*. Then the two high-speed combatants became a series of streaks and blurs that collided with nearby shelves and sent objects flying in poltergeist-like bursts of rage.

The advancing humans continued their charge, doing their best to dodge the blur of motion that was their leader going toe-to-toe with a vampire. On my other side, the man whose batons had sent us both flying and the soldier with the bullet hole through her shoulder joined the still standing guards. We were surrounded.

Gripping my knife to keep it from slipping out of my sweaty palm, I sprang to my feet and shouted, "We've got more incoming. Hortense, how are you doing?"

The court tutor spat in a most unladylike way and wiped a sleeve across her bloody chin. "I can still fight."

Her voice sounded raw enough to make me wince, and her face was pocked with lighter patches of green where her skin had blistered, but if Hortense said she could fight, I wasn't going to call her a liar.

A deafening crash echoed far to my right. We weren't the only ones engaging enemy forces. Somewhere in the warehouse, the others were also fighting.

I opened myself up to the flow of energy around me. I'd hoped to avoid using my magic since, despite Ash's blood, a week's worth of calories, and half a day of rest, I wasn't fully recovered. But these guards were both stronger and faster than I'd anticipated, and they used dirty tricks. We needed every advantage we had.

"Double dosing!" The woman with the hole in her arm pulled something out of a pouch on her belt and slammed her fist against her thigh. Her eyelids fluttered. Her breathing sped up. Veins bulged along her neck. When she straightened, an empty syringe clattered to the floor.

Of course. That's why the guy I'd fought had been able to match my speed and strength despite my fae advantage, and why Hortense's superior sword skills hadn't obliterated all opposition in the first few seconds. Not everyone who took Fantasia manifested magical powers, especially in small doses. Some just got a physical boost and a sense of invincibility. Others went completely nuts. It made sense that Purity would cultivate soldiers who could take Fantasia without losing their minds.

"Double dosing," said the man who'd zapped me. He too jabbed a syringe into his thigh.

A chorus of "double dosing" sounded among the approaching guards, sending a chill down my spine.

"Fae suppression!" came a call near the back of the advancing troop.

Three spheres shot into the air, shattering against the rafters in a shower of iron dust.

Hortense and Pete stood back-to-back beside me, directly under the descending cloud of glittering metal. I didn't know what kind of magic goblins usually had, but Targe's comment about them being sturdy made it seem like physical combat was Pete's main superpower. The only magic I'd really seen Hortense do had been ritualistic—powerful but slow. Not ideal for a fight. Like the goblin, she seemed more comfortable with the sword in her hand. That left me to handle the magic.

Blue-gray fog rolled across my vision as I drew more power. The warehouse lights seemed to dim. Faces peeked out of the shadows—distorted masks made by beings with only a vague impression of what faces should look like. I pulled the flowing energy through my center, filtered it with the ruby glow of my fae magic, formed the spell I wanted in my mind, then directed it with my raised blade.

"Hold your breath," I shouted.

Pete and Hortense crouched into defensive postures and did their best to shield their faces from the iron rain.

An unnatural wind howled through the aisle, snatching up the glittering dust and carrying it away. Hair whipped across my face. Fabric snapped and fluttered. A few people stumbled in the sudden gust. The iron shavings covering the floor stirred and shifted, heavier than their drifting counterparts. It took a second gust to clear them. When the area was free of the toxic dust, I lowered my arm. The wind cut off, leaving an eerie silence that rang in my ears.

The guards might have been surprised by my indoor squall, but it hadn't slowed them down. While I'd been clearing the air, they'd closed around us. Hortense fended off the remnants of the original group, while Pete faced the new threat. Both were clearly experts—no fae who'd reached adulthood had less than a century of experience with a blade—but they were barely holding the space around us. The man who'd sent me flying earlier matched Hortense's sword swing for swing with his electrified batons, while his friends harried her from either side. Pete was losing ground to the onslaught of new bodies, dodging batons as his curved blade slashed wildly to keep them at a distance. The space between them, the space *I* occupied, was shrinking fast.

Pulling in another wave of energy, I dropped to one knee, pressed my knuckles to the ground, and sent my magic into the earth. My pulse raced. Sweat drenched my forehead. Concrete rippled in a wave that sent several of the advancing guards stumbling into their neighbors. Two charged batons met, setting off a concussive blast that knocked several soldiers to the floor.

The fog swirling through my vision thickened.

Welcome back.

I jerked at the words then shook my head, trying to dislodge the creepy feeling of someone whispering in my ear. The beings in the Rift were dangerous, but I couldn't let them distract me.

If only Emma were here to act as my paladin. . . . Guilt and remorse followed that thought. Being my paladin was what had cost Emma her sight, and her magic, in the first place.

A guttural cry on Hortense's side brought my attention to the woman I'd shot in the arm. White froth bubbled from her lips and streaked her chin. Thick veins bulged beneath her skin. Bloodshot eyes looked on the verge of popping out of their sockets. Blood trickled from the woman's nose, mixing with the froth to turn it pink. It seemed a double dose of Fantasia had been too much for her.

She'd remained at the back as her companions advanced, probably fighting not to be overwhelmed by the drug. Now she charged . . . straight at me.

Gulping Rift energy like life, I compressed my magic into a dozen razor-sharp blades and shot them through the tip of my physical knife.

The rabid woman jerked and jolted with each impact. Blood bloomed from a dozen new wounds where my ephemeral blades had pierced her, but she didn't stop.

I staggered, panting. Sparks danced in the darkness closing around the edges of my vision.

You've been avoiding us, said a multilayered chorus of voices. A grinning face overlaid that of the crazed woman rushing toward me.

Hortense's blade sliced through the air. The side of the woman's neck opened. Crimson life spilled out, but she still didn't stop. She didn't even slow down.

Blue lightning arced over Hortense's rigid body as one of her opponents took advantage of the opening.

Dropping my knife, I slammed both palms against the woman's chest as her arms closed around me. I opened myself fully. Energy rushed in. The ruby glow at my core shrank and stuttered, flickering like the last light in a storm. Then it winked out.

Power surged through me. I pushed it all through my open palms, into the mindless woman who was trying to bite me like some B-movie zombie after brains.

My hands grew warm, then hot. The woman seemed to vibrate. With a *pop* like the cork flying free of a champagne bottle, the pressure under my palms gave way. My hands sank into the cavity, scraping raw bone where the woman's ribs abruptly ended. Viscous blood dripped down my wrists. I yanked my hands away.

The woman dropped to her knees then folded backward over her lower legs. I could see the floor through the perfect, six-inch hole seared through her chest. Speckles of viscera dotted the concrete behind her like confetti—all that remained of the woman's missing heart and lungs.

Turning away, I reached up to cover my mouth but quickly thought better of it when I smelled the blood on my hands.

The nearest attackers took a collective step back, clearly shocked by the violent dismemberment of their companion.

Hortense, freed from the muscle-cramping electricity of her attacker's baton, took the opportunity to separate her opponent's head from his shoulders. The man's severed head hit the floor with a heavy thud and a wet squelch, a look of surprise frozen on his face.

The guards snapped out of their momentary stupor. One man turned and fled. The rest doubled down on their attack to a chorus of shouts and almost animal howls. No one was without injury at this point, but those still on their feet showed no signs of stopping.

A wave of dizziness and enervation swept over me. I sank to one knee, hard enough to bruise, and braced my hands on the floor to keep from kissing it. This was more than nausea or horror at what I'd just done . . . this was magical backlash.

Chapter 21

I CHOKED ON bile. Sweat poured off my skin, and I shivered till my bones ached. Panic chased the chills as images of Garrett in his wheelchair and Emma waking up blind in a hospital bed filled my mind . . . and they were the lucky ones. Worse were the walking shells left from a full burnout. Since I was still conscious, I could probably rule that out, but even a minor backlash could do serious damage. It had been stupid of me to draw so much energy without a paladin to help channel it.

I forced myself to stand, exhaling in relief when my limbs responded. I could see Pete and Hortense keeping the guards at bay, protecting me while I recovered. I could hear the clang of metal on metal and smell the sharp tang of blood. I could taste the salt from my sweat and feel its dampness on my skin. I exhaled in relief, but . . . *something* was wrong.

I tentatively prodded the conduits that allowed me to channel magic, afraid of what I might find. They seemed intact. Rift energy swirled sluggishly through my body, drifting without direction.

Pete cursed, snapping my attention back to physical reality. He'd tripped over one of the unmoving guards on the ground and lost his footing. His remaining attackers swarmed. One took Pete's sword through his gut, then Pete disappeared under a hail of batons, knives, and steel-toe boots as the guards overwhelmed him with sheer numbers.

A woman with sharp features and a long black braid turned toward Hortense's now-exposed back.

I grabbed my knife off the floor and dove between them, catching the blow on my blade an inch from Hortense's shoulder.

Pete thrashed and flailed, kicking my ankle as he tried to break free of the mob beating him bloody. Hortense dropped another body, but two guards circled around Pete's skirmish to join her fight. Another broke off and turned to me. Further up the aisle, streaks of lightning burned afterimages across my vision as the speedy practitioner from the market kept Blondie engaged with her electrified gloves.

I didn't want to cast more magic until my system had a chance to recover . . . but a single knife wasn't going to save Pete, and both Blondie and Hortense were busy.

Dropping into a low stance, I reversed my grip on my knife and called my magic. Carefully this time. Only a little.

Icy fingers scraped my insides, digging into my flesh.

Hey there. The voice wasn't mine, but it was in my head.

I gasped and stumbled.

The woman whose attack I'd blocked jabbed her baton toward my face. I managed to twist to the side, but the metal scraped my cheek. A *zing* of electricity danced across my skin like the zap from a doorknob when I wore slippers in winter—not enough to drop me, but it made me itch.

I was here first, said a different voice, though the words registered more as thoughts than sounds.

That doesn't matter if you can't keep her, said a third.

The lazy currents of Rift energy that had been swirling inside me took on a sense of purpose, surging through my body in a race for control.

Shit. That backlash might not have done any physical damage, but it let in some uninvited guests.

I reached for my fae magic—the magic I used to filter Rift energy when I wasn't panic casting—but the ruby glow was nowhere to be found. Fear gripped me. Had it been snuffed by the torrent of energy that let the demons in?

Bony knuckles connected with the side of my face. I stumbled into Hortense, which earned me a curse but kept me on my feet.

Blinking though watery eyes, I managed to block a kick to my side. The second of my attackers seemed to have lost his shock stick, which was great, but his punch had been plenty painful. I'd be lucky if my cheek wasn't fractured.

My female opponent swung her baton at my head. I ducked, which forced the man who'd punched me to dodge as his companion's momentum carried the crackling weapon in his direction.

Still in a crouch, I slashed out with my knife. The blade connected with the woman's thigh, but the metal threads in her riot gear deflected most of the force, leaving only a shallow cut as she jumped away. Using the momentum of my slash, I spun and kicked at the man. He shifted his weight at the last moment to save his knee. I wasn't sure if these two had double dosed or not, but they were definitely faster than standard humans.

A sickening numbness spread through my limbs as the demons who'd invaded my body jockeyed for space. Every anchor they sank into my flesh sent a shockwave through my system, and I lost a little more mobility. If I left them unchecked, I'd eventually lose control of my entire body, and worse, my magic. I'd become a rifter—a mindless meat puppet for a demon's holiday in the Mortal Realm. There was a small chance I could maintain some level of control, like my father had, but the odds weren't great, and I really didn't want to take that chance. I needed to get them out before I lost more ground.

The glowing rod swung toward me in a backhanded arc.

Rather than dodge or block, I matched its pace and rotated with the swing, sliding my hand along the woman's forearm to guide the movement. Back-to-back, we came full circle. The tip of the baton connected with the shoulder of the man who'd been closing in from the side. His eyes went wide. He fell back as his muscles went rigid.

Continuing my pivot, I slid the tip of my knife into the woman's side, just below her ribs. She screamed and jerked away, clutching her free hand to the bloody wound.

Pouncing on the moment of breathing space that strike earned me, I diverted my awareness to the battle being waged *inside* my body.

The bluish fog I'd grown used to seeing when I tapped into the Rift swirled like dark storm clouds around my core, battering against each other as the demons sought access to my deepest center. Tethers bound those clouds to my body, anchored by twisted barbs from which darkness spread like an infection. As I sank toward the anchors, the buzzing, white noise that filled my head resolved into voices.

You had one at that thing on the hill.

A corpse. This one's better.

She's too much for you to handle.

I'll devour you both.

I'd like to see you try.

Focusing on the nearest anchor, I wrapped my energy around the barb and yanked. The tether resisted, digging into my flesh, but a second tug jerked it free.

I gasped, doubling over around a sudden pain in my chest.

One down. I looked around the swirling mess of my core and felt an overwhelming sense of dread as I tried to count the demonic anchors twisted among the writhing threads of my soul.

Whatever. They all have to go. I raced to the next anchor and pulled it free, invoking another shudder-inducing lance of ice through my heart.

A jolt of pain, hotter than an iron straight from the fire, lit up my nervous system like a Christmas tree.

My lungs seized. I slashed blindly, the attack made clumsy by rigid muscles and numb fingers.

My knife clattered to the ground, but the pain retreated. Apparently even a sloppy attack had been enough to bluff a credible threat.

I wobbled on gelatin legs. The skin over my abdomen felt seared. Strong arms pulled my elbows back, forcing my shoulder blades together.

My vision cleared to reveal the woman with the baton. Electricity crackled along its length as she waved it in front of my face. She bared her teeth in an expression too feral to be called a smile.

Behind her, Pete had stopped moving, though several guards continued to kick him. Hortense was holding her own, but barely. Even with the guards she'd dropped, we were still outnumbered four to one, and I couldn't use magic till I got the demons out of my system. But even as I hung there, I could feel the anchors I'd pulled resetting, spreading their influence as I was overwhelmed in both battles. I needed to focus to defend my core, but that blue lightning was streaking toward my face.

Demons. Humans. I couldn't fight them both.

A snarling streak of gray-white fur soared overhead, and oversized paws tipped with two-inch claws slammed into the woman's smirking face.

The baton's tip whizzed past my nose, close enough to smell the static.

The woman screamed and stumbled back, rivulets of blood pouring from a dozen gashes across her face. Jynx dropped lightly to the floor. The scent of singed fur and cooked meat filled the air.

The guards pummeling Pete scattered to a chorus of shouts, tripping over each other in an effort to avoid the thick ax tearing through their ranks. Targe yanked his bloody blade out of the rib cage of a man who hadn't moved quickly enough. The hand clutching that shaft looked as if it had been dunked in a deep fryer—charred skin peeling off his knuckles and angry red welts up to his elbow.

Using the distraction of my friends' arrival, I head-butted the man pinning my arms.

He jerked, but didn't let go, so I dropped my weight, stepped deeper into his space, and pivoted. The man tumbled over my hip, finally releasing my arms in order to break his fall. Except he never hit the ground.

The man's startled gaze met mine as he passed straight through the slightly distorted concrete floor and vanished from view. A second later, his scream sounded in the rafters above, cutting off abruptly at the end of his two-story fall.

"Can't leave you alone for a second." Ava dusted her hands as she straightened. The floor between us no longer shimmered. Blood matted the hair on one side of her head, and her lip was split.

"I appreciate the assist," I said. "Can you keep them off me for a minute?"

"That's why we're here," Targe said. He threw his ax into seemingly empty space only to have it embed itself in the back of the woman Jynx had mauled.

Damn, teleportation is cool.

"We've got you covered," Ava said with a smile that opened the split in her lip.

It went against every instinct I had to close my eyes in the middle of a fight, but I needed to deal with the battle inside me. My friends would take care of the rest.

The certainty of that thought startled me. I'd spent most of my life alone, keeping people at a distance, even the people I considered my friends. I'd been determined not to rely on anyone else, because the people you were counting on might not be there when you needed them. That independence made me strong, but it also kept me small. Some wars couldn't be won alone.

I smiled. I'd changed a lot in the past year.

Tuning out the battle raging around me, I settled cross-legged on the floor, took a deep breath, and focused on myself.

The corruption had spread to nearly every corner of my body, turning healthy pink to bruised purple. If I'd lost that much ground to a single demon, my friends might have found themselves on the wrong side of my magic. Luckily, I wasn't the only one who'd been distracted by a second fight. The demons who'd set up shop in my body were too busy trying to outmaneuver one another to pay much attention to me.

Since demons didn't have bodies, it took me a moment to distinguish the three beings fighting for dominance as more than storm clouds of mist and malice, but the thickest patches of darkness moved with intent, each with a distinct energy. Razor talons slashed out from the densest of the clusters, ripping a chunk of blue mist off another like pilfered cotton candy. The shredded energy folded into the larger mass, blending until it was indistinguishable. The third demon swooped in from above, diving toward the creature who'd just taken the hit like a falcon after a field mouse. The two collided, and when they split apart, one was distinctly smaller, though I couldn't tell if it was the falcon or the mouse who'd come out on top.

Something bumped against me in the physical world, but I kept my eyes closed, ignoring the grunts and shouts of the battle I couldn't see. Cooling sweat made me shiver.

Doing my best to stay small, I slipped past the dueling demons and wove through the webs of corruption gumming up my insides. It felt wrong to pass the caustic tendrils anchored in my flesh without ripping them out, but dealing with them one at a time would be like playing a game of whack-a-mole, and I didn't have time for games. Now that I could concentrate, my best option was to remove them all at once, so I choked back my revulsion and raced toward the glowing white core at the center of my being. That's where I was strongest, so that's where I'd stage my counterattack.

The last time I'd had to kick someone out of my body, I'd dueled Ash's manifestation in an all-or-nothing battle in the deepest recesses of my soul—the vault that stored my true name. But Ash was a crafty bastard older than dirt. I didn't intend to let these squabbling interlopers anywhere near my name.

Searching the threads of energy that made up my core, I found what I was looking for—the barest flicker of a ruby glow.

Thank the stars. I nearly wept in relief. Fae magic was antithetical to demons; the two could not occupy the same space. I'd worried the flame of my magic might have been snuffed out during my unbridled channeling, but the flood of Rift energy hadn't overwhelmed it completely.

Cradling the precious ember in my incorporeal hands, I blew softly, feeding it energy. Not Rift energy—that would only damage the spark further. No, I poured my life into the ember, and the ember glowed brighter. This was the one protection I had against demons that no other practitioner could claim . . . the reason I still had a chance to reclaim my body despite being so far gone.

A prickling sensation told me the demons had finally noticed my presence, but they were too late. Flickering flames wrapped my hand, dancing along my fingers and up my forearm, growing as I fed it.

What is she—?

The demon's question cut off as I reached out with my blazing hand and grabbed one of the thick, red strands of my central core. Memories flooded me, the foundation of who I was—watching my father drive away for the last time; playing chess with Uncle Sol; walking into my mother's hospital room; buying my mountain sanctuary; exhibiting my art in James's gallery; finding out I was part fae; standing up to the PTF directors; meeting Bael; defying the vampire council; falling in love; losing friends; finding a family; fighting, failing, and getting up to fight some more.

People say your life flashes before your eyes when you die . . . but I had no intention of dying. I was reminding my body that I was still alive. Still fighting.

Ruby flames ignited the thread, racing along it as I rode the wave of emotions that accompanied my core memories. Rift energy came from without, a force to be channeled. Fae magic was fueled from within. The only way to use it was to give yourself over to it. My fae magic spread like wildfire, jumping from thread to thread, gaining momentum as my memories—my *life*—fed it. My core became an inferno, searing away the darkness and burning the demons' anchors to ash as I took back what was mine.

Two swirling clouds of blue-gray energy shied away from the blazing onrush. The third, the largest, attacked.

Brave or foolhardy, the demon latched onto one of the healthy tendrils near my core, pushing against my consciousness. Bubbling corruption spread from its touch, holding back my flames even as they licked at the demon's essence.

A face from a nightmare formed in the mist, all teeth and bones. *You're a thousand years too young to beat me, child.*

I felt the demon's grip squeezing my soul, choking off my power. But this demon didn't know who it was messing with. I'd defied bigger bads than this body-snatching vagabond.

"Maybe if I were human," I whispered back. I welcomed the part of me that was fae, spreading it like a protective coating over my mortal vulnerability, letting the ruby glow infuse every inch of my being.

My heart raced. My breath came in quick, short bursts. This type of magic was hell on my physical body, but I focused all my energy into one final push.

The crimson blaze flared around the defiant demon as I tossed another log on the fire. For a moment the demon stood its ground, holding the conflagration in check, then its corruption boiled away. My flames consumed the roiling mass of angry energy, turning it to so much smoke. Breaking past that hurdle, my magic surged outward, licking at the tails of the other two demons as they fled ahead of my firestorm.

The cleansing flames crashed against the shores of my body and rolled back to me, cauterizing the demon's breach points and confirming nothing remained that shouldn't. My fae fire shrank back to the soft ruby glow I was used to, though it seemed a bit brighter than I remembered.

Rough concrete slapped my cheek.

I opened my eyes. The world was on its side. Legs danced in and out of my field of vision.

I blinked and tried to sit up. My muscles were jelly. My stomach cramped, sending a wave of bile to the back of my throat. Jynx's bloody paws left red prints as she landed in front of me then catapulted toward one of the few remaining guards. Targe's group had turned the tide of battle while I dealt with my pest problem.

I tried again to rise and made it to my elbows, then my hands. Breathing was difficult. Still, I was alive and in control. I would recover.

A section of shelves on the far side of the aisle crumpled, contents spilling to the floor alongside the limp body that had impacted them. Electrical sparks danced over the speedy girl's gloves. Blood glistened on her shirt, though the dark fabric hid the color. Her neck ended in a ragged line of torn tissue and snapped vertebra. Her head dangled several feet away, where Blondie the vampire stood with his back to the rest of us, fingers tangled in his opponent's hair.

Pete, who'd apparently crawled to the edge of the battle once free of his mob, glanced around. I did the same. The others were busy finishing their fights. With the practitioner dead, this war was as good as won. I exhaled.

When I looked back, Pete was moving toward Blondie. His blade arced toward the vampire's exposed neck.

Shit!

Vampires could heal from a lot of things. Decapitation wasn't one of them.

I shouted and tried to stand, willing my enervated limbs to hold my weight. The world seemed to slow as my focus narrowed to the scene unfolding before me. Blondie turned at my shout. Too late. Realization twisted his features as Pete's sword connected with his flesh.

A silver flash dropped like a curtain between the two combatants. A crimson fountain showered them both.

The dead practitioner's head hit the floor with a *squelch*.

Pete howled. His sword clattered to the concrete, severed hand still gripping the hilt.

A dagger zipped past my ear, embedding in the throat of a soldier who'd been about to smash his baton over Hortense's head. She'd turned away from her own fight to slash Pete's arm. The baton landed beside Pete's sword as the guard clutched both hands to his throat, gurgled, and collapsed.

Targe's ax bit into the shoulder of the last guard standing. He yanked it free as the guard dropped to her knees, then he sidestepped as she fell on her face. The battle was over . . . or was it?

Pete retrieved his fallen sword, pulling it from his own severed grasp to wield in his remaining hand. He seemed barely slowed by his missing limb or the thick, almost black blood dripping from the wound.

Blondie pressed his fingers to the side of his neck, then lowered his hand to look at his spilled blood. The gash was already healed, but I doubted the feeling of having his throat cut would fade so quickly. He glared at Pete.

Hortense raised her bloody blade, poised to strike at either man should they make a move.

"Stand aside." Blondie's voice was dangerously low.

"I will not," Hortense said.

"He tried to kill me."

"He did not succeed," she replied.

"My blood was spilled."

"Not nearly enough," Pete muttered.

Blondie hissed, baring his fangs.

Targe hefted his ax and stepped closer, adding a fourth corner to the tense standoff. Ava and Jynx shared a worried glance.

My first impulse was to step in and act as peacekeeper, but I held back. Once the vampires came out of hiding, these groups would come into contact more and more often. Pete wouldn't be the only one to lash out. I needed to know if, on an individual level, fae and vampires could work out their differences without a referee. We all did.

"The attack was cowardly," Targe said, "and a breach of trust."

"You side with the abomination?" Pete pointed the tip of his sword at Hortense. "She is the traitor here, spilling fae blood to protect an enemy."

Targe shook his head. "We agreed to work together for the success of this mission."

"You agreed," Pete said, "not I."

"The promise was implied when you walked through that portal," Targe argued.

"I swore no oath and broke no vow. My only shame is my failure to finish the job."

Blondie balled his fists. "He admits his crime with every breath. I demand justice."

"Killing vampires is no crime; it is the duty of every true fae." Pete cast a pleading look at Targe. "Hate me if you must, but this die has been cast. Your ceasefire is already over. We must finish him before his bloodsucking brethren return or we lose the advantage."

Targe hesitated, seeming to study the whorls in the shaft of his ax.

My breath caught. Had I miscalculated? I moved to intervene, but Ava grabbed my elbow, holding me back. I shot her an accusing glare. She just shook her head.

"I cannot condone your actions," Targe said at last. "Nor will I compound them by shedding more blood."

I exhaled.

"Then you'll hand him over so I may dispense justice?" Blondie asked.

Targe shook his head, tightening his grip on his ax. "I can't do that either. As he said, he broke no vow, and attacking a vampire isn't a crime among our people." He met Blondie's gaze. "I won't attack you, but if you press this, you'll meet my steel."

The blare of the alarm, which had faded to the background of my awareness, abruptly cut off. My ears rang with the sudden silence. A moment later, three vampires rushed up the aisle from the left, coming to an uneasy stop at the edge of our tense tableau. The sides were now balanced.

A vampire with a long, narrow nose and dark, shoulder-length hair pulled into a ponytail stepped cautiously closer. He held no weapon, but his stance showed he was ready to fight. "Everything okay here?"

Blondie assessed the fae assembled before him. Vampires were faster, which gave them the advantage in hand-to-hand combat, but Targe and Ava's teleportation might even the odds. Whatever the ultimate outcome, if these groups clashed, both sides would sustain heavy casualties. I swallowed the lump in my throat and prayed to any god listening that no one else would die tonight.

Blondie nudged Pete's severed hand with the tip of his shoe. He turned to Hortense. "You would fight as well?"

"If I must," she said without hesitation.

"Do you regret protecting me?"

"No."

He pursed his lips, nodded, and said, "I will leave the coward's fate to the fae."

Targe met Pete's gaze. "You're done here. Put it away."

For a moment it seemed Pete might prefer to fight them all, fae and vampire alike. Then he sheathed his blade. *Now* the fight was over.

I shuffled forward, slightly more stable than I had been a moment ago. Ava released me, moving to help Pete wrap his stump with a sleeve torn from his jacket.

"You made the right call," I said.

Blondie grunted. Turning to the newcomers he said, "Have you secured the facility?"

The ponytail vampire nodded. "We're in a warehouse on the outskirts of town. Nikolai is in their security office keeping tabs. There's a second building that was being used as a barracks. We found more beds than the staff here can account for, but the occupants seem to have fled during the commotion. Probably through another portal since there's no evidence of a large-scale evacuation."

"The quarantined guests and vendors from the market," I said. It would have been nice to arrest them all and deliver them to the PTF with a bow, but I was glad the fighting was over. At least we'd put a serious dent in their merchandise. The black market baddies were a problem for another day.

"All remaining hostiles are dead or secured," finished Mr. Ponytail.

"Did you find fae captives?" I asked.

Again he nodded. "Kept in a separate room. We breached the door but haven't released them yet."

"Then what are we waiting for?" Jynx stepped up beside me, fully nude except for the blood coating her hands, feet, and face. "Let's go get my brother."

Chapter 22

"THE FAE ARE through here," said Mr. Ponytail, stepping past two unconscious, zip-tied guards to open a pair of double doors behind them.

The stench hit me first—a sour mix of ammonia and body odor. I pulled my shirt collar up to cover my nose as I stepped inside. Cages of varying types and sizes lined the walls, including several enormous, glass tanks. A single horse-faced kelpie floated in one, while a second held a school of grindylows—two-foot creatures with eel-like tails, long, webbed fingers, milky-white eyes, and razor-sharp teeth. Several racks supported glass globes that held a variety of tiny sprites. Most of the cages were composed of iron bars lined with plywood floors—simple but effective. Many held single occupants, though a few housed groups of smaller creatures, while others stood empty. As soon as we entered, a deafening chorus of shouts, pleas, threats, and promises rose up as captives called for their release.

Blondie grabbed my sleeve, pulling me to a stop on the threshold as Targe and the other fae rushed into the room. The vampires remained in the hall.

I gave him a curious look. "What's the matter?"

He glanced past me to the room of imprisoned fae. Once those cages were opened, the fae would outnumber the vampires six to one. Blondie was probably wondering how many would try to kill him, as Pete had, despite his participation in their rescue.

"Our orders were to provide backup while you searched for your missing fae. It's time for us to go." He gestured to his companions, and as a group, they turned away.

"Hey, Blondie," I called after him.

He glanced back, arching an eyebrow. "My name is Anatole."

"Anatole," I amended. "I'm sorry about what happened with Pete. I'm glad you're okay."

"It has been an interesting night." His gaze shifted to Hortense. He frowned. "I never imagined a fae would save the life of a vampire."

"The world is changing," I said.

"We shall see."

I watched the vampires leave, then joined Jynx—still barefoot, but with the tattered, single-sleeved remains of Pete's jacket hanging to her thighs in a passable imitation of clothing. We peeked in cage after cage, looking for Chase while the others started breaking locks.

A few of the freed prisoners took off through the open doors, but most grouped together near the entrance.

Fae weren't the only prisoners. In the third cell, I spotted the young practitioner who'd been sold on the auction block before Chase. He knelt in the center of his cage, chains on his wrists and a control collar around his neck.

"We're going to get you out," I promised. The boy didn't respond.

"Found him!" Jynx shouted.

I hurried down the row. Chase sat stiffly in the center of his cage, ears flat, tail wrapped around his legs. He stared at me with the combination of fondness and disdain that seemed to come naturally to the feline face.

Ava hurried over, positioning her hands on either side of the lock. A shimmer rippled through the metal, and the bottom half of the lock fell free. I tore off the remaining link and opened the door.

Chase sauntered out as though he didn't have a care in the world. Once clear of his prison, he shifted, stretching and twisting into his human shape.

I wrapped my arms around his neck and squeezed for all I was worth. "I'm so sorry, Chase. I should never have put you in danger."

He hugged me back, then pushed me to arm's length. "You presented an opportunity. I chose to follow this path, knowing full well that it would be dangerous."

"Still, I—"

He shook his head. "You came back for me. You kept your promise. That's all that matters."

"Well, not *all* that matters," Jynx said. She braced her fists on her hips and leaned forward, grinning so wide it made my face hurt to look at.

Chase met her stare for stare. "What?"

"Aren't you going to thank me?" she asked.

"Why would I do that?"

"Because I just saved your fuzzy butt."

Chase snorted.

"Admit it," Jynx said. "You were stuck, and I rescued you."

"Technically, Ava rescued me."

"Whatever. You totally owe me."

"I disagree," Chase said.

Jynx stuck out her tongue.

I left the siblings to argue and returned to the cage with the practitioner boy. Targe had sheered the lock with his ax, but the boy remained inside. I opened the cage and offered my hand.

"Come on out now. You're safe."

He wouldn't meet my gaze, but he took my hand and crawled out. When he straightened he came up to my shoulder.

"What's your name?"

He stared silently at the ground.

"Do you want me to take that off?" I pointed to his control collar.

He didn't respond.

What did they do to this kid?

"Who is your companion?" Hortense asked, walking up to us.

"I'm not sure," I said. "He seems a little shy."

What he seemed was broken, but I didn't want to say that out loud.

"And your *other* companions?" she asked warily. "Where are they?"

"They thought it best to leave before they were outnumbered."

"A wise decision," she said. "Despite your intentions, I doubt vampires will ever be safe among the fae."

"I don't know," I said. "You saved Anatole."

"For the sake of the mission," Hortense said. "We could not fight the guards *and* the vampires without sustaining casualties."

While that was true, I knew Hortense well enough to guess that wasn't the *whole* truth. "I think there's hope, especially on an individual level." I cast her a sidelong glance. "Anatole seemed quite taken with you."

She rolled her eyes. "I shall leave the necrophilia to you."

"Baby steps. You could start as pen pals."

"Hmph."

We fell into a companionable silence as Targe corralled the last of the freed fae.

"I do appreciate you saving him," I said, "whatever your reasons."

She crossed her arms and exhaled. "I don't know if the future you imagine is possible, but I respect what you are trying to do." She shook her head. "Vampires and fae have long lives and long memories. We are slow to change. In that regard, humans may hold the advantage. Perhaps your perspective, however naive, will help us move beyond our history rather than simply perpetuating it."

Targe joined us. "That's everyone."

I looked over the motley group of freed prisoners. "Will you open a portal back to Crossroads?"

He shook his head. "Not enough juice. We'll make our way to the Great Lakes Reservation, then disperse to our own realms."

Chase walked up while Targe was talking and joined the conversation. "A quick jog through the Shifter Realm should see us back at Crossroads in a day or two." He looked at me. "You're welcome to join us."

I couldn't meet Chase's gaze. Despite what he'd said, I still felt responsible for what had—and had almost—happened to him.

"Hey." He shoved my shoulder. "Don't make this weird."

"Sorry." I forced myself to look into his yellow-green eyes. "The summit is tomorrow, and I need to be there for it. I'll ask Everly to send some agents to secure this place and see if I can bum a flight back to Colorado with them."

"Probably best if we're gone before the PTF arrives," Chase noted.

"Agreed."

"What about the items in the warehouse?" Targe asked. "I saw several magical artifacts on those shelves."

I hesitated. The warehouse was full of weapons, both magical and mundane, that could do a lot of damage in the wrong hands. The question was: whose hands were the right ones? *What I'd really love is for all those dangerous devices to be destroyed, but that's not going to happen.*

Turning to Targe I said, "It'll take some time for the PTF to get here. Make a pass of the shelves and take whatever you want and can carry with you. Anything left will be confiscated by the PTF."

"Fair enough." Targe walked to the milling fae and explained the situation. "Ten minutes and we're gone." They dispersed into the warehouse to claim their treasures.

Chase bumped my shoulder with his. "Now that Crossroads is taken care of, I was thinking of moving back to your cabin."

The knot of guilt constricting my chest loosened a little. I smiled and bumped him back. "You're always welcome."

"Then I'll see you in a few days."

I pulled my phone out of my pocket as Chase trotted after the others. My heart hurt with the relief of seeing him safe.

It's almost over.

Everly's phone rang six times before she answered. "What now, Alex. I'm a little busy planning the massive global collaboration you just dumped in my lap."

"Have your agents reached Hayes's lab yet?"

"Yes. They should have it secured within the hour."

"Great. I have another location for them to lock down."

"The market site?"

"Oh. Make that two more sites, I guess. And I need a ride home."

* * *

"HURRY UP," EMMA called from the front of the house. "The broadcast is about to start."

I wrapped a towel around my wet hair, pulled on my bathrobe, and rushed to the living room, dropping onto the couch beside Emma.

"I still think you should be there," she said.

I shrugged. By the time my plane landed, I'd have needed to head straight to the conference to arrive in time. I was exhausted, covered in blood, and had a black eye. Not a great look for a press conference. Besides, I'd had enough time in the spotlight—a place I had never wanted to be to begin with. I'd chosen home and a shower instead, with a short detour to drop the mute practitioner I'd rescued off at Luke's. Hopefully he could help the kid.

The television showed a stage set up on the grass outside the Denver PTF building. Open-sided tents provided shade for the audience, but the main area was bathed in sunlight. Several uniformed security officers stood at attention around the stage. Director Harris, wearing a pastel-blue business suit and practical pumps, strode to the podium. Lights flashed as reporters snapped pictures.

"Thank you for coming out today. As you all know, tomorrow marks the beginning of the interspecies peace conference. What you may not know is that, until a few hours ago, that conference was in danger of being canceled due to an impending attack by a group of Purists utilizing the drug Fantasia. I'm here to tell you that, thanks to a collaborative effort by the PTF and a group of previously unidentified paranaturals, we were able to eliminate this threat, cripple Fantasia's distribution network, and apprehend the drug's creator, Doctor Calliope Hayes." She gestured, and more flashes ensued as James and David escorted a handcuffed Dr. Hayes onto the stage.

I recalled the doctor's annoyance when we accused her of "creating" Fantasia. *"I'm a scientist, not a drug dealer."* I shook my head. *Hayes may have developed Fantasia, but she didn't distribute it. She didn't plan the attack on the summit. She was trying to save people, in her own messed-up way, but now Fantasia is probably all she'll ever be known for.*

My heart seized when James stepped into the camera frame. His skin was more tan than I remembered, which made me think Ash hadn't been exaggerating about the beach in Spain. His black hair was gelled and styled, and his perfectly tailored suit screamed "respectable." His cobalt gaze swept over the crowd, and for a moment he seemed to see me through the screen. My breath caught. The thrum of our connection reverberated in my soul, sending shock waves through my system. He was so close. My chest ached. My fingers twitched. I wanted to touch him, to hold him. I wanted to crawl through that TV screen and kiss him and never let him go.

"With this threat behind us, the peace summit will take place tomorrow as planned," Everly continued. "And in gratitude for the assistance provided by our new acquaintances in bringing this matter to a successful and timely close, I, on behalf of the PTF, hereby endorse their participation in the upcoming peace talks."

Murmurs spread through the crowd.

"Their representative will now introduce himself."

She stepped to the side, and James took her place in front of the microphone.

"Good afternoon," he said.

Even distorted through the television, his voice brought both a blaze and a balm to my soul. I leaned forward, eager for more.

"My name is James Abernathy. I own the Souled Art Gallery in Boulder, Colorado. I was born in Italy, and I have lived and worked among humans all my life. Some of you may recognize me from footage of the attack on this very facility"—he gestured to the building behind him—"during which I defended a delegation of Church officials. Or from when my friends and I tried to warn the PTF board of directors about dangers beyond their understanding before the events at Arlington. I stand before you now having worked alongside the PTF last night to secure over thirty Fantasia facilities across the globe in a coordinated effort the likes of which this world has never seen. I hope that these actions, more than my words, prove to you how devoted I and my people are to forging a peaceful coexistence with humanity." He braced his hands on either side of the podium, took a deep breath, and said, "I am a vampire."

Chaos erupted in the audience as reporters jumped to their feet shouting questions—most of which, unsurprisingly, had to do with drinking blood.

I clenched my hands and pressed my knuckles to my lips. *That's it,* I thought. *Now everyone knows.*

"Sounds like they're taking it well," Emma said sarcastically.

James stepped back, and Everly returned to the microphone. "Mr. Abernathy has agreed to full PTF testing to map his abilities." I could barely hear Everly's words above the din. "The paranatural registry will be updated accordingly once we have those results. In the meantime, we've released footage from last night's military action that should shed some light on their capabilities."

"How long has the PTF known about the existence of vampires?" shouted a woman in the front row.

"What's the vampires' relationship to the fae?" demanded a lanky reporter near the back.

"Will the vampires join the summit on their own, or as part of the Paranatural Alliance?" bellowed a man in a bowler hat.

"There are many questions about where vampires will fit, both in human society and among the other paranaturals. That's one of many topics that will be discussed at tomorrow's meeting. For now, we ask you to remain calm and remember that everyone here is working toward the same goal. *Peace.*"

Everly exited stage left, followed by James, then David and Dr. Hayes. They all filed into the PTF building while the rest of the security force held back the crowd.

Cole Barlowe climbed onto the vacated stage, gesturing with both hands for the audience to quiet. "Friends, I know you want answers. We all do. That's what tomorrow's summit is all about. I for one am just grateful that, through the PTF's quick and decisive actions, these proceedings can carry on, undaunted, and I pray that the representatives of the other races are brave enough to join us. Humanity is on the cusp of something great, something that all our guns and bombs could never accomplish. Tomorrow's summit will be a turning point in history, the moment when humans evolve beyond the limits of our past and take our first steps into a new and brighter future. I can't wait to share it with all of you."

The audience applauded.

I frowned, recalling Dr. Hayes's parting comment. *"Humans must evolve to survive."* I drummed my fingers on my armrest. *A scientist working for Purity and a philanthropist working for One Earth. What are the odds they'd share the same philosophy?* Then again, sometimes the only difference between an ally and an enemy was the path they took to reach their goal. I squinted at Barlowe on the screen. Sometimes it was hard to tell which path a person was on.

"Won't announcing the vampires' participation ahead of time make some fae choose not to attend the summit?" Emma asked.

I shook my head and turned away from the broadcast. "On the contrary. The fae lords will want to get the vampires kicked out, which means they're pretty much guaranteed to show up. The question is: can we get them to stay and talk once it's clear the vampires aren't going anywhere?"

My cell phone buzzed. James's text lit the screen. *I'm heading home. Join me?*

A flutter of anticipation warmed me. I smiled and wrote back, *On my way.*

* * *

THE STREET IN front of James's house in Golden was swarming with reporters.

I circled the block, parked on a somewhat quiet section of road, walked to the back side of James's property with my head down, and hopped the fence. When I straightened from my landing, James was standing in his back doorway.

My breath caught as my eyes roved over him, drinking in the familiar angles of his face, the dark gloss of his hair, the welcoming blue of his eyes, and the trim strength of his frame. I'd longed for this moment. Now, I feared some terrible trick—a dream from which I'd wake only to find myself alone as I had every morning since we were separated. I touched the knotted-fabric ring on my finger for comfort, a habit I'd repeated every time I thought of James over these past few months, but the memories stored there by my magic paled before the reality of him.

He opened his arms in invitation.

The tether between us, which had grown steadily stronger the closer we got, pulled me forward like a rubber band. I raced across the yard and slammed into him.

His arms snapped closed like a steel trap, pinning me to his chest. The scent of blackberries and cloves washed over me. His mouth sealed over mine—eager, insistent, ravenous. My knees melted under that heat, but the cage of James's arms kept me upright. I ran my hands along his sides, over his shoulders, and through his hair, gripping the silky strands in my fists to reassure myself that he was alive, and here, and *mine*.

Cradling my cheek in the palm of his hand, James pulled back enough to meet my gaze. His cobalt eyes seemed to assess my very soul, then he pressed his forehead to mine and said in a breathy whisper, "By all that is and all that was, you are the most beautiful sight in creation."

I grinned, sinking into the ocean of his gaze, and whispered back, "I've missed you, too." Though "missed" didn't begin to cover what I'd felt in James's absence. I let him experience the full force of my emotions through our connection as I pressed against the length of him and laid claim to his mouth once more, giving myself over to the hot ache searing every inch of my body.

James's desire reflected my own, building as our shared sensations amplified one another in a rolling crescendo. A deep groan tore out of him, or maybe it was me. I was having trouble telling where one of us ended and the other began. Gripping my thighs, James lifted me effortlessly off the ground. Clinging to him as though my life depended on eliminating every molecule between us, I wrapped my legs around his waist, and he carried me into the house.

* * *

I STARED AT my hand resting on James's bare chest, slick with sweat, and thought about the amulet that used to hang there. "I'm sorry I couldn't free you from the council. I tried, but . . . I wasn't strong enough."

James turned his head, staring into me with those sky-blue eyes. "You, my love, are absolutely perfect. Don't let anyone, or anything, convince you differently."

I smiled weakly. "But I couldn't save you."

He rolled onto his side, shifting the sheets around his waist, and propped his head on his bent arm. "Do you love me?"

"Yes."

"And will you continue to love me despite my becoming the vampires' public representative?"

"Of course."

He brushed a hand over my cheek. "Then I don't need 'saving.' "

I frowned. "But—"

He pressed his fingertips to my lips. "As much as I disagree with some of their policies, the vampires are my people." His words resonated deep in my core. Just as Ash considered themself fae and I considered myself human, James would always consider himself a vampire, daywalking or no. "I'm in a unique position to help them. All of them." He shook his head. "I'm not sad about how this turned out."

I pushed his hand away. "Even if you have to live in captivity on the other side of the world?"

"That part isn't ideal," he admitted. He slid his hand down my side until the heat of his palm rested against my hip. "But there's nothing in our agreement that precludes you from visiting."

"And all the Purists who'll be gunning for you?"

His smile flashed fangs. "Let them come. You and I have taken on the world before." He pulled me into a kiss.

I strummed the silver cord that bound our souls as our lips met. Words could mask the truth. Emotions, not so much. Underneath the waves of desire rippling through James was a flush of . . . pride.

"You're actually happy to be representing the vampires, aren't you?"

He shrugged. "I've never liked letting other people speak for me. This way, I can make sure the message is delivered clearly."

"Mm hmm." I tipped my chin as he trailed kisses down my neck. "And what message do you plan to so clearly articulate tomorrow when you face the fae?"

"That it's time to put old feuds to rest." He kissed my shoulder. "We're all attending the summit for the same reason." Another kiss. "We want to save lives."

I froze.

He pulled back, searching my face. "What's the matter?"

I shook my head. "It's just . . . Dr. Hayes said the same thing."

I flopped onto my back, my mood spoiled.

James resumed his lounging Adonis pose. "That bothers you?"

"It bothers me that I don't think she was wrong." I frowned. "I mean, obviously what she was doing was wrong . . . but I think she really was trying to save lives. Her research, terrible as it was, could actually help people."

"Even villains have reasons for the things they do. Sometimes damn good ones."

"Yeah . . ." I chewed my lower lip. Dr. Hayes created Fantasia, but she'd been focused on the research, not the drug itself. Someone else had been behind the drug's distribution. Someone who'd seen its potential as an evolutionary shortcut to put humans on even footing with the fae.

That thought struck a nerve, casting what Barlowe had said in his speech about humanity being on the cusp of accomplishing what guns and bombs couldn't in a new light.

Swallowing the sudden lump in my throat, I asked, "What do you think of Cole Barlowe?"

James frowned. "The One Earth activist? I don't know much about him. Why?"

"He said something in his speech today about humans needing to evolve."

"And?"

"Dr. Hayes said something similar back in her lab."

He sat up and turned to face me. "You think Barlowe is somehow involved with Dr. Hayes?"

"I don't know. Maybe it's nothing."

His cobalt gaze searched my face. I could sense him prodding our bond, detecting my unease. "Does it *feel* like nothing?"

I sighed. When I met Barlowe, he seemed exactly how I imagined a philanthropist and vocal advocate of paranatural rights would be. But humans could lie, and the way he talked about humans evolving and accomplishing what weapons couldn't . . . maybe he was talking about a philosophical evolution, as I'd originally assumed, but what if he was talking about physical evolution, like the kind Dr. Hayes was researching?

I shook my head. "I don't have any evidence, but something feels off. And Barlowe's been working closely with David on the security measures for the summit. His staff will be interspersed with David's PTF agents, right at the center of the event. If he *is* a threat, he's in a perfect position to do some serious damage."

James gave me a grim look. "What do you want to do about it?"

I squirmed. I couldn't just accuse one of the most influential people in the paranatural rights community of conspiracy without concrete evidence, and I couldn't risk word reaching the fae that I suspected an attack, or they might pull out of the summit. I needed to get Barlowe to show his hand while keeping the delegates in the dark. The beginnings of a plan percolated in my mind, but to pull it off I'd need help from a master of deception. Luckily, one was sleeping just down the hall, pretending to be one of the thralls the council had sent to keep tabs on James.

* * *

PLUSH, BLUE CARPET rippled with golden thread absorbed my steps as I made my way to the waiting room set aside for the paranatural delegations. I checked my watch.

Any minute now.

I nodded to another pair of security guards standing at attention along the resort's wide hallways. They looked out of place among the elegant glass sculptures and water features decorating the building's many nooks and alcoves.

"Hallway cameras are down." Barlowe's voice came through the earpiece David had given me to communicate during the event. Barlowe was helping coordinate from the resort's security office. He knew the building better than anyone, after all. "I repeat, cameras are down."

I smiled. *Right on time.*

"Seriously?" David said. "I double-checked that whole system last night."

More like sabotaged, I thought. "Should we delay the start?"

David waited long enough to appear to consider. "No. We weren't recording in the ballroom anyway, and we have enough personnel to secure the delegates' routes. We'll proceed on schedule. Liaisons, get to your groups."

"Understood," I said.

I stopped in front of the door to the paranaturals' waiting room and let myself inside. Sarah and Ken—the alpha of the Appalachian werewolf pack—sat at a table with Garrett and a petite woman with short, russet-brown hair who must have been his chosen second to represent the practitioners. James sat at a separate table, while one of the thralls sent by the vampire council—a slender woman with long black hair and porcelain skin wearing a sleek gray dress—stood behind him.

I smiled at the PTF agent standing at attention just inside the room. She, along with her counterparts in the two other waiting rooms, had been specifically assigned this duty because David trusted them. They'd each been told just enough of our plan to prevent them calling out any discrepancies between what they heard over the comms and what I was about to tell the delegates.

"There's been a slight delay," I said. "Some glitch with the security cameras. Nothing serious, but it's going to take a few minutes to sort out." The guard nodded. Sarah gave me a curious look but didn't say anything. Had her werewolf hearing picked up our earlier communication through the guard's earpiece? I felt bad keeping my friends in the dark, but the fewer people who knew what was about to happen, the better. At least Sarah seemed content to trust me. David and Everly had the far less enviable jobs of keeping the human and fae delegates contained during our little ruse. I doubted either of those groups would take news of a delay well.

Turning back to the guard, I said, "I need to borrow James for a second."

The guard motioned to James, who stood and walked over. His thrall shadow attempted to follow.

"Just James," I said. "Don't worry. I'll take full responsibility for his safety."

She narrowed her eyes and frowned, but what could she do? I was one of the coordinators of the summit. If I said I needed James, I needed James.

The guards stationed in the hallway didn't so much as look up when James and I stepped out. Illusions couldn't make a person invisible, but the results were close enough. While James was nowhere near as powerful as Ash, he could mask our presence for a short trip across the hall. Now that the cameras were out of commission, no one would be the wiser.

We ducked into the bathroom where we'd left Ash the night before. I walked to the last stall and rapped my knuckles against the "out of order" sign.

Ash came out wearing the features of a heavyset woman with short, chestnut hair, dark freckles over light-brown skin, and hazel eyes—a dead ringer for the guard I'd just talked to in the paranaturals' waiting room. The jeans and T-shirt Ash had been wearing when we set our trap last night had become a standard-issue PTF uniform, complete with tactical belt and weapons, though I suspected the accessories were only for show.

James dropped to one knee and bowed his head as soon as Ash stepped into view. The gold and silver tethers connecting me to the two vampires hummed in my core. Neither Ash nor James was comfortable in the other's presence, but where James felt awe, Ash felt only sadness.

Telling James the truth about Ash had been a risk, but circumstances had changed since Canada, when Ash threatened to murder any and all who learned their secret. Now that James was the recognized representative of the vampire race, and Ash knew there was no chance of me making daywalking amulets, James had become indispensable—a fact that Ash had grudgingly accepted, though they were far from thrilled. James had taken the introduction to his creator well enough, though he seemed incapable of not groveling in Ash's presence despite being commanded repeatedly to stop. I supposed, for a vampire, meeting Ash was something akin to a Christian meeting God.

I had no such hang-ups. "You ready?"

Ash stepped around James and moved toward the exit. "And eager to get this over with."

"You and me both." I pulled James to his feet. "Stay out of sight till we get back."

"Be careful." James pressed a quick kiss to my forehead, glanced at Ash, then averted his eyes. "Both of you."

Ash and I exited the bathroom and backtracked to the paranaturals' waiting room, but we didn't open the door.

I touched the device in my ear. "Ready to commence procession."

"Confirmed," David replied.

"Confirmed," said Everly.

I nodded to Ash, and they activated the complex spell we'd spent the better part of last night setting up while David "checked" the security system to ensure we weren't caught on camera. The door to the waiting room seemed to open, and the waiting delegates seemed to file out. The illusions weren't perfect. Their clothes didn't quite match what the delegates were wearing, and every now and then, something would flicker, but the decoys only had to fool the guards stationed outside the ballroom, and their attention would be focused outward, looking for potential threats, not scrutinizing the guests. I hoped.

Ash and I fell into step at the back of the procession. We walked past the guards at the first intersection, then merged with Everly and the human delegation. Like the paranatural representatives, the illusions for the humans weren't perfect, but they were as close as we could get with the pictures and documents we'd been working from—close enough to pass a cursory examination.

David led the fae delegation toward us from the opposite side of the resort. The fae had been the most difficult to mimic, having such a variety of claws, scales, feathers, builds, skin tones, and clothing. Luckily, the human guards would likely find the fae's unglamoured appearances shocking enough that small mistakes wouldn't raise red flags. If the Church representative had turned up with green skin, that would have been a problem, but among the fae such oddities were easily dismissed.

Two dozen security guards stood at attention in the area in front of the ballroom. A three-tiered fountain trickled over carved marble at the center of the space, surrounded by low, padded benches. The fae were admitted to the ballroom through the east entrance. The paranaturals and humans were ushered through a set of heavy oak doors on the west. Ash and I were last to cross the threshold. The doors were secured behind us.

I'd seen the ballroom last night, as we'd marked the routes for Ash's illusory army, but the room had been empty and only the sconces around the walls had been on. Today, light danced from five crystal chandeliers that hung from the ballroom's two-story vaulted ceiling. Pearl garlands hung in graceful arcs that created a pinwheel effect when I looked up, and tapestries of rich burgundy swathed the dark wood walls to prevent the vast space from becoming an echo chamber. Barlowe's resort had been designed for awe and elegance, and his architects had certainly hit their mark. As it was, the grandeur of the ballroom felt a bit wasted on just me, Ash, and the light puppets around us. Hopefully the real guests would get to enjoy it soon enough.

The pretend delegates took their seats around twelve tables that had been arranged in a loose circle at the center of the room, while the PTF agents, Everly, and David took up positions around the perimeter. Ash and I moved to our marks at the absolute farthest corner of the room. As the only real people present, we were the only ones in any danger if my suspicions came to pass.

"So far, so good," I said. Maybe I'd been wrong about Barlowe.

Ash gestured to the illusions, who were taking turns introducing themselves in whatever Ash imagined their voices might sound like. "How long do you want to let this run?"

No one expected peace to be brokered in a single day. This initial meeting was planned to be a short affair, focused on establishing the participants' authority to negotiate on behalf of their respective groups and outlining their general goals—a formal ground-breaking of sorts, with more in-depth negotiations to follow. That worked perfectly for my purposes, since it meant any attack would have a relatively short window in which to occur. Right or wrong, I'd be able to put my suspicions about Barlowe to rest in the next few minutes.

"Give it ten minutes. If nothing has happened by then, I'll call it."

Ash's prerecorded summit played out before us for several minutes, and I started to relax. Hopefully the real thing would go this smoothly. As I watched fake James stand and introduce himself, I found myself wondering again what our future would look like. A fae-practitioner hybrid and the daywalking spokesperson for the vampire race.

I cast Ash a sidelong glance. "Assuming all goes well today, what's the plan for after? Will you take James back to Spain until the next session, or now that he's been established as your representative, could he stay here?"

I tried to keep my desperation in check, but Ash felt it. Or maybe it would have been obvious to anyone. A flicker of sympathy darted through our connection, there and gone almost before I registered it.

"All the more reason to take him back to Esteban's compound," Ash said. "James will be an important political target moving forward. He needs to be protected."

"We can protect him here," I said.

"Esteban's stronghold has fortifications and hundreds of loyal troops, both human and vampire. James chose a life of simple solitude. He has no such support."

"So, give him some bodyguards. Heck, *you* could be his bodyguard. Stay here with him, with us." I touched Ash's arm, strengthening our connection. "I know you've spent your whole life yearning for the home your mother showed you as a child, but maybe you could find a home here."

"I don't belong here."

Ash's words resonated inside me, reminding me why I'd fought so hard to make this summit happen and reinforcing my resolve to create a more inclusive future . . . for everyone. "James, Emma, me, we're all unique; we don't fit anywhere, but we fit together. Maybe you could, too."

Ash shook their head. "There's nowhere in this world where I can ever be myself and still be safe."

The weight of Ash's words rippled through our connection, and again I sensed that overwhelming exhaustion that made me want to curl up on the floor and never move again.

I forced myself to keep breathing until the pressure threatening to crush me eased. "Maybe, if the negotiations go well and the fae give up their vendetta, you can finally stop hiding."

"Even if the fae sign a treaty that includes vampires, such a promise would not protect me. While all vampires come from me, I am no more one of them than I am a fae or a demon." Ash gestured to the illusions surrounding us. "This peace will be for them. You and I . . . we aren't represented here. Such is the burden of being unique."

Ash's words hit me like a punch to my diaphragm. I'd argued with Everly and David that I could legally participate in the black market infiltration because I wasn't *technically* part of the paranatural alliance. It hadn't occurred to me that that argument could be turned against me. As both a practitioner and a fae halfer, where would my rights fall in this new treaty?

I opened my mouth to reply.

The service doors at the back of the ballroom exploded inward.

Chapter 23

TWENTY PEOPLE RACED through the breached doors. They all wore either security uniforms or the black slacks and white shirts of the resort's staff.

A man from Barlowe's administration team slammed his palms against the ballroom wall. Blue light rippled over the surface, spreading like a wave until it crashed against itself on the far side of the room. It left a blue sheen in its wake. I touched the wall beside me and received a static shock that made me hiss and shake my hand. The crackling glow covered the entire room. So long as that spell was active, there'd be no way out, and no way for help to get in.

A woman dressed as a caterer raised her arms. A dozen metal spikes hovered above her outstretched fingers, each pair connected by a length of chain. The spikes shot forward, piercing the decoy delegates. Ash's creations screamed as iron pierced illusion.

Two men lifted grenade launchers to their shoulders and shot bundles into the ceiling that burst on impact. Fine metallic mist rained down. Half the infiltrators drew swords or knives and charged the seemingly stunned fae lords. The remainder drew guns. Three peeled off to secure the human delegates, three came toward the paranatural illusions, and another three headed directly for Everly, David, and me.

"On your command," Ash whispered.

The Fantasia-fueled extremists fell upon the fake fae lords, slashing with speed and strength boosted by Dr. Hayes's drug. I stared at the man running toward me, gun pointed at my head. Soon, he would be too close. I wished there were some other way to stop these fools, but a drawn-out conflict would only claim more lives and further endanger the summit.

"Do it." My voice cracked on the words.

Ash whispered into their closed fist then lobbed the contents toward the center of the room. The tiny jade stone I'd recovered from the black market and forgotten in my pocket during the chaos that followed soared through the air. A sphere of green light expanded around it.

It took three beats of my racing heart for the light to envelope the room, falling just short of where Ash and I stood. Ash's throw had been perfect. When the light dissipated, Ash's illusions were gone, leaving only the two of us and twenty stone statues waging a one-sided war. Utter silence rang in my ears. I stared down the barrel of a Glock six inches from my face and met the blank stare of the statue holding it. The last threat to the summit had been neutralized. I wanted to cheer. I also wanted to vomit. Ash had thrown the stone, but I was the one who'd killed these people. And given my options, I'd do it again.

When a full minute passed and no new threat entered the room, I pulled out my cell phone and texted David. *Attack neutralized.*

His reply was immediate. *On our way.*

I tapped the wall behind me to make sure the sealing spell had ended with its caster, then I turned to Ash. "Time to change."

The PTF guard beside me morphed into James's familiar features. He was almost perfect, right down to the little crease on his brow and the curve of his lips. His eyes were the cobalt blue I expected, but they weren't *his*. As perfect as the illusion was, I would never look into those eyes and think this was James. That gaze had too much weight behind it, which was saying something considering the centuries James had survived.

David and Everly came through the east entrance with a handful of PTF agents. David looked over the ballroom's morbid sculpture garden and whistled. "Damn, you really pulled it off."

"You doubted us?" Ash asked in James's voice.

David shook his head. "I just had no idea you could make an illusion on this scale . . . that anybody could."

I bit the inside of my lip. Hopefully no one ever asked James to duplicate this process, since there was no way he could. Ash was on a whole other level of magic, maybe as strong as the fae lords.

"Probably best we downplay the fact that your show fooled the PTF agents outside," Everly said. "People are nervous enough about what vampires may be capable of without adding fuel to the fire."

"If it's any consolation, this level of illusion is rare," Ash said, "and it's impossible without significant planning and preparation."

"Good to know." Everly gestured to the statues. "What about the attackers? Can we revive them to stand trial?"

I shook my head. I'd asked Ash the same thing when I came up with this plan. "As far as we know, there's no cure for this curse."

Everly nodded. "And the artifact?"

I picked up the jade stone and set it on her palm.

"I'll see that it's locked in the PTF vault for dangerous magical items."

David cleared his throat. "If we're done here, we should probably get the real summit underway before the delegates rip each other apart."

"Agreed," Everly said. She frowned at the statues frozen in poses of aggression and violence. "We'll use the secondary location."

"What about Barlowe?" I gestured to the statues—all members of his resort staff. "Is this enough to connect him to the attack?"

"It's enough to detain him while we get to the bottom of this," Everly said. "I have a team picking him up as we speak. I've also ordered the rest of his people escorted off the premises and held for questioning. But that can wait. The rest of us have a peace summit to attend."

David pressed his fingertips to the device in his ear. "The summit is a go. All teams, wait for your liaison to return, then proceed to location two." Turning to me he said, "Head back to your group. We'll do the same and see you in a few minutes."

Ash and I hurried back through the halls, avoiding eye contact with agitated staff who were being led away in handcuffs by local PD. Some of them might have been ignorant of the attack, but for now, everyone Barlowe had brought in was a suspect. Once the coast was clear, we ducked into the bathroom where we'd left James. His arm snaked around my waist as soon as I stepped through the door. His palm cradled my cheek, and he pressed his forehead to mine.

Ash cleared their throat. "Save the lovey-dovey for later. You two still have a job to do."

James released me and knelt before his creator, which was a little disconcerting since they were both wearing the same face. "I'll do my utmost to utilize the opportunity you've created for our people."

"You'd better." Ash looked at me. "Both of you. Now get going."

James and I met up with the rest of the paranatural delegation in their waiting room, then proceeded as a group to our backup location. I scanned the halls constantly, but no one jumped out and tried to kill us. Hopefully, we'd foiled the last attack planned against the summit.

"Location two" was, or would one day be, a reservable event space attached to one of the resort's three restaurants. The event room was smaller than the ballroom, but still large enough for our purposes. Like the ballroom, tables had been set up to create a roughly round space with chairs around the outside. The colors in this room were muted blues and neutral grays, and the carpet was a deep navy-blue that made me feel as if I were underwater.

James, Sarah, Garrett, and their aides took seats along one side of the curve, while their PTF guard and I took up positions behind them. Everly guided the human delegates to the six seats to my right, and David directed the fae to fill out the remainder of the circle.

"Deja vu," I muttered. Except for the change in location, I could have been watching Ash's illusion on replay.

Bael and I exchanged curt nods as he walked past. Rhoana, who was attending as his aide, ignored me, keeping most of her focus on the gray-skinned shadow walkers who came in next.

I caught Morgan's amber gaze for a moment, then turned to her brother, who would be speaking on behalf of the Realm of Shadows. "Representative Galen, I'm glad you could join us."

"As am I," Galen inclined his head, cast a surreptitious glance toward James, then hurried on.

Morgan leaned close and whispered, "Vampires? Really? Not the direction I would have gone."

I shrugged. "I used what I had."

She chuckled. "One thing I'll say for the Mortal Realm: you always deliver an interesting time." She winked and trotted after her brother.

Since "interesting" was the highest compliment I'd ever heard Morgan give, I assumed that meant she was pleased with the way things had turned out.

"I thought we were meeting in the main ballroom?" That question came from Thomas Parson—an elderly man with a silver tonsure and drooping, freckled skin who sat as chairman of the PTF board of directors.

"Someone made a mess in the ballroom," Everly said smoothly. "I didn't think anyone would want to wait longer for it to be cleaned up."

"I should think not," said the representative from the United Nations. Her blond hair was swept into a professional updo that gave full focus to her anxious expression as she pulled a laptop from her bag and set it on the table. "We're already behind schedule." The United Nations and the Unified Church of Humanity had both insisted their representatives be allowed to stream the event, to ensure all their voting members had access to exactly the same information.

"If everyone's ready," Everly said, "We can call this session to order."

"Not yet." The Lord of Illusion had yet to sit down. At three feet tall with long, drooping ears, wild caterpillar eyebrows, and enough wrinkles to make a Shar-Pei jealous, Lord Ridhan looked every part the ancient forest guardian he was. He wore a tunic of dried leaves and carried a walking stick taller than he was topped with a milky crystal. "There is a matter that must be rectified before we can officially begin."

"Oh?" asked the representative from the Church of Humanity—a pencil of a man with round, wire frame glasses and a push broom mustache. "And what is that?"

Lord Ridhan pointed his staff at James. "We have an interloper."

"This is James Abernathy," Sarah said, "representative of the vampire race."

"We know who he is," Bael said, a slight smile curving his lips. "But vampires have no place at this table."

"On the contrary," Garrett said. "They have been accepted as members of the Paranatural Alliance."

"Since when?" asked Annabrae—an Undine general with dark-brown skin, gill-like nostrils, and lips as black as her hair who was speaking on behalf of Lord Nadeera while the queen dealt with civil unrest back home.

"Since yesterday," Garrett replied.

"Then you have made a grave mistake," said a sharp-featured woman cloaked head-to-toe in raven feathers—Neilee, the Aerie representative. "I will not treat with vampires."

"Nor shall I," said Lord Ridhan.

James cleared his throat. "If I may?" He waited until everyone's gaze was focused on him. "My people have earned our seat at this table by proving our willingness to work with other species toward a common good, and none have benefited more from our recent actions than the fae, hundreds of whom were saved from a slow and torturous death. Surely such a debt outweighs your stale prejudice?"

"Better those fae had died than allow themselves to be indebted to you," said Ridhan. "Regardless, their debts are theirs alone and not nearly enough to bargain for what you seek." He turned to the human section of the table. "We fae have come to treat with humanity in good faith, but we shall not stoop to dealing with vampires. Banish them now or lose this chance for peace."

Ridhan nodded to his companion, a slender pixie with hair like silver moonlight. She stood, fluttering long iridescent wings that draped her back like a living cape. The Aerie representative and her aide also stood. Then, to my horror, so did Galen and, more reluctantly, Morgan. Half the fae present were threatening to walk out of the summit.

The human delegates leaned together, whispering. Would they reject the vampires in order to placate the fae? Would the entire Paranatural Alliance be excluded from the summit now? The worried look Sarah shared with Garrett told me they were thinking along the same lines, wondering if they'd made a mistake.

Annabrae nudged the blue-skinned man by her side and started to rise. The summit was falling apart.

I have to fix this!

But how? The fae hatred of vampires ran deep. So deep that even saving hundreds of fae lives and stopping the Fantasia trade wasn't enough to sway them. What could they possibly care about enough to make them stay? Then it struck me. The only thing the fae hated more than vampires . . . was one *specific* vampire.

"What if I could offer you something?" I blurted.

Everyone froze. All eyes were on me.

Swallowing the lump in my throat, I stepped away from the wall to stand beside James. "Something you've been seeking for a very long time."

The lords exchanged looks, some irritated, some curious. Annabrae settled back in her seat.

"What, exactly, are you offering?" Galen asked.

I looked at James. He stared back.

What are you doing? The question thrummed through my soul. This close, I could hear James's thoughts clearly, as well as the emotions behind them. *Concern. Confusion.*

I shifted my gaze to include the thrall beside him. As the progenitor of the vampire race, Ash had access to every thrall ever created—a sort of back door to their brain that allowed Ash to spy on their masters, muck about in their memories, send commands, or even take full control of their bodies. Ash might not be physically sitting at the table, but through that thrall, they were there just the same.

I brushed the golden thread anchored at my core. My connection to Ash wasn't as strong as my connection to James, but I could feel their cold panic. Ash realized what I was suggesting. They were trapped in this building by the afternoon sun, surrounded by powerful enemies, and completely at my mercy. My heart hammered. *Betrayal.*

I have a plan, I whispered into that link that bound our souls, projecting truth and confidence for all I was worth. Out loud I said, "Do you trust me?"

"Always," James said.

Hope. Doubt. Anger. Then that deep exhaustion that threatened to pull me into its crushing depths. *Do what you will.*

Taking that as consent, I faced the fae, lifted my chin, and said, "I can give you the identity and location of the vampire progenitor, the one who spawned their entire race."

A stunned silence settled over the room, making my racing pulse all the louder.

Ash's unease increased, tightening my chest.

I hope you know what you're doing, James whispered in my mind.

Me, too.

The fae had always assumed that, due to their linked souls, killing the vampire progenitor would eliminate the entire race. Even Ash wasn't sure if that was true or not. I was betting these lords wouldn't be able to pass up the opportunity to test their theory once and for all, even if it meant bruising their pride in the short term. After all, if they were right, there would be no vampires left to negotiate with once Ash was gone.

"How did you come by this information?" asked Anika, the chimera Shifter Lord who'd chosen to attend in her humanoid form since her golden-furred lion, spiked tail, and massive wings would have been difficult to accommodate indoors, though her horns and claws were still visible, and the deep pools of ink she stared out of were far from human.

"A reliable source," I said. "A source whose life could become very uncomfortable should the vampire council discover what I'm proposing. Therefore, I would require certain assurances regarding the safety of my informant."

"Such as?" Bael asked.

I met his gaze and tried to squash the nervous anxiety fluttering through me. *I really hope this deal works out better than our last one.*

I set my hand on James's shoulder, giving it a reassuring squeeze. "The fae lords must grant sanctuary to my informant and a small group of companions in a realm and location of my choosing, and the lords must do everything in their power to protect that person's safety from any and all threats, indefinitely."

As I'd hoped, every gaze was drawn to my hand on James's shoulder.

Let them make that connection, I prayed. It was common knowledge that James and I were in a relationship, so of course he would be the logical source of my information. One I'd do everything in my power to protect.

Guilt, relief, and surprise fluttered through my connection to Ash. They were far from calm, but they understood. I hadn't betrayed them. Now I just needed to make this deal stick.

"No vampire would give up their master," said Galen.

"Except perhaps one who had already broken those bonds." The corners of Bael's mouth curved up, making him look like a contented cat. He'd taken the bait. "So, now that your first plan has failed, this is how you intend to secure your lover's freedom from the council? By using us as a shield?"

I kept my mouth shut.

Bael spread his hands. "I will offer my realm as refuge for your informant and accept vampires at this table in exchange for up-to-date information about the creature who has eluded us for so long."

"The decision has to be unanimous among *all* the fae lords," I said.

"I will accept those terms," said Lord Anika.

"On behalf of my father, the Lord of Shadow, I also accept your terms."

I was a little nervous about accepting the words of the Shadow, Aerie, and Undine representatives in place of the actual lords of those realms, but those lords had given their representatives full authority to speak in their stead. To refuse to abide by the agreed-upon terms after the fact would undermine the lords' credibility and jeopardize any future deals.

The Aerie representative and Annabrae voiced their assent. That only left Lord Ridhan. He looked side to side. Of all the realms represented, Illusion and the Aerie were the only ones with whom I'd never interacted. Like Bael, the others probably assumed I'd choose Enchantment as the location for the sanctuary. That would make the most sense. . . . *if* James were my informant.

"If you want Illusion's cooperation," said Ridhan, "I require more than just a name. You must deliver the abomination directly into my hands so that I may kill them."

I swallowed, choosing my words carefully. "I will give you the who, where, and when to find the person you're looking for. How you use that information will be up to you."

He narrowed his eyes at me. "Very well. I agree to the terms."

"Then it seems the parties attending these treaty negotiations have been set," said Garrett, "and will include the vampires as part of the Paranatural Alliance."

The human representatives, who'd been muttering among themselves, each nodded.

"So long as she holds up her end," said Lord Ridhan, jabbing his staff in my direction. "Give us your information."

"Once my informant and their companions are safely established in their new home," I said. "If I fail to deliver, you can always evict your unwanted guests and ban the vampires from future sessions of the summit. I can hardly take the information back once I share it with you."

"That's reasonable," said Galen. "Let us finalize the details of our deal so that we may commence with this summit."

We ended up drafting two contracts that day. The first spelled out my deal with the fae lords down to the finest detail, and boy, were they surprised when I told them where I wanted my informant's sanctuary to be built. The second was a simple document bearing the signatures of all twelve representatives, their aides, and six witnesses, declaring everyone's intentions to negotiate in good faith toward the establishment of a sustainable peace treaty between all the represented peoples. That first session of the summit lasted a total of eight hours as we nitpicked over every word. In the end, all that was agreed upon was that we were willing to talk to each other. Still, it was a step in the right direction.

* * *

NEEDLE-LIKE LEAVES CRUNCHED underfoot, stirring an earthy scent of damp plant life and musky loam into the night air. I craned my neck, seeking the tops of the towering redwoods that dominated this region of California to which we'd been summoned. The organic sentinels seemed to touch the stars. My foot caught on a root, and I stumbled. James grabbed my arm to steady me. Giving his hand a grateful squeeze, I returned my gaze to the path and the jittery speck of light ahead. The tiny sprite who'd introduced themself as our guide at the edge of the dark forest darted back and forth like a pinball ricocheting off the trees, leading us deeper into the unknown. The heavy, uneven tromp of dozens of humans overwhelmed the natural sounds of the night, muted slightly by a hazy fog that coiled around the massive trunks and dampened my skin.

"How much farther?" Emma asked.

I glanced over my shoulder. Emma walked beside Ash, once more in their female persona. The two of them had grown quite close in the three weeks we'd all been living together. Once the first session of the peace summit ended, the fae had needed time to prepare their end of our deal, and Ash had arrangements of their own to make. Desperate for more time with James, I'd argued that Ash's arrangements could be handled from the comfort and convenience of my spare room. It hadn't been as difficult to convince them to stay as I'd expected.

The orange sprite darted back and spun a halo over Emma's head. "Not far now. Not far." It buzzed off once more.

Emma sighed and trudged on. Hiking was not her favorite pastime. I, on the other hand, would have loved the experience, if not for the overwhelming anxiety of what was coming.

The past three weeks had been like a dream—quiet mornings, family meals, and no one trying to kill us. I visited Maggie and little Alex twice a week, even working up the courage to babysit so the exhausted parents could have a night off. David finally introduced us to his new boyfriend, proving things were getting serious. Crossroads officially reopened, and Chase returned to claim his favorite spot on the back of my couch. For the first time in a long time, the future was looking bright. Especially now that Barlowe was behind bars.

After the summit, Everly's forensic accountants tracked down a dozen shell companies that Barlowe used to funnel charitable One Earth donations into offshore accounts. Those funds had single-handedly supported Dr. Hayes's research, as well as numerous Purity operations all over the world. Once those facts came to light, Barlowe stopped denying his Purist connections. He spouted rhetoric about human potential and evolutionary imperatives to any journalist who'd interview him. Like Dr. Hayes, Barlowe insisted he was acting in humanity's best interest.

Barlowe's betrayal and subsequent arrest sent ripples through the One Earth community. Several other influential members came under intense scrutiny, and there was even talk of disbanding the organization. While I was confident Barlowe's trial would put him behind bars for the rest of his life, we couldn't be sure of the scope of his network or the full extent of his influence. One thing I *was* certain of: we'd be dealing with the fallout of Barlowe's lies for years.

Sometimes I wished everyone were as bound by the truth as the fae. Then again, the inability to lie hardly made them trustworthy.

I stepped around the ridiculously large base of a tree and stopped dead. Seven fae waited in a small clearing ahead. They stood so spread out that I had to turn my head to count them all, but the fact that all six representatives had come was a very good sign. The final fae had midnight skin that shimmered when she moved and platinum hair that hung to her knees. She wore a gown of liquid moonlight.

"Finally," said the harpy representative from the Aerie Realm. "The sky here is too crowded." She shuddered, sending a ripple through her dark feathers.

"This is everyone crossing over?" Lord Ridhan stood in the center of the area with his arms crossed over a green tunic belted with leather braids and wooden beads.

"We won't all be staying," I said quickly. Best to deal in specifics where fae were concerned. "Some of us will require safe passage back, once we've determined that all the parameters have been met."

"Yes, yes." Ridhan waved my words away. "Any who choose to return will be allowed to do so."

"And you guarantee this portal won't harm vampires?" I indicated James.

"Leetha's spell has not been keyed to bar any species," Bael assured. "All may pass unhindered."

"Let's get this over with," said Ridhan.

The unknown fae bowed and gestured to her side as though inviting Ridhan into a building. He walked past her and vanished. The rest of the lords followed.

David, who was attending as a witness to our deal, stood with James and me as we ushered the rest of our group through. I held my breath when Ash approached the portal. Despite Bael's reassurance, part of me feared the fae would use this as an excuse to kill the vampire representative. If they'd had any inkling who Ash really was, we'd all be dead already.

Ash met my gaze under the starlight. Their smile was only visible thanks to my fae vision. The golden bond between us had faded, as they'd promised it would, but I didn't need that magical connection to recognize the nervous hope hiding behind their eyes. Ash had waited centuries to set foot in their homeland. Tonight, they would fulfill their mother's promise.

Ash vanished from sight. I exhaled. Not that I could be sure they'd survived, but we were one step closer to ending this farce.

Emma followed Ash, and the remaining humans streamed through, carrying backpacks, suitcases, and crates of supplies—a total of thirty volunteers who'd agreed to leave their lives behind to start the first human colony in a fae realm. I'd sat with Ash and James through each interview to ensure everyone knew exactly what they were signing up for.

Some joined for the adventure, some for the generous compensation given to their families, and some because becoming a thrall could cure what even magical medicine could not. These people weren't just a food supply; they were the foundation of a community, one in which I hoped Ash could finally find a sense of belonging.

When the last of the immigrants walked through, David nodded to me and stepped into the portal.

"See you on the other side," I said to James.

He squeezed my hand and stepped into oblivion.

I strummed the silver thread in my soul. The response was faint, but reassuring. I braced myself and stepped forward.

The familiar, though no less unpleasant, sensation of being turned inside out and stitched back together washed over me as I stepped into the Realm of Illusion for the very first time.

"Holy hell!" David spit onto purple grass and wiped his sleeve over his mouth. "Is it always like that?"

"Pretty much," I said.

A fae who looked like an inverted copy of the one I'd just left stood beside me. Their skin sparkled like diamonds and their long hair was abyssal black. The humans murmured and turned, taking in their new surroundings.

We stood in a forest nothing like the one we'd left. Prismatic leaves chimed in the wind, creating rainbow lights and a song that made me want to close my eyes and listen forever. Above the crystal canopy a deep-green sky sparkled with strange constellations, and a marbled moon hung in the sky. The trees seemed to collect the moonlight, lighting the forest with a soft glow that reminded me of the gems I'd trained with in Bael's workshop. The gurgle of water drew my attention to a nearby stream flowing toward a collection of buildings nestled among the trees.

"Kevkolusa." Lord Ridhan's voice was tight, as though naming the village hurt him. "I suppose it's a fitting end for the place that spawned such evil."

"This isn't an ending," I said. "It's a beginning."

"Tell that to the families your demand has displaced."

"We never required that anyone leave."

Ridhan made a choking noise. "As if any would choose to remain beside a vampire."

I clenched my fists. "Then they made their choice. Fortunately, that should mean plenty of vacant houses to get the new residents settled."

I did feel bad for the fae who'd been relocated, but thinking about how Ash's family disowned their daughter and hunted her child across centuries made it more palatable. These people had had ample time to find a reasonable solution. Since they preferred genocide, we were left with this.

"Your vampire's domain starts where the rivers merge and extends for one mile in every direction," Bael said. "The spell's border redirects anything that approaches from inside to a point exactly opposite within its boundary. All who approach from without will be instantly transported to the far side, bypassing the middle entirely."

The Shifter Lord stalked forward on golden paws, though she kept her massive bat wings furled at her sides so as to fit between the trees. "We six have woven our magic into this sanctuary so that none at all may pass its borders. Not even a lord."

"And none may leave," added Bael. "This bastion of shadows shall act as both sanctuary and prison. Once we leave, the portal we came through tonight will open for twenty-four Earth hours once every hundred years, to allow for stock replenishment." He gestured to the humans who'd come with us. "There will be no other way in or out."

James stiffened at my side.

"Wait," I said. "That wasn't part of the deal."

Lord Ridhan smirked. "This was the most effective way to ensure the occupant's *absolute* safety. A stipulation that you were most adamant about." The smirk grew to something closer to a snarl filled with loathing. This was Ridhan's revenge for ousting his people and contaminating his land with someone he considered an abomination. He thought he could deprive the vampires of their champion, and me of my lover.

I dared not look at Ash to gauge their reaction.

Bael gave me a sympathetic look. "I think you'll agree that we lords have provided a sanctuary that meets or exceeds what was agreed upon. Therefore, our part in this deal is done." He rested his hand on my shoulder. "However, your informant is under no obligation to utilize our creation. Should everyone here choose to return through the portal, we will not stop them." His face split in a wolfish grin. "There are other options that would secure your informant's safety. Ones that may be more palatable to you both."

So that was Bael's play. He and Ridhan had probably schemed this together, thinking I would agree to hide James in Enchantment rather than say goodbye to either him or the Mortal Realm. Well, the joke was on them. James would be staying in the Mortal Realm. But how would Ash feel about being entirely cut off? I should have stipulated that the portal remain accessible at all times, but there'd been so many details to keep track of when we made this deal, I couldn't see every possible outcome.

I wrung my hands.

"This place is great." I started at Emma's words. I hadn't seen her approach. "We *all* think so," she said. She took my hands in hers and squeezed them reassuringly. "You made a good deal."

I glanced over her shoulder to where she'd been standing with the waiting humans. Ash was looking right at me. With their enhanced senses, Ash would've easily been able to follow my conversation with the lords. Ash nodded. A weight lifted from my heart. "Thanks, Em. That's good to know."

"Regardless of whether you utilize this sanctuary or not," Ridhan said, "we've fulfilled our promise. It's time for you to deliver the information you owe us."

I exhaled. This deal hadn't turned out exactly as I'd expected, but Ash should be safe for the time being, and they'd have an opportunity to leave when the portal opened in a hundred years. That was hardly anything to a vampire. Maybe by then, the world would be a safer place.

"Very well. Since we all agree that my informant will be *absolutely* safe here . . ." I glared at Ridhan. "I promised you the who, where, and when to find the vampire progenitor." The fae were so still they could have been statues. Statues with *very* hungry expressions. I took a deep breath, the soothing song of the crystal trees giving me confidence. I extended my arm to the group of milling humans. Ash stepped forward and let their glamour drop, revealing the narrow-faced, androgynous fae I'd sat with in the farmhouse. "Meet the source of my information. Ash. The first ever vampire. Right here, right now, and totally untouchable."

"The . . ."

"Your . . ."

"Source?"

Ridhan bellowed.

Bael burst out laughing.

I waited with my friends—James and David on one side of me, Ash and Emma on the other—until the fae lords quieted down. Then I said, "Per the terms of our deal, you have all sworn to protect this person to the best of your abilities." If looks could kill, I would have dropped dead on the spot. I certainly wasn't making any friends here. "Since that concludes our business, I suggest we all take our leave so this lot can get settled."

"We cannot let this stand." Ridhan turned, seeking backup from the other fae.

"The terms were set and signed," said the Shifter Lord. "The oversight was ours."

Bael shook his head. "Face it, Ridhan. She outmaneuvered us."

"And you're okay with that?!"

"Proud even." He winked at me. "There's always next time."

I held my breath until all six lords passed, mumbling and grumbling, through the portal. Ridhan shot one final look of hatred over his shoulder before he disappeared.

I doubled over and gasped. My heart raced. My knees shook. Dealing with fae lords was like playing chicken with a locomotive. Yet, somehow, I'd won.

James rubbed my back. "You did it, Alex. It's over."

Ash took both my hands and pulled me straight, staring into my eyes. "Alex . . . thank you. In the most fae sense of the word. Truly, thank you. Not only have you helped secure the future of the vampire race, but you've given me something that I'd long since given up any hope of achieving. More than a safe home, you and your friends have given me a sense of belonging. These past few weeks with you have been some of the happiest of my very long life. I'd like to return that favor."

I frowned. "What do you mean?"

"We discussed before that James could not remain in Colorado because he didn't have the necessary assets to support his position."

James cast me a curious look.

"Now that I will no longer be among my children, I would like to name James as my heir."

"What?" I asked.

"What?" James echoed.

"With me staying in this realm indefinitely, Esteban's powers, his entire being, will eventually unravel, but for now, there is enough of me in him to enact my will and facilitate the necessary changes. James will be reinstated as a full member of the council, no longer a prisoner, no longer restricted, and named as my direct successor."

Ash turned to James, and I could see James's struggle not to drop to one knee—a habit he'd finally managed to break after the first three days of cohabitation. Ash placed their hands on James's shoulders and looked up at him. "My son, I charge you with leading our people into the future. All my Earthly resources and connections will be yours. I've already laid the groundwork for your transition."

Tears sparkled on James's cheeks, catching the starlight like the prism leaves singing around us.

Ash moved one of their hands to my shoulder. James twined his fingers with mine, closing the circle. "The future is in your hands," Ash said. "Make it a good one."

Want more?

Try the RIFTER SERIES, starting with:

DEMON RIDING SHOTGUN

About the Author

L.R. Braden is the bestselling, multi-award-winning author of the Magicsmith series, the Rifter series, and several works of shorter fiction. When not writing, she spends her time reading in a multitude of genres (speculative fiction is her favorite), playing games with her family, enjoying Colorado's great outdoors, and weaving metal into intricate chain mail jewelry that she sells through her Etsy shop, Wimsi Design.

Connect with her online at https://www.LRBraden.com.

www.ingramcontent.com/pod-product-compliance
Lightning Source LLC
Chambersburg PA
CBHW020946260626
47169CB00006B/1840